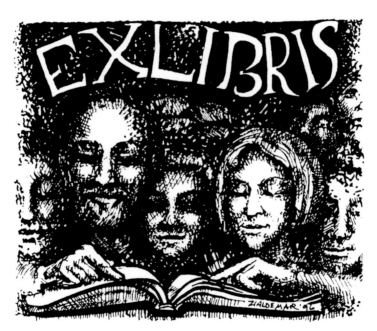

ALSO BY PAUL BEATTY

The White Boy Shuffle

TUFF

TUFF

A NOVEL BY

PAUL BEATTY

ALFRED A. KNOPF   NEW YORK 2000

Grateful acknowledgment is made to the following for permission to reprint previously published material:
ABC Entertainment: Excerpt from "Schoolhouse Rock" theme song. Schoolhouse Rock® and its characters and
other elements are trademarks and service marks of American Broadcasting Companies, Inc. Reprinted by
permission of ABC Entertainment.

Universal Music Publishing Group: Excerpt from "My Melody," words and music by Eric Barrier and William
Griffin, copyright © 1987 by Universal—Songs of PolyGram Int., Inc., a division of Universal Studios, Inc.
(BMI). International copyright secured. All rights reserved. Reprinted by permission of Universal Music
Publishing Group.

Library of Congress Cataloging-in-Publication Data
Beatty, Paul.
Tuff : a novel / by Paul Beatty. — 1st ed.
p.   cm.
ISBN 0-375-40122-9
1. Afro-Americans—New York (State)—New York Fiction.   I. Title.
PS3552.E19T84   2000
813'.54—dc21   99-40358 CIP

Manufactured in the United States of America
First Edition

To paraphrase the immortal Biggie Smalls —
This book is dedicated to all my niggers in the struggle, both literary and
real: Nigger Jim, Queequeg, Dilsey, Candide, Uncle Tom, Teacake, Dan
"Spook" Freeman, Stagolee; Al and Ronald, Jerry, Charlie and Billy,
T. Morrow, DCP, D.W., Lawson, and Toi Russell.

Thanks to Shelah, Pam, Jordan, Jürgen, Anna, Sharon, Ma, Grandma, and Ainka.

A special thanks to Shawn Wilson and Yuri Kochiyama for their perseverance and inspiration.

TUFF

1. TUFFY AND SMUSH

When Winston Foshay found himself on the hardwood floor of a Brooklyn drug den regaining consciousness, his reflex wasn't to open his eyes but to shut them tighter.

Instead of blinking until he reached a state of alertness like a normal person, he stood up, and eyes still closed, hands splayed out in front of him, blindly searched for the full-length mirror he knew was somewhere between the leather couch and the halogen lamp. Feeling like a birthday boy playing pin the tail on the donkey, Winston found the mirror, gently touched the glass with his fingertips, and slowly opened his eyes, his suspicions of what the donkey looked like confirmed in full.

The jackass staring back at him has the drum-weary, heat-darkened face and heart of a Joseph Conrad river native. A thin beard of nappy curlicues worms from his chin. Deep worry lines crease his forehead. His eyelids droop at half-mast. His thick tight lips hint at neither snarl nor smile. Winston's is a face that could just as easily ask you for the time as for your money. So impenetrable, so full of East Harlem inscrutable cool is his expression that usually even he doesn't know what he's thinking, but this time it's different. This time his thoughts are as plain to him as the cracked likeness in the mirror. He probed the bullet hole that had smashed his nose into a shock-white dimple of crushed glass and thought, *Niggers will be niggers.*

TUFF

Moments before he'd been as unconscious as a white heavy-weight and, like the boxer, a debit to his race, so he didn't quite trust the healthy appearance of his reflection. He frantically patted himself down as if he were looking for a cigarette lighter. Finding no bullet holes, Winston thumped a fist on his chest. "Damn, a nigger still breathing like a motherfucker."

Scattered about the small Brooklyn apartment were three other ghetto phenotypes, soulless young outlaws posed stock-still, mouths agape, eyes open, like figurines in a wax museum's rogues' gallery. The room was Zen silent, save for the sound of the tattered curtains flapping against the wall and the steady gurgle of an aquarium filter. The cocksure composure Winston had lost only minutes before, during the shooting, was returning fast. Cupping his testicles with his left hand, Winston strode over to the nearest body, a man he'd known only as Chilly Most from Flatbush. Chilly Most was slumped over the coffee table, his forehead resting midway between the baking powder and the metric scales. Five minutes ago Chilly Most was fiddling with the dram weights, waiting for the base cocaine to arrive, pontificating on the idiocy of the incumbent mayor guesting on a radio talk show, taking credit for the city's falling crime rates. "The mayor think rhyming sound bites, community policing, and the death penalty going to stop fools from getting paid. Don't tell me, a criminal, eight credits shy of an associate's degree in criminology, that stupid slogan 'Stop the heist, love Christ,' a cop on a moped, and the gas chamber will make you think twice. Please, once you decide to commit the crime you've already had two thoughts. Sneak attack or frontal assault? Should I say 'Run your shit, nigger,' or the more traditional 'Stick 'em up'? You put the gun barrel up a nigger's nostril, you think, *Damn, I shouldn't put skylight in this motherfucker's dome*, then you say, 'Fuck it.' That's two more thoughts, right there. Man, the death penalty make you kill more. You spark one fool, you going to smell the vapors, might as well not leave no witnesses. Any fool with a modicum of reasoning ability would draw that conclusion. And if the city is so safe, why the mayor still traveling with nine bodyguards? All this empty election bullshit—if crime is down it's only because niggers killing other niggers. Like when food gets scarce, alligators eat other alligators, trimming the population."

Chilly Most had indeed been trimmed. There was a golf-divot-sized cavity in the crown of his head and a thick layer of blood and junior-college brain tissue seeping over the charcoaled entry wound. Recoiling from the carnage, Winston sucked his teeth, popped a piece of gum in his mouth, and muttered, "Goddamn, I hate Brooklyn."

To celebrate Winston's eighth birthday, his father had taken him and his rowdy Brooklyn cousins on a day trip to Coney Island. Winston's present was the entry fee to the annual hot-dog-eating contest. He won first place only to be disqualified for washing down thirty-three foot-long frankfurters with his father's tepid beer. Instead of a year's supply of all-beef wieners, he received a fifty-dollar citation for underage drinking.

The party moved to the sideshow tent, where Harry Hortensia, the Bearded Lady, let all the other children parade over her stomach as she lay on a bed of nails. When Hortensia spotted Winston out of the corner of her eye, trundling toward her like a baby hippopotamus, she shot up, rubbed his tummy for a cheap laugh, and gave the disgruntled boy his first kiss. While Salamander Sam, the Amphibian Boy, juggled flaming truncheons, Cousin Carl, imitating a talk-show host, ran up and down the bleachers, shoving an air microphone in the faces of strangers and asking, "Since the bearded lady kissed my cousin Winston . . . does that make him a faggot?" Then it was on to the Hellhole.

The Hellhole was an upright metal cylinder that by spinning at high speeds used centrifugal force to pin the riders like refrigerator magnets against its metal walls. The operator took Winston's ticket and glanced at the roly-poly black boy and then at the rusty guide wires dangling overhead. "How much you weigh, son?"

"Not that much," Winston answered, tears welling in his eyes. "Please, mister, it's my birthday." Against his better judgment the operator waved Winston through. "Make sure you stand away from the door. The rest of you little shits stand opposite Buddha Boy to balance things out." Winston placed himself against the cold steel wall, trying to avoid the glare of his thrill-seeking cousins. "See, Winston, your fat ass going to slow the ride down." There was a high-pitched whine and the Hellhole began to turn, gaining speed until the g-forces stuck even big Winston to the walls. All was forgiven, and his cousins shrieked and laughed, yelling for the operator to "drop the floor!" With a pained mechanical groan the floor began to recede, and for a moment Winston's weight was not a hindrance: he was sticking to the wall like a swatted fly, just like the rest of the riders. Then, almost as soon as he allowed himself a smile, he began slowly sliding down the wall like a drop of paint. What, the ride was over? No, Cousin Julie was still horizontal, swimming her way around the cylinder. "Look at Winston," she yelled, "he falling like a motherfucking dead bird!" The kids spun around and above, raining insults down on the helpless pudgy eight-year-old caught in the vortex of the metal eddy. Winston coughed up a ball of saliva and spat in the direction of his effeminate cousin Antoine, the loudest of his tormenters. The wad of mucus hung in the air for a tantalizing second, then snapped back, splattering on the bridge of his nose. Even his father laughed. Winston began to cry. The tears didn't run down his chubby cheeks, but streamed backward, past his temples, canaling through the ridges of his ears. The sounds of ridicule from thirteen summers ago replaced the reverberations of gunplay in Winston's ears. "Fuck Brooklyn, and fuck all you Brooklyn niggers!"

Now on this, the last cool night of summer, Brooklyn was short three more niggers for Winston to hate. Although he addressed all black men as "God," Chilly Most, apparently less than divine, was unable to resurrect himself. Zoltan Yarborough, who was always running off at the mouth about his proud Brooklyn roots, "Brownsville, never ran, never will," had become the rigid embodiment of his slogan. He had one leg over the windowsill, and a bullet hole in him that, like everything his mother ever told him, went in one ear and out the other. Demetrius Broadnax from "Do-or-die Bed-Stuy" was shirtless on the floor with a column of bullet holes from sternum to belly button in his muddy brown torso. Winston gloated over Demetrius's body, looking into his ex-boss's glassy eyes, tempted to say "I quit" and ask for his severance pay. Instead he walked to the aquarium, pressed his nose against the glass, and wondered who was going to feed the goldfish.

Like most of the jobs Winston had taken since graduating high school, this one also ended prematurely, after a job interview only two weeks ago where the look on his face was his résumé and two sentences from his best friend, Fariq Cole, were his references. "This fat nigger ain't no joke. Yo—known uptown for straight KO'ing niggers." There was no "So, Mr. Foshay, how do your personal career goals mesh with our corporate mission? Would you consider yourself to be a self-starter? What was the last book you read?" Demetrius simply handed Winston the inner-city union card, a small black .22 Raven automatic pistol, which Winston coolly, but immediately, handed back.

"What, your ass don't need a burner?"

"Naw."

"Look, fool, maybe you can body-slam niggers out on the street, but in this business, people don't walk in the door shaking their fists in your face."

Winston shrugged.

Demetrius studied him up and down and asked, "You ain't shook, are you? You don't seem the scary type."

"Never back down. Once a nigger back down, he stay down, know what I'm saying? Just don't like guns."

"Well, when some niggers do come in blasting, your big ass be in the way and shit, two, three motherfuckers can hide behind you. Be here tomorrow afternoon at four."

When Winston started work, he was "in the way and shit," but not in the manner Demetrius had hoped. Winston's job description was simple: four to ten, five days a week, answer the door, look mean and yell, "Pay this motherfucker, now!" at the balky customers. But the trip into Brooklyn made him edgy. His childhood traumas kicked in, undoing his cool. Instead of suavely sauntering around counting his money every five minutes, Winston fumbled about the drug den, stepping on people's toes, toppling everything he touched, and talking nonstop. He tried to lighten the somber felonious atmosphere by telling embarrassingly bad jokes. ("You hear the one about why Scots wear kilts?") After the flat punchlines ("Because sheep can hear a zipper open from one hundred feet away") there would be a barely audible metallic click, the sound of Demetrius switching the gun's safety to the off position.

Winston had trouble keeping track of the Brooklyn drug mores. Which colored caps went with what size plastic vials? Were portable televisions an acceptable form of payment? He was unable to distinguish one crew's secret whistle from another's. How often had Demetrius yelled at him, "You moron, don't flush the drugs! That's the mating call of the ruby-crowned kinglet!" Then Chilly Most and the others would join in with their snide castigations: "As opposed to our secret signal—"

"The flight song of the skylark."

"A gentle *woo-dukkadukka-woo*."

"Good ol' *Alauda arvensis*, indigenous to Eurasia, but common in the Northwest Territories of Canada, if I'm not mistaken."

"You are not, you nigger ornithologist, you."

The last time Winston heard the cherished secret whistle, he answered the door and two niggers he'd never seen before, brandishing firearms, rushed past him and, before they could be properly announced, introduced themselves with a bullet in Chilly Most's newly shorn bald head. Winston did what his coworkers always said he'd do if he ever found himself face-to-face with a gun: he fainted "like a bitch."

Three minutes had passed since Winston regained consciousness, and he couldn't leave the apartment. It was as if he were spacewalking, tethered to some mother ship treading Brooklyn ether. He would clamber for the door and a muffled sound in the hallway or a distant siren would drive him back into the living room. He began to mumble: "This like that flick, the bugged-out Spanish one where the rich people couldn't leave the house. Luis Bustelo or some shit. What is it . . . surrealism? Well, I got the surrealisms."

A creak in the floor behind him stopped Winston's babbling. He quickly about-faced, balling his shaky hands into fists.

"Who dat?"

"Who dat?" came the response. Winston relaxed. He smiled, "Nigger," unclenched his fists, and plopped down on the sofa.

Fariq Cole hobbled into the living room, his crutches splayed out to the side, propelling him forward. Fariq's friends called him Smush because his nose, lips, and forehead shared the same Euclidean plane, giving him a profile that had all the contours of a cardboard box. Each herky-jerky step undulated Fariq's body toward Winston like a Slinky, alternately coiling and uncoiling. A solid-gold dollar-sign pendant and a diamond-inlaid ankh whipped about his neck in an elliptical orbit like a jewel-encrusted satellite. Fariq stopped next to the doorjamb, tilted his head to the side, and cut his friend a dubious look.

"Who was you talking to?"

"Nobody. Just trying to figure out why I was still here."

"You still here because you couldn't leave without me, your so-called boy."

"You is. But it wasn't you—I barely got to work ten minutes ago, I didn't even know you was here. Naw, it's something else."

Fariq was the coolest of the many cool handicapped East Harlemites. His appearance was inner-city dapper, functional and physically fit assimilationist. Despite the soft spot in his head where his skull had never fused, it'd been a long time since he'd worn a cyclist's helmet. The bill of his fiberglass-reinforced Yankee baseball cap hung over his left eye, shad-

owing the surgical scars. The baggy corduroys covered up his leg braces.
His clubfeet were squeezed into a pair of expensive sneakers, though he'd
never run a step in his life. Fariq ran his tongue over his precious-metal-
filled mouth, the front four incisors, top and bottom, capped in a gold-
and-silver checkerboard pattern. Etched on his two front teeth were small
black king and queen chess pieces, christened "Fariq" and "Nadine" in
microscopic handwriting.

"Now look at these no-money motherfuckers—who going to take
care of their families?" Fariq said, a rubber-tipped crutch sweeping across
the carnage. "That's why a prudent motherfucker like me has an IRA
account, some short-term T-bills, a grip invested in long-term corporate bonds and high-risk foreign stock. Shit, the twenty-first-century
nigger gots to have a diversified portfolio—never know when you gon'
have a rainy day. And look like it was thunderin' and lightnin' in this
motherfucker."

Winston and Fariq had known each other since the subway cost
seventy-five cents. Fariq was an enterprising shyster who dragged Winston, the muscle, along on all his moneymaking schemes, the first of which
was a fifth-grade dognapping operation so immense it required the use of
every rooftop pigeon coop on 109th Street between Park and Second
Avenues for kennel space.

The idea was to stalk the parks and streets of Manhattan luring
unleashed dogs into the bushes with whistles, kindhearted "Here, boy"s,
and hickory-smoked slabs of beef sausage. The poor, whining creatures
left tethered to parking meters while their owners kibitzed over cappuc-
cino were liberated with garden shears. Then the boys waited for the
rewards to be posted and returned to collect the bounty. "Yeah, lady, the
dog was wandering the streets of Harlem. Some crackheads had put an
apple in his mouth and was fixing to skewer him with a barbecue spit up
the ass, talking about 'pooch du jour,' when we rescued him and brought
him here. Would fifty dollars be enough? Well, frankly, no."

Winston ran up to Fariq and with one flabby arm buried his friend's
head in a boys-will-be-boys headlock. Fariq's eyes bulged with pain, "Ow,
Tuff! You know better than to do that shit."

"Sorry, man—just trying show you some love, glad you alive and shit.
Was it the spina bifida or the rickets flaring up? I can never remember
which one you got."

"Both, nigger, both. But I'm just sore from hiding in the tub. Heard that first shot, I belted my pants, fell into the tub, and pulled the shower curtain closed. Thank goodness those niggers didn't have to piss."

"We need to be out, son. Rollers going to show up any minute now."

"The po-po ain't here by now, they ain't coming."

"Well, them shoot-'em-up cowboys might be back to get me—don't want to leave no witnesses behind."

"Man, after they sparked up these clowns, I could hear them laughing at your big ass passed out on the floor. They ain't worried about no swooning motherfucker coming back to get them. I thought I was going to come out and have to splash water on your face. Slap you around a bit, James Cagney style."

"I didn't faint. I was playing possum and shit."

"Yeah, right. Let's get ghost."

"Who you, the leader now?"

"Fuck you, Tonto. Hi-yo, Silver, and away, nigger."

"Robin."

"Batgirl."

"Al Cowlings."

"Oh, a low blow."

They left the apartment with a bravado that belied their fear. The halls normally filled with kids and the sounds of blaring televisions were silent. The refugees were holed up in their urban-renewal hovels waiting for the occupying forces to leave. A little girl, wearing a belled choker, peeked out of a doorway, stuck out her tongue at the two boys, and was snatched by her ponytails back inside so quickly the bell didn't even tinkle. The building's elevators never worked, so Winston carried Fariq in his arms down twelve flights of stairs, gently setting him down next to a battered block of mailboxes. Readjusting the collar on Fariq's shirt, Winston stepped back and snapped his fingers. "Wait here. Now I know why I couldn't leave—I forgot something. Be right back." Before Fariq could say, "Naw, nigger, don't leave me," Winston was springing up the flight of stairs two and three steps at time.

Fariq was nervous about being left alone, but pleased to see Winston's famed agility return. *Nigger was fumbling around the spot telling jokes like he Henny Youngman and shit. Talking to himself. I know the boy don't like Brooklyn, but goddamn, fainting? Many times fools pulled guns on him? Tuffy be like, "Shoot me, motherfucker!" I guess the good thing about fainting in the face of death is that it keeps you from begging. That's the old Tuffy, running them stairs like the big Kodiak bear of a brother he is.* Fariq grinned, recalling how during the summer-long games of tag, only the fastest kids on East 109th Street could outrun Tuffy, avoiding his painful, heavy-handed tag back. Fariq's toes began to tingle. He could feel the vibrations—the vibrations from the scraping of his corrective shoes as he dragged them over the craggy pavement, trying to run. Fariq was It for an entire summer: lumbering after screaming hordes of children on his crutches, feeling like the neighborhood leper, never catching anyone. On the first day of fifth grade Fariq had to resort to ringing Sharif Middleton's doorbell at six-thirty in the morning, tagging the unsuspecting mope with a crutch in the gut as he answered the door wiping the sleep from his eyes. *Tuffy, my nukka, where you at?*

Winston entered the apartment, stepped over a body, and grabbed a brown lunch bag from the rear of the refrigerator. He reached inside the sack and gobbled down a cold, soggy ham-and-cheese sandwich. His mouth still full, Winston flipped the plastic sandwich bag inside-out, walked over to the aquarium, sprinkled the crumbs into the water, and when the fish rose to the surface, deftly scooped it out, barely wetting his hands.

Winston was knotting the plastic bag and on his way out when he heard a tinny ringing sound. The girl from the hallway was cowering in the corner of the living room, holding three puffy wallets, some jewelry, and Demetrius's .22 Raven pistol in the folds of her dress. Winston bristled. "You little vulture, these fools ain't cold and you rifling pockets."

"Finders keepers, losers weepers."

"Christ, everybody and they mama got a hustle. Give me the gun."

The girl scrunched her face and backed even further into the corner, sticking her tongue out again. Winston walked up to the girl and took the gun from her hands, then lifted her to her feet by the elbow.

"Go home."

She skipped down the hall to her apartment, the door opened, and a thin hand reeled her inside by the hem of her dress. The door slammed shut. Winston waited for the click of the lock, stuffed the gun into his pants pocket, gently placed the fish into the lunch bag, and hustled back down the stairs.

"Where you been, man?" Fariq said in a nervous whisper. "Somebody's out there."

"I told you, I forgot something," Winston answered, holding up the bag.

"You forgot your lunch? Here we are . . . niggers trying to kill—"

TUFF

"Shhh! *Cállete*, man." Winston peered around the corner. The security guard was sitting at his desk, scribbling phony names on the visitors' sign-in sheet. The putrefied zombies of Al Capone, King Kong, and Mao could have entered the building, loading tommy guns, pining for Fay Wray, and talking about a Cultural Revolution, and this minimum-wage watchman was going to wave them through, no questions asked.

"Ain't nobody out there, just the rent-a-cop—let's see if he know what the fuck up." Winston, still out of sight, called the guard's attention. "Hey yo, Barney Fife, couple of niggers come this way telling war stories?"

"Yup, came through a few minutes ago saying they now have to find and kill some crippled motherfucker. Asked me if I wanted to feel the guns. I did, and they was hot as a preacher's brow Sunday morning."

Fariq's body buckled at the pelvis, the crutches slipping out from under his arms. As he righted himself, his peptic ulcer rumbled like an active volcano and a small accumulation of warm, lumpy excrement flowed into his underpants. "Shit."

"Which way did they go?" Winston asked the guard.

"No way."

"What?"

"They're right out front, smoking Phillies and talking to some honeys."

Fariq's yellowed eyes closed softly as every affliction kicked in at once. His arrhythmic heartbeat grew more erratic, pumping his sickle-celled blood in stops and starts. Bracing himself against the broken elevator, he cursed his mother for drinking, smoking, and shunning prenatal care during her pregnancy. Swallowing hard, he repeatedly pressed the Up button and castigated his father for thinking that his two-month-premature birth meant that he was born "ready for Freddy." *That boy don't need no incubator. He's not no chicken.*

Winston chewed his bottom lip and watched his friend shake, then suddenly zipped past the guard and raced for the fire exit. He pushed on the latch, swinging open the heavy door into the dusk. A zephyr of spring air gusted in and, for a moment, cooled Winston's sweaty face. The alarm sounded, its deafening ring filling the cinder-block hallways. Winston hurried back to Fariq and in one motion hoisted his friend onto a shoulder and ran toward the front door. Pausing in a cranny, he watched the gunmen head for the back of the apartment building. Carrying Fariq like a wounded war buddy, Winston tore out for Bushwick Avenue, hurdling bushes and slipping around the mottled Brooklyn trees like the tag player of yore. The clap of the gun pounding against his thigh, the jingle of loose pocket change, and the squeaks of the metal brackets holding Fariq's body together at the joints sounded to Winston like the score to the climax of a Hitchcock thriller. He stole a glance behind him, half expecting to be buzzed by a crop duster.

At the intersection of Bushwick and Myrtle, a line of public buses were impatiently queued up behind a lone drunk ranting in the middle of the street. Like a column of Tiananmen Square tanks, the buses tried to maneuver past the man, but he halted each advance, stepping in front of the buses and boldly waving them off with a raggedy sports jacket. From his drug errands Winston knew the man usually confronted his pink elephants about this time of night, and he counted on him being there, challenging the powers that be with non sequiturs. "I am black, it is raining. Warren Commission, I presume. Incoming!" Winston and Fariq skirted past the man ("You men, return to your positions"), hopped on the third bus, and headed for the back. They sank low in the plastic seats, gasping for air and waiting for the bus to move. Fariq was wheezing. He frantically removed his inhaler from his jacket and took two long hits.

"Shit, nigger, you didn't have to do all that! You should have told me you was going to make your move, I could have followed you on my own."

"Hah," Winston snorted.

Fariq moved to whack Winston with a crutch, but it was wedged underneath the seat in front of him. "Naw, money, I'm serious. Shit is humiliating. I can take care of self, know what I'm saying, Tuffy?"

"Spare me, bro. I'd had to rescue your ass like in *Deer Hunter*. Wasn't for me you'd be in a bamboo hut playing Russian roulette with the Brooklyn Viet Cong. Didi, mau! Mau!" Winston sniffed the air, then checked the bottoms of his sneakers. "Hey, did you poot?" he asked Fariq. Fariq said nothing, rolling his tongue in his cheek. For most young men this gesture was the sign for oral sex; for Fariq it was code for "I had an accident." Winston reached under the seat and freed Fariq's crutch.

The bus rolled onto Broadway, honking its way out of Bedford-Stuyvesant and into the fringes of the more cosmopolitan Williamsburg. As the projects receded into the distance the two survivors straightened in their seats, looking out the grimy windows. On the crowded sidewalks the people looked tired and angry, fighting for space on their way home from work. Bohemian whites weaved in and out of traffic, heads down, pissed off they couldn't afford to live in Manhattan. Pairs of Hasidic men, dapper in black pin-striped coat-and-tail suits, walked like dandies, holding attaché cases and rehashing last night's Knicks game. The only people Winston could differentiate as individuals were the Puerto Ricans. To Winston the whites, Jewish and Gentile, had the same general physiognomy. With callous, tight-lipped expressions, they marched as one, lockstep, arms linked at the elbows. The Puerto Ricans reminded him of people he knew. They were more or less from around the way, more or less niggers, more or less poor. The Puerto Ricans had faces he could say hello to. And he said a big silent "What's happening?" to the woman in the green rayon sweater. *Yes, you, honey dip, with the shopping bag. Why you walking so fast? Hurrying to help the kids with their homework? I feel you. The capital of Kansas is Topeka, that's all I remember.*

Winston peered into the flitting eyes of the colored boys who had sprouted and grown up along market walls like vines. He could tell which ones were filial home-by-eleven mama's boys, which ones were walking the tightrope between rebellion and sainthood. Some, like the young man about Winston's age, diddy-bopping against the foot traffic, had surrendered to the streets. Winston knew that one well, a lost warrior looking for an arena to test his skills. Winston grinned and delivered a whispered challenge: "You lucky I ain't out there. We could bump shoulders and squab. Wax that ass, nigger." Then a bit louder: "Sucker."

Winston pressed the expanse of his back against the engine-warmed seat. The motor's churning caused the seat to vibrate and he relaxed for a moment, enjoying the free massage. Fariq looked at his friend. He knew that smirk, the satisfied look after Winston had beaten the crap out of someone. "Tuffy?"

"Mmm."

"You really did faint back there, didn't you?"

"Battle fatigue, I guess. Saved my life, though. Maybe it was God reaching down and touching me. Saving me for some higher purpose." Winston laughed. "Quick, Smush, cheer me up." Fariq drummed his fingers against his jawbone. "Remember the cat-ass punk you beat down last week in front of the Old Timers' Lounge?"

"Yeah, waving that box cutter, '*En garde*, motherfucker,' like he going to do somethin'."

"I heard to avoid the neighborhood embarrassment the punk tried to join the armed forces. Been to all the motherfuckers—Navy, Marines,

Coast Guard—but he can't pass the psychological. You bruised his brain or some shit. Every two minutes for no reason at all he yells out '*La Mega!*' like he a DJ on that Spanish station. He be taking the repeat-after-me oath, 'I solemnly swear to uphold *La Mega!*' 'Yes sir, I'm really interested in flight mechanics and *La Mega Noventa y siete punto nueve!*' Nigger a permanent radio jingle."

Winston smiled. "So let's call that nigger La Mega from now on, okay?"

"Yeah."

Tuffy pulled a crinkled brown paper bag from his jacket pocket and offered it to Fariq. "You hungry?"

"What you got?"

"Pork rinds and fish."

"You might has well got shot. The way you eat, you killing yourself anyway. How much you weigh now?"

"I don't know—three-ten, three-twenty. It's been a while since I've been to the meat-packing plant on Edgecombe to sit on the scale. Anyway, these are fat-free pork rinds."

Fariq threw up his hands. "You idiot! Pork rinds are pieces of pig fat deep-fried in pig grease. How can they be fat-free when they're one hundred percent fat? See, dumb niggers like you keeps the white man in business."

Winston shrugged his shoulders and pulled out a small clear plastic jug of a light blue syrupy punch. "And now you drinking a Thirstbuster? How many times I told you the Klan owns that shit. That junk will make you sterile. How you think the company can afford to charge only twenty-five cent for the stuff? CIA subsidizes that fucking poison. You ever see Thirstbusters in the white neighborhoods? Hell no. What, white folks don't want a bargain?"

There was something to what Fariq was saying. Whenever Winston was in Midtown, doing the things he couldn't do in Harlem, such as seeing a movie or shopping for logo-free clothes, and got a craving for a Thirstbuster, his favorite drink was impossible to find. Stocked with colas and nectars, the shelves in the clean East Side delicatessens had natural waters from every lake in Europe, but no Thirstbusters. Winston would ask the shopkeeper for a grape or pineapple Thirstbuster and get a blank stare in return, forced to exit the store examining his two-dollar bottle of melted glacier water for mastodon hairs.

Winston downed his prized drink in two gulps, slowly pulled the container from his mouth, and let out a loud "aaaahhhh." "Dag, Fariq, you right, my sperms is fizzing."

"Fuck you."

Winston crushed the empty plastic container in one hand and bowled it down the aisle. The bus continued down Broadway.

"I got an idea how to make some cash. You down, Tuff?"

"Don't know."

"This drug insanity is played out. Shit is a hassle. You have to develop a regular clientele, the inventory is all complicated, one connect is LIFO, the other is FIFO. Too many unorganized crazy motherfuckers to deal with. We need to be into some self-contained shit. Make a quick strike and be out. Hit and quit it."

"LIFO and FIFO? What the fuck you talking about?"

"Last in, first out; first in, first out. Man, I'm talking about revolutionizing the drug business. Inventin' a product that if you look at it for more than two seconds, you're addicted. Something that stays in your system forever, like PCP, and maybe throw in some trace amounts of Prozac to make it attractive to the upper-class-white market—ta-da, a drug that keeps losers high for life." Fariq touched Winston lightly on the forearm like some used-car salesman with the deal of a lifetime. "A one-time, mind-altering gold mine. I'd call it Eternal Bliss, the dope fiend's Everlasting Gobstopper. I'd be Willie Wonka up it this motherfucker. I'm tellin' you."

Winston pushed Fariq away. "You tripping."

Undaunted, Fariq continued, his voice rising a couple of octaves to an overzealous infomercial pitch. "Tuff, think of the long-term savings for the consumer."

While Fariq rambled on about his marketing strategy, Winston ignored him and watched the Manhattan skyline creep closer, lapsing into a funk somewhere between semi-alertness and sleep. The images of the dead bodies he'd left behind flickered in his head like science-class slides. He closed his eyes and began counting the number of dead bodies he'd seen in his twenty-two years. Including Fariq's grandmother in the funeral home: sixteen.

After a warm weekend night, at 109th and Fifth Avenue, the border of Spanish Harlem and black Harlem, bodies turned up on the streets like worms on sidewalks after an afternoon shower. Sometimes the coroner pulled junkies stiff as Styrofoam from the abandoned apartments on

116th Street, or a group of kids on their way to school found a homeless person frozen to death under the brick railroad trestle of Park Avenue. Two weeks ago, on his way to buy an Italian ice at the pizza shop at 103rd and Lexington, Winston heard the screech of truck brakes. He looked up to see little Ursula Huertas, seven years old, flying across Lexington Avenue as if she'd been shot out of a circus cannon. She lay there in the gutter, a crumpled, unmoving ball of black hair and bony brown limbs, her mother and the purple flowers on her bleached white Sunday-school dress doing the screaming for her. Winston planted a sandalwood punk in the cardboard shrine Ursula's relatives erected on the spot where she died. Filled with burning candles, assorted kitsch pictures of the Virgin Mary and angelic saints Winston didn't know, the shrine was one of many forever-flame memorials that pop up on Spanish Harlem's street corners and last for about two weeks.

The encroaching skyscrapers of the city began to look to Winston like tombstones for giants and he grew strangely homesick. Niggers die everywhere, Winston knew, but he longed to be back home among the tragedy of the familiar. Drinking brews on a corner where he knew or had at least heard of the names mentioned in the spray-paint cenotaphs that dot the neighborhood. Watching the children flick skelly caps over the sidewalk epitaphs where so-and-so's nigger got dropped. Mourners with money to spend hired local graffiti artists to paint huge murals on hand-ball walls or tenement sides. A larger-than-life-sized portrait of the deceased accompanied by Day-Glo renditions of luxury cars and the styl-ized signatures of his friends. The neighborhood women were never memorialized on the walls. Winston wished he could draw. He would have painted a three-story mural dedicated to his older sister Brenda. Winston was twelve when Fariq called up to his window, "Nigger, you bet-ter come on, Brenda getting dogged up on Seventeenth." Winston arrived on the scene just as the ambulance was leaving. He walked to a public phone, one from which, thanks to deregulation, he could call anywhere in the United States and speak for thirty seconds for a quarter. Winston dialed local, his mother's work number. "May I speak to Mrs. Foshay? . . . Ma, go to Metropolitan. I'll meet you in the emergency room."

Winston took out an indelible marker and absentmindedly scribbled his grade-school tag on the bus's frayed upholstery: TUFFY 109. "So you down, kid?" asked Fariq, elbowing Winston in the ribs. "We talking goo-gobs of money. Scads o' cash."

TUFF

"Shit ain't going to work."

"And why the fuck not?"

"Because addicts is looking for a reason to get up in the morning, and crack, heroin, whatever, is the reason. Lipping that pipe like falling in love every day—maybe a little better. Can you imagine what it's like waking up in the morning and knowing that soon as you hustle up ten dollars, you going to be in always-and-forever love? To do that you can't wake up already in love. You got to get up in a cold room, mad as fuck you been sleeping on a flat pillow, or without a pillow, convinced that life hates you, and you hate life. Then you can cherish the high. You want the high to last, but not forever, yo."

Fariq punched his friend in the shoulder. "You sound like you know what you talking about."

Winston thought about confessing to the time, the fifth anniversary of his sister's death, he experimented with crack and spent four days in his bedroom closet tweaked out of his mind. Like an addicted jeweler, he held powdery rocks to his eye with a set of tweezers, examining each brownish-white marbled facet for imperfections. When he ran out of cocaine he pronounced the bread crumbs and balls of lint flawless and stuffed them into his pipe. On day four Winston realized he'd been masturbating with paper-towel rolls and petroleum jelly for entertainment, and quit his mini-addiction out of sexual shame. But whenever Winston heard the line "I wanna rock right now" from Rob Base's hip-hop classic "It Takes Two," his throat parched. Turning away from Fariq, Winston mopped his brow. "I don't know nothing about it, but I've heard people talk."

Fariq paused for a moment. "Maybe what Eternal Bliss needs is some type of time-release-cold-remedy-type mechanism."

Winston groaned, and the bus jolted to a stop. "Broadway Station, last stop."

From there it was the J train across the bridge to Canal Street, then a long walk through the dank algae-laden tunnels to catch the uptown local. Once on the train, Fariq leaned down and glared at a middle-aged man seated next to the door. "Can't you read, motherfucker?" he shouted, pointing to a sticker that read, THESE SEATS RESERVED FOR THE HANDI-CAPPED AND ELDERLY. The embarrassed man rose and politely offered Fariq his seat. Winston laughed, and the tweed-jacketed man standing next to him nonchalantly checked his wallet. Winston took a deep breath and, to keep from slapping the man upside the head, grabbed him firmly by the wrist, digging his watchband into his skin. "I had a long criminal-activity-filled day. One more crime ain't going to hurt me none. Crime down, but it ain't stopped." The man rushed out at the next stop. A woman two seats away tucked her brooch beneath her blouse and twisted her engagement ring so the stone's brilliance was doused in the dark of her palm.

"Uptown bound, yo."

"No more Brooklyn Rambo niggers in camouflage pants."

"Word. Fuck Brooklyn."

"Spike Lee, Jackie Robinson, Barbra Streisand, Woody Allen, Mary Tyler Fucking Moore can all kiss my black Manhattan ass."

Winston tossed the last piece of bubble gum into his mouth, unfolded the comic that was, as usual, unfunny, and then read the fortune. *Don't carry grudges—they can weigh you down.* Unmoved, Winston blew bubbles till the subway doors opened at 116th Street.

2. PAQUETES DE SEIS DE BUD

Like prairie dogs fresh out of their burrows, welcoming the cool desert night, the duo popped out of the subway station and stood motionless, gazing at a Spanish Harlem just emerging from its early-evening siesta. A foursome of sturdy tank-topped old-timers played a staid game of dominoes in front of the Laundromat. A frenetic salsa fell out of an upper-floor window like a Boriqua waterfall. Winston, roused from his momentary trance, giddily splashed around in the Latin percussives, stutter-stepping, shaking his hips, and singing the lyrics. *No tengo miedo, tengo bravura, tú y yo, tenemos amor pura.* Winston was back on the block.

"That's Hector Lavoe."

"You say everybody's Hector Lavoe. That's the only Spanish singer you know. It might be Marco Manteca from down the street."

"Just change your drawers, son. You smell."

Fariq pulled out a spare pair of underwear and walked into Kansas Fried Chicken to use the bathroom. Winston headed straight for the T&M Tienda, *"Dos paquetes de seis de Bud, por favor,"* then reimmersed himself in the nighttime bustle, snapping the gray hood of his sweatshirt over his head. After Fariq finished tidying up, the duo headed east toward Third Avenue, Fariq insanely jealous because Winston could walk and drink, while Fariq had to wait until they arrived at their destination before he could sip his beer. Winston stopped and held the can of beer to Fariq's lips. Fariq took two gulps.

"My brother."

"Tastes good, don't it?"

"True, that."

With a firm brush of his thumb Winston removed the suds from Fariq's mouth. He considered telling Fariq about the gun but decided against it. Once people knew you had a gun, it was like having a car— everyone begging to borrow it, wanting you to use it to make their lives easier. Winston pointed to their usual drinking spot by the empty pool in Jefferson Park. They liked to sit on the edge, their legs dangling in the void, reminiscing about taking turns feeling up Henrietta Robles in the shallow end. Even Fariq risked rusting his leg braces for a few blind gropes.

Winston figured four, maybe five beers and Fariq would agree to lend him enough money to get him through the rest of the month. There was a pulse against his hip and Winston peered down at his beeper, illuminating the numbers. Fariq knew, from the sour look in Winston's face, who was paging him. "You better get home, nigger, you a father now."

"Mmm."

Winston shut the beeper off and wrested another beer from the plastic ringlet, and thought back to that Sunday years ago at Coney Island, walking away from the Hellhole, crying and cursing his cousins. He recalled his father soothing him with promises never kept. That day was the last time he'd cried, the last time he'd held his father's hand.

The beer slid solidly down Winston's throat and bubbled in his nose. Winston pointed the half-empty can at the diving board. "Remember when Raymond Vargas dove off that fucker and smashed his mouth on the edge of the board?"

"Yeah, he used to talk about diving in the Olympics. Toe the edge of the board and say, 'This is a Dominican Escape-from-the-Ghetto Inward One-and-a-Half Twist with a Cry-on-the-Gold-Medal-Stand-During-the-National-Anthem Pike. Degree of Difficulty: the fact white people think niggers can't swim.' Then, blam, the kid was at the bottom of the pool unconscious and toothless. Didn't you go to the bottom and drag him up?"

TUFF

"Uh-huh. Rebroke Raymond's jaw a month later when he said that when I swam I looked like a big black oil spill."

With some effort Fariq lifted himself to his feet, finished his beer, then, with one crutch, golfed the empty can toward the far end of the pool. It nestled about two feet from the drain and Fariq mimicked a golf announcer's whisper: "That leaves Fariq Cole a short putt for a birdie."

"Sit, you're making me nervous."

Fariq sat back down. "Tuff?"

"What?"

"Golf a game or sport?"

"Goddamn, you're restless. Don't you ever stop and chill? Look up at the stars? Look, if you can wear a watch at the professional level—golf, tennis, bowling—it's a game or a pastime, not a sport."

"I just wanted to say, good looking out today. Thanks, that's all."

Winston returned Fariq's gratitude with an embarrassed nod. Taking his own advice, he lay back over the pool's edge, gazing up at the twenty or so stars visible in the hazy New York City night. Using the can propped on his stomach as a sextant, Winston charted a course through the black sea above him, navigating an out-of-body escape from the madness.

> **TEN YARDS UP:** I'm floating next to a middle-aged woman looking out her third-story window, elbows folded on a bath towel, and wearing nothing but a flimsy white slip, looking over the block like an urban hoot owl.
>
> **TEN THOUSAND YARDS:** I'm riding a double-seater bike with E.T. the Extra-Terrestrial. I'm in the back, E.T. steering through some thin cigarette-smoke-looking clouds. I tell him, "Pedal faster them pesky white kids gaining on us."
>
> **ONE MILLION YARDS:** The earth's surface looks as if it's been smoothed with wood-shop sandpaper. The Himalayas are the same height as the Indian Ocean and the Grand Canyon. The whole planet look like it's been shellacked with sunlight.
>
> **ONE BILLION YARDS:** I'm on the moon. I hot-wire the lunar buggies and joyride from the Sea of Tranquillity to the Bay of Rainbows.
>
> **TEN MILLION MILES:** From here the earth is one of many small moth-eaten holes in a raggedy interstellar theater curtain. When does the show start?

ONE HUNDRED MILLION MILES: Allergic to the space dust in the asteroid belt, I sneeze. Fifty years from now a meteor will land in the desert with traces of mucus on it and scientists will lose their minds.

ONE BILLION MILES: The tilted ring around Saturn is the felt brim on the gaseous head of the solar-system pimp. Those bitches Venus and Uranus betta have my money.

TEN BILLION MILES: From here the sun is the size of a flickering match two football fields away. Goddamn, it's cold.

ONE HUNDRED BILLION MILES: Set the boom box adrift, tune in radio static. Me and the constellations listen to an aircheck from 1937. *Good evening to the East Coast, and to the West Coast, good morning. This program of ultramodern rhythms comes to you from the Savoy Ballroom, known as the Home of Happy Feet, located in Uptown New York City. It's Count Basie and His Orchestra featuring Billie Holiday, and here's "They Can't Take That Away from Me."* The constellations jitterbug, entrants in a dance marathon that's been jumping since the dawn of time. Orion swings Cassiopeia around his hips. I slide Andromeda through my legs.

ONE TRILLION MILES: Color disappears. Everything is black-and-white. My mind and the universe are the same size. My father is holding court in a faraway lounge, conferring with ancient poets, saying, "See I told you so, everything is everything."

ONE LIGHT-YEAR: The time it took for Daddy to send that first child-support check.

ONE HUNDRED LIGHT-YEARS: Depth perception disappears. Nothing in the universe seems more than an arm's length away. The universe must be handled gently, like the oldest vinyl record in the collection. I pull it slowly from a worn cardboard jacket. Holding the universe by the edges, I blow on its scratchy surface. Flipping the universe over, another puff and the dust from side B is a new galaxy. If you could play creation on a turntable, what would it sound like?

ONE THOUSAND LIGHT-YEARS: I see the souls of Demetrius, Zoltan, and Chilly Most trying to find the happy hunting ground. "Where are we? Alpha Centauri? Nigger, we want Alpha Cygni! Give me the map, motherfucker!"

"You see your heaven up there?" Fariq was propped up on his crutches, which formed a makeshift cruciform on the chain-link fence behind him. Ankles crossed, arms to the side, a can of beer in one hand, a cigarette in the other, Fariq began yelling, his voice carrying throughout the empty park: "Beer and fish for everyone! Who sold me out? Judas? I knew it—greedy bastard! Before I die I leave you with this last holy piece of advice: Never, never let a nigger kiss you in public."

Uncapping his marker, Winston jammed his forearm into Fariq's throat and scribbled on his friend's wrinkled brow. He stepped back to admire his work. "There, now you're Jesus." Fariq wet his hands with beer and tried to rub the inky scrawl from his forehead. "Come on, man, what'd you write?"

"I-N-R-I."

"What does that mean?"

"I don't know, but it's always at the top of any Jesus-on-the-cross painting I've ever seen. A Rasta once told me it means, 'I Negro Rule I-ternally.' "

Fariq stopped rubbing his brow. " 'I-ternally'? Now what the fuck does that mean?"

"No idea. I thought you would know—sound like that crazy Five-Percenter 'White man is the devil' madness you be talking."

Fariq pirouetted on his clubfeet and removed the crutches from the fence. He was about to right himself when he lost his balance, teetered, and fumbled away his walking sticks. Before he could pick them up, Winston scooped the metal stabilizers off the ground and waved the poles in Fariq's face, snickering, "Drunk?"

"Drop my shits, fat boy. I can pick 'em up myself."

"Fat boy?"

Winston tossed the metal poles about ten feet away from Fariq's twisted legs. "Fetch, punk. If Jesus Christ could walk on water, a fake Jesus can at least walk on two legs." Without hesitating, Fariq released the fence and boldly ambled forward, his feet pointing inward at an angle that made his toes touch, his thin legs bent at the knees, forming an X. Feet never leaving the ground, Fariq took three wobbly steps, stopped, and exhaled. Winston couldn't restrain himself. "Why are you holding your breath? You're not swimming underwater—breathe."

"Don't be watching me walk," Fariq cautioned Winston. "I hate it when motherfuckers be watching me walk."

"You ain't walking, nigger. You ice-skating or something. You so shaky it looks like there's an earthquake but you're the only one who can feel it."

Reaching out for his crutches, Fariq pounced on them like dollar bills in the street, clutching the supports to his chest before they could blow away in the wind. "Told you I could walk."

"You better quit bragging, track star, before I call Social Security tomorrow and tell them to stop sending you them disability checks. Let's go get some more drink."

They headed back to the store in silence, listening to what passed for a quiet night in the city. A streetlight sputtered and hummed. Rats scaled mountains of trash bags. Caught up in the headwind, sheets of loose paper and debris blew past the boys' feet. A campaign flyer for the upcoming election plastered itself to Winston's chest. He peeled it off. The handbill read: VOTA WILFREDO CIENFUEGOS, DEMOCRAT POR COUNCILMAN DISTRITO 8. SEPTIEMBRE 9TH. ¡PARE LA VIOLENCIA! *Pare la violencia:* Stop the Violence—a phrase that prior to the Brooklyn incident was part of the ecumenical white noise he'd heard and seen since grade school. Don't Smoke. Just Say No. Safe Sex. Be a Father to Your Child. Friends Don't Let Friends Drive Drunk. *Pare la violencia.* Winston didn't have a problem with Mr. Cienfuegos's advice, though he didn't find it very practical. How? he wondered. Would an impassioned plea from a politician turn Winston into a pacifist? Could Wilfredo Cienfuegos have convinced the Brooklyn henchmen to put away their guns and allow a cripple and a sluggard to walk off with Bed-Stuy's money in their pockets, beneficiaries of the ghetto's free-market economy?

But Winston had the power to stop the violence. Oftentimes when he came upon a scene of aggression the combatants stopped pummeling each another, unsure on whose side Tuffy, the neighborhood superpower, might intervene. Winston imagined himself dressed in a suit and tie, his face superimposed on the political circular. But the daydream quickly slipped away from him. In his mind the handbill yellowed into an Old West wanted poster. "Wanted for Councilman Eighth District—Winston Foshay. Start the violence!" Winston released the flyer into the slipstream. *I'd be a good-ass politician, though.* The sheet of paper boomeranged in the wind and reattached itself to his hip like a house cat afraid of the backyard wilderness. Winston folded the flyer and stuffed it into his back pocket.

TUFF

"Tuff, it was dead bodies, the whole nine."

"Yup."

"We still alive."

"Yup."

"Culture cipher, my brother. The fundamental black man manifest as the elemental hierarchy of the earth-sun dichotomy—"

"Don't start."

"Yacub—"

"I'm serious, don't start."

Fariq gave up trying to enlighten Winston to the ways of the knowledgeably holy five percent, and ran through possible acronyms for I-N-R-I to occupy his hyperactive mind. If Needed, Resurrect Immediately. Idolatrous Necrophilia, Religious Intercourse. Inspected—Natural Redwood Immobilizer. Is Nothing Really Important?

"Tuff, I bet you that I-N-R-I is Latin for some shit."

Tuffy's head was buried in the market's night box, trying to talk to the proprietor through three inches of Plexiglas; if he heard Fariq he didn't answer.

I Negro—Remedy Intoxication.

3· TUFFY AND YOLANDA

Winston didn't realize how drunk he was until he arrived at his apartment and couldn't insert his key into the lock. After a few misses he resorted to the method he picked up from watching his next-door neighbor return home after a payday binge. Bending down and closing one eye, Winston placed his left index finger on the keyhole. With his right hand he pressed the tip of the key into his left shoulder. Using his left arm as a guide, he slid the key into the lock with his right hand. Winston opened the door as quietly as possible, rehearsing his excuse to Yolanda for why he didn't call. "I was at Keith's crib and that nigger's phone is off, so I sent Taurus to tell Jamilla to tell Yusef to tell Laura to call you. But I didn't know Yusef got a restraining order against Jamilla after she set him on fire for fucking Wanda. Turn out that fool under house arrest anyway, and couldn't tell Laura or nobody else nothing, nohow." He was slowly making his way down the dark hallway when a block of light from the bedroom illuminated him like an escaped convict.

"Don't worry about trying to creep, the baby woke."

"All right."

Walking past the bedroom, he hurriedly made his way to the bathroom.

"You not going to come see your son?"

TUFF

"What, he got a mustache? I know what he look like."

Winston took a no-handed piss. He held up the sandwich bag. The goldfish was swimming in water murkier than Winston's alcohol-laden urine. Wedged in one corner, the fish opened his mouth every two seconds, as if he had something to say but couldn't remember what it was. Flushing the toilet, Winston dangled the bag over the whirlpool, contemplating ridding himself of one more responsibility. "Seat," Yolanda called out.

"Down," he grumbled, a long, whispered "Fuck" lingering behind him as he headed for the kitchen. Taking a deep casserole dish from the cupboard, he filled it with tap water and spilled the goldfish into it. The fish swam an appreciative lap in its new home. Winston flicked the glassware, calling the fish to attention. "Is it safe?" Yolanda was giving him time to fix a quick meal before she went into her de rigueur Impertinent Black Mama act. Winston went to the refrigerator and removed a stick of margarine and two large flour tortillas. With a match he lit the gas burners and flipped the tortillas over the open flames. When the tortillas showed the first signs of charcoal burns, he whipped the hot disks onto the counter and ran the margarine stick over the doughy circles. Rolling the tortillas into dripping tubes of oleo, Winston chewed and tried to think of a name for the fish. Yolanda's voice rushed into the kitchen, demanding obedience like God talking to Abraham. "Turn off the stove, wash your hands, then bring me some Kool-Aid."

"Dustin," he said to his pet. "Since you're a survivor, like Dustin Hoffman in *Marathon Man*." Winston dipped his finger in the water and began poking the fish in the head. After each jab he'd lean close to the water and ask his light-headed pet, "Is it safe?"

Yolanda was sitting on the edge of the rumpled bed breast-feeding their eleven-month-old son, Bryce Extraordinaire Foshay, Jordy for short. Upon hearing his father enter the room, Jordy released Yolanda's nipple with a loud, wet smack. A bridge of drool sagged between the tip of the mother's teat and the baby's chin. As Jordy turned toward his father, the link of saliva snapped and the spit rope swung into the baby's chest. Winston looked at the clock radio on the nightstand; it was two-thirty in the morning. A happy little gurgle bubbled from Jordy's throat and the males greeted each other with puffy-cheeked smiles. "What up, little nigger?" Winston said, bussing his son on the forehead.

"I told you about that. Where you been . . . *big* nigger?" Winston sheepishly opened his mouth to speak, ready to unravel and inflate his prefab excuse like a passenger jet's emergency slide. "Don't even feel it, Tuff."

Winston closed his mouth, offered Yolanda the Tupperware glass of Kool-Aid and a bite of his tortilla. She waved him off. He sat next to her. She had the gruff look of a cop standing two steps away from a car pulled over on the highway, one hand on her gun, asking to see a driver's license and inquiring how many drinks were had this evening. Winston sobered up quickly and told his story, spraying tortilla crumbs over Yolanda and the baby. Whenever he reached a turning point in the tale, he illustrated the episode by removing the appropriate item from a pocket, then tossing it on the mattress: first the gun, then the empty bag of pork rinds, followed by the bubble-gum fortune, and lastly a thick rubber-banded roll of bills. Winston finished his tale, stuffing down the last of his tortilla. He licked his oily fingertips and waited for a reaction. Yolanda examined each piece of evidence carefully, looking for a flaw in the story. She read the bubble-gum fortune, snickering at the comic: "Bazooka Joe's hilarious." She placed the bag of pork-rind crumbs over her nose and mouth and inhaled, testing it for freshness. Whipping the bag behind her back, she snapped, "What's the expiration date?"

"Yolanda, please."

"I know your ass, you always check."

"July nine."

Yolanda examined the date and grunted. She inflated the bag with a quick breath of air and loudly popped it against his head. Handing Jordy to Winston, she picked up the gun, expertly ejected a bullet from the chamber, aimed at her reflection in the bureau mirror, then, with cowboy élan, spun the firearm around her finger. Anticipating a misfire, Winston tucked Jordy into his chest and ducked beside the bed.

"Baby, what the fuck you doing? That thing's loaded!"

"Don't worry, I put on the safety. You been running around with a loaded gun in your pocket with the safety off. Lucky thing hamburgers don't have legs, 'cause you might have had to chase one down and shot your dick off."

"Take a bigger gun than that—magnum maybe."

"Yeah, sure." Yolanda put the gun underneath the mattress, then yanked the rubber band off the roll of money. Licking her thumb, she quickly counted the money into neat little hundred-dollar stacks. Winston was whisking a giggly Jordy through the air and making airplane noises. "Stop it, you going to keep him up."

Winston sat back down on the bed, bouncing the baby on his knee.

"You mean to tell me Smush just lent you seven hundred dollars."

"He didn't want to at first, talking about he would have to liquidate some stocks, but I liquored that nigger up and guilted him into it. Besides, it's his fault I almost got killed."

"How is it his fault?"

"Nigger know I didn't want to work in Brooklyn."

"Tuffy, why can't you tell Smush no?"

Yolanda started to pout and busied herself restacking the money. Pretending obliviousness to her irritable mood, Winston nuzzled Jordy's snot-encrusted nose. Yolanda placed the money in the top dresser drawer, removed the baby from Winston's arms, and walked into the living room. As she belted her black satin nightgown with one hand, she issued Winston a caveat: "Better be a goldfish in here." Winston kicked off his shoes, folded his arms behind his head, and lay back on the pillow, awaiting the tirade. "How this stupid nigger get to be my baby's father?"

"You know damn well how—I wooed the fuck out of you."

Yolanda had been working as a cashier at the Burger King on Fourteenth and Sixth Avenue, the filthy one around the corner from the YMCA. It was her first job since she'd started going to school part-time at York College, and even after six months she was still a gung-ho serf in the Burger King's fast-food realm. She wore her paper crown with pride, pretending that every customer was possibly a mysterious Burger King plain-clothed inspector making a clandestine inquisition of her franchise. Super-sizing the Whopper Combo orders with a smile, and never forgetting the "Thank you, come again" salutation, Yolanda had a reputation to live up to—her photo Scotch-taped to the Employee of the Month plaque.

She didn't notice Winston and his posse enter the store, each hooded druid bundled in overstuffed down jacket, ski mask, headphone earmuffs, shaking the December snow from their bodies like wet dogs and stomping their boots on the just-mopped floor. The group was bunched up at the counter jostling for position when Winston spotted Yolanda salting the french fries. He'd only gotten a glimpse of her, but already there was an expanding hollow in his chest. A machine in the kitchen emitted a long beep and Yolanda's thick, tight body glided over to a silvery panel. She pressed a button, mindful of her long cherry-red fingernails, and removed a batch of breaded chicken pieces from a deep fryer. Winston saw several rings on each hand—a sign, he thought, that she might have a man. Yolanda placed the chicken in the warmer, and her squat profile revealed the arc of her right breast. The brown polyester pants gave her buttock a sexy sheen in the store's fluorescent light. Her face Winston couldn't see, since her head was turned. She was talking to the manager about some take-out trivialities. Winston stared at the nape of her neck, exposed by a granny-bun hairstyle. He shivered. Yolanda turned, topped off a soda, and faced Winston. Seeing him standing there transfixed, she started, then smiled. Their eyes met, and they were instantaneously on page 6 of a Harlequin romance novel on a spinning pharmacy book rack.

As she made her way back to her register, Winston retreated a few steps and let his hungry friends surge ahead of him in line. *That wasn't no "Welcome to Burger King" smile,* Winston thought. *Baby trying to say a little something.* Yolanda avoided Winston's stare. As she took the orders of his friends, she absentmindedly stroked the thin baby hairs meticulously greased to her temples, silently repeating the dating mantra passed down by generations of black women: *Niggers ain't shit. Niggers ain't shit. Niggers ain't shit.*

"Next person in line, please," Yolanda politely called out. Winston bellied up to the register and gazed at the menu. He took his time, carefully choosing his opening words to the woman he knew would be the love of his life: "One Whopper cheese, no pickles, no onion. Two king-size chicken sandwiches, light on the dressing."

Yolanda repeated the order into the microphone, hiding the thrill she felt in the back of her throat. "Will there be anything else, sir?" Oops, she walked into it, the lounge lizard's classic window of opportunity. Yolanda gripped the microphone tightly and steeled herself for the inevitable pickup line.

"Yes—large onion rings and two apple turnovers."

Yolanda felt both relieved and disappointed. Maybe he didn't like her. Maybe he wasn't staring at her but at the conveyor belt of greasy burgers behind her. She looked into Winston's cupcake-brown face and repeated his order. Remembering her customer protocol, Yolanda pushed the fries and beverages. "Would you like to try our new cheddar cheese curly fries and something to drink?"

"I'll take an orange soda."

"What size?"

" 'Bout your size."

Yolanda blushed but didn't waver a second. "That be about a medium."

Winston laughed, leaned over the countertop, and shouldered his way into her life. "You from Queens."

Normally Yolanda would ask a customer to step aside so she could take the next order. Now she glanced from Winston's face to his hands, marveling at the smoothness of his skin. "How can you tell?" she asked.

"The dolphin earrings, the cellophane-crimped bangs, more silver than gold on your wrists. Might even have a little Long Island in you." Though Winston's deductions were correct, Yolanda pretended to be unimpressed with a sassy "Sooo."

"Where at? Hollis? Kew Gardens?"

"Queens Village, near the track. That okay with you?"

"Long as you ain't from Brooklyn, I'm straight. You got a man?"

Yolanda held up her hands, showing off her collection of department-store promise rings.

"But can he be burnt?" Winston asked.

"Light a match."

Holding trays of lukewarm burgers in wax paper and brimming with more jealousy than they'd care to admit, Winston's boys chided him into hastening his mack.

"Let's be out, Chubbsy Ubbsy."

"Oh, Miss Crabtree, I have something heavy on my heart."

"You going to have something heavy on your lip in a minute."

"Baby girl going to have something heavy on her lap in minute."

Winston struggled to resist the gravitational pull of his boys. He didn't want to succumb to the forces of friendship physics, huddle up and get into a bitch-this-and-bitch-that round-table synopsis. Yolanda rescued the conversation by acknowledging the nappy-headed ballast hindering the weightlessness of puppy love. "Your team cock-blocking and shit."

"Yeah."

"What's your name?"

"Winston."

"What they call you on the streets?"

"Tuffy."

"Yolanda."

Yolanda slid Winston a brown tray overflowing with food he didn't order. Jammed into a forest of french fries, a two-inch figurine of the Burger King surveyed his cholesterol domain. Impaled on the king's lance was the receipt with Yolanda's phone number scribbled over the subtotal. Winston dropped a bundle of crumpled bills in her hand and assured her of a phone call that evening. A macho "All right then" and he was off to share his spoils with the homies, forgetting the change. As Yolanda watched him plod away, she wondered what her friends would say when she showed up at the club with a big-boned roughneck. She could hear Tasha now: "That huge nigger sure is ugly, hope he can sing." With a smile at her musing, she called out, "Next," and without looking back Winston answered, "Me, goddammit!"

Their first and only date was a Christmas Eve boat tour circumnavigating Manhattan. Yolanda and Winston met at the Battery Park marina, Winston punctual for the first time for an appointment that didn't involve a court proceeding. Yolanda arrived an independent woman's mandatory fifteen minutes late. Winston flashed the tickets he'd bought a week in advance and the giddy couple ran down the gangplank, elbowing past the out-of-towners and racing up the spiral stairs to the upper deck. Yolanda sat next to a porthole window and Winston squeezed in beside her.

"Got enough room?"

"Plenty."

Winston lifted Yolanda's curls and a cold sea breeze raised goose bumps on her neck. She braced for a kiss; instead, Winston slapped a Dramamine patch behind her ear. "What's that?" Yolanda asked.

"In case you get seasick."

"Thanks, but the boat don't go but two miles an hour."

"Knots."

"I know."

As the boat chugged around snowy Gotham, they talked over the droll tour guide, defining the landmarks for themselves. "See that building?" Yolanda asked, pointing at a limestone-and-steel skyscraper, "I used to work there two summers ago—thirty-second floor, in the cafeteria."

"For real? You know that tan building right next to it? I used to slave there, Strudder, Farragut, and Peabody."

TUFF

"What'd you do?"

"Kept the fax machine from getting clogged."

"That's it?"

"My shit was high-tech, right? I lasted two whole days on that one."

The roof speaker crackled, "Ladies and gentlemen, I know it's a cloudy night, but those of you with binoculars can see the Rikers Island guard towers just past the Triborough Bridge. Commissioned in 1936, Rikers Island jail is the former residence of nefarious felons such as the Son of Sam, alias David Berkowitz, child-killer Joel Steinberg, the Cosa Nostra don John Gotti, and Harlem drug lord Nicky Barnes—"

Yolanda stood up and waved at the distant jailhouse. "Ahoy, Luscious and Tabitha! Jasmine, what up, girl?" Winston hissed and looked down at his feet. "You okay?" Yolanda asked, knuckling the brooding boy on the chin. "You know somebody in Rikers?"

"Please, I know much niggers on the rock."

" 'Many niggers,' or 'a lot of niggers,' " Yolanda corrected.

Winston nodded, blinking to hold back his tears and a slew of sins past, present, and future. "You got bad memories?" Yolanda asked. Winston kept looking at his feet. Yolanda pulled on Winston's earlobe, stroked his eyebrows, looking for the hidden lever that spins the bookcase, revealing the secret room. Winston raised his head and took a deep breath. He unlocked his chest plate and removed his armor piece by heavy piece. *Fuck it.* Winston started with his first arrest at age thirteen after a summer's day spent shoplifting and chain snatching with every teenage boy from the block. At dusk, he and the posse were walking down Forty-fifth Street, nineteen deep—pissy drunk, brash and boisterous as soldiers on a three-day pass. Someone shouted "Pockets!" pointing at a man exiting the movie house. Before the sex fiend noticed the red-eyed wolf pack surrounding him, they were on him. Four kids grabbed a pocket and yanked. With a loud Mama-making-Sunday-morning-dustrags tear, the man's pants fell apart at the seams. His billfold dropped to the ground and vanished before he had a chance to shout "Hey!" Coins and peep-show tokens clattered onto the sidewalk and raced around his shoes. The man scrambled after what remained of his belongings, trying to hold up his shredded pants, and fight off the boys, who descended upon the coins like pigeons upon breadcrumbs.

Somehow, one boy, Dark, a fresh-off-the-Greyhound-bus émigré from Duarte, California, left the robbery with pearls of errant masturbatory ejaculate in his hot combed hair. Eager to diffuse the taunts of the other boys and prove that his thick pigtails were "gangster" and not "sissified," he backtracked four blocks and found the victim reporting the crime to two patrolmen. Ignoring the officers, Dark began pummeling the man, shouting, "You got sperm in my perm, now I'm full of germs." Winston was rolling on the sidewalk in a fit of laughter when the police handcuffed him. He snickered all the way to the police station: "AIDS in my braids, now I'll never get laid!" Giggled through the fingerprinting: "Nut on my haircut, like I been butt-fucked!" The city went through a roll of film before finally settling on a mug shot of him sporting an Uncle Ben smile, tears running down his face.

Things ceased to be funny when the cops refused to believe that a boy Winston's size could be thirteen, and since budget cuts had made night court a liberal memory, he'd have the weekend on Rikers to prove his identity. It didn't take long. Winston disembarked from the bus, suffered through the indignities of a strip search, and strolled into building C-64. There, playing toilet-paper checkers on a bunk underneath the clock, was a double-jumping birth certificate: his father. Father and son played checkers with rolled-up balls of toilet tissue, arguing about who would call the wife, the mother. "I haven't spoken to you or her in three years, I didn't go to your sister's funeral, so phone her, boy."

"Fuck you. King me, bitch."

Unlike Winston's father, Patrice Foshay kept her promises. The last one, delivered behind an ironing-board pulpit, was: "Winston, you keep getting into trouble, I'm not going to kick you out the house, I'm going to leave my damn self and you're not coming with. You'll be living on your own. Understand?" Monday morning Mrs. Foshay posted bail on the two delinquents. She dropped Clifford off at his girlfriend's, raised a "Power to the People!" fist in the air, and moved to Atlanta, assuring Winston she'd send rent and food money until he turned eighteen.

It took Winston two years to move his belongings into his mother's bedroom. When the phone rang every two weeks at precisely ten o'clock, after the black sitcoms went off the air, his mother would ask why he couldn't be more like "those nice boys on TV."

Winston was just finishing the tale of his dysfunctional upbringing with a blasphemous "Fuck a Cosby" when an immense marble-white yacht christened *Jubilee* in bold black letters sailed alongside the tour boat. With sleek helicopters perched bow and stern and a radar dish spinning above the bridge, the boat looked more like a war vessel than a luxury craft. "So you're all alone?" Yolanda asked. Winston shrugged, his gaze cast out toward the bay. Yolanda knew the right thing to do was to put her head on Winston's pillowy shoulder and say, "No, you aren't." But she had long since learned to let the man make the first conciliatory move. Instead she filled the uncomfortable silence with cynicism: "Every nigger's father say they was in the Panthers. And if they was, they didn't do shit but hand out flyers."

"Crazy? Nigger was down." Winston flipped open his wallet and showed her a photo of a goateed black man dressed beret-to-boots in black, crouched behind a Volkswagen Beetle, his leather-gloved hands positioned over the hood, aiming a shotgun at some unseen enemy of the Revolution. Yolanda grabbed the wallet and fawned over the Polaroid. "Yo, your pop groovier-than-a-motherfucker. Look at those pointy kicks and the tight-ass straight legs." She flipped through the rest of the wallet, pausing at the food-stamp ID card to verify that Winston wasn't lying about his age. She studied the more recent photos of Latino and black boys grouped around firearms, posing in front of London-gray school lockers. Interspersed with the group shots were portraits of the same solemn-faced teens at the steering wheel of the communal vehicle or the local arcade, looking directly into the camera, holding the pistols to their temples. Winston introduced the boys on the block by proxy: "Rude, Kooky, Shorty-Wop, Point Blank—right there's my ace, Fariq." Going through the contents of Winston's wallet, Yolanda realized what made him attractive, other than his cute button nose. He was comfortable with who he was and wasn't. You don't meet too many casual black people. Winston was honest—maybe not with the rest of the world, but he was honest with her and himself. He didn't embellish or rationalize his exploits, talking in pipe-dream slang about him and the crew "coming up," "blowing up," "bubbling," and "living large." No sob-story brooding about inner-city lassitude—"You can't understand, it be mad crazy stress on a nigger"—as if Yolanda were on the outside looking in on a black man's world. She understood self-pity and self-doubt; there was no need to talk over her dookie-braided head.

Yolanda tapped a purple-and-pink fingernail on the food-stamp ID and said, "You mind?"

"No, everybody at the store know me. Go ahead." As she slipped the card from the plastic holder, Yolanda noticed there was another photo tucked underneath it. Oh, my competition, she thought; then she noticed it was a picture of a gray-haired woman who looked to be in her late fifties. She was standing in front of the Apollo Theater. Snuggled next to her, a young Winston, his nappy head resting atop her pageboy.

"Who's this Oriental lady?"

"Asian."

"Who is she?"

"Ms. Nomura. She's my unofficial guardian. She looked out for a nigger after Moms jetted."

"Mmm-hmm."

Yolanda handed the billfold back to Winston and turned her attention to the partygoers dancing on the *Jubilee*'s poop deck, one ear cocked for the explanation. "Yolanda, you ain't got nothing to be salty about—Ms. Nomura like my auntie. She live right across the street, knew my father when he was in the Panthers. I told you, she's like my second mother. If you jealous of a sixty-year-old, you got issues."

Yolanda folded her arms and peered out the porthole window. "Fucking boat move too slow." Winston pulled a bright orange life jacket from underneath the bench and carefully slipped it over Yolanda's head, fastening the buckles across her chest and knotting the cotton straps behind her back. Yolanda's shoulders visibly relaxed. Oh, this fat motherfucker smooth, she thought.

Winston flamboyantly doffed his jacket and cloaked it over Yolanda's shoulders. He was entering player mode and about to unleash his rap, the rap being the black man's equivalent of a lion tamer's whip crack to straighten out a headstrong feline, or a Buddhist monk's koan to further confuse a disciple. What's the sound of one man rapping? "Yolanda, stop fronting. I can tell by your reaction you in a brother's corner. That's on point, but let's not play no games. We all need to be rescued to some extent. You going to school, that's rescuing yourself. Just seeing a strong black woman such as yourself going head-up with the bullshit makes me wonder what can I do to straighten my game out. So listen here, I ain't now, and never will, trip off nothing in your life that makes your life better. That's not a promise, that's factoid, baby. Like the sky is blue, the summer's hot, and you fine as hell. No question. Ms. Nomura is like this life jacket, kept me afloat when times was hard. But I was just bobbing up and down in the stormy sea of the streets. You're my rescue ship plucking me out of the water—all ahoy-and-shiver-me-timbers like."

TUFF

Yolanda put the palm of her hand in Winston's face. "Save it. You're right, I like you—more than I should, but let's not get into it tonight, we got the rest of our lives to kiss and make up. Let's be carefree, like those white folks on that boat. Look, they kicking it."

Winston reached into his backpack, pulled out a frosted black bottle of Freixenet champagne, two paper cups, a brown teddy bear with a hot-pink ribbon knotted around its neck, and a Christmas card. "Shit, *we* kicking it."

Sipping her champagne, Yolanda opened her handmade card. On the cover was a surprisingly decent watercolor of a black couple sitting on a mountainside outcropping, hugging and kissing to the amusement of a brood of sad-eyed Disneyesque forest animals. On the inside, written in twiggish block lettering, was the following inscription:

> *The essence of beauty is —*
> *[pocket mirror]*
> *you.*

Yolanda saw her reflection framed by the sentimental bromide and succumbed to the wanton manipulation that is romance. With a cheery "Clink," she touched paper cups with Winston. "Let's make a toast," Yolanda said, trying to hide her wistfulness. "A toast to love. A toast to the man who got me open with no promises, no handsome-muscle-flexing tight-butt-wiggling, and no money."

Winston rubbed his chin, trying to determine if he'd been insulted or not, then raised his cup. "Then a toast to the woman who loves me for me, though she don't know me from the next man."

"Fuck the next man."

"A toast to a woman who knows what she wants."

Yolanda and Winston unclenched from that first kiss, tongues numb with champagne, sex organs swollen with lust, and the axes of their young worlds permanently tilted. Or as Winston so delicately phrased it, wiping lipstick from his mouth, "Everything's going jibbity-jibbity."

"How did I fall for that bullshit, Tuffy? 'Everything's going jibbity-jibbity.' It's all jibbity-jibbity, because you always drunk, you wino." Yolanda was still carrying on, and Winston found himself on the living-room sofa, obediently enduring his censure. Listening to Yolanda denigrate him was like going to church Easter morning. He didn't want to do it, but he sat still out of obligation, hands folded in his lap, hoping his headache would prevent the sermon from seeping into his brain.

As Yolanda edged toward the bookshelf, Winston froze. "Come on, Landa, don't." Yolanda's substantial archives consisted of well-kept stacks of *Essence, Ebony,* and *Chocolate Singles* magazines crammed with articles entitled "Hypnotize with Pumpkin Pie," "Atlantis, Unicorns, Black Love—Fact or Fiction?" and "Ten Good Qualities About Black Men Other than Penis Size." Next to the periodicals were the self-help books, all written by short-Afroed women from Philadelphia: *Sisters Doing It for Themselves—How to Masturbate to an African Orgasm; The Black Women's Guide to Finding a Real Man;* and Yolanda's bible, *Nigger, Please Please Me.*

What bothered Winston about Yolanda's choice of reading material wasn't all the doctoral-cum-beauty-shop research—anthropology seeking the missing link between prehistoric Stepin Fetchit man and the genetically engineered Denzel Washington that fossilized him, or the parascientific diaries that monsterized him. *I collected the instruments of life around me, that I might infuse a spark of being into this lifeless thing at my feet. . . . I saw the dull yellow eye of the creature open*—behold, I, Dr. Eula Frankenstein-Barnes, author of *The Good Black Man: Some Assembly Required,* have created life!

What irked Winston was that Yolanda started buying this trash after they'd married, when the relationship was problem-free, at least in his mind. When Yolanda sat up in bed after sex reading *The Black Woman's Guide to Finding a Real Man,* he'd explode. "What, I'm not a real man? How come there's never any doubt about you being a real woman?" . . . *And I had selected his features as beautiful. Beautiful! Great God!* Yolanda would try to calm Winston with a lecture about the problems unique to black-on-black love. Winston argued that there were no differences between black, white, Puerto Rican, or kangaroo relationships. "Problems is problems," he'd say. "The difference is, black couples have their bedroom behavior studied by every stuck-up bitch with a degree and a word processor."

Yolanda blithely ran her hands along the paperback bindings of her library, drawing energy from the fiction section, like an Irishwoman kissing the Blarney Stone. Winston swore on the graves of every relative he could think of that he'd change his behavior. Pulling a slim volume entitled *Pimp-Slapped to Oblivion* off the shelf, Yolanda opened to page 1 and cleared her throat. Winston cringed, grabbing the arm of the sofa and awaiting the literary castor oil. The words *"Clockwork Orange"* involuntarily escaped from his mouth. Yolanda looked up from her text. "Tuffy, I'll work your clock. After I read this, you'll know what time it is." Yolanda began reading in a voice so strong it pressed Winston into the upholstery. He was feeling a special kinship with the useless button in the middle of the pillow cushion. " 'Chapter One.' " Yolanda licked her lips. " 'Giorgio Johnson knew better than to disrespect the pussy.' " Winston stood up and objected with a stamp of his foot. "There ain't no niggers named Giorgio!" Yolanda sat him back down with the cut-eyed look. Winston wondered why he hadn't married a woman who solved word-search puzzles on the train instead of reading this trash. Yolanda continued: " 'The pussy is mighty-mighty, and Giorgio Johnson was letting it all hang out, his supplication total. His prickly tongue spelunked into the nether regions of my hot, drippy pubes. . . .' " As Yolanda read, Jordy crawled along the floor toward Winston and latched onto his ankle like a koala bear to a eucalyptus tree. "Shit is awful, isn't it?" Winston said quietly to the boy, lifting him to his knee and dandling him about. "Ever notice that none of the female characters have names? They're called Sister Child, Mama Doll, Cousin Girl, Queen Auntie Woman Purity Love. All this we-are-family, sisterhood bullshit. Fucking books should come with needle-point and kinte-cloth headwraps. Don't worry, boy, I'll read you some Pippi Longstocking later." Jordy responded with a toothless smile. "Ah, you like that, hunh? You remember my girl Pippi don't wear no panties." Covering his son's ears, Winston gave thought to countering Yolanda's redemption literature with the authors in his canon. He imagined tearing the book from his wife's hands, pinning her to the carpet, and haranguing her womanist sensibilities with some macho, gonadal writing. A dose of Iceberg Slim's or Donald Goines's pimp/ho prose would restore some gender-role balance to the relationship.

"Winston!" Yolanda yelled.

"Hunh?"

"Look at the baby!"

Jordy had burrowed under Winston's shirt, suckling and kneading his father's fatty left breast. Yolanda was livid. "See, boy a year old and he don't even know what parent is what."

"He know I'm his father," Winston said, wiping the spittle off his nipple.

"Then he don't know what a father is for, because you be gallivanting the streets at all hours." Exasperated, Yolanda massaged the bridge of her nose. "Winston, what are you going to do?"

Winston said nothing and eyed Jordy, who was straddling his thigh, for manly approbation. But the look on his son's face seemed to say, "Yeah, nigger, what *are* you going to do?" The child's forlorn expression triggered some handyman impulse in the father. Winston had an urge to fix a leaky faucet, sweep the sidewalk in front of his building, maybe check to see if the window guards were all securely fastened to their mounts. He'd been warned that having a kid would change him. Make him more responsible. Less impulsive. Winston had vowed that fatherhood wouldn't change him, at least not permanently. He knew for most young fuck-up dads the post-partum conscientiousness lasted a year. After that they reverted to the old ways with even more zealotry than before: *I gots mouths to feed, brother, mouths to fucking feed.* So what if the individual changed—what did it matter if his circumstances remained the same? An angel in hell was still in hell. He removed the Wilfredo Cienfuegos handbill from his pocket. He read the tag line: Stop the Violence. *Why?*

Yolanda ran her hands through Winston's greasy hair and kissed him on the cheek. "You staying up?" Winston nodded. "Leave me some money on the dresser for the movies, okay?"

"Just don't read Jordy that Pippi Longstocking—turn the boy into a white-girl lover." Yolanda scratched the back of her head. "I can trust you with him tomorrow?"

"Of course."

"No drinking, no reefer. Jordy is your son, not some nigger you know from your program."

"It only happened once, go to sleep. One damn tattoo."

As she turned to leave, Winston grabbed her by the sash, reeled her in like a yo-yo, and puckered up for a good-night kiss. Yolanda obliged. Winston's lips mole-hopped from Yolanda's mouth to her breasts with soggy pecks. Flicking a crusty nipple with the tip of his tongue, he covered the spigot with his mouth and took a long pull. A streamlet of milk coated his tongue. Yolanda moaned in soreness and pleasure. Winston sat back, a globule of milk pooled in the corner of his mouth. "You had arroz y abichuela con pulpo from Dalia's for dinner, didn't you?" Yolanda shook her head in disbelief and boxed his ear with a solid smack. Winston raised his arms, basking in self-adoration. "I know my breast milk. I should be on TV. I could suck women's titties and say what they ate for breakfast. Now that would be a good-ass job. 'Scrambled eggs with cheese and onions, blueberry pancakes, lightly buttered.' "

"Be careful with him tomorrow."

"One tattoo."

Yawning, Yolanda disappeared into the darkness of the hallway. "Good night, Tuffy."

"Don't be dreaming about Giorgio Johnson."

Winston adjusted Jordy on his pelvis and pointed the remote control at the dark television set. The screen lit up with a satisfying instantaneous pop. A frail-looking white boy was playing catch with an offscreen partner. The camera zoomed in for a close-up. Two features dominated the boy's sullen face: a set of knobby cheekbones and a pair of fly-wing-thin varicose eyelids. His shriveled head was covered with a baseball cap five sizes too big. The camera zoomed out and someone lobbed the kid a baseball, which, using two hands, he clumsily caught in the palm of his brand-new mitt. After tossing the ball back, the boy turned to the camera to make his plea. "Hello, my name is Kenny Mendelsson. I'm ten years old, but I have the brittle hips of an eighty-seven-year-old woman and the hairline of a chemotherapy patient."

"You got a sense of humor too," Winston said, turning to Jordy. "That nigger got—what's that disease called? Geezeritis or some shit." Winston gingerly lifted each of Jordy's limbs, checking behind the joints, in the concave pits, for skin blemishes or irritations that might be a sign of some such congenital malady. "I feel you, G," Winston said to the television. "Believe me, I know what it's like to get old before your time." He ran his hand over his son's back, reading the ridges and fatty folds in his soft skin like a familiar braille. Winston stopped at the right clavicle, where the lizard-green block letters embossed on Jordy's Kahlua-brown skin read, DA' BOMB. He sighed. *Da' Bomb. Man, nobody don't even say 'Da' Bomb' no more.* Hopefully, it'll fade as he gets older. And anyway, these light-skinned babies get darker when they get to be about five or so.

The next public-service announcement was for the Big Brothers program. A bald-headed black actor Winston was familiar with from some bit parts in a long-canceled television show walked down a tenement row in measured, authoritative strides. Speaking in a dinner-theater baritone, the actor strode up to a young black boy in a striped polo shirt. He clamped his hands on the boy's shoulders. "Providing guidance in an environment bereft of direction is the moral mandate, nay, the incumbent duty of African-American men. Isn't that right, Clarence?" Clarence looked up at the man's chin and smiled. "Yes, sir!"

"Show them what I taught you."

"Now?"

"Yes, now."

"Once upon a midnight dreary," Young Clarence began reciting an extremely abridged version of Poe's "The Raven," doing a laudable job with just the slightest hesitation at the word "surcease," and delivering the last lines with the appropriate morbid panache: "And my soul from out that shadow that lies / floating on the floor, / Shall be lifted—nevermore!" Clarence took a deep bow and the actor, his eyes welled with tears, looked into the camera and said, "Isn't he the little Eliza Doolittle? Make a black boy's dreams reality, call now." Winston concentrated on memorizing the number sailing across the bottom of the screen.

Serenaded by the canonical poesy, Jordy had fallen asleep. Winston pressed his ear to his son's heaving chest and listened to his heartbeat. "You know, little nigger, you was almost fatherless today? A hot second away from growing up to be one of those hard-to-handle motherfuckers. Having to listen to your mother whine, 'Oh, ever since your daddy died you've been impossible.' Yeah, I saved you from much grief. You'd be crying at night, cursing me because I left you. But I ain't going nowhere, dog. I got a plan to get my shit together. Put all my caca in one big pile."

Lifting his right pantleg, Winston scratched the surface of his tattoo: a cherry-red heart, ventricles and all, looking as if it could really pump blood, sitting atop a flaming Grecian torch, coiled concertina wire binding the disparate items together. The tattoo sat about an inch above his ankle and just below the tan line created by cotton crew socks—next to his palms and the bottoms of his feet, the lightest places on his body. Above the heart, in an elegantly smooth cursive, flowing like a solitary ribbon trailing a Red Square gymnast on May Day, was the epigram: BRENDA—I KNOW YOU DIDN'T LEAVE ME ON PURPOSE. I AIN'T MAD AT YOU. Winston told the tattoo artist that he wanted the words legible. "You know them notes in the old black-and-white movies? The star never opens the note and starts squinting, and moving the paper every-which-away, going, 'What the fuck does this say?' "

TUFF

Winston pressed gently on the borders of his handiwork, as if the skin were still reddened and tender. "What you think about an uncle, Jordy? Get a Big Brother who'll teach me how to spell, so I can be a movie critic. No, wait. That's out. You never see no black movie critics. Matter of fact, you never see niggers talk about anything that don't involve other niggers—well, there's that fag weatherman on Channel 7. 'Scattered clouds and drizzles through early morning, oh joy.' But that's the move though. Get a designated nigger in my life. An educated motherfucker who'll provide me with some focus and guidance and shit. Channel 7 will have a real nigger doing the weather. 'Yo, it's brick out there today. Cold as hell. You niggers with security jobs dress warm or sneak in the lady. Better yet, quit.' And Jordy, whatever I learn from my Big Brother I'm going to pass down to your ass. Boy, your father going to be one of those pipe-smoking, *Wall Street Journal*–reading motherfuckers, because I'm tired of being one of these bummy *Raisin in the Sun* niggers."

4· THE STOOP

The clicks and buzzes of the lottery machine conveyed an almost telluric importance as it hiccuped the pastel-colored tickets into the operator's hand one by one. It was as if its grinding sounds somehow helped to keep the world spinning on its axis, or least the neighborhood from collapsing into total ruin. "Okay, 2-2-1 dollar box, 8-4-7 dollar straight, 3-7-3-1 both ways a dollar." The operator dutifully punched in Winston's numbers. "5-2-2-4 dollar straight, fifty-cent box." Yolanda knocked the operator's hand away from the panel. "One second, Denesh. Winston, where did you get these numbers from?"

"I told you, I'm changing my life. And I'm starting with changing my numbers."

"But you're changing *my* numbers."

"*Our* numbers, baby."

"How much did you put in the pot?"

"Two dollars."

"Okay, then you get to change two dollars' worth of numbers."

Yolanda handed Winston a stubby green pencil and a computer punch card and shoved him away from the counter. "Winston, fill out this week's Lotto, and stop messing with my numbers." He pretended to reel from Yolanda's push and stumbled toward the rack of vacuum-sealed pastries. "I hate these stubby fucking pencils, they don't have any erasers. If I fill in '44' instead of '45,' I might fuck up the rest of my life because these stupid pencils for midgets don't have erasers."

Yolanda laughed. "You thought you were slick, '5-2-2-4 dollar straight, fifty-cent box.' Like I wouldn't care because it was only a fifty-cent play. Hoo boy, between you and this Big Brother crap and changing my numbers."

"Almost had your ass, though."

"You didn't have shit."

"Shit, for a second you was like, 'Hmmm, I like when my man is assertive. Listen to my nigger, "Fifty-cent box." Doing his thing.' " Winston stuffed a cupcake into his mouth and hurriedly filled in his application for a worry-free future. Fariq and the rest of the gang were waiting.

Fariq sat atop his concrete rostrum, the top stair of his 109th Street stoop, poring over a magazine. His eyebrows gull-winged in concentration, Fariq spat business jargon from his mouth like the morning remnants of last night's tortilla chips. "Earnings per share, decent. Median operating margin, about average. Market value, twenty-four-point-six mil. Profits as of . . . nothing special. Stockholder's equity, fifteen-point-seven percent, no shit?" Fariq's girlfriend, a thin, swaybacked woman named Nadine Primo, slid in closer to him, deposited her chin on his shoulder, and, pointing to the page, said, "This one has a nice employee-to-sales ratio."

The three men lounging on the stairs below were growing impatient. "What the fuck you talking about, Smush?" asked Armello Solcedo, a lanky half-Dominican, half–Puerto Rican. "I didn't come out here to waste my Sunday watching you read a magazine, *entiendes*?" Jabbing a thumb at their skeptic friends, Nadine said to Fariq, "Show them." Fariq removed the magazine from his lap and, with the infinite patience of a kindergarten teacher for his charges, panned it slowly past the blank faces of his boys. "My brothers, this is what we need to be about this summer— major dollars. Economic self-reliance."

"What the fuck you tripping on?" Asked Winston, rolling down the sidewalk, hand in hand with Yolanda, cradling Jordy like a football. "Your crippled ass *still* reading them kung fu mags? I don't know why you all excited, they been printing the same articles since I was five. 'Bruce Lee's

One-Inch Punch and Other Powerful Jeet Kun Do Techniques Revealed Here—for the First Time Ever.' With a picture of him doing a one-finger push-up."

He stopped at the base of the stoop. Every important decision Winston had ever made had been made while sitting on this stoop, from saying yes to his first beer to deciding not to ask Yolanda to get an abortion. He looked over at the kids playing stickball in the street. A boy who had just finished legging out a triple used the last of his breath to gloat in front of the third baseman: "I'll hit your pitcher all motherfucking day!" If all the world's a stage, the stoop at 258 East 109th Street was his proscenium of Ghetto Tragedy. Yolanda guided her sheepish man by the elbow. "C'mon, Tuffy, let's sit." The couple, dressed alike from sneaker to fisherman's hat in matching green-and-blue-striped cabana suits, worked their way up the stairs, gingerly stepping over and around the bramble of knobby knees and spindly legs until they settled in a space next to the wrought-iron rail reserved for them. Pleased to see them, the crew, excepting Fariq, greeted Winston and Yolanda with handshakes and cheek kisses. Fariq frowned, looking down and away from the tardy pair. Winston drew his friend's attention with a smack atop his head. "Never take your eyes off your opponent, even when you bow."

"Man, you an asshole."

Winston continued, his voice taking on a clichéd Chinese lilt. "It's like a finger pointing away to the moon: don't concentrate on the finger or you will miss all that heavenly glory."

"Enough with *Enter the Dragon* bullshit. You late. And this ain't a copy of *Karate Illustrated*." Fariq held the magazine in the crook of his arm like Moses on the mount holding the commandments. "This is the June issue of *Black Enterprise*."

"No, not the *June* issue, my bad," Winston said, sarcastically dipping his head in apology. "What so special about the June issue, son?"

"The June issue lists the one hundred largest black businesses. If we going to make some real money this summer, we need some inspiration, and here"—Fariq slapped the magazine with the back of his hand—"are one hundred moneymaking entities run by punctual niggers who've achieved something in this doggy-dog world."

" 'Dog-eat-dog,' " Yolanda corrected.

"Don't mock me, Yolanda," Fariq said, continuing his harangue, "Money and Allah are the keys—the keys that open the chains wrapped around our hearts and minds. The Koran teaches one how to be a lock-smith, and money allows one to buy the tools a locksmith needs. Then you can make the key to freedoms."

Yolanda's lip curled into a lioness's snarl. " 'Freedoms,' the plural?"

"Hell yeah, the motherfucking plural." Fariq rubbed his chin, searching for an example. Finding it, his hands chopped the air, accenting each word. "When Lincoln gave the slaves their freedom, singular, could they vote? Own property? Fuck who they wanted to fuck? No. So it must be more than one freedom."

"So now it's 'the right to truths, justices, and the pursuit of happinesses.' "

"College fucking you up, girl. What's your major, anyway?"

"Undecided."

"See, them crackers bending one of your free wills right there. Undecided. Black people ain't got time to be undecided. And at the college you go to it's only two majors anyway, undecided and tricknology."

"Trick who?"

"Anyway, we, and niggers in general, need to keep everything in the community—lie black, die black, and buy black. Emulate the Jew."

Growing incensed, more so at Fariq's rhetorical illogic than at his religious insensitivity, Yolanda glowered at him and asked, " 'The Jew,' singular?"

"Yes, singular. Jew."

"You mean there's one huge Superjew out there?"

"You know what I mean, Little Miss Grammar. The Jew is like that—Tuffy, what's the name of that three-headed monster that be fight-ing Godzilla?"

"Ghidrah," answered Winston.

"The Jew is like Ghidrah—three heads, one body working toward the same goal: kicking Godzilla's ass."

"And who's Godzilla—the black man, I suppose?"

Fariq rolled his rheumatoid eyes at Winston. "I told you we shouldn't have brought the women. Women don't know shit about making money."

"Fuck you, Smush," Yolanda said, looking to Nadine for gender solidarity.

Nadine shrugged her shoulders. "He's right."

"You know I'm right. Moneybags will back me up. Ain't that right, Moneybags?"

At the mention of his name, Moneybags, momentarily aroused from his stupor, sat upright. His soiled and skinny frame was crammed into the width of one mid-stoop stair, knees folded tightly into his chest, and the spongy souls of his flip-flops overlapping the stair like owl talons around a redwood bough. "Ain't that right, Moneybags?" Fariq repeated. Mummi-fied from a life of failed business ventures, crack, and old age, Moneybags stiffly raised his paper-bagged pint in agreement. "Ain't but two bitches ever made money on they own—Oprah Winfrey and—I forget the other bitch's name. Bitch invented the hot comb or some shit."

It was through Moneybags's curbside lessons in big business that Fariq had learned to decipher the stock pages, when to lowball a buyer, and if he were dumb enough to pay taxes, how to leap through the gaping loopholes. All Winston knew about the supposed oracle of commerce was that he didn't dress as sharply as he had in the past. Moneybags made his early fortune selling milk-crate seating for a dollar a pop to overflow crowds during the legendary basketball tournaments held at Rucker and West Fourth Street parks each summer. Despite Fariq's claims that Money-bags possessed infinite economic knowledge, Winston had never seen him offer any jewels of his wisdom other than the semiprecious baubles he'd snatched off the necks of groggy subway riders. Only once had he heard Moneybags engage in a coherent conversation. Two years ago, upon leav-ing a retrospective of Italian comedy at Lincoln Center, Winston spotted Moneybags's showroom, a one-man open-air bazaar on the corner of Broadway and Sixty-sixth Street. Dealing in vacuum-wrapped electronics, Moneybags hopscotched over his smorgasbord of off-brand home phones, answering machines, and cassette decks to barter with the tourists. Win-ston was about to nod a covert hello when a potbellied black man pointed at a video camera box sealed in seamless cellophane. "How much?" the man asked, picking up the medium-sized carton, examining each side as if the sharpness of the corners conveyed something of the product therein. Moneybags smirked, answering the buyer sotto voce, "Crazy?"

"Naw, man, how much for the camcorder?"

"This merchandise ain't for the brothers," Moneybags said, grabbing the box from the man's hands and placing it behind his back as if he were a suitor hiding a bouquet of roses, searching for an excuse to renege on an ugly blind date. The man backed off, a glint of understanding spreading across his face. "Your kindness is appreciated, brother." Walking down-town, the portly man took one last look at Moneybags haggling with the bargain hunters. He guessed the tourists would be returning to Munich, Osaka, and Rome, arms laden with gifts: transistorless radios and red clay bricks wrapped in newsprint.

Government attempts to revitalize minority small business through free trade agreements and tax breaks had failed Moneybags. He was no longer a one-man electronics warehouse. The effects of trickle-down economics had reduced him to peddling ghetto bric-a-brac: stolen cheese, browning meats, and over-the-counter pharmaceuticals. It wasn't uncommon for East Harlem residents to see Moneybags zigzagging across Lexington Avenue hawking a small bottle of red cough suppressant: "I got that Robitussin, baby. Got that Robitussin. Cough syrup. Cough syrup."

Today it was flimsy wooden picture frames. Moneybags placed a heavy mahogany frame around his neck. He was preparing to leave. As he squared his shoulders toward Fariq, the sun silhouetted Moneybags's dark profile against the partly cloudy sky. For a moment, the sickly sheen on his face and the graying mustache made him look like an oil portrait in the boardroom of a multinational corporation come to life. Moneybags excused himself. "I need to be going. Apparently none of you boys has any crack rock. But if I hear anything happening where you all might make some loot, I'll let you know." The proud CEO of nothing walked away from the stoop, steering a metal pushcart, one wobbly rear wheel alternately turning and sticking.

"I admire that motherfucker," said Fariq. He shouted at the slouched back of the wiry tradesman, "Moneybags, stay up, God."

"Why do you admire him?" Armello asked.

"Nigger could be out here selling drugs, doing something negative like the rest of us, but he's down with the downtrodden, bottle hustling, redeeming aluminum cans and souls at the same time. Allah be praised. All praise due."

"Fariq deep today," commented Nadine.

Fariq began thumping on the magazine again. "This list is going to give us some ideas. This summer we ain't fucking around, it's time to build the foundation. Let's get this money, hear me?"

Armello, sitting to Winston's right, said, "Word is bond, son. What the first company on the list, yo? Bet money it's a record company."

Winston turned, threatening to smack Armello. Armello flinched. "Stop it, Tuff."

"Record company—you thinking small, yo," said Winston. "Niggers own bigger shit than a record company."

"I know. I know. You right."

Armello was the only member of the crew ever to have any of what they considered "real" money. As a high-school senior Armello was a twenty-year-old all-city shortstop and fourth-round draft choice of the Toronto Blue Jays. To boost his worth, Armello's agent had him shave three years off his age and pretend he was a seventeen-year-old hurricane refugee who spoke no English and grew up on the dirt roads of Barahona playing ball with a chocolate milk carton for a baseball mitt. The ruse worked. The Blue Jays, thinking they'd found the next barefoot phenom, offered Armello one hundred thousand dollars to play minor-league base-ball in Knoxville, Tennessee. Five years, four hundred ninety-two errors, a career batting average of .074, two hushed-up charges of statutory rape, and one very public conviction for battery of a third-base umpire later, all Armello had to show for the bonus money was a worthless lamin-ated baseball card of himself, the lime-green Kawasaki Ninja parked a few feet away, and an overabundance of I'm-not-going-to-blow-my-next-opportunity determination. "I'm with you, Smush, we can do this. All we need to do is focus. Shit, I remember playing Chattanooga in late August, we were down two–one, bottom of the sixth, man on second, two out, I steps to the plate—"

"Strike three!" Yolanda yelled, jabbing a fist past Armello's chest and pointing at an imaginary dugout somewhere near the El Tropical social club. "Armello, you ain't giving no Hall of Fame speech, so shut the fuck up."

While Armello sulked, Yolanda impatiently extended an upturned palm to Fariq and said, "Well, nigger, you got the floor, the steps, what-ever." Fariq looked over at Winston. "Damn, nigger, you need to check your girl."

Winston shrugged. "What you waiting for, Smush, a drumroll? Get on with it."

"The number-one black company in America is"—Fariq paused, locking eager eyes with the rest of the crew—"TLC Beatrice International Holdings." The gang's chests sank in a collective exhalation. Everyone had expected to hear the name of a familiar conglomerate: Texaco, Colgate-Palmolive, Zenith, Schlitz beer, thinking niggers must own something they'd heard of. Seeing the crew's racial pride crash and burn, Fariq tried to swell their deflated egos. "The company is worth two billion dollars."

"So," snorted Yolanda. "Who ever heard of TLC Beatrice? What in hell do they make?"

TUFF

Fariq explained, "TLC makes orange juice. They distribute groceries all over Europe, especially in France. International foods, supermarkets, know what I mean?" Fariq immediately realized he'd set himself up for ridicule by mentioning such a staid venture as the supermarket. He steadied himself for the inevitable pillory.

"What, nigger, you expect us to go to France to deliver and sell groceries all summer? This is going to make us rich?"

"Remember eggs and bread go on top."

"Manager to register seven, I have an overring. I need the key. *La llave, por favor.*"

"Shit, none of us even speaks French."

"Speak for yourself, nigger." Yolanda said. She stood up, whipped her braids behind her back, and started singing the chorus from an old soul classic into her hairbrush. " '*Voulez-vous coucher avec moi ce soir.*' "

"We going to be broke this summer."

"Dead and stinking."

" '*Gitchi gitchi ya ya da da.*' "

Shaking his head, Fariq bemoaned the shortsightedness of his friends. "That's why niggers don't have shit. You know, the average white man holds on to a dollar for one-point-six-five years. Guess how long stupid niggers like yourselves hold on to a dollar?"

"How long, motherfucker?"

"Thirty-eight minutes." Fariq wearily leaned back against the sloping stairs. He lifted his head and said, "My people . . . my people," hoping someone would see fit to put him out of his misery. From the bottom of the stoop, Charles O'Koren, who'd remained silent until this point, willingly delivered the death blow. "TLC Beatrice ain't even a black-owned *entity.*" He waited for the gasps of disbelief to subside, then continued: "I seen a special last week—the brother who owned it been dead for years. Money was worth a couple hundred mil at least. Hear me, 'Money was worth'—ha, ha. I got jokes, right?"

Charles "Whitey" O'Koren was an American anachronism, the last of a dying breed: the native, destitute, inner-city white ethnic. The O'Korens moved to East Harlem in the mid-twenties when it was still a haven for scab labor. The slack-shouldered Whitey lived on 111th and Third Avenue with his mother, Trish; stepfather, Felix Montoya; and Grandpa Mickey. During the postwar forties Mickey O'Koren had watched tidal waves of REO Speedwagon trucks crash upon the streets, then recede into night, leaving wiggly hordes of indistinguishable young Puerto Ricans skittering and writhing on the streets like exposed grunion. "Better than more wops," he'd say optimistically, waving goodbye to the Giamattis, the Lambresis as they closed the doors to the Packard and headed for the lily-white sanctuary of the South Bronx. Soon the package stores were called bodegas and the food stocks on the local shelves were unpronounceable. Cables of cured brown longaniza puerpoiquena replaced the red links of kielbasa and bangers. In the clash of cultures pidgin arguments with Spanish *tenderos* in blood-splattered lab coats were commonplace. "Listen, jocko, I want yellow bananas, not these unripe, snot-green plátanos. Who do you think you're calling 'Mofungo'? And give me a pound of *papas*, Chico."

The headstrong patriarch ignored pleas from friends and family to move. So long as there was a local barbershop that cut "non-burrhead" hair and Guinness came in the can, Mickey saw no need to relocate. When his grandson was born, Mickey wrapped him in a green, white, and orange blanket and lobbied for a Gaelic name—Eamonn, Colin, or Paddy. Trish, wanting something less Hibernian, plied Grandpa Mickey with creamy stout and stated her case for a soft euonym, *español* perhaps, a name that sang racial armistice, so the boy wouldn't feel so different from the other kids—Miangel, Panchito, or Ramón, she suggested. After three weeks of debate they settled on the classically safe Charles Michael O'Koren. It was the neighbors who revived the old Anglo-American sobriquet and dubbed the boy Whitey.

Whenever a stranger asked Charles whether he found the ethnic blatancy of his nickname a hindrance, the hard-hearted, freckled boy of nineteen replied, "It makes me no nevermind." In private he preferred to be called C-Ice or Charley O'. But there were paranoid tendencies lurking underneath his b-boy scowl. Often while walking the streets of Spanish Harlem minding his business, Charles flinched upon hearing a frustrated local curse the living gods with a "Fuck whitey!," forcing him to ask what he'd done wrong. Charles implored his friends not to call him Whitey, and they begrudgingly agreed. However, old-timers such as Winston, Fariq, and Armello sometimes slipped and called him that, out of equal parts habit and condescension.

"For real," Winston asked Charles, "a black man don't even own the business?"

"Word. A nigger *used* to own it, but like I said, the nigger dead, now his wife running the company."

Winston could almost see the word "nigger" come out of Charles's mouth. Normally Winston chastised him with a punch to the chest for using "nigger" in his presence, but he didn't know this dead executive, and he let the trespass slide. "His wife ain't black?"

"No, Tuff, the bitch is Filipino or some shit."

"Filipina," said Yolanda, angrily snatching the magazine from Fariq's hands. She scrutinized the chart as if she were reading the bylaws of a clearinghouse sweepstakes to decide if she'd really won ten million dollars. "You mean the largest black company in America is owned by an Oriental bitch?"

"Asian."

"Shut up, Winston. Where's the sense in that? Just because a black man used to own the business, to act like the shit is still black! If that's the logic, then the damn Indians still collecting rent on all this," Yolanda spouted, sweeping the cement expanse of 109th Street with a real-estate-agent wave of her hand. "I swear to God, niggers is retarded."

Armello didn't like the defeatist tone Yolanda was setting and tried to put a positive spin on the proceedings. "Come on now, no need to be upset—so the largest black company is owned by a Chink, so what? We still got the number two company. What's *número dos*?"

Yolanda scanned the full-page chart; sucking her teeth in disappointment, she tossed the magazine back in Fariq's lap. "Norman Kearny's Automotive Group. A goddamn car dealership in Detroit is the largest truly black-owned business. This is sad; I feel like crying. A fucking used-car salesman! The next business down is probably them African niggers selling fake Rolex watches at the Statue of Liberty."

Fariq looked crestfallen. Nadine slung a sympathetic arm around Fariq and glared at Yolanda. "Well, bitch, at least my man trying. Ever since they almost got shot everybody been like 'Life too short. I got to get paid, now.' What ideas *your* man got?"

All heads swiveled toward Winston, who had tuned out soon after the "Asian" "Shut up, Winston" exchange and was now busy filling out a wrinkled pink form with the short green lottery pencil, using Charles's back for a hard surface.

"Tuffy, what the fuck you doing?"

"Filling out my unemployment sheet. It's obvious dealing with you *estúpidos*, I'm going to need the two months I got left. Anyway, I got my own program in the works. I don't need y'all. I'm just out here for the camaraderie and the excitement. Let's see, 'Date of Search'—last Tuesday."

Armello snorted, "*Coño*, why you got be so negative, Tuff? The city going catch you in a lie—last Tuesday you was sleep all day because we broke night Monday."

Winston licked the point of his pencil and scribbled on. " 'Name and/or Title of Person Contacted'—Lester Muñoz's—no, wait, Maldonado's Auto Body, 5881 West 147th Street, Harlem, New York."

Charles started to straighten up. "The numbers on Forty-seventh only go up to five hundred something."

Winston cuffed Whitey sharply on the back of head. "Stop moving, nigger." Charles placed his elbows back on his knees. " 'Contact Method'—C-lo game in back room. 'Work Sought'—speedometer adjuster, stolen parts inventory taker."

"You playing yourself, Winston."

"*Resultado*—offered position, but unable to accept position because I'm too fat for the available jumpsuits, also allergic to carbon monoxide/dioxide, whatever." Winston folded up the sheet and slipped it into his back pocket. Yolanda scooted away from the banister, putting a bit of distance between her and her lazy man. "Winston, why you acting like this?" she whined.

Reaching into Yolanda's purse, Winston pulled out the Raven .22 automatic and flashed an evil sneer. He wondered if he was once again challenging his destiny on the stoop of 258 East 109th Street. "We need to get back to what we do best, the roughness. I'm feeling scandalous, like Richard Widmark in *Kiss of Death,* fixing to push the old lady in the wheelchair down the stairs. I about get my hustle on. I know my life was spared because I'm destined for a higher purpose."

"You bugging. After it happened you couldn't even imagine a higher purpose. Now listen to you."

Winston held the pistol to his mouth, fogged the muzzle with a gust of hot breath, then began polishing with the underside of his shirt, rotating the gun in the sunlight. "Man, these things are instant imagination. It's like having a good idea, but you don't know exactly what it is yet."

5 ▪ INEZ

he gun altered the general mood of the gathering. Charles and Nadine reacted to the pistol in much the same way a childless couple reacts to another person's baby. "My boy, where you'd get that? That shit is nice. Yo, son, let me borrow it."

Yolanda and Fariq maintained wary yet indifferent cool, respectful of the gun's power, but knowing that without any immediate provocation there was no real cause for alarm. "Tuffy, that's Demetrius's gun. You stupid? You know that piece got bodies on it." Chambering a bullet, Winston pointed the gun at three uniformed men and a dog about thirty yards away, cavalierly approaching the stairs. Armello panicked and let out a bluesy moan. "Ooooohhhh. Fuck you doing, Tuffy? Drawing down on some cops! Why didn't you tell me you was dirty? You know I'm on probation, man. I'll get a bid 'cause your fat ass traveling dirty."

Armello turned to Fariq, speaking quickly and with a note of urgency in his voice: "Smush, I ain't trying to go back to jail. I didn't know Winston was carrying that piece, you my witness, right?"

"Relax, Armello, it's only Bendito and them."

As the three men and a dog came closer, Winston lowered his arms, frowning as he hid the gun under his leg. "Thought you were afraid of guns?" whispered Charles.

"Yolanda been working with me. I'm confronting my fears. Doing things to get me used to the piece a little bit at a time. What's it called, Boo?"

"Phobia densensitization," said Yolanda, happy to show off one of her Introductory Psychology terms. "But I can tell guns still make you nervous. You're perspiring and your eyelid is twitching. Wish I had my galvanic skin response equipment from the lab, then I could measure your progress with some objectivity."

The Bonilla triplets, Bendito, Miguelito, Enrique, and their brown, pink-nosed pit bull, Der Kommissar, stopped at the foot of the stoop. The brothers grew up on 109th Street, two buildings down from Winston; their complexions and politics covered the Hispanic spectrum. Bendito was as handsome as *novela*'s leading man: gigolo white, his dirty-blond hair permanently tousled by a tropical breeze that seemed to follow him wherever he went. He was enough of a nationalist to spurn the annual Puerto Rican Day parade as an affront to *la patria*. Every July he'd say, "When we march up Fifth Avenue with guns, like young lords preaching Taino love, then I'll sing 'Oye Como Va.' *Tú sabes?*"

Miguelito was a swarthy Cuban-boxer black, but a loyalist to his supposed Spanish Majorcan roots and to the United States. He felt Puerto Rico's admission to the Union would dignify his beloved isle: "We'll no longer be dirty. We'll be exotic, *como* Hawaii," he liked to say.

The middle triplet, Enrique Bonilla, suffered from vitiligo. His skin was a splotchy calico of every shade on the melanin palette, and his politics were as convoluted as his complexion. He waffled between all three Puerto Rican destinies: independence, statehood, and its status quo as a United States protectorate.

The triplets were, however, united in their hatred for Winston. The animosity between him and the Bonillas started in elementary school. One day Tuffy noticed Enrique's face looked like a beginner's jigsaw puzzle of a map of the United States. He shoved young Enrique into the custodian's closet and with a felt-tip pen placed a black dot in each sector of Enrique's face, scribbled a state name in each patch of skin, and labeled every dot with all the capitals he could remember: Sacramento, California, was near Enrique's right ear; Topeka, Kansas, under his right eye; Indianapolis, Indiana, beneath the left; and Tallahassee, Florida, on the lower left jaw. Winston turned his human political map into the teacher as a makeup assignment for a missed quiz, explaining that the squiggly black line running down Enrique's forehead, over the bridge of his nose, and ending at the cleft in his chin was the Mississippi River. The feud was set in motion, and thereafter Winston honed his pugilistic skills on the Bonilla triplets.

Despite the Bonilla boys having enrolled in every karate and boxing school in Manhattan, Winston beat the brothers viciously and regularly, pulverizing every zygotic permutation: individually, Bendito and Enrique, Bendito and Miguelito, Enrique and Miguelito, all three at once. Like many bullied city kids, the Bonilla brothers had become auxiliary police officers right after finishing high school. Their civil servitude stemmed not from any sense of social justice; rather, it was a state-sanctioned training course for a job that would serve as an outlet for their vengeance and pent-up rage. Armed only with handcuffs, a flashlight, and a ticket book, the Bonilla brothers had a well-deserved neighborhood reputation for being the last ones on a crime scene, sucker-punching the suspect in a chintzy display of cop solidarity.

The Bonillas and their dog stopped in front of the stoop. The two factions, police and policed, looked at each other in silence for a few moments. Bendito, the oldest brother by three minutes, placed one shiny patent-leather shoe on the bottom stair. The hellhound, Der Kommissar, followed with a stumpy paw. Winston spat, the globule landing inches away from the tip of Bendito's shoe, and the dog's paw snapped back to the sidewalk.

"Afternoon, *morenos*," came the greeting from Enrique.

"*Buenas tardes a los tres pendejos. Ahora, vete por carajo,*" answered Winston. Der Kommissar, whose Spanish was better than the Bonillas', growled.

"Yo, Tuffy, you better be glad this dog is on a leash, else you'd be in trouble, bro," cautioned Bendito.

"That dog is leashed for its own protection, because I'm a dangerous nigger. He comes near me, it's over for him."

"Don't you people see the No Loitering sign?" asked Enrique, using his flashlight to point out a rusty metal placard that since the turn of the century had been ignored by the poor and used by the police as an excuse for harassment. Both parties overlooked the broadsides sloppily wall-papered beneath the No Loitering sign. Still wavy and wet with paste, the block of posters read: ON ELECTION DAY EMPOWER YOURSELF AND YOUR COMMUNITY—VOTE FOR MARGO TELLOS DEMOCRAT COUNCIL-WOMAN DISTRICT 8—LIMPIANDO NUESTRAS CALLES.

Fariq made a halfhearted peace offering to the officers. "We're not loitering. We're having a board meeting. Planning how to make money this summer."

"That wouldn't include drug dealing, would it?" asked Miguelito, both hands tugging at Der Kommissar's leash.

"I doubt it. We thinkin' 'bout going legit this summer. Actually, Tuffy was just about to share with us his brainstorms."

Winston lifted his leg and pulled out the handgun. The Bonillas hurriedly stepped back, falling over each other in a dither. As the triplets disentangled themselves from the dog's leash, Winston pressed his advantage. He held the small pistol in the flat of his hand, showing it off like a downtown gunsmith. "Way I figure it is, we buy a shitload of guns, paint the noses and barrels that street-cone orange so they look like toy guns. That way when kids about to spark up an officer of the law, such as you all, the cop will freeze for that crucial second, thinking his assailant is holding a plastic toy. Surprise!" Winston stuffed the gun into his pants pocket.

"That's not a bad idea," commented Yolanda, throwing a "so there" glance in Nadine's direction. The testy young gun molls cinched in closer to their respective men.

The Bonilla brothers straightened their ties and badges. Miguelito strummed his flashlight across the wrought-iron balusters, turning the railing into a cacophonous harp. "Any more bright ideas, fat boy?"

"*Sí, claro, mamao.* I was thinking we could pool our resources and make a movie," Winston said, slipping the gun into his front pocket.

"Here we go." Fariq perked up, temporarily suspending the discord with the Bonilla triplets. "Ever go to the movies with this motherfucker? My man be at the movies in places you didn't even know had a theater. I went one time with this weirdo to see some Japanese flick at the YWCA, no less."

"*Stray Dogs,*" added Winston fondly.

"They showing the film on a wall. I'm not excited about having to spend the afternoon reading in the dark, but to make matters worse you couldn't even read the subtitles."

"Too fast?"

"Naw, in a movie where everybody is pale as Swiss cheese, sittin' in a white room, wearin' a white linen suit, they got the subtitles written in white letters. I was lost from the giddy-up—trying to read that shit was like trying to find Whitey at a hockey game. The nigger with the big lips could act, though."

TUFF

"Takashi Shimura."

"That was the last time I went to the movies with Tuffy. I don't feel comfortable. Don't be nobody in the audience but retired old white people. Not a nigger in the entire place. Maybe one or two toothy mother-fuckers flossing some white bitch. 'Oh yes, Cannes this year was *incroyable*.' Faggots. No black couples in there, that's for sure. How in the fuck you get interested in them foreign shits anyway, Tuff?"

"Playing hooky in the Village one day. Walked past a marquee on this little place that said *400 Blows*. My ignorant ass thought *400 Blows* was one of them kung fu joints, so I was like 'One adult. Where the popcorn and soda at?' Ready for some drunken-monkey style, know what I'm saying? Turns out the film—"

"Hear this nigger? 'The film.' "

"Whatever. As I was saying, this French nigger and his crimey are . . ." Winston mumbled something under his breath.

Fariq cupped his ear. "What, son? I can't hear you."

Charles, who was sitting closer to Winston than Fariq, gladly explained, "I think Winston said, 'looking for a poetry to explain their misunderstood lives.' Then something that sounded like 'Balzac.' "

Winston knew better than to give a heartfelt synopsis of a grainy black-and-white film that had inadvertently touched his heart and caused him to empathize with a loafer-shod French boy, Doinel, the young, unloved Parisian, running toward the sea in the last reel. Winston had wanted to chase behind him, clasp him on the shoulder. *Wait up. Where you going? Can I come with you? What's the story with this fat motherfucker Balzac?*

Winston vibrated his lips in disgust. "I didn't say nothing about no Balzac, I said, 'Him and his boy be like balls out.' "

"But you did say something about poetry, though."

Ready to resume his tête-à-tête with Bendito, Winston walked toward the cop. "Anyway, I got two ideas for movies, one underground, one commercial." Bendito, growing testy but feeling the security of his badge and a partisan court system, held his ground. Winston and Bendito stood forehead to forehead, nose tips touching like Eskimo lovers. Tuffy spoke, his voice cold and steady. "My underground joint is going to be straight-up guerrilla filmmaking. A snuff film where masked niggers go round ambushing police officers, field-testing those bulletproof vests. The boys come out the *Chino's* wiping they chins—*kack! kack!* Shit going to be called *Officer Down*. Sell them on the corner next to the bootleg Disney cartoons. All profits go to the families of those killed in police custody." Winston took a deep breath and began reciting names drummed into his head by his father during the "police brutality" lectures he delivered during his infrequent custody weekends. "Ernest Sayon, Jason Nichols, Yong Xin Huang." Droplets of Winston's hot spit landed softly on Bendito Bonilla's face and cooled in the light crosstown breeze. "Leonard Lawton, Frankie Arzuaga, Annette Perez."

Bendito and his brothers slowly drew their flashlights from their holders. Winston backed up two steps, planted a loud kiss on each fist, and eyed the bludgeons dancing in front of his nose. Bendito lunged forward, eyes closed, hacking wildly at the space where Winston had stood a split second earlier. "I'm going add your name to that list."

Fist cocked near his ear, Winston was poised to unload a punch when two thin arms grabbed him from behind and wheeled him back toward the stoop. Inez Nomura's touch was as familiar to Winston as Yolanda's. Emboldened by the sight of a small woman walking Winston away, the triplets raged on: "Let him go, you slant-eyed bitch!"

At one time Inez had admired the Bonillas' spunk; at least the boys tried to stand up to Winston's bullying. But the brothers had committed the unpardonable sin of joining the police force, becoming conspirators with the capitalist oppressors. Enrique stepped to Inez, his badge sparkling in the afternoon sun. "You goddamn zipperhead, don't you watch the news? Communism is dead. The cold war is over. Cuba's going to be the fifty-first state."

"Fifty-second, man, *después* Puerto Rico!" corrected Miguelito.

"Fuck you—and shut up that dog!" snapped Winston. Inez and Yolanda calmed him with soothing words the Bonillas couldn't hear.

"What y'all sayin' to him?"

Yolanda turned and flipped a lavender acrylic talon at the trio. Inez raised a V for Victory into the air and teasingly shouted, "Workers of the world, unite!"

Bendito Bonilla replied, "None of these motherfuckers have jobs, so what you talking about, 'workers'?"

The brothers turned to leave, scattering the crowd with shoves, snarls, and threats. "*Maricón*," hissed Armello to Enrique, who, tugging Der Kommissar's leash, turned and replied, "That's *Mister* Maricón to you."

TUFF

When the triplets resumed patrol duty against a nearby brownstone wall, Inez asked Fariq what had happened. "It wasn't nothing, Ms. Nomura. We was discussing moneymaking."

"Why are you guys so preoccupied with money?"

"Because we don't have none."

"I don't have any money either, Winston, but you don't hear me complaining about it."

"That's because you too busy complaining about the system. And what you mean you don't have *no* money?"

"You know how much I make running the school? Thirty thousand dollars a year. Not a whole lot of money."

"Yeah, but you got a framed uncashed check for twenty thousand dollars on your bedroom wall next to the picture of you and your kids."

"Doesn't count. That's blood money—a bribe from the United States government to be quiet, forget about the camps, and fall in line like a good American. A bribe that I never accepted. That restitution check is not my money, it's a memento."

Fariq shook his head. "You Chinese. If it was me I'd cash that check and put it right into the Hang Seng."

"I'm Japanese."

"The Nikkei then."

"I get a restitution check too," Nadine said meekly.

Fariq squinted at his girlfriend. "Fuck you talking about, Nadine? Niggers ain't never got, ain't never going to get, any restitution money."

"My welfare sounds like the same thing Ms. Nomura talking about. And it's more money in the long run."

"Funny."

Nadine, pleased with her joke, worked Jordy's arms up and down like water pumps, producing a foamy saliva that bubbled from the baby's mouth. "Tuffy, you sure this kid ain't got rabies?"

The afternoon wore on, the shadows lengthened, and the tension died down. The neighborhood kids resumed playing stickball. The adults chattered like patrons in a theater lobby waiting for the bell to signal the next act. As veterans, they knew the edges on a rough East Harlem weekend were never smooth. "Tuff, what your commercial idea for a movie?"

"That's right, Boo, you never said."

A smile lit up Winston's face like a camera flash. He pretended to close one eye around an Otto Preminger monocle. "Okay, picture this: *Cap'n Crunch—the Movie.*"

"What? The cereal, yo? You buggin'," Nadine said, tapping her index finger on her temple.

"Hollywood's remade all the cartoons—*The Flintstones, Popeye, Batman*—but nobody has done a cereal. The commercials are just as popular as the cartoons. Captain Crunch sailing on an ocean of milk, having adventures and shit. Shit would be slamming."

The gang started to giggle, seeing the appeal of the idea and unable to fight off Winston's infectious enthusiasm. "You got the Carlisle and the little white kid sailor motherfuckers for that matinee PG feel." The group closed in around Tuffy, peppering him with questions. "Who gonna play Cap'n Crunch?"

"Danny DeVito."

"What was the thing that steered the boat?"

"Sea Dog, fool. And I'm going to have Smedley the stupid elephant rampaging to get to the Peanut Butter Crunch. The fucking Crunchberry Beast, all yellow with strawberry polka dots and shit. You know who going to be the costar?"

"Who?"

"The invisible motherfucking Goo-Goo!"

The group convulsed with laughter, giddy with the reminiscence of how important breakfast cereal was to a kid's sanity.

Inez folded her arms and looked at Winston and his friends high-stepping around her. Their glee was contagious, and she wanted to join them, but age and psychological distance immobilized her. She felt as if she were tied to the stake while the natives whooped and pranced. Tuffy wiped the tears from his eyes with his wrist. "Don't give me that look out of the corner of your eye, Ms. Nomura. You about to start that 'If you'd only channel your energy, harness your intelligence, you could be the next Malcolm X' bullshit. Remember how you sent me the Koran when I was in jail? Well, I never told you this, but I traded it for some astronomy magazines stolen from the library. So you can forget about that by-any-means-necessary bullshit."

Almost four decades ago Inez was in her early twenties, a University of Washington dropout, and procrastinating in New York

TUFF

before returning to the drudgery of her parents' chicken farm just outside of Olympia. There was no better place to put off poultry raising than Manhattan in the early sixties.

Every morning she would go to the observation deck of the Empire State Building and place pennies into the power telescopes, bringing into focus the beatnik far-out, bebop outta-sight—and New Jersey. A week before the spring molt, she received a letter from her mother. It was in English—the language her mother often bragged was taught to her by her personal tutor, Lionel Barrymore, who held class in Seattle's Rialto Theater. The letter's curt B-movie telegram prose was all too clear. There was no salutation.

> Return home. This is final plea to only daughter. Born March 19th, 1943, in Tule Lake, California. Named after half-Japanese, half-Peruvian midwife, and not after the months (April, May, June) or flowers (Rose, Daisy, Iris, Violet) like the rest of the Japanese girls your age. Too young to remember barbed-wire fences, redheaded sentry who manned the machine gun in guard tower making sounds like he is strafing Japanese. We know you are rebellious, it's in your blood. Descendant of Choshu clan, whose children slept with smelly feet pointed toward the Tokugawa's Tokyo for two hundred and fifty years. During war Father and I were repatriated from Heart Mountain, Wyoming, to Tule Lake with other "no-noes," though he insists he was not a "no-no," he was a "hell no, fuck no." The War Relocation Authority give us questionnaire: Are you willing to serve in the armed forces of the United States on combat duty, wherever ordered? "Hell no!" Will you swear unqualified allegiance to the United States of America and faithfully defend the United States from any or all attack by foreign or domestic forces, and forswear any form of allegiance or obedience to the Japanese emperor, or any foreign government, power, or organization? "Fuck no!" You are born rebel, but our daughter nonetheless, one does not "forswear" allegiance to family. The kindness of gods is only reason Father got the land back. We have just placed this season's pullets in the pen. You are smart. You can help with courts and Mexicans, who are on strike with the Filipinos. They

want one dollar forty cents an hour. Father, chicken-king of Olympia, Washington, orders you home. We thinking of adding turkeys.

Mother loves you.

Enclosed with the letter were two Rhode Island Red feathers.
Ma never talks about the camps.
From the top of the Empire State Building Inez gazed past the Central Park greenery and into the clay-brown Harlem horizon. She envisioned herself driving the family acreage in the sky-blue convertible Oldsmobile, ordering the migrants about in her clipped Spanish, hoping the silk scarf would keep the mosquitoes off her face and the guano dust out of her lungs.
I've been everywhere in New York but Harlem.
She walked up Central Park West looking for street signs directing her to Harlem. Crossing 110th Street, she stumbled over a fissure in the blacktop and fell into a pothole the size of an army soup kettle. A group of girls in gingham dresses stopped jump-roping to giggle at her, laughing shyly into their palms. Welcome to Harlem.
After dusting herself off, Inez inhaled deeply; the air was thick and heavy and smelled of gasoline. She traipsed the brownstone-lined streets, tarred, narrow tributaries that all flowed into the big river, 125th Street, black America's Nile. At the corner of 125th Street and Lenox Avenue, a faded banner hung limply from two lampposts: BLACK UNITY RALLY. A gathering of about forty people was huddled around a wooden tribune. The speaker, a clean-shaven, bespectacled man, was dressed in a clean but well-worn gray suit and trench coat. He was the color of the Rhode Island Red feathers in her pocket and seemed to have butane for blood, gas fumes for breath, and a flint for a tongue. As he spoke his words burst into flaming invective, burning the ears of anyone brave enough to listen. The man paused, wiped his sweaty brow, then narrowed his eyes as if he'd spotted an approaching enemy hidden in the brush. A woman moved away from the throng, downcast and shaking her head. "That man crazy. He going to get us all killed."
Inez filled the void. Malcolm X smiled, showing off an equine set of teeth. "I'm a field Negro," he said. "The masses are the field Negroes. . . . Imagine a Negro saying, '*Our* government.' I even heard one say, '*Our*

astronauts.' They won't even let him near the plant. '*Our* astronauts.' "
After two weekends Inez was in the front row of the weekly rally, mouthing "I'm a field Negro" to herself. She soon moved into the Theresa Hotel on 125th Street and began working part-time for Malcolm X's Organization of Afro-African Unity. Her duties were mostly editing press releases, inserting a semblance of Anglo cogency into the rambling colored rhetoric. Exasperated, Inez often confronted Malcolm, clutching heavily revised speeches and essays. "Malcolm, you can't just jump from theme to theme, you need a transition." Malcolm would chide her, saying, "Now, Inez, you've been here long enough to know niggers can't never stay on the topic."

Despite all the organizational infighting and bad grammar, nothing else made sense to her. What organizations other than OAAU were thinking globally, had a charter for racial brotherhood—and a cache of weapons? The yippies had explosives and California pot connections, but lived off trust funds. The Peace Corps was a Kennedy front fraught with peaceniks too naive to understand they were nothing more than hut-to-hut corporate salespeople, setting up company trading posts in virgin markets, installing just enough electricity to power the soda machines. The Communists? The first two years were fun: the thrill of being subversive; tossing around Party vernacular in the cell meetings; the vodka; pretending to have read all the Trotsky; outing Hollywood auteurs; posing for a Communist Party ID card photo. Then things took a turn for the worse. Cynicism and paranoia took precedence over revolutionary praxis. Everyone became a possible infiltrator; the vodka was no longer used to toast union victories, but to drown the sorrows of African corruption; the bull sessions became "Ralph Ellison is a traitor" laments; and the ID card became an orange "Go Directly to Jail" card in a deadly game of Monopoly.

There was a strange dissonance in the fact that though Inez was poor, fatigued, and immersed to her neck in the world's misery, life in the OAAU was good. Hands in her sweater pocket, her chicken feathers rubbed to the quill, she ignored her mother's daily ultimatums, busying herself with plotting the Revolution. Dissidents from around the world were her lovers: South American grenadiers, African middle-class Bolsheviks, and one long-term relationship with a Chinese spy whose cover was serving as Lyndon B. Johnson's valet. The secret agent ended the relationship with a note stuck to the refrigerator with a carrot magnet.

Dearest Inez,

     LBJ is growing suspicious. Always asking, "Isn't Nomura a Japanese name? How can this woman in New York be your cousin if she's a Jap and you're a Chink? Where are my slippers?" We must part before El Jefe gets the bright idea to call Hoover. In addition, you sleep too late and your eggs are runny. No regrets my sweet, we remain united in our love for the workers' struggle. Go outside and have fun.
Big Hug,
Agent #9906 M.I.D.

P.S.
By the time you read this, the Knicks will have beaten the Cincinnati Royals by five points, and Malcolm X will be dead.

     The day Malcolm was shot, Inez drank herself numb at Showman's Tavern, listening to the jukebox shuffle between Lunceford, Holiday, Eckstine, Parker, and twenty nickels of Etta James. The regulars commiserated over long-neck beers, thankful they still had Martin Luther King Jr.'s persistence and Father Divine's ten-cent dinners. *Told you they'd get that nigger. Shit, I give the playboy reverend four years tops. He talking about poor people and Indochina—that's fucking with The Man's money.*
     Returning home, Inez drunkenly stumbled through the Theresa's lobby. The once-lavish hotel struggled to hold on to its glorified past. Its cracked and pitted marble pillars barely supported the sagging ceiling; a cave-in looked inevitable. If the structural decay didn't bring the walls down, then the newly integrated downtown hotels would. Now that Malcolm had been shot, the secret was out: more than the spokesperson for black pride had been slain; Harlem itself was dead.
     Inez followed a rutted trail that swathed through the faux-Turkish carpet to the lounge for one last gin-and-tonic to brace her against a temperamental radiator and a thin blanket. On the white Philco television Ed Sullivan was introducing a wonderful, wonderful entertainer, a Texan who'd be a really, really big star. Shyly Trini Lopez strode on stage wearing a rhinestone jacket and a warm smile, the oversized electric Gibson guitar held to his breast like a six-string shield. In a soft, chirping voice he began to sing. *I like to be in A-mer-i-ca! . . . Ev'rything free in A-meri-ca!* Inez

decided she too would like to be in America, start a community center in Harlem. Find the next Malcolm in Harlem.

The laughter had died down. Now Winston was sitting two steps below Yolanda, her crotch serving as his headrest. "Ms. Nomura?"

"Yes, Winston?"

"You like my Cap'n Crunch idea?"

"It's ingenious, but impractical and scary. When are you going to call me Inez?"

"Inez? What kind of name is that for a nigger?"

As Yolanda toyed with Winston's eyebrows, his shoulders began to sink from his earlobes. To Inez he looked a spoiled seraph—Lucifer a week before the fall from grace.

"I'm not a nigger," she said.

"You used to be."

Two years ago, before he met Yolanda, Winston and Inez were in some ways closer than he and Fariq. After a neighborhood scrap or a bad day at school, he'd often seek her out for solace. They'd walk into the bowels of Central Park, Winston cursing a storm and working off his anger with sets of chin-ups on a thick cottonwood branch belonging to his favorite tree. Finally he'd drop to the ground, more tired than angry, and tell stories about the tree. It was underneath these boughs a ten-year-old Winston watched a group of boys rape and beat a jogger, kicking her motionless body into the mulberry bushes and leaving her for dead. When he was a little older he nearly decapitated bicyclists by knotting the ends of a section of fishing wire to carpenter nails, stretching the filament across the footpath, and hammering the nails into the trees about shoulder high. At night the line was invisible. An unsuspecting cyclist would pedal past the trees and the fishing line would catch him under the chin, lifting the biker off the bicycle so cleanly, the riderless bike would coast straight down the hill and into the waiting hands of Winston and his friends. There they'd pile on the bicycle, one on the seat, one on the handlebars, one on the rear lug nuts, two on the frame, a troupe of Chinese acrobats forming a jittery pyramid and riding into the night. Then Winston would begin to cry. It was under this tree Winston had shanked Kevin Porter. Holding his hand, Inez would ask what it was like to stab someone. "It's like putting your hand into shower steam. Weightlessness.

Nothing on the other end of the knife but a nigger's sticky body heat."
Winston would read the disappointment, envy, and fear in Inez's face, and
would feel the need to ease her conscience with the rationalization: "You
know, it's not the stab wound that kills them, it's the bacteria. Most motherfuckers that get stuck die from septic poisoning and shit."

From the bottom stair, Charles pulled out a cigar and looked up
through the ghetto's version of the glass ceiling. Winston, Fariq,
and the rest of the colored executive board were still debating exactly
what would be this summer's business venture. Using his box cutter,
Charles dissected the cigar lengthwise, spilling the tobacco onto the sidewalk. While he peeled away the inner leaf to thin the wrapper, the irides-
cence of the diamond stud in Fariq's ear caught Charles's eye. "Fariq, how
you get that earring?"

"Scrambling, nigger, you know that."

Charles nodded. "Okay, then can we cut dreaming about this Cap'n
Crunch, *Black Enterprise* madness and talk about how we really going to
make some ends meet this summer?"

Winston knew what Charles was hinting at: a return to drug dealing,
this time him doing more than steering customers. "Stop right there, I
ain't selling no drugs this summer."

"We don't sell no heroin or coke. We'll sell this shit." He held the
bag of marijuana in the air. "Won't make as much money, but hey."

Charles sprinkled marijuana onto what remained of the tobacco cas-
ing. Rolling the blunt tightly, he expertly licked an edge, applying just the
right amount of saliva, and sealed it like an envelope. "Pharmaceutical's
good money, kid. Tuffy, Brooklyn got you shook, son? Shit, some niggers
bum rush my spot and put a gun to my wig, I'd be jumpy too."

Winston bristled at Charles's suggestion that he was scared of drug
dealing. "I told you, no. Just the drug thing is embarrassing. There's no
dignity standing on the corner saying 'What's up?' 'What you need?' to
every person who passes by, like I'm really a friendly motherfucker.
'Smoke? Smoke? Red Top. Jumbo. Double Up. You straight, my man?'
People ignoring you, pretending you're invisible, stepping over and
around you like you a piece of dog shit on the sidewalk. But you be caught
up, chasing that dollar. Raising your eyebrows at everything that move.
Pushing product on kids, stray cats, and old women on they way to

church. And every now and then one of them old holy-rolling bitches bites, be like, 'Hit me off with a twenty.' Man, that shit depressing as fuck. The worst is when these rides with out-of-state plates pull up packed with twelve white boys, like a damn Ringling Brothers clown car. 'What's up, you got that rock, bro?' "

"Hate it when a white boy call me bro," concurred Armello, to the head-nodding agreement of Fariq and Charles.

"True indeed. They only call you bro when they want something," Fariq empathized.

"I be wantin' to stomp them fools. Why you got ask me for drugs—I look like a dealer because I'm black?"

Nadine frowned. "But you *was* dealing, Tuffy."

"That makes it all the worse. I *am* the stereotype, angry about being stereotyped. Then when five-o blow up the spot, they treat the white boys like day campers. 'You fellows go home, you don't belong out here, it's dangerous. These people will eat you alive.' Turn to me like I'm a cannibal shaking salt on some white kid's leg—'If I see you out here again, chief, you gonna go down.' My pathetic ass strugglin' to get out an understandable 'Yes, sir' because I'm gargling crack rock wrapped in cellophane, tryin' not to swallow unless absolutely necessary."

Winston grabbed the joint from Charles, inhaled, and began to speak without breathing. The words seemed to come from his nostrils: "I ain't selling no drugs."

Inez was in disbelief: Tuffy refusing to deal drugs? Maybe her homilies suggesting how Winston should channel his street savvy into political action were finally sinking in. This was a different boy than the one who at the mention of Che, Zapata, and Gandhi would screw his face and say they didn't sound like revolutionaries but like soccer stars.

"Come on, Ms. Nomura, why you keep looking at me like that? Wipe that smile off your face—it's not like I've seen the error of my ways and shit. I'm still the same nigger. No shame in my game."

"That's right, no shame in his game," echoed Yolanda, though she, too, was relieved that Winston had renounced dope peddling.

"I haven't changed, y'all. You remember how in junior high you used go into the bathroom and there'd be one bold-ass, foul, don't-give-a-fuck nigger taking a massive shit in a doorless stall and smoking a cigarette? Well, that nigger was me. No shame in my game. I'll still mug a nigger, take a dump in a public toilet in a second."

Charles rose to his feet. "Don't play yourself, Tuff—how you think Derrick opened that Laundromat? Tito, that shitty taquería? I say we ask Diego and them to put us down."

Armello waved Charles off. "Whitey, I'm with Winston on this one. You ain't got shit to say, because every time we get popped you don't never no real time. You get reprimanded to your mama's custody. Besides we ain't got to do the drug thing nohow. Do we, Smush?" Armello hit the joint. The marijuana's potency doubled him over with a hacking cough. A plume of smoke spewed from Armello's mouth, immediately followed by a violent eruption of a clear, viscous slime that fell to the sidewalk in globs. Armello wiped his mouth, beamed, and handed Fariq the weed. "Hit this, G, my God."

Without puffing on it, Fariq handed the joint to Yolanda. "I'm going to talk to Moneybags, y'all. Come up with a hustle somewhere between dope selling and banking."

Nadine asked Yolanda for a puff, but Winston intercepted the pass, lipped the blunt, took a strong hit, then handed it to Nadine. "Damn, nigger, you got it all soggy."

Bleak, he thought, *my shit is looking bleak. Damn, that is some good-ass weed.* Involuntarily his eyes closed. His brain seemed to solidify like drying cement, and his head grew heavy. A passing cloud blotted out the sun. Even with his eyes closed Winston noticed the sky darken. "You know what would be cool right now?" he said in a dreamy voice. "A fucking solar eclipse."

"Whatever, nigger."

Tuffy imagined being camouflaged in an umbra that matched the pitch blackness of his skin, the abysmal blackness of his mind, and the mysterious blackness of space. He took one more puff. *I'd be lost in space then. I could disappear like a motherfucker. Harlem, we have liftoff.*

ONE HUNDRED THOUSAND LIGHT-YEARS: The Milky Way looks like a discarded hubcap by the side of the night road.
ONE MILLION LIGHT-YEARS: All quiet on the eastern edge of the universe, 109th Street between Lexington and Third Avenue. The front line of the war on everything, and the end of creation. In space no one can hear you scream. In New York City everyone can hear you—but will anyone pay attention?

6. THE BICYCLE THIEF

My purse! He stole my purse!" The shout shattered what remained of the afternoon's fragile tranquillity, a rock thrown through an already broken window. And pedaling in its wake was a skinny, graham-cracker-colored black boy. Shirtless and wearing only sneakers and a pair of denim cutoffs, the boy weaved his mountain bike through the stickball game. He held a leather purse to the handlebars, the cleaved straps flapping in the wind like streamers. Running down the middle of the street giving chase was a husky woman taking short, lung-burning, end-of-the-marathon strides. "That's Big Sexy," remarked Nadine, biting her nails. "That boy stole her purse." The last time Winston had seen Big Sexy was at Jordy's baby shower. She'd been thoughtful enough to buy Jordy pajamas that he'd grow into. Her daughter Lydia DJ'd, mixing salsa, merengue, and hip-hop into a seamless concerto that glued her mother to the dance floor the entire night. A pink Spaldeen sailed past the cyclist's head. "Fuck you doing, man? You fucking up the game." The purse snatcher bunny-hopped the bicycle onto the sidewalk, nearly knocking over Inez and Armello. Winston glanced over at the Bonilla brothers, who sanctioned the crime with their idleness. "Anyone know that nigger?" Winston asked. No one said anything. In painstakingly slow slow motion, Winston dug his gun from his pocket, cocked it, then slipped the small pistol onto his trigger finger like a wedding ring. "What the hell this fat fool doing, Smush?" Nadine asked. "I think he thinks he's starring in one of those Chinese gangster movies. You know how they move in slow motion for no apparent reason."

Slapping Armello on the butt, Winston nodded at his friend's motorcycle. "Uncle, but still. Let's go."

Armello acknowledged his orders with a snappy, Cantonese-accented "Yes, sir!" and the vigilantes leapt onto Armello's motorcycle. Armello stomped the kick start and gunned the bike into gear. Winston placed one hand on Armello's hip and with the other held the gun aloft. Firing a round into the sky, he yelled, "You can't get away with the Crunch, because the Crunch always gives you away! *Il ladro! Il ladro!*" The quip was barely audible over the screech of the skidding rear tire as the motorcycle peeled off into the street. Big Sexy pumped her fist, too exhausted to deliver any words of encouragement.

Inez appeared a bit worried as the two-man posse leaned into a left-hand turn and ran a red light, disappearing into the Lexington Avenue traffic. Yolanda offered her the joint roach. Inez refused, and removed a bottle of Bacardi 151 rum from her handbag. "Ain't that warm?" asked Yolanda.

"I don't give a fuck, I need a drink."

Her thumb on the nozzle, she shook the contents, then took two strong gulps that wrinkled her nose. The roar of Armello's mufflerless motorbike could be heard in the distance. What if Tuffy managed to catch the boy? Would he shoot at the kid just for appearances' sake, to show the block he'd completely overcome his fears: guns, jail, the sunrise? "Yolanda, you're not worried?"

"About what?"

"Winston."

Yolanda shrugged.

"Ms. Nomura, they're just bored and broke. Armello can handle that bike. Plus, ain't no use worrying about something that hasn't happened yet. Right or wrong?"

After a few minutes there was a war whoop from the far end of the block. Winston was twirling the recovered purse overhead like a Pony Express rider. He flung the bag to Big Sexy, the bag flying over her head and landing in a pile of discarded furniture. Winston hopped off the motorcycle before it came to a complete stop.

TUFF

"Nigger, you ill."

"You shoot that man?"

"Nah, it was mad weird, yo. I thought about it. Pointed the gun—
'Yeah, nigger? What? What? Playing stickup, kid? On my block? What?'
But I felt stupid. Shoot no nigger for no purse. I felt like a dog chasing a
car. What am I going to do with it if I catch it, know what I'm saying?"

Armello dismounted, swaggering over to the stoop, narrating his
way up the stairs. "So I pulls alongside that fool and nigger's eyes like to
pop out his head. Tuffy sidekicked the bike in the sprocket and B
slammed headfirst into a parking meter. Wasn't no resistance from Papi
after that. Where's that dank at?"

Charles handed Winston a freshly rolled blunt.

"I never could figure out," Ms. Nomura pondered aloud, "when do
you call somebody G and when you call them B?"

"You call a *moreno* you don't know Papi, B, or G, but Puerto Ricans
is strictly B, whether you know them or not. A Puerto Rican rarely calls
another Papi in public, but a non-Rican trying to be down can call another
Rican Papi and maybe get away with it."

Der Kommissar ambled up to the group, his leash taut from dragging the deadweight of his three masters. The dog wheezed and panted
like a diesel engine pulling slag. Miguelito pointed his fingers at Winston
and Armello. "You *callejeros* think you the police? Why don't you go down
to the precinct and pick up an application? You *sucias, también*. The
department needs a few good men."

"*¿Qué jodiendo?*" Nadine asked, flipping a middle finger at the
brothers. She glared at the Bonillas. "You *cabrones* didn't do a damn
thing. What if one of these two had been hurt doing your dirty work?"

Winston blew a dense puff of marijuana smoke in Der Kommissar's
face. The dog snapped at him, its jaws closing with the force of a sprung
animal trap. Winston slapped Der Kommissar across his foamy jowls with
the butt end of the handgun. The dog barked and turned in frantic Chi-
huahua circles. "Y'all want to hear a joke?" Winston asked his friends.

"Yeah," they answered in unison.

"Why do cops hang out in threes?"

"Why?" asked Enrique to the chagrin of his brothers.

"One to do the reading, one to do the writing, and the other just
likes to be around intellectuals."

Bendito slackened Der Kommissar's leash and the dog leapt for

Inez's forearm, its yellowed incisors just missing Jordy's face. In a blur of reflex, Winston caught the dog in midleap by the collar and body-slammed him off the stairs. Der Kommissar yelped but didn't stop struggling as Winston pinned his stocky carcass to the sidewalk by kneeling on the dog's hindquarters and neck. Jamming the barrel of his gun into the dog's ear like a metallic swab, Winston drilled until the muzzle disappeared. Without being asked, the Bonillas backed off. The dog squirmed and simpered.

Again a crowd gathered around the stoop to watch the Bonilla–Foshay rematch. "That motherfucker ain't barking now," commented a little girl who'd gathered to watch the skirmish, "he going, *hmmmm himmm mm himmmm*. I wonder what that means in dog talk?"

"That means 'Somebody get this fat motherfucker off me,' " Charles joked.

"Ever notice dogs in movies never die," Winston asked the crowd, pressing his knee into the dog's groin. Der Kommissar yelped. "People be drowning, burning alive, tornadoed, laser-beamed, and the dog always lives. Fucking mutt runs through a wall of flame, gets crushed by a falling car, rammed by a runaway ocean liner, and the dog comes out wagging its tail. The audience goes crazy. That's manipulative Hollywood bullshit. But this ain't Hollywood, this East Harlem, the fuckin' barrio." There was a muffled crack and Der Kommissar's carcass bounced once on the sidewalk: a forced sneeze spewed a mist of blood and mucus from his black nostrils. With some effort Winston yanked the gun from the dog's ear. He swabbed the ear wax and blood-clotted gun barrel on his pants leg, then punted the dead dog into the gutter. "Bet you won't be snapping at little kids no more."

Forgetting all of his police training, Bendito rushed Winston like a berserk third-grader, arms windmilling, propelling him headlong into battle. Like a pawn making an *en passant* capture, Winston flanked Bendito's frontal assault with a sidestep, and uncorked a right hand that caught the officer flush on the chin. The crack of the cop's jaw dislocating was louder than the gunshot. Bendito lay on the sidewalk, eyes closed, the brass badge on his chest slowly rising and falling. Seeing their oldest and strongest brother supine, Enrique and Miguelito turned heel and ran, catcalls of "Mommy!" flogging them down the block. It was a neighborhood beef; no one worried about the beaten officers calling the cops.

One stickball player cautiously touched Der Kommissar's gummy nose and exclaimed, "Hey, it's cold. I thought when a dog's nose is cold that meant they was healthy." Another boy pressed his hand to Bendito's nose and remarked, "This one's warm. What that mean?"

Yolanda brushed aside the circle of stunned children staring at Der Kommissar's carcass. She grabbed one of the dog's cropped ears, lifted its head, then dropped it back into the gutter. "I knew it—no exit wound. These pits got thick-ass skulls. Learned that in my animal husbandry class."

Nadine downplayed Yolanda's observation. "You're not taking into account the size of the gun—it was only a two-fifth."

"But I am taking into account the size of your brain, bitch."

"Heifer."

"Ho, ad infinitum."

"Speaking of animal husbandry, Yolanda, you better check your man," Charles said, rolling another marijuana cigarette. Winston was in the middle of the stickball infield, standing on the manhole cover that was second base. He stared directly into the sun for few seconds, then looked down at the manhole cover as if he were comparing their dimensions. "He having a breakdown like an '89 Ford."

"Shut up, Whitey!" Yolanda called out to Winston: "Honey, what's the matter?"

"I killed a dog."

Unmoved by Tuffy's behavior, Fariq questioned his friend's sincerity. "You've put niggers in comas, and you feeling guilty about shooting a fucking dog?"

"It was just a dog, it didn't know no better. I mean, it took a minute, but now I'm like damn, that dog could have been me back up in Demetrius's spot two weeks ago. Niggers could've been looking at my dead body. Talking about, 'It's just some nigger, he didn't know no better.' "

Fariq tossed Winston his cellular phone. "Well, call somebody who cares, you big bitch."

"Don't be like that, Smush," Yolanda pleaded. "Say something to him. He just trying to turn his life around but he don't know how."

Fariq waved her off. "Tuff like a big ol' battleship that sees some torpedos heading right for it. He want to turn on a dime and spin out the way, but he can't. Too much momentum. Nigger too big. Moving too fast. Tuff gots to deal."

"And y'all supposed to be boys. You not right, Fariq."

Winston had Fariq's slightly damaged cell phone pressed to his ear. "Hello, Big Brothers of America? . . . Yeah, I need a Big Brother. . . . No, I don't want to *be* a Big Brother, I *need* a Big Brother. . . . How old am I? Twenty-two . . . Too old? To whom am I speaking? . . . Mr. Russo? Mr. Russo, you don't send a nigger to 291 East 109th Street, you going to wish you had. . . . Foshay. Winston Foshay." Laughing, Fariq flipped his business magazine in the general vicinity of the trash barrels. "Motherfuckers is hopeless."

Feeling better, Winston walked back to the stoop. He handed Fariq his phone and took the bottle of rum from Inez. Unscrewing the pink top, he downed a capful of liquor. "Wooo! Yeah, this'll do." Slowly, he circled Der Kommissar, liberally splashing the pungent spirits around the carcass.

"Winston, what are you doing?" asked Inez.

"Standing on that manhole cover, looking down, I had a thought." He took another sip, this time eschewing the cap. "Ms. Nomura, how many books have you given me to read over the years? About thirty?"

"I guess."

"You know how many of those I read? Two: *Go Tell It on the Mountain* and *Musashi*. And out of those two books I remember nothing from *Go Tell It on the Mountain,* and one chapter from *Musashi.*" Winston asked Charles for some matches. He struck one and threw it onto the ring of rum. Suddenly the dog was encircled by an ankle-high wall of fire. "Miyamoto Musashi a samurai, right? Nigger trying to find the way of warrior and shit. Killed umpteen motherfuckers and still don't know any more than when he hadn't killed nobody. So one day he asks a monk for some advice. 'Show me the way' and shit. With a stick the monk draws a circle in the dirt around Musashi and walks away. Musashi like, 'What the fuck?' "

Charles handed the blunt to Nadine. "Nigger, I'm like, 'What the fuck?' "

Winston pressed on. "Musashi stood in that circle for hours trying to figure out what the monk meant. Finally he has a revelation; he and the universe are one. The circle is like time and space, never-ending."

"Yo, Tuff, you do not need to be smoking no weed. You have lost your fucking mind. On the strength, just say no to drugs."

Winston spread his arms out wide as he could. "Extend the circle, its edges go the ends of the universe." He closed his arms and made a small circle with hands. "Shrink the circle, it becomes size of your soul."

Inez and Winston shared a knowing smile: the Big Brother from the agency would be his monk. Winston poured the rest of the rum over Der Kommissar's body, inadvertently spilling some on Bendito Bonilla, who, still unconscious, was perilously close to the fire. Winston nudged him out of harm's way with the side of his foot, then tossed the bottle back to Inez. But before he could light another match, Charley O' flicked the remainder of his joint onto the dog. A column of black smoke rose into the air, and underneath it the dog's fur crinkled and its hide sizzled.

"You a hostile person, Tuffy. You got some issues," Yolanda said from behind Winston, stepping over Bendito Bonilla and joining him outside the funeral pyre. She saddled Jordy on Winston's shoulders. Fariq was bent over Bendito, probing the officer's slow-breathing torso with his crutch.

Peering over his shoulder, Inez swallowed a mouthful of rum and asked how long Bendito would be unconscious.

Fariq stood up and said, "I don't know, but he ain't been out that long, about five minutes."

"I thought knocking someone out with one punch was some 'manipulative Hollywood bullshit.'"

"No, that shit is on the real. Cockstrong nigger, nice with the hands, like Tuffy, catch you right, forget about it. I seen niggers knocked unconscious for twenty, thirty minutes. Motherfuckers pissing on 'em and shit." He unzipped his fly and straddled Bendito. "Come to think of it . . ."

7 ▪ A SPOONFUL OF BORSCHT

abbi Spencer Throckmorton cajoled his temperamental 1966 Ford Mustang onto East 112th Street. "There it is," he said aloud, turning down the volume on his eight-track player and leaning across the passenger seat for a closer look at a brick building in the middle of the block. "It" was Congregation Tikvath Israel of Harlem, the last synagogue in Harlem. Six years had passed since Spencer had visited Spanish Harlem, and in the temple's place was La Iglesia de Santo Augustine.

Spencer double-parked the car. He stood on the sidewalk and stared at the brownstone. The building's remodeled facade was in excellent shape. A new gutter lined the roof and ran down the sides of the church. The cracks under the second-story windows were filled and smoothed with spackle. The cement Star of David carved in the pediment above the doorway was gone, replaced by a generic etching of the Son of God and two hovering angels in prayer. But to Spencer's joy, buried under countless coats of paint, a small mezuzah remained nailed inside the doorjamb. In restoring the building, the Catholics, as usual, had done an excellent job of presenting the big picture without paying much attention to detail.

During his last year of rabbinical school Spencer served his internship under Rabbi Abe Zimmerman at Congregation Tikvath Israel of Harlem—or Constipation Tic Bath Unreal of Harlem, as the rabbis liked to refer to it while dusting the holy scrolls. The Jewish population of Harlem, once numbering over 100,000, had long since evaporated. When Spencer interned at Congregation Tikvath, the membership rolls listed twenty worshipers, twelve of whom were ambulatory, the rest attached to life-support systems at Mount Sinai Hospital. Two of the more regular worshipers weren't even Jewish: Oscar and Rosa Alvarez, a Puerto Rican couple who loved to listen to the cantor, Samuel Levine, sing his solos ("*Dios mío*, he sounds like Caruso"). Sometimes in the midst of Levine's chanting "Shema! Adonai elohenu, Adonai echad!" Oscar, moved to the depths of his soul, would wail "Changooo!"—his invocation of the Yoruba god—momentarily bringing the solemn services to a halt. "*Lo siento! Lo siento!* It won't happen again."

On the last Rosh Hashanah Spencer celebrated in the temple, he convinced Rabbi Zimmerman to let him bring in the New Year with a call from the shofar that would rattle the windows. He blew from the diaphragm, as Rabbi Zimmerman had advised, but all he produced was a garbled, flatulent tone. A quarter of the congregation died that year, and Spencer felt as if he were the most undesirable of God's chosen people.

Spencer started the Mustang's ignition, then leaned on the horn for a solid minute. Blindly plunging his hand into the mountain of cassettes on the dashboard, he shoved a pink Loggins and Messina tape into the eight-track player and double-checked the address taped to the sun visor: Winston Foshay, 291 East 109th Street, first floor.

Why the media paid so much attention to the crisis of the black family was a mystery to Spencer. His father, a successful mortician, was a constant presence in his life, and the parade of greedy wives had provided Spencer with an overabundance of mothering. Spencer grew up in Palmer Hills, a black upper-class enclave of Detroit. Well-rounded and comfortable as his childhood was, it prepared him for nothing but cocktail-party patter and entry into a prestigious university. When he wasn't attending weekend classes in classical piano, jazz trombone, ice skating, Chinese calligraphy, or conversational Swahili, he was drag-racing through town in his sixteenth-birthday present, a mint-condition Mustang convertible.

The first family rift occurred over two decades ago, when Spencer spurned legacy status at the alma mater of his father and grandfathers before him, Morehouse College, and chose to attend Theodore College, a small, overpriced New England white liberal-arts school geared toward molding the minds of the wealthy A-minus student. During his freshman year Spencer became what his dad termed "a lapsed Negro" and fell in love with Belgian ales, easy-listening radio, and a ponytailed, athletic red-head named Hadar Nepove.

Hadar and Spencer met in front of the dorm during a late-night fire drill, two sleepy first-year students waiting for the all clear. Hadar's frisky bosoms were poking out of her cotton nightgown like curious kitten heads. Spencer's pants bulged like a wind sock in a hurricane. Hadar stuffed her breasts back into her frock and winked at a leering Spencer.

"When opportunity knockers . . ."

"What?"

"You know, that's the first time anyone has ever winked at me. It's very unsettling. I'd rather you grabbed my ass. Then I'll know I'm not misinterpreting your signals."

"You wanna get a beer?" Hadar asked, nodding toward the campus pub, the Rathskeller.

Spencer bowed. "After you, m'lady."

They waited out the remainder of the fire drill dressed in their pajamas, drinking wheat beer and listening to German oompah-pah music. The conversation was brisk, since Spencer had prepared for such a moment by spending most of his free time at the local kiosk reading every magazine and was ready to fake a knowledgeable discussion on any topic from the situation in the Middle East to Victorian antique furniture.

Hadar was not as eager to please. Though Spencer's Motor City swarthiness was of some primal appeal, she didn't quite trust him. He seemed too comfortable. Here they were, Jew and black, in a loud faux-Bavarian beer hall, drinking from steins served by Rubenesque barmaids clad in dirndls, and Spencer was saying how relaxed and at home he felt: "It's like I'm really Lutheran." Spencer never questioned whether he fit in; if he was there, he belonged. A southern Jew surrounded by New England bluebloods, Hadar put up a brave front. She felt obliged to throw herself into the bastions of Gentile superiority—Theodore College, the Rathskeller, the crew and rugby teams—not sure whether she was being self-affirming or self-hating. Sometimes when Hadar phoned her family in Nashville, she'd say "regatta" and her grandmother would cry.

Spencer was agendaless, and his cultural neutrality made Hadar uncomfortable, yet envious of his unwillingness to be labeled. "Hadar, the only time I feel black is when I look at my hands," Spencer said, spreading his fingers out in front of him.

"How do you feel when you aren't looking at your hands?" Hadar asked.

"Normal."

For three years Spencer loved Hadar from afar, happy to lend her his notes and cheer on her scull from the riverbank. Late one night, after a regatta victory party, a drunk Hadar asked Spencer to walk her home. Sitting cross-legged on the floor, he flipped through her music collection. "Hadar, we've got identical taste in music. Every album you have, I have—well, not the album, but the eight-track."

"No way! Nobody listens to my music—my friends won't let me near a radio," she said, packing the bowl of her bong with a soggy clump of black hash.

"Then your friends don't have any taste. This is real music. Music that puts you in touch with your feelings. Man, you can't hide from Barry Manilow, Dan Fogelberg, Art Garfunkel, Karla Bonoff, Jackson Browne. And this Leo Kottke album is—dare I say it?—nonpareil."

"Hold this." Hadar passed Spencer the bong and pulled a top-of-the-line Ovation acoustic guitar from under her bed. She placed the guitar on her lap and expertly plucked a few familiar chords. She began to sing, "All we are is dust in the wind. . . ." Spencer lifted his thumb from the bong's air valve, carbing the thick column of smoke into his lungs. He exhaled just as Hadar was fading out of the last chorus as if a sound man were hidden away in the closet. When the *d* in "wind" melted away like a snowflake on her tongue, Spencer proposed.

Spencer and Hadar moved out of their respective dorms and scheduled the marriage for a year hence, the day after graduation. They took turns announcing the impending nuptials to their parents. Spencer went first. "Hello, Dad, I've got a new girlfriend, her name is—"

"That's great news, son, but I've got something to tell you. You've got a new mother, Niecee Walters. Say hello to the boy, you fine, foxy thing, you." Spencer squeezed Hadar's hand, swearing lifelong allegiance, no matter the sacrifice.

The call to the Nepove household went somewhat smoother than the one to Spencer's father. "Hello, Mom, Dad, Grandma—can you hear me? Everyone all there?" Hadar's mother answered in an exaggerated southern accent: "We's all assembled, darlin', like kittens in a basket. What is it you is so giddy about? Vandy's playing Georgia in two minutes—got a new running back this year, Clovis Buckminster. Boy big as the sultan's house, so be quick about it."

"Mom, I'd like to introduce my fiancé, Spencer Throckmorton."

"Hello," greeted Spencer from the extension phone, exuding confidence, "Mom, Dad, Nana." From the other end came the sound of something tumbling to the ground.

Hadar gasped, "Mommy, what happened?"

"Uh, nothing, *bubeleh*. Everything's fine." Mr. Nepove responded, "That's, er, good news," then to the hired help, "Melba, prop Grandma's head up with a book or something and get her some water."

"What's wrong with Nana?"

"Nothing—she had an attack. Hadar, this Throckmorton isn't a member of the tribe, is he?"

"Nothing to fear, Mr. Nepove, I'm very sympathetic to the plight of Jewish people around the world. You've heard of Jews for Jesus, well, consider me a—" Spencer racked his brain for an appropriate alternative alliteration. "Consider me a Zairian for Zionism."

"Spencer, you're black?"

"Yes, sir."

"Well, you know what they say: 'If you're not part of the solution, you're part of the problem.' "

"Mom?"

"That's wonderful news, Hadar. And don't worry about Nana, she'll come around. Christ, our kick-return coverage is pitiful this year! Someone tackle that boy!"

Grandma did come around, on the condition that Spencer convert to Judaism. During that last semester before graduation, Spencer began his conversion by meeting with the Hillel House's clergyman, Rabbi Eisenstadt, on alternate Thursdays. Together they studied the tenets of the Jewish faith, reciting passages and prayers applicable to the conversion. One Thursday, Rabbi Eisenstadt asked Spencer how he, as a Jew, would spend Christmas Day. Spencer said he'd go to the movies like everyone else, and Rabbi Eisenstadt pronounced him fit to be an American Jew. *Mikveh*, the ceremonial cleansing, was held in a stagnant pond on the college's south campus. Spencer exited the waters, sopping wet, dripping with algae, silt, and soggy underbrush, physically dirtier than when he went in, but spiritually purified. "Congratulations, Spencer," Rabbi Eisenstadt said proudly. "I've forgotten to ask you one thing, Spencer, but it shouldn't be a problem. You're circumcised, aren't you?" Spencer blanched, slowly shook his head no, and was handed the business card of a Mr. Epstein, emergency mohel.

The bris had all the backroom horrors of a 1950 Mexican-border-town abortion: the mailed instructions, code words to be exchanged at the rendezvous point in front of a corner pharmacy. Spencer and Hadar climbed into a minivan already seating two other blindfolded goy/Jew couples. During the long, meandering ride to the clandestine medical offices, Spencer tried to memorize auditory landmarks, just in case.

"The mohel will see you now," the nurse said, guiding Spencer down a dim corridor lit with buzzing and blinking fluorescent tubes.

"Relax, my friend. I'm Mr. Epstein." Mr. Epstein's breath smelled of gin and lime, and to Spencer's disappointment, he was clean-shaven. Spencer had pictured a man with an Eastern European accent and a full beard. With a callous, ungloved hand Mohel Epstein tugged on Spencer's penis as if he were ringing a church bell. "Oww!"

"You're penile sensitive—we'll use the anesthesia." Mohel Epstein peeled back Spencer's foreskin and took a sip of his drink. "A bit of smegma buildup—Nurse Lacey, the novocaine." Mohel Epstein plunged the needle into the tip of Spencer's penis, and the last thing Spencer felt was Epstein stenciling a very crooked line around what he called the "turtleneck" of his penis.

As a blindfolded Spencer groped his way into the van for the return trip, he felt Epstein place a hand on top of his head. "Hold up a second, son, you need a name. Henceforth, you shall be known by the Hebrew name of Yitzhak." Spencer was disappointed, having hoped for a short, sporty three- or four-letter name: Ari, Zev, Seth. He'd never known a Seth who wasn't cool.

For the next two weeks, Hadar treated Spencer like a wounded war veteran come home. She cooked, sang, and teased him into painful erections. One night she drew a pair of dark sunglasses on the white gauze bandage that covered his dick head, playfully addressing Spencer as "Yitzhak, the invisible penis." On unveiling day, Hadar unwrapped the bandages. Instead of saying "ta-dah" and welcoming Spencer's new penis into the world with a little fellatio, Hadar covered her mouth to stifle a scream and ran out of the bedroom sobbing. Spencer examined his new member. His dick looked as if it had been mutilated by a broken grade-school sharpener. He vainly tried to blow and brush away the corkscrew bits of scar tissue from his penis as if they were wood shavings. "Not to worry, honey—it's just a little bruised, is all."

Despite the newfound carnal pleasures she received from Spencer's penile mangling, Hadar left him at the end of the summer. "You're too Jewish," she explained, leaving him to a pile of law-school rejection letters.

As a result of his conversion efforts, Spencer's grades had dropped so dramatically that despite his skin color and his ability to pay for three years of graduate education without financial assistance, he couldn't get admitted to even the chintziest law schools. Spencer thought of appealing the decisions but knew no admissions board in the country would be willing to acknowledge the mind-numbing rigors of a black male in an interracial relationship. "But you don't understand, dating a white girl *is* an extracurricular activity!"

Not wanting to waste his conversion, Spencer moved to New York and enrolled in Hebrew Union's rabbinical program. Four years later he graduated, second-to-last in his class, and with one job prospect— "kosherizing" the steers in a slaughterhouse in Ames, Iowa. Turning down the offer, Rabbi Throckmorton supplemented his modest trust fund by guest-lecturing at the more liberal synagogues. His most popular address was entitled "The Ignored Indispensability of Jewish Support for African-American Politics and Art Forms: Without the Observers of Shabbat There'd Be No Martin Luther King Mountaintop, Bebop, Hip-hop, or Bad Shakespeare Productions." Soon word of the existence of a hip young rabbi "who just happens to be black" spread. Spencer obtained notoriety as a freelance rabbi, speaker, and journalist, and New York City's leading Jewish and secular publications, mistaking his innocuousness for intelligence, competed for his services. Spencer was the only black friend of many of the city's political organizations. And since there was only one degree of separation between him and the Manhattan activists, but an immeasurable distance between them and the rest of mysterious black America, officers of various organizations would ask Spencer to recommend like-minded and like-tempered black folks for those high-paying display-window positions for which qualified black candidates were invariably hard to find. "Rabbi Throckmorton, do you know any black people qualified to head up our financial department in Milwaukee?

TUFF

Remember, they must be smart as a whip." No one ever called Spencer looking for qualified *white* candidates who were smart as a whip, or even fellow Jews who were dumb as a doorknob; but he didn't mind so long as they called.

Spencer's junket to East Harlem was no altruistic act. The trust fund was petering out, and Spencer was on assignment, as one of the few black writers who, as his African-American editor at a local paper put it, "possess a command of *the language* that most of *us* don't have. Can describe the perverse ghetto mentality in a vernacular familiar to our readers. Doesn't write in music-magazine expletive." Spencer had been shocked by his editor's elitist banter, but the banknote on the condominium was due, and with a gracious smile he played along. "I'm just keeping it real, homeboy."

Having schmoozed up the editor, he pitched an idea for a Sunday feature, using the tried-and-true derisive-article-about-minorities-written-by-a-minority approach. "Let's capitalize on the city's decreasing crime rate," he said, straightening his tie to convey his seriousness and urbanity. "My sense is that your readership wants reassurance that this drop is more than just a lull. They're seeking a guarantee that the criminal element—and let's be frank, I mean the feral African-American and Hispanic youth, and one or two Italian boys—isn't in hibernation like locusts awaiting nature's signal. Who's to say that one day without warning the hatchlings won't swarm and devour the city?"

The editor tilted back in his chair, thumbs linked under his suspenders. "A CAT scan of the sleeping giant. It's a bit alarmist—where's the human interest angle?"

"A sidebar on the history of African-American paedogenesis."

"Big-bellied black girls—always good fodder for the editorial page. But what makes you think you'll be able to mingle with the nitty-gitty element? Blend in and become one of the gang?"

Spencer hunched his shoulders, folded his arms tightly across his chest, and delivered a line of classic hip-hop meter, laying out the verse as if he were a tap dancer challenging another hoofer to match a complicated step:

> *I'll take seven MCs*
> *Put 'em in a line*
> *Add seven more brothers*
> *Who think they can rhyme. . . .*

The editor, taking his cue like a pro, finished the verse off like a Japanese court poet exchanging haiku with Bashō.

> *Well it'll take seven more*
> *Before I go for mine.*
> *Now that's twenty-one MCs*
> *Ate up at the same time.*

"You're good, Throckmorton. You're very good."

Two stern-faced teenage boys flanked the entrance to 291 East 109th Street. Studies in asymmetry, each lad sported a single pant leg hiked up to knicker height, exposing a thin calf lotioned to a mahogany sheen, one earring, one nose ring, and one shaved eyebrow. To further the sense of fashion imbalance, the taller kid's T-shirt read, I AIN'T GOT TIME FOR NO FAKE NIGGAS, and the other's shirt said, I LOVE BLACK PEOPLE, BUT I HATE NIGGAS.

Spencer felt his world listing. "Hello, boys." He raised his arms like a shaky gymnast on a balance beam and the wooziness abated. "Your shirts bespeak a bit of a familiar paradox. The quest for the real nigger within us, and the simultaneous hatred for that selfsame nigger as other. As in 'I'm a real nigger, but I hate all other niggers who aren't like me in ways that fit my idiosyncratic perception of essentialist niggertude.'"

" 'Boys'?" said the short one. The other kid stared past Spencer, eyes fixed on the Mustang's vintage hubcaps.

"Not 'boy' in the pejorative sense of the word—I meant like 'homey,' 'brother man,' 'compadre,' 'nigger' even. Do you know where I can find the Foshay family?"

The young man turned to his partner and began speaking as if Spencer weren't there. "You hear *this* nigger, brother man. How much you think them rims is worth?"

Feeling somewhat anxious about the future of his automobile, Spencer pulled out his *Tiny Tome of Jewish Enlightenment* and comforted himself with a passage from the Talmud: "God detests a man who rushes to accuse a neighbor." Squeezing between the two boys, he entered the building.

The lobby was an atomic cyclotron: kids flocked about the hallways, black and brown molecules sliding along the linoleum, bouncing off the walls, reacting to boredom, the summer catalyst. "Anyone know Winston Foshay?" At the sound of Spencer's voice every child froze, instantly inert. Spencer tried another tack. "Winston Foshay? *Buenas tardes, muchachos. Yo buscando para el niño negro,* Weeenston Foshay?" Nothing. At the end of the hallway a door opened. "In here," said a faceless voice. The children didn't move until the door shut tightly behind him.

Spencer didn't receive the fanfare he'd expected. He'd prepped for his mentorship by rereading his collection of pauper literature—Steinbeck, Bukowski, Hansberry, Hurston—hoping to gain some insight into the lives of the working poor. Spencer thought he'd walk into a welcoming party atmosphere—balloons and a paper banner hanging over a representative sampling of the dignified poor. The sturdy matron would offer him a party favor, a one-candle cupcake, and, after a bosomy hug, introduce her ragamuffin bastard.

He followed the voices down the hallway and into the cramped living room. There was a chesty black woman inside but this one took one look at Spencer and muttered, "Oh, hell no," and plopped down onto the couch, shaking her head in disgust. An obviously physically handicapped gentleman held up the magnifying glass he was using to examine some counterfeit twenty-dollar bills, and cast one enlarged eye toward the rabbi. "Tuffy, they sent you one of them alternative-hippie-goofball niggers."

"I tried to find the apartment, but the kids in the hall wouldn't tell me where Winston lived."

The black behemoth in baggy jeans and tank top motioned for Spencer to sit in the lawn chair next to the bookshelf. "They probably thought you was a cop. If you'd have asked for Tuffy, they'd have told you which door to knock."

Spencer carefully sat in the creaky chair and faced what he guessed by the stoic look on his hosts' faces would be his tribunal. "I'm Spencer Throckmorton. You folks must be Winston's siblings. And where is the lucky protégé?" Spencer pointed to the child, who was doing the suspect lean against the television screen, hands on the tube, legs apart, eye-to-eye with an R&B diva, shaking his diapered behind to the beat. "Surely that tyke isn't little Winston?" he asked. No one answered him. He looked about the stuffy, windowless, stiflingly hot room, feeling, for one of the few times in his life, out of place. "This motherfucker got dreadlocks!" yelled the woman.

The big man placed his chin in his hand, "Man, I hate niggers with dreads. A coconut motherfucker, all right, but an American nigger? They too stuck-up."

"Think they playboys."

"But if they didn't have dreads they'd look like plain old mailman niggers from around the way."

"Wouldn't be so special."

"So fucking spiritual."

"So fucking revolutionary."

"So together."

"Self-actualized."

"Bracelet-, bangle-wearing, bitch-ass niggers."

"Don't even listen to reggae music."

"Most of all you can't trust 'em."

"True."

The baby stopped dancing, climbed onto Spencer's lap, and tugged violently at one of his knotted strands of hair, dislodging the yarmulke from his head. The crippled kid dropped his magnifying glass and sounded the alarm:

"Je-e-e-w!"

Everyone looked at Spencer and waited for him to explode like a terrorist grenade rolled into the midst of a gathering of innocents. Jordy scooped up the knit cap and waddled over to his father. "What up with this?" asked Winston, flipping the yarmulke back to Spencer.

"The nigger is a Jew," said Fariq.

"I can speak for myself," Spencer said, popping the inside-out cap back into position. "Obviously, I'm a member of the Jewish faith. Not so evident is that I'm also a rabbi. But how does my religion bear on my ability to provide guidance to a troubled teen?"

"Teen?" Winston shouted.

"Winston Foshay." Spencer was growing impatient, waving the referral paper in the air. "The boy I'm to be a Big Brother to."

"I'm Winston."

Spencer leaned forward in his chair. "Come again?"

"You heard, Jewboy, he's Winston Foshay, your Little Brother."

"Relax, Fariq. Look, Rabbi, I know you didn't expect no big, three-hundred-pound-plus nigger like me, but I called the Big Brother program because my thing, my shit, is confused. I saw the commercial and I thought I needed a Big Brother, a father figure. You know, try to do something with my life."

" 'I need a father figure,' " Fariq cackled.

"Shut up, Smush!" Yolanda scolded, flinging her hairbrush at Fariq, which he deftly knocked out of the air with his crutch.

Spencer began to see the gravity of the task he'd undertaken. Here in front of him was a young, uneducated black man over twice his size looking to forge his way in the closed society that somewhere along the way he'd decided to join.

His rabbinical duties were a cinch compared to this. You give a thirteen-year-old a phonetically transcribed script, he makes his bar mitzvah speech, counts the cash, and skips into young adulthood. Spencer wasn't sure he wanted the responsibility of showing someone how to be responsible for himself. Jordy, still in front of the television, squatted and jabbed his hands in the air, furiously imitating the rapper in the video.

"That's all right, Mr. Throckmorton. You can go now." Winston was at the front door, door handle in hand. "Sorry for the inconvenience, but I've decided I don't need you. It's been almost two weeks since I called Big Brothers of America and now I've changed my . . . changed my mind about this Big Brother stuff."

Spencer gathered his belongings and made his way to the door, seeing his Pulitzer disappear and feeling somewhat offended that a person in Winston's position didn't want his help. "What do you mean, you don't need me?"

"We don't have anything in common."

"How do you know?"

"That was you driving up, car stereo blasting some song about Winnie-the-Pooh? Some shit about counting bees and chasing clouds?"

"Loggins and Messina, 'The House at Pooh Corner.' "

Winston rubbed the back of his neck. "We from two different worlds, Rabbi. Plus, I think I'm more mature than you."

"Excuse me?"

"Look, you might have few years on me, but compared to you, my game is trump tight. I mean, I got a wife and kid, a goldfish."

"I thought these people were your sister and brother. You two are married? Where are the rings?"

"We ain't got no rings because this cheap, flabby motherfucker says he don't believe in wedding rings."

"That's right—wedding rings are signs of materialistic something or other."

"I swear, sometimes I could kill Ms. Nomura," said Yolanda, rubbing the tension from her temples. "Wasn't much of a wedding—we got married over the phone."

"The phone?"

Winston was ushering Spencer outside, saying his thank-yous, when Yolanda asked Spencer to sit and told Fariq to bring him something to drink from the kitchen. Spencer returned to the rocking chair. "We were never properly introduced. I'm Yolanda, Winston's wife; this is our son, Jordy; and the anti-Semitic motherfucker who'll be carrying a six-pack in his teeth is Fariq." Fariq exited the kitchen with the beer balanced on his head, sashaying his ass in the limited range of motion that his calcified bone structure allowed. "Check me out, toting the brew African-style. *Baba laaay. Ta daa laay boo buubuu.* That means, 'I ain't carrying nothin' in my teeth like some fucking dog.' I'm Afro-centric to the core. Y'all better take some African lessons from me, because I'm the epicenter of Afro-centricism."

Yolanda snatched a beer from Fariq's head, opened it on the edge of his crutch, then handed it to Spencer.

"Damn, girl, you don't have to do that—the fucking bottles are twist-off."

"I know."

The stale malt liquor wasn't one of the Trappist ales Spencer preferred, but he thanked everyone just the same. As Fariq and Yolanda continued to bicker, Spencer drank his beverage, his face reddening and growing warmer with each sip. His rising body temperature combined with the blast-furnace effect of the unventilated apartment made him feel like Pliny the Elder running headlong toward the eruption of Mount Vesuvius. In the Foshays, Spencer saw the story of a lifetime. He encouraged Yolanda to continue her tale. "So you two got married over the phone?"

"Yeah, the fool—"

"Come on, Landa, he don't want to know this."

"Winston married me while he was in jail. He'd lost his visitation privileges and called me at work one day. I'm eight months pregnant, he's lonely, talking all lovey-dovey, 'Let's get married, Boo.' When? 'Now.' Some friends hipped me to this reverend who does quickie marriages for inmates. Your phone got three-way? Call this 900 number.' Boom, we gettin' married for one ninety-five a minute. And you know what this idiot said instead of 'I do'?"

"No, tell me."

"After the reverend said the 'Do you take this lawful wedded bride to have and to hold' and all, he said, 'Well, she's the first woman I've been with for more than two menstrual periods, so fuck it.' "

" 'So fuck it'?"

"Next thing I know, I'm married and this nigger making kissing noises into the receiver."

"That's beautiful."

"You got a wifey, Rabbi?" Winston asked.

"You mean wife? No."

"I'm saying, you got a girl?"

"Yes, I do."

"She black?"

"Of course," Spencer confidently answered, not mentioning that his girlfriend, Natalie, wasn't exactly what the T-shirted boys outside would call a "real nigga." She chewed gum like an understudy for a college production of *Grease*, and ended every sentence with the exclamation "Fuck, yeah!," "Cool!," or "Excellent!" Natalie had recently confided in Spencer that she dated him only because his Caucasian sensibilities were muted by his black skin. She'd grown tired of unadulterated white boys making tanning jokes, buying her leopard-skin panties for her birthday, and asking why her pubic hairs weren't as straight as the hair on her head. "Hey, it's hard dating a sister. Give me some skin on that one," said Spencer, thrusting his palm toward Winston, waiting for him to acknowledge the black man's covenant. Winston remained still, looking at Spencer warily out of the corner of his eye. "You going to leave me hanging? Aw, man, that's cold-blooded." Winston reluctantly pounded a fist on Spencer's upturned palm.

Tuffy sensed that Spencer was trying too hard to be accepted. The man didn't even know brothers don't give one another five anymore. Yolanda, meanwhile, was beginning to be swayed by his genteel dreadlock manner. She patted a spot on the sofa between herself and Winston. "Spencer, come on over here. Smush, bring in some more beer!" Spencer sat down on the couch, trying to hide his apprehension, with a long pull at his bottle. "You know, after the first few sips this malt liquor isn't so bad."

Yolanda reached over to finger his cowrie-shell necklace. She tucked a couple of loose dreads behind his ear, and imagined herself as the love-starved protagonist in one of her sisterhood novels. "I'm beginning to think it might do Winston some good to have a Big Brother. Are you big? I mean, Spencer, are you a *big* brother?"

Winston looked at the amount of beer remaining in Spencer's bottle. It was about half full. Ten more minutes and Spencer Jefferson would be out of his life forever. Winston had an ergonomic chess move of his own. Like a gracious host Winston scooted away from Spencer, so his guest could make himself comfortable. As soon as Spencer's back touched the sofa cushions, Winston leaned in on the rabbi until he heard Spencer's ribs creak under his weight. He spread his legs until Spencer's knees were cinched together like a schoolgirl's on her first date. Lifting the remote, Winston shut off the television, which slapped Jordy from his cathode funk and sent him waddling to his mother in tears.

"Sensory deprivation," commented Yolanda.

Fariq set the beers down on the coffee table.

"Fariq," said Winston, grabbing a beer.

"What up?"

"This stringy-headed nigger a Jew."

"No doubt."

Using his crutches like gondola poles, Fariq rolled his chair over to the sofa. "I thought the motherfucker smelled like new money when he walked in."

"Speak on the Jew, God."

"The Jew is the black man's unnatural enemy."

"Unnatural?" asked Spencer, gasping for air, fighting for elbow room. "How can you can say a people who have been systematically hunted are the 'unnatural enemy'?"

Feigning camaraderie, Winston placed his arm on Spencer's shoulder, then quickly bulldozed his forearm into the rabbi's neck, cutting off his oxygen flow and hence his rebuttal. Fariq, thinking his opposition had been humbled into silence by the irrefutable logic of his statement, pressed his advantage.

"The Jew isn't a hunter in the spear-throwing sense, but an opportunist, a circling vulture, an egg-stealing muskrat, a germ-infested, night-crawling parasite. Tuffy, I'm telling you, don't let this Hebrew motherfucker in your life. He'll use you up and spit you out. The Jew always got an ulterior motive. Why you really here, Rabbi, spying among the enemy?"

When he tired of Fariq's vitriol, Winston eased off the rabbi just enough so Spencer could fill his lungs with air and free one hand. Spencer inhaled greedily in short quick breaths. He restored the circulation in his numb hand by clapping it against his thigh. After a few moments, Spencer spoke. "There's a saying in the Talmud, 'If two men claim your help and one is your enemy, help him first.' "

"So that's why you here? Your presence is an admission that the black man, the original man, is your enemy."

"Look—Fariq, is it? I don't know what you have against me and my people, but if you want, I can send you some ADL pamphlets chronicling the commonalities and historical parallels of Jews and blacks."

Fariq grew excited, rubbing his ankh with one hand and pointing in Spencer's face with the other. "ADL? Oh, you playing the acronym game? JDL and JDO. We got some initials too. I-S-L-A-M—I Self Lord and Master. F-O-I—Fruit of Islam, but when the jihad starts, F-O-I going to stand for Fariq Obliterating Infidels."

Fariq's inchoate ranting became impossible to distinguish from the baby's wails. It wasn't often Spencer found himself confronted with rabid anti-Semitism, and he didn't know how to respond. He regretted that rabbinical school offered no course on effective conflict resolution with the Jew hater. With his free hand he managed to remove his copy of the *Tiny Tome of Jewish Enlightenment* from his shirt pocket. He began reading aloud. "The Talmud says, 'A guilty man who denies his guilt doubles it.' "

"The Talmud." Fariq rubbed his palms together and said, "Let's break down that word, 'Talmud.' 'Tal' from the Dutch *taal*, or to talk. 'Mud,' a filthy, slimy substance. 'Tal-mud,' talking in a muddled way. Talk that confuses, abuses, and ruses the black man. 'Hebrew': He brew. He who brews. Brews, stirs. Wherever he goes, the Jew be stirring up trouble. I know my lessons, son. 'Mint Julep': Mint equals money. Jew lip. Lip, kiss. Jews kiss money. Kiss, love. Jews love money. 'Ed-jew-cate': Teach the ways of the Jew. 'Jewlius Caesar' . . ."

Using one hand as best he could, Spencer hurriedly flipped through his small book, searching for a calming aphorism that would also refute Fariq's slander. " 'Accept your afflictions with love and joy'—Eleazar ben Judah of Worms."

Silently, Fariq drained his beer. He removed the bottle from his lips with an audible pop. "Afflictions? How dare you say that to a handicapped motherfucker like me? That's some typical patronizing Jew chicanery."

" 'Chicanery.' " Spencer was momentarily taken aback, impressed by the vocabulary. Fariq continued, ignoring an obvious example of exactly the haughtiness he was speaking of, "Everybody got they little book—the Jews, the Communists. Well, niggers got a little book too." From his back pocket Fariq pulled out a tattered, photocopied, and shoddily stapled book the size of a travel postcard. He shoved the book so close to Spencer's face, Spencer could taste the grit of pocket lint and copy-machine toner on his lips. "I can't read the title," Spencer announced. Fariq pulled the treatise away from his nose until the title came into sharp focus—*The Little Black Book of Sophism: Fucked Up Things Jews Say About Black Folk*. Like warlocks practicing ancient witchcrafts, Spencer and Fariq held their tiny books to their chests, taking turns hurling their spells back and forth.

" 'I saw the best white minds of my generation destroyed by madness, starving hysterical naked, dragging themselves through the filthy, cum-stained, loud, over-sexed, Negro streets at dawn like Edgar Rice Burroughs Tarzans looking for an angry fix.'—Allen Ginsberg."

" 'If you truly are a Jew, you will be respected because of it, not in spite of it.'—Samson Raphael Hirsch."

" 'Fee, fie, foo, fum. I smell the blood of a nigger!'—Andrew Dice Clay."

" 'I am a Jew. When the ancestors of the right honorable gentleman [Daniel O'Connell, member of the British Parliament] were living as savages on an unknown island, mine were priests in the Temple of Solomon.'—Benjamin Disraeli."

"Hold up a minute—that 'My people were doing shit while your people lived in caves' is our line! 'Nigger, nigger, nigger . . .'—Lenny Bruce."

" 'I am a Jew because in every place suffering weeps, the Jew weeps.'—Edmund Fleg."

" 'Shvartze, shvartze, shvartze . . .'—Jackie Mason."

" 'Man's good deeds are single acts in the long drama of redemption.'—Abraham Joshua Heschel."

" 'Every prostitute the Muslims convert to a model of Calvinist virtue is replaced by the ghetto with two more. Dedicated as they are to maintenance of the ghetto, the Muslims are powerless to effect substantial moral reform.'—Bayard Rustin.' "

"Fariq, Bayard Rustin wasn't Jewish, he was black!"

"So what? He was probably working for the Jews when he wrote it. Besides, there's a triangle by his name, which means he's a homosexual— just as bad as being a Jew. Rabbi Kahane! Rabbi Kahane! Rabbi Kahane!"

Winston could see his plan to let Fariq badger the rabbi into leaving was backfiring. "Rabbi!" he yelled, rising up from the sofa and flicking on the television. "Fariq! That's enough with the 'Jew,' 'Muslim,' 'he say,' 'she say.' Y'all giving me a headache."

Fariq stuffed his book into his back pocket like a victorious boomtown gunfighter. "C'mon, Winston, you can't tell me you never felt the Jew's foot in your ass. Let that shit out, my brother. Ease your burdens."

Winston thought a moment. "Naw, man, I ain't got Jews on the brain like your ass. Really I never have no dealings with Jewish people."

"Because the Jew is an invisible threat. I'm going to hip you to something called the Protocols of the Elders of Zion. Lays the Jew master plan thing out."

"I don't have to take this crap!" Spencer shouted, but he made no effort to leave.

"And you've had some Jews in your life."

"Who?"

"The judge who sent you up on that shit that went down on Twenty-fourth Street."

"Berman?"

"There you go."

"And the one who tried get me on parole violation, when my public defender didn't show, was he Jewish?"

"Judge Arthur Katz."

"Damn, that's two cases and two Jews. Smush, you better hurry up and tell them motherfuckers down at Muslim headquarters you've uncovered a new conspiracy."

"You think I won't tell the Minister."

"That's right, run to your leader," wisecracked Spencer, seeing that Winston wasn't entirely on Fariq's side.

"This nigger ain't even Muslim," said Winston, pointing to Fariq's crutches. "The Muslims don't want this motherfucker. He too crippled. Neither Muslim headquarters or Mecca has handicapped parking."

"Fuck you, Tuff!"

Winston turned to Spencer. "But Smush do raise a good point. Why are you here, Rabbi, for reals?"

Spencer looked shamefully down at the floor and confessed, "I became a Big Brother so I could write a feature article on ghetto youth for the newspaper. I didn't know any ghetto youth, so . . ."

His honesty was welcomed with palpable resentment. Yolanda no longer felt the need to use Spencer as a sounding board for her problems with her husband. Under his breath Fariq spoke of a consortium of Jews controlling the world's media.

"I'm sorry," Winston and Spencer mumbled simultaneously.

"Winston, what are you sorry for?" Yolanda snapped. "Don't apologize when you haven't done anything wrong."

"I know. But I just feel sorry."

Yolanda and Fariq waited for him to ask the clergyman to leave. After all, Spencer was his guest. Winston stayed on the couch, hands clasped behind his head, lips pursed, eyes closed. Spencer's deceit left a bitter taste in everyone's mouth, and Jordy ran around the room in circles, a cherubic ladle stirring the soup of bitterness, disillusionment, and summer heat.

On his fourth circuit he picked up his See 'n Say, pulling the string on the plastic toy designed to teach toddlers the rudiments of farm-animal communication. "The cow says, 'Mooooo!' This is how a dog sounds— 'Woof! Woof!' This is how a turkey sounds: 'Gobble! Gobble!' " After each bark or bellow Jordy would stop in front of his father and try to reproduce the animal's characteristic call. His quacks and meows were a welcome distraction. For a moment Winston forgot about the dreadlocked rabbi's duplicity. "The rooster says, 'Cock-a-doodle-doo!' What's the rooster say, Jordy?"

"Thabba-thubba-ooo," mimicked Jordy, yanking on the string.

Winston wondered, if the machine imitated a person, what would be the human equivalent for cock-a-doodle-doo?

Spencer, hoping to make one final stab at a partnership, broke the silence. "Anyone seen any good movies lately?" And Winston had an answer to his question.

"Jewboy, don't you know when to be quiet," Fariq said, his patience run dry. "Better yet, leave."

Tuffy opened another beer. "Ain't no such thing as a good movie. At least not since the price of a ticket went past seven dollars."

"Oh, God, now the nigger going to start talking about 'the film.' "

Fariq said "the film" in one long wispy breath, as if enunciated by a Public Television cinéaste. Then he returned to passing his magnifying glass over the counterfeit money, occasionally scissoring slivers from spools of blue and red thread, arranging them haphazardly on a bill, and dusting the money with a coat of spray-on polyurethane. " 'The film.' "

Yolanda whisked Jordy from his aimless rounds and sniffed his diaper.

Spencer could see in the sparkle in Winston's eye and the wry smile a subtle erosion in the rocky landscape that separated them. "What do you mean?" he asked.

"Why do most people go to the movies? To be entertained, right? Maybe to learn something. But most motherfuckers go to guess who the fucking killer is. And it's always the same person."

"Who?"

"The motherfucker you least expect, of course."

"So why do you go? Why waste your money?"

"I don't even know. I knew when I was little. I went to the show to see some famous movie star's titties. Now movies is so bad they've even ruined that simple pleasure."

"How?"

"You sit down, popcorn in one hand, soda pop in the other. You wait a bit, look at your watch, and say, 'Forty-five minutes, and this bitch ain't showed no titty? This flick sucks.' If she flash her chichis *before* forty-five minutes, then the movie *really* sucks."

"So any film with a female lead is a bad film?"

"Except for *La Femme Nikita.* Some of them old Natalie Wood shits is all right too. That bitch was fine."

"And if the lead is played by a man?"

"If it's a man, especially if it's a white man—and it usually is, even if a nigger is the star—then the film has to be about right and wrong. And whiteys is the last motherfuckers on earth to be teaching me about right and wrong. Much less charging me for the lesson."

"But why do you go?"

"I go for the disappointment, I guess. I'm used to being disappointed, and I know I'll find it in the movie theater."

Spencer reached for a unopened beer. Winston didn't mind.

"Winston, can I ask you something else?"

"Yeah."

"Why did you call Big Brothers of America?"

"Suppose I knew I'd be disappointed."

"Maybe subconsciously you did, but that's not the reason you made the call."

"True. I guess I really called because I'm looking for someone to explain shit. I don't understand nothing about life, me—nothing."

"Kind of like someone to say, 'Meanwhile, back at the ranch . . .' "

"Yeah."

"You know, when the Japanese used to show silent films the theater owners paid someone to stand next to the screen and explain the action."

"For reals? Didn't they have those cards?"

"Intertitles. I supposed they did, but, you know, sometimes those aren't enough."

"That's true. Whenever I go see one of those silent jammies, Charlie Chaplin or something, I be trying to read the lips. Figure out what's really going on. So they had a motherfucker lip-reading or some shit?"

"The guy was called a *benshi*. They'd show *Battleship Potemkin* and he'd say, 'Note Eisenstein's simple yet masterful contrapuntal statements in this scene. The rectangular lines of sailors and officers standing on the quarterdeck, bisected by the battleship's guns—the state's guns, if you will."

"I seen that. 'All for a spoonful of borscht.' Baby carriage going down the stairs. Good fucking movie. *Benshi*. That's deep." Winston was stalling for time. He was enjoying the conversation. Here in front of him was the only person he'd ever spoken to who'd also seen *Battleship Potemkin* and was willing to discuss it in detail. But that was no reason to let a dreadlocked Yankee into his life. He asked Spencer why he knew so much about film. The rabbi told him the role of Jews in Hollywood was one of his lecture subjects. He then proceeded to assert that the recent independent film explosion was a Gentile assault on the perceived Jewish domination of Hollywood. This proclamation was followed by a thin segue into the argument that the popularity of the remake was more than a function of the dearth of Tinseltown originality; it was the movie industry's veiled attempt to recapture its image as art. Moviemaking, once a highbrow craft associated with the creative goyishe genius of Tennessee Williams, Nabokov, Dalí, and Faulkner, was now painting by numbers, dependent on the guile of moguls, computer geniuses erasing the distinction between actor and animation, and a slew of out-of-work nephews.

TUFF

Winston was having some difficulty following Spencer's argument—
not because he didn't understand the artistic references or failed to see
what Jewishness had to do with what Spencer was saying, but because he
was having an epiphany. He interrupted Spencer's speech. "Hey, Rabbi.
Meanwhile, back at the ranch . . ."

"What?"

"You remember when I told you I was looking for understanding?"
Spencer nodded.

"I now understand that understanding is not something you look for,
it's something that finds you. You understand?"

"What made you think of that?"

"You was talking and for some reason I thought of *Fugitive from a
Chain Gang*. You ever seen it? Paul Moody."

"Paul Muni."

"So you seen it?"

"No."

"Paul Muni down South, running from the police for a murder he
didn't commit. Gets caught and put in prison. Right there, you know I can
relate. But one scene fucks me up. It's late at night, he's on a wagon with a
bunch of white boys coming back from breaking rocks or picking cotton,
and as he comes back to the jail, there's a wagonload of black niggers
about to go out to pick cotton, break rocks. And Muni and this pitch black
motherfucker catch eyes for about two seconds. Oh, the shit is deep."

"That's it?"

"Hell, yeah, that's it. Muni give that nigger a look like 'Damn, now I
understand the bullshit you black motherfuckers go through. People
falsely accusing you of shit you ain't done. Forced to pick cotton.' But he
don't start crying. He don't call nobody 'brother' or wish him luck, try to
shake his hand, or talk about how they've got to unite. He don't say not
one word. Just gives Money a look that says, 'I feel you, homey, but I gots
to get mines.' That's real. That's how it be in jail or in life. Sometimes you
catch yourself feeling close to motherfuckers you not supposed to feel
close to, but you can't afford to play the humanitarian role. But I realized
I'm waiting for someone to look at me like that or for me to look at someone else like that. I'm not sure which."

"Didn't I look at you that way when I came in?"

"No, Rabbi, you looked at me like you felt sorry for me."

"And what's wrong with that? I do feel sorry for you."

"You need to also feel sorry for yourself."

"You're saying I'm hollow, shallow, like today's movies."

"Nothing wrong with being shallow, just shouldn't be shallow when you trying act like you about something."

Spencer felt shamed, but there was no lingering anguish pressing on his shoulders, forcing him to his knees to beg for forgiveness or spiritual guidance. He begged his religion for a sign of contriteness. And his heart began to pound, the hairs on his arms to stand on end, his knees start to shake. "Did you feel that?" Spencer asked.

"Feel what?"

"A buzz, an ethereal presence in the room, like something was passing through."

"That's the malt liquor talking to you. You getting fuzzy-faced. Take a piss, you'll feel better."

"Shit, I was hoping God was about to say something to me."

"God ain't never spoke to you?"

"I don't believe in God."

"You're a rabbi, how can you not believe in God?"

"It's what's so great about being Jewish. You don't have to believe in a God per se, just in being Jewish."

Winston had a strange, slanted smile on his face. He threw his arm around Spencer's shoulders and escorted him to the door like a kind bouncer saying good night to the village drunk. "Rabbi, let's start next week. I'll put you on six months' probation, but I ain't making no promises." Here would be the monk Winston needed. He had dreadlocks, but so what? He'd have a person in his life to whom he wasn't emotionally attached. Who knows, Spencer could be an impartial voice-over that would cut through the white noise of Yolanda's bickering, Fariq's proselytizing, and Ms. Nomura's good intentions. "Can I ask one thing before you go?"

"Sure."

"What's borscht?"

"Borscht is beet soup."

After shutting the door behind Spencer, Winston sat down on the couch, took out his marker, and drew a circle on his palm. Inside the circle he wrote his name. Yolanda stopped scouring Jordy's anus and was about to place a fresh diaper, then the baby, on Winston's lap, when he shot up and ran to the door. Spencer was ten paces past the threshold, trying to figure out how a young man with a child to support, living in an apartment with bedsheets for drapery and mayonnaise jars for glassware, could afford to see so many films. *Maybe he walks in backwards,* he thought, *like Cacus stealing the cattle from Hercules.*

"Yo, Rabbi!" Winston's head was sticking out of the door. "Since you thought you were going to be a Big Brother to an eight-year-old, what were you planning to do with me this afternoon? Take me to the zoo?"

Spencer reached into his haversack and whipped out a glow-in-the-dark Frisbee, which he expertly flung at Winston at warp speed. Winston laughed, and swiftly slammed the door. The disk bounced off the metal door frame with a thud and skidded to a wobbly stop at the feet of a young boy. The boy picked it up and offered it back to Spencer. "Keep it."

Spencer Jefferson walked to his car feeling as if he'd just interviewed for, and landed, a job as an urban mahout. He'd walk alongside the elephantine Winston Foshay, beating on his rib cage with a bamboo cane, steering him past life's pitfalls, prodding him into performing the tricks required by respectable society.

8· THE GAS THEORY

here's a certain quixotic calm to an empty school hallway. Even though he wasn't enrolled in Ramón Emeterio Betances Community Center and Preparatory School, Winston felt privileged. Cruising the hallways while class was in session was as close as a city kid got to experiencing the serenity of Huck Finn guiding his craft down the Mississippi. *Thank God I'm not in one of those classrooms. And summer school to boot?* The baby stroller squeaking, Winston wheeled Jordy down the halls on his way to a meeting Spencer had organized on his behalf. On the phone, Spencer had compared the meeting to a football huddle. Winston and the important people in his life would get together, discuss the best strategy for scoring a touchdown, then execute the play. "Winston becomes a success, on five, ready, break!" Spencer had said. Winston doubted it would be that simple.

He stuck his head into a second-floor room. Inside, a teacher stood in front of a pull-down map of New York City, reviewing the day's social-studies lessons. "How many boroughs in New York City?"

"Five! Staten Island, the Bronx, Queens, Brooklyn, and Manhattan!"

"Which ones are islands?"

"Staten Island!"

"And?"

TUFF

"Manhattan!"

"What's the northernmost borough?"

"The Bronx!"

"Now, which way is north?" Every student in the class thrust a finger high in the air, pointing toward the heavens. The beleaguered teacher's head dropped slowly into his hands. "No. No."

"Damn, this year's crop is dumber than we were," Winston said, pulling his head from the door frame and walking abjectly toward the teachers' lounge. Ms. Dunleavy looked up from her lunch and saw a round silhouette pause on the other side of the fire glass. She opened the door. "Good eve-ning," Winston said in a slow Hitchcockian drawl.

"Winston, good to see you." Seeing Jordy curled in his stroller, she asked, "Is that your son? He's so cute, may I hold him?" Winston turned his back to her, wheeling the baby out of reach. "Can't do that. No white person has ever touched him. If one does, I'll have to kill him. Like a mama rabbit does when a human handles her kid."

Ms. Dunleavy had been Winston's teacher last fall when he attended the GED preparatory program at the community center. Her notions of English didn't feel right in his mouth. For Winston language was an extension of his soul. And if his speech, filled with double negatives, improper conjugations of the verb "to be," and pluralized plurals (e.g., womens), was wrong, then his thoughts were wrong. And oftentimes her corrections had the effect of reducing him to ethnic errata.

In an alternative school whose faculty were mostly ex–flower children still mad at Bob Dylan for going electric, Ms. Dunleavy was a tolerable teacher. She just taught. She never grilled Winston about his home life, digging for literary fodder to be used in a persona poem or a condescending novel so orchestrated for political correctness it read like *Uncle Tom's Cabin* meets a televised broadcast of the President's State of the Union Address.

She didn't conduct her geography lessons from a summer Sandinista intern's perspective and in a Public Radio accent: *People, today I'm going to place a red flag in every Latin American country where the United States has conducted covert operations to assassinate its leader. Say the names of the countries with me as I insert the flag: Cuuu-baaa, Ar-hen-tee-na, Neek-kar-rah-ghgxgwhaw.* During arithmetic Ms. Dunleavy didn't adopt a faux street attitude to explain how to divide fractions in the local vernacular. *So peep this, when you be like wanting to divide fractions, you take the reciprocal of the divisor, "reciprocal" means flip the script, find the highest common digit, squash the common denominators, then multiply across. That's stupid dope, right?* Unlike the male teachers, she didn't compound her sins by being constantly late for class, and not-so-discreetly fucking the students on the weekends.

Despite his resistance to Ms. Dunleavy's ministrations, Winston was on the verge of reaching the delinquent's equivalent of the four-minute mile, a two hundred score on the GED, when he quit school. When Ms. Dunleavy asked him why, he replied that he was afraid of what he'd do if he failed the test. "I know I'll hurt somebody." He also said he was afraid of what he'd do if he passed the test. "I know I'll hurt myself. Sabotage my life."

Winston could hear the overlapping small talk coming from the conference room next door. "My father in there?" he asked Ms. Dunleavy.

"Yes, he is. Are you going to stay for the reading?"

"Hell no—my father's poems is worser than shit you used to make us read. You all be falling for that Black Panther Up-with-People bullshit too."

"Your father is an inspiration to thousands of people involved in the struggle."

"All I know is when that nigger starts reading, I be struggling to stay awake. First thing he does, every time, is put his watch on the podium, all serious-like. As if what he has to say is so important. Like the Revolution might start at any moment, so there's no time to waste. Then Pops proceeds to ignore the watch and read for three hours. Whitey could put us all back in slavery and the nigger would still be reading."

"Winston, you need to come back to school—it's never too late."

"But it's always too hard."

Winston lifted Jordy from the stroller, then walked into the conference room, wedging himself in the nearest corner. His entrance went unnoticed by everyone except Fariq, who silently acknowledged his friend with a raised eyebrow and an almost imperceptible lifting of his chin. Winston's "peoples" sat around an oak table like off-Broadway dramaturges planning the last act of his life. Inez sat at the end of the table nearest him. On her right were Yolanda, Fariq, and Spencer. To her left a hedgerow of fluffy salt-and-pepper Afros crowning the heads of Winston's father and his Panther cronies, Gusto, Dawoud, Sugarshack, and Duke, each with a steel Afro pick tucked over one ear. At the foot of the table, in front of an empty chair, sat a speakerphone.

Spencer was proud of himself. It had taken him a week to make the arrangements but by gathering all of Winston's loved ones in a single room, he'd performed his first mitzvah, and he wasn't going to let Clifford Foshay's brutish tactics sour the miracle. He knew of Clifford's Panther reputation for being an intimidator, and the square-shouldered leather jacket and Mennonite beard only enhanced it. It wasn't hard to see where Winston had learned his bullish ways. "Where this fucking boy at?" asked Clifford without bothering to even look at the door. He reached for Spencer's arm and, leather sleeve creaking menacingly, seized Spencer by the wrist. "Fuck time is it?" He hiked up Spencer's sleeve and, not finding a watch, sank back into his chair. "Where's your watch, brother? You know, Brother Malcolm said, 'Don't trust a man who doesn't wear a watch.'"

Spencer didn't flinch. "Where's *your* watch, Mr. Foshay?"

"Nigger, my watch is in my bag with my poems. Where it's supposed to be. And don't puff your chest out at me, I know who you are. You that fucking Negro rabbi white folks drag out every time they need a reasonable black opinion."

"That's right, that's right. Why should we trust you?" echoed Sugarshack. Clifford's squires sat back in their seats, stroking their goatees and finishing one another's sentences. "Do you understand what Mao meant when he said—"

"'In the relationship that should exist between the people and the troops, the former may be likened to—'"

"'—water, and the latter to the fish who inhabit it'?"

Clifford held up his hand for quiet. "You a Tom. One of those political, cultural, social theorists. And now you cozying up to my son?"

Spencer sat upright in his chair. "I do subscribe to one theory. A metatheory, if you will. That is, I think a good theory should be generalizable, accurate, and simple."

"Fuck kind of theory is that?" Clifford groused, finally letting go of Spencer's wrist.

"It's the GAS Theory, a theory about theories. But no theory meets all three of the criteria: generalizable, accurate, and simple."

"Einstein's theory of relativity!" shouted Sugarshack, pleased with himself for citing the grandest of theories.

"Generalizable and accurate, but not simple," Spencer answered.

"What about the theory that fags and Hindu people talk a lot?" volunteered Gusto, unsheathing his Afro pick from his head and forking out his natural. Clifford frowned and asked, "Whose theory is that?"

"It's *my* theory, mofo," Gusto answered, burying his metal-toothed rake in his now lopsided hairdo.

"Sounds more like a prejudice than a theory," Spencer said. "But for the sake of our getting-to-know-you discussion, we'll call it a theory— though a simple one, it is definitely not generalizable, or accurate."

Tired of playing the wallflower at a party supposedly thrown in his honor, Winston uprooted himself, placed Jordy on the table in front of Inez, and sauntered to his seat. Jordy crawled down the length of the tabletop and nestled himself in his father's lap. "Man, the only theory that satisfies all three bits of the GAS Theory is the GAS Theory itself."

"Where in hell you been, smartass?" asked Clifford.

"Where in hell *you* been?"

"Boy, don't get uppity with me. Back in my day we didn't need an intervention to straighten no young black boys out. Things was together. The community raised the children. If Mrs. Johnson saw you wasn't acting right, she called you, you came. She put the stick to your behind, and you took it. Sent you home, called your mother. When your mother said, 'Is what Mrs. Johnson said true?' you said yes, and took another beating from your parents."

Tuffy casually waved off his father. "If shit was so righteous and *together* back in the day, how come *you* turned out so fucked-up?"

Clifford stood up, his hand raised high overhead. "Nigger, don't disrespect me!" The speakerphone crackled to life and the scratchy voice of Winston's mother called out, "Clifford, you leave Winston alone!"

"Tell that nigger something, Ma," Winston said, pulling the speakerphone closer to him and adjusting its volume upward, "before I have to stuff them 'We Shall Overcome' civil rights sunglasses up his ass."

"How you doing, son?"

"Good, Mama. I miss you."

"I'm here for you, baby, but I only got another thirty minutes until my lunch break is over."

Spencer scooted in closer to the table. "Speaking of theory, I think we've just seen a bit of Freud's Oedipal theory at work."

"Now that's one theory that isn't generalizable," said Yolanda. "It surely doesn't apply to black folk. True, a nigger might want to kill his father, but he sure as hell doesn't want to fuck his mother. He might fuck a cousin, but Mom is out."

Spencer picked up his pen and pad and began. "I'm pleased everyone could make it. We are here to help Winston Foshay get on what is called 'the right track.' We all know him to be a troubled youth with loads of untapped potential. And Winston, I know that you are cynical about this process and it probably feels like a funeral to you, but please keep in mind that whatever you hear said today, we, unlike Antony, Brutus, come not to bury you, but to praise you."

Fariq twisted the bill of his baseball cap to a rakish angle. "Tuffy, I don't know what this fool talking about, but I came to make sure you find a job so you can pay me my ends, nigger."

"Fuck you, man. You get it when I got it."

"Let's get started. Winston, one of a Big Brother's initial duties is to alert the members of his Little Brother's support group, assess the strength of the social network, then formulate a plan of action."

"One minute."

"Yes, Mr. Foshay."

"I cannot in good conscience agree to be party to this without knowing where your political sympathies lie, Mr. Throckmorton. How do we know that you're not leading Winston down the road to black apathy?"

"For the record, okay, I don't believe in labels."

"You still a Jew asshole."

"Thank you, Fariq. As I was saying, before I was so rudely labeled, is that political terms such as 'left,' 'right,' 'Democrat,' 'Republican' have no meaning to me. They convey nothing about one's political personality or motivations. I judge one's political savvy on whether or not they capitalize the *b* in 'black' and can pronounce 'Ntozake Shange.' "

"Who?" asked Dawoud.

Gusto nudged his stolid partner. "You know, that sister who wrote that play—*Rainbows for Colored Chicks Whose Arms Too Short to Slap Box with God.*"

"Yeah, I remember. Some bitch talking about how brothers don't respect them. That shit was pretty good—I saw it while I was coked up."

"Can we return to discussing Winston's welfare?"

Clifford drummed his fingers on the table. "I just don't want my son's integrity as a strong black man compromised. We must ensure the boy develops himself as a black man, a descendant of African aristocracy, the southern working class, and some hellified Brooklyn niggers who took no shorts."

Waving a mindful finger, Spencer interrupted him. "I think we shouldn't take this black-man's-right-to-self-determination thing too far with Winston. It's like calculating pi to the five-billionth place—so what?"

"Wait a goddamn minute!"

Like channelers at a séance, everyone looked around to see where the disembodied yell was coming from. "Hey, anybody out there?"

"Oh shit, it's Moms on the speaker phone. Everybody shut up! Go 'head, Mama."

"Listen up. It's Winston's life. Let Winston decide what he wants to do with it. I've got to go—bye, son. I'll call back in a few minutes."

"Love you, Mama."

After Mrs. Foshay's reproach the gathering sat upright in their chairs, waiting for Winston to take command of the meeting and his life. Winston, oblivious to the restlessness surrounding him, rummaged through his backpack and removed a box of food. He set a tin of pernil, habichuelas, and arroz amarillo topped with gandules aside. He unwrapped a thin, flimsy burrito and bit into it. After just one bite he spit out the mouthful of food. "Taco Bell will definitely fuck up your order. I told them no onions." Winston took his time rewrapping the rest of the burrito. He wiped his mouth with a napkin and said, "First, these niggers gots to go."

"Who, us?" asked Gusto, Dawoud, Sugarshack, and Duke, flabbergasted, their index fingers pressed to their breastbones. "How you going to act?"

"You four draft-dodging dashiki-wearing brown-car-driving leather-trenchcoat-in-the-summer-sportin' stuck-on-stupid-played-out-1970s reject motherfuckers need to raise. You all ain't none of my social support network."

Clifford defended his friends. "Winston, you've known these brothers all your life. Who looked out for you when I was gone? They did. Who turned you on to Miles and Monk? They did."

"Them niggers didn't turn me on to shit. They only came over to the house to crash, smoke weed, and flirt with Moms. And when the electricity was turned off, they'd steal my boom box since it ran on batteries and force me to listen to all that fucked-up plink-plink-bong music."

Clifford covered Winston's hand with his own and squeezed. "Winston, these are four brothers who've been around the block. Proud black men who've sacrificed their youth so young people like yourself wouldn't have to go through what they did. Do you remember?"

Winston's resolve began to weaken as he recalled how comforting it

was having the four men requisition the tiny apartment like Allied libera-
tors. Their cocky banter made him and his mother laugh. Their menthol
cigarettes dangled from ashtrays he'd made in school like smoking cannon
from castle ramparts. Winston felt protected. And though he was too
young to know the war had been over for more than a decade, he longed
to be old enough to fight on the Revolution's frontlines. After dinner the
men would sit on the couch and clean their weapons. Carefully, they'd
place dabs of brown oil on the guns' mechanisms, smearing the droplets
with their fingertips.

"I remember when Gusto shot me, cleaning his fucking rifle. That's
what I fucking remember."

"You know that was an accident."

"Dead in my fucking thigh."

"Shit was an accident."

Clifford shook Winston's shoulder, and Winston blinked away the
memory of his leg pulsing blood. Brenda tying a bathrobe-belt terry-cloth
tourniquet around his leg.

"Winston."

"What?"

"We're all black men here, and men, especially black men, make
mistakes. We need to forgive each other and work together. You're a
smart enough young man, not so different from Malcolm, Huey, and
Eldridge when they were your age. Many a great black man has been in
the same position you're in now. Jesus, Hannibal, Pushkin, Babe Ruth,
and Beethoven all listened to their elders, and you must do the same."

Winston looked at the man he had designated to be his elder.
Spencer was wearing a stonewashed blue oxford shirt. He looked under
the table: his new mentor's sockless feet were shod in pewter Sperry
Top-Siders. Sugarshack, noticing the look of chagrin on Winston's face,
reached across the table and fingered Spencer's collar. "Nigger look like
CIA, don't he? This the type nigger you want on your team?"

Winston popped off the plastic lid to his Spanish food and placed his
face in the rising steam. Wrestling the slabs of fatty meat with his plastic
utensils, he spoke without looking up. "Look, maybe y'all was throwing
grenades, toting shotguns, feeding kids and shit back in the good ol' days,
but now you ain't doing a damn thing but playing off-beat bongos and a
dented-up saxophone behind my father's wack-ass poetry, so even if
Spencer is a CIA agent, you ain't got nothing to worry about, because the

statute of limitations has long expired on whatever revolutionary shit you've done."

Clifford shook his head. "Son, you're missing the point. I know you think we're old-fashioned, paranoid, and who knows what else—"

"No, I know what else. Yolanda, what's that word you always using for people who can't function without certain other motherfuckers in they lives?"

" 'Codependent,' " she shot back.

"Right." Winston turned to face Clifford and his rat pack. "Y'all codependent. . . . Yolanda, what's that word you always use to describe me, Smush, Whitey, and Armello?"

" 'Homoerotic'?" she said, a little unsure of her answer.

"Yup, that's it. Daddy, you, Sugarshack, and them are all old-fashioned, paranoid, codependent homoerotics." Winston started flicking green snow peas from atop the mound of yellow rice at his father's friends. "Now bounce! Before you motherfuckers start talking about John Coltrane."

"That's wrong, Winston."

"Pops, you go too if you want."

Clifford remained seated while Gusto, Dawoud, Sugarshack, and Duke got to up leave, pulling their collars up around their necks, tugging on the sleeves of their jackets, and patting down their Afros, trying to maintain their expired seventies insouciant chic. "No need to bring Coltrane into this," said Gusto, licking his fingers, then matting down his eyebrows. Winston beat a rhythm on the tabletop, mocking their poetry as they skulked into the hallway.

> *Coltrane be superbad.*
> *Coltrane be black love.*
> *Coltrane be a love supreme. A love supreme.*
> *Coltrane be a burrito supreme. A burrito supreme.*

"You call that poetry? I admit, when y'all used to bogart my tape deck, I liked that nigger's music. That fucking horn would calm you down like a back rub. But after listening to you clowns write about his shit, I can't stand his music. Whenever I hear one of his tunes I think about your bullshit poetry. Y'all must be killing the nigger's record sales."

Extremely satisfied with himself, Winston returned to shoveling food into his mouth. "Man, that felt good, yo." Everyone was staring at him with varying degrees of incredulity. "What y'all looking at?" he demanded, speaking with his mouth full.

Spencer waited for Winston to swallow, looked him in the eye, and asked the question that forever has hounded any miscreant who's ever tried to set his or her life straight. "Winston, what *do* you want to do?"

A grim look of concern crossed Winston's face. This question had been asked of him countless times, and for the first time in his life he didn't respond with his stock answer: "I don't have to do nothing but stay black and die." He couldn't verbalize it, but Winston was feeling the onset of the freedom his father and Inez were always saying his ancestors died for. "What do I want to do? I don't know, but I want to do something."

"You want to make money," blurted out Fariq.

"True."

"You want to set a good example for your son," suggested Yolanda, refilling Jordy's baby bottle with apple juice and sliding it down the table as if it were a mug of beer in a saloon. Winston sipped from the bottle, then handed it to the baby.

"Sure, you right."

"You want to emulate them," Inez said, pointing to a set of posters including Ho Chi Minh, Marx, Menelik II, and Emma Goldman, lined up on the wall like a radical Mount Rushmore.

"If you say so," Winston teased, looking over at the posters. "Who's that?"

"Which one?" asked Inez.

"The one at the end—the crazy-looking white man."

"That's Eugene V. Debs. He was a labor leader at the turn of the century. He ran for president a few times too."

Winston stared at the black-and-white photo of the bald, craggy-faced agitator. Eugene Debs was standing on an unseen soapbox, leaning over a sea of people like a figurehead lashed to a frigate bow, his fist beating the air, his mouth open in mid-mandate. You could almost hear the rabble rouser begging the crowd to overturn everything from corporate oligarchy to the horizon. The blown-up photo of Debs's exhortations reminded Winston of himself: the pushy nigger who threatened and bitched and moaned and fought until he got his way. "That old motherfucker look like he about to have a heart attack. Nigger better calm down."

Inez nervously tugged on one earlobe. "Winston, you've mentioned money, family, social activism as possible goals and aspects of your life you want to work on. Where do you plan to start?"

"Right here with my seed," he answered, lifting Jordy up by the scruff of the neck like a mother lion lifting her cub. "This little nigger here is my first responsibility."

"I don't think so."

"What do you mean, Ms. Nomura? I ain't got to take care of Yolanda—she grown, she can look out for her own self."

"Winston, it's like being on an airplane."

"I never been on a plane."

Winston knocked his fist on his forehead and let out a groan. "I fell into one of your moral traps, didn't I? Go ahead, tell me what happens on a plane."

Inez winked. "Well, when you board the airplane they wait until everyone is seated; then the flight crew shows the passengers a safety video: how to fasten your seat belt, where the closest exit is, the life jacket is under the seat. Then on the screen are a mother and child sitting side by side. The narrator says, 'If the cabin pressure falls, yellow oxygen masks will drop from directly overhead. Place one over your head and breathe as you would normally.' "

Fariq objected. "How can you breathe normally? If the plane is fucking going down, you'd be hyperventilating and shit." Inez offered Fariq a cigarette, hoping the smoke would occupy what little air he had in his asthmatic lungs. When Fariq started coughing, she continued.

"The narrator goes on to say, 'If you are traveling with a small child, put on your mask first, then place the mask on the child.' "

"You trying to say I have to be responsible for myself first before I can do anything else?"

"Exactly."

Yolanda folded her arms and sat back in her chair, bottom lip protruding. "Dag, Winston, I've been trying to tell you the same thing for the past year. Why when Ms. Nomura says it, instantly you understand?"

"It's not her saying it; it's when and where she said it. You say it right after we've had sex. I'm not really listenin' to your 'Honey, when are you going to learn' shit. I'm rubbing my dick against your thighs trying to get another hard-on."

"Tuffy!" Yolanda screamed, slapping the table in an effort to keep from laughing. Winston apologized with a kiss on the cheek. Although he hadn't fully answered the question of what he wanted to do with his life, in deciding to take responsibility for himself he felt he'd made some progress.

However, the unavoidable, but rarely acknowledged, corollary to the what-to-do quandary loomed unspoken in everyone's mind as they watched Winston wolf down the rest of his lunch. Winston knew what they were thinking. *Now that I've said I'm going to do something, the real question is what can a high-school-dropout short-tempered nigger like me do? I ain't starting over. No way.* Using his thumbnail he picked at a piece of meat lodged in his teeth. "So I suppose I have to get a job?"

Winston spun about in his chair and looked at the cork job board on the wall behind him. Nestled among sheaves of multicolored flyers, the job board promoted everything from political rallies to a charity sumo demonstration in a local park to the candidates running in the upcoming election. Thumbtacked to the board were the job listings. Written with black felt-tipped pen on yellow three-by-five index cards, the listings were neatly arranged in columns under the headings Clerical, Child Care, Service, and Miscellaneous. Winston shuddered, thinking of the last time he'd found himself face-to-face with the dreaded job board.

Just after Jordy was born, Winston, feeling the pressures of an extra mouth to feed, joined up with a chain-snatching ring that operated in the tony Chelsea/West Village area. Although the baby was good subterfuge, he quickly tired of lugging Jordy to work with him, but was averse to leaving him at the day-care centers in his neighborhood. He couldn't bring himself to entrust his child to places that sounded more like halfway houses or reclamation institutions than nurseries: Bridge the Gap Day Care, Family Restoration Through Faith, Empowerment House, Sheltering Arms Children's Service. Even Ms. Nomura's day care at the community center was called the Crack Is Wack Children's Center. Winston wanted to drop Jordy off at one of the Chelsea spots he passed while running from the cops—child-care centers whose names seemed to emphasize preparing kids for the future: the Multimedia Preschool, the Piaget Discovery School. The implied mission of the other nurseries was simply allowing children to be children: the Acorn School, City and Country School, Kids Curious, and Buckle My Shoe. Winston had fixated on Buckle My Shoe. To him it sounded like a luxury rumpus room where the staff called the kids "toddlers" and "youngsters," not "clients" and "crumb snatchers." He'd seen the name somewhere before. *The job board!*

The index card termed the position as "custodial in nature," one day a week, and ten cents over the minimum wage. Winston accepted the job, negotiating free child care two days a week for Jordy in return for an eighth of top-grade marijuana a week. On his first Tuesday, at precisely one-thirty, while Winston was cleaning the windows, Diedre Lewis, his supervisor, took a break to smoke her weed on the roof. "Watch my kids for me, Mr. Foshay." The moment Diedre left the room, all fifteen brats started wailing like tripped-up security alarms, and no amount of cradling, lullabies, or "Aw, there now"s would silence them. Next Thursday, on his way to work, Winston grabbed a crusty brown bottle from the medicine cabinet—a bottle he hadn't opened since his dognapping days. That afternoon when Diedre went on break, the kids cried like beaten seals. Winston twisted the cap off the bottle and poured the clear, dense liquid onto a cleaning rag. Shaking a box of Chiclets as if it were a hunting rattle, he lured Kyle Palmetti into striking distance. Quickly, Winston pounced on the boy, covering his mouth and nose with the towel. The child fell instantly into a deep sleep. Instead of fleeing after seeing one of their brethren incapacitated, the other kids clamored to be next. "How'd you do that?" "Do me next." "No, me!" "Me!" When Diedre returned from her break, the entire brood were asleep in their cubbyholes. Winston sang the latest radio hit to himself and ran his squeegee over the windows. "How?" she asked.

"Chloroform."

Convicted of child endangerment, the state sentenced him to six months' probation.

"**A**ny of those jobs interest you, Winston?"

"Ms. Nomura, can I get a job putting up jobs on the job board?"

"No."

"This sumo sounds interesting. Is there a sumo school near here? Maybe I can be professional sumo wrestler."

"Get serious!"

"Chill, Pops."

Winston put a beefy hand to the side of his face, a makeshift horse-blinder blocking out the distractions on his determined run for the roses.

"If you're going to get a job, get one you look forward to going to," suggested Spencer. "Winston, what *do* you look forward to?"

TUFF

"This documentary called *Seven Up*, where they follow these British people around. But it only comes out once every seven years."

Winston got up from his chair and, hands on knees, studied the board. Reading each card carefully, he hoped something in the text would jump out at him, showing itself from among the overabundance of data-entry positions. NEW YORK CITY PLANETARIUM — ASTRONOMER'S ASST. "Hey, I like this one," he said, tapping the card with his finger. "Look into the sky all night. Naming stars, look for spaceships—who knows, maybe I'll discover a comet. Tuffy's Comet. Sounds kind of ill. This might could work."

"You should be a comet, 'cause niggers like you don't come around too often."

Winston frowned at his father's insult. Inez asked him to read the bottom of the card, trying her best not to sound too discouraging.

His voice hesitant, Tuffy began reading. " 'Excellent math skills required. All applicants must have working knowledge of basic physics.' Is my math that bad?"

Fariq, who during games of twenty-one always knew when Winston had over fifteen in his hand because he'd roll his eyes into his head, count his fingers, and take forever to say "Hit me," spat out, "You ain't never even had pre-algebra, kid. What x stand for?"

Winston shrugged. "I don't know."

"Actually, that's right—x stands for the unknown."

"Told you. Ask me another one."

"What's an average?" Inez said impatiently.

"Average? Let's see . . ." Winston answered cautiously, gauging the correctness of his response by the twists and frowns in Inez's expression, "that's like the most regular. If you put everything together and picked out the most typical. I'll use it in a sentence. 'The *average* black man can whip four or five white boys.' " A look of skepticism swept over Inez's face. "I mean, because of the anger," Winston said quickly.

Yolanda pointed at the job board. "Once more."

"I'm just playing." Winston giggled. "I know what average is. That's when you add the numbers, divide, and come up with the number in the middle. Ha, I'm about to be an Astronomer's Assistant. Later for all y'all."

"I have one," said Spencer. "In the equation $E = mc^2$, what does c represent?"

Clifford waved his hand in disgust. "Forget that. Ask him what's physics."

Winston said nothing and returned to the board. Embarrassed, he read one of the campaign flyers aloud, as if to prove a point. "Collette Cox—City Councilwoman for the 8th District. Vote Social Democrat for Justice. September 9th." He looked back at the poster of Debs, then ripped the handbill from the wall and sat back down. "You all would back me in anything I do, long as it's positive, right?"

"Of course," said the collective.

He slid the campaign flyer across the table and announced, "I'm going to run for City Council." The assuredness in his voice surprised him. Everyone but Inez scooted away from the table like tapped-out poker players. Winston had a satisfied smirk on his face. *Politician. Don't need to know physics to run for some bullshit office.* Jordy scrambled up his father's face, using Winston's ears, lips, and eye sockets for toe- and hand-holds.

"You stupid?" asked Fariq. "This is a waste of time, this boy is hopeless." Clifford added, "This shit isn't funny."

"I'm serious. Ever since I can remember, you, Moms, Yolanda, my counselors been going on about how I need to meet the challenges of life. That I need to stop taking the easy way out. Well, here go my challenge."

"Tuffy, leave me out of this."

"Didn't nobody say nothing about you, Smush."

"I just challenge you to pay me back my money. Anyway, I don't know why you talking this nonsense about running for City Council when you don't even vote."

Having reached the top of Winston's head, Jordy planted a flag of saliva on the bristly peak. "I vote," Winston said, wiping the top of his head with a napkin.

"Who you voted for?"

"Voted for president."

"The one we got now?"

"Fuck I look like? I walked in the booth, looked at the bullshit candidates, and said to the lady at the desk, 'What if I don't like none of these motherfuckers runnin'?' She gave me a big ol' ballot and said I could write in whoever I wanted."

"And?"

"Nigger."

"What?"

"I wrote your crippled ass in. 'I, Winston Foshay, vote for my man, Fariq Cole, for president. If you don't know, you better ask somebody.

And in case you still don't know, he lives at 154 East 109th Street, first floor. When he walks his knees bend backwards like a flamingo's.' "

"Damn, yo—you voted for me for president?"

"Yeah, bro. Swear on my mother."

Flattered, Fariq looked away, blinking his eyes. "Damn, yo. That's lovely, kid." Winston, already assuming victory at the polls, began doling out political patronage. "Don't sweat that, dude. When I win, you going to be chief of the fire department, Armello going to be chief of police, Whitey chief of white people. Ms. Nomura, you my chief of education. No, scratch that—chief of fair play. Somebody should be in charge of fair play, don't you think?"

Swinging a leg over Winston's shoulder, Jordy used his father's arm like a fireman's pole and slid down to the floor, where he untied Winston's shoelaces.

"You showing your ass, son."

"That's all right, I got a lot of ass to show."

"Get real and get this thought of running for City Council out of your head, because you're unqualified, boy."

Yolanda bunny-hopped her chair closer to her man. "Now, Clifford, I'm not saying Winston should run, but think about it—who's qualified? That black man they always talking running for president in the *next* election? Because he gives a good press conference he's qualified? If he ever does decide to run, you know what the first thing he's going to be— *un*qualified."

Although he didn't know what black man Yolanda was talking about, Winston nodded his head. Ms. Nomura, her hands clasped together like a nun administering to a bedridden child, said, "Winston, maybe you should get involved in politics at a more basic level." Tuffy shook his head. "I already tried that. Every time you ask me to go to one of your demonstrations I go. I picket the army recruiting station when you tell me the U.S. fixing to bomb some defenseless country for no reason. What happens? The fuckers get bombed anyway. Remember, I went hunger-striking with you for them goddamn refugees?"

"What refugees?"

"Some dirty jungle motherfuckers in some country I never heard of was getting mistreated. We were in front of the UN Building."

"I don't remember."

"The time I was the only one who got arrested, because that man was heckling me. 'That's not fair, hunger-striking with the fat kid. It'll take him a whole year to die.' I had to beat that man's ass."

Spencer, who'd been quiet since Winston had announced his candidacy, finally spoke. "I feel that we must admit to ourselves that we've laid out some stipulations and guidelines for Winston to follow: his vocation should pay a decent living wage, contribute to the social good, be an exemplar to his son, and be racially, I don't know—righteous. I think Winston has chosen to pursue a course of action that while on the surface is infeasible and bullheaded does meet the agreed-upon exigencies. I have only one question. Winston, are you certain this is what you really want to do?"

"No, but it's what I'm *going* to do. The only people who want to become politicians are the third-grade snitch-ass hall-monitor types. Why can't I do it? You just put up some posters in the neighborhood and people vote for you. All I need to know is how much does the job pay."

"I'd say about seventy-five thousand dollars a year," Ms. Nomura said.

He stamped his feet and pumped his fist in the air. "Oh, that's crazy money. After I win I'll be making more than all y'all combined."

"You won't be making more than me, believe that shit, motherfucker."

"But you can't win. Winston, listen to me for one second." Clifford stood up and pointed a finger in his son's face. "Be practical. I know I've always told you pursue your dreams, but you got to understand the difference between fantasy and reality."

Winston slapped away his father's hand. The loud, stinging crack caused those at ringside to cringe. "Man, I'm tired of you getting up in my face." Clifford backed off but continued preaching about the costs of running a campaign and the number of votes needed to win. Winston ignored him and stared at the poster of Debs. He tried to imagine what the old Socialist was saying. Used the buildings in the background to figure out where in New York City he was speaking. *Lower East Side?* He counted the number of blacks in the crowd. *Two. I bet those niggers had it hard. Calling everybody "boss."* "Daddy, how many times have we met face-to-face?"

"I don't know—"

"I'm going to tell you: thirty-three times in twenty-two years. Eight in the last eleven. That's counting today, and the last time I seen you, you was sleeping on the A train at four in the morning, snoring your ass off, your head banging against the window, an empty bottle of Wild Irish Rose rolling between your feet."

"What are you getting at?"

"I bet you in at least thirty-two out of those thirty-three times we've had the same conversation: 'Why you fucking up in school? Why don't you stay out of trouble?' And I always said, 'Because I can't do the work,' or 'I can't stop hanging out with my friends.' You would tell me I can do anything I set out to do. And what I'm setting out to do is run for City Council. Why can't you just say, 'Son, I'm proud of you, I know you can do it.' "

"Because you can't."

"Ms. Nomura, how many votes it take to win?"

"Four thousand votes in the primary, you'd win for sure."

"That's it?"

"I know it doesn't sound like a lot, but the primary is in September, that's right around the corner—and besides, not many people in this neighborhood vote."

"That's because I never ran. Look, I know more than four thousand people in this place. I know at least half of every project. Woodrow Wilson Houses, first floor: Gilbert Osorio raising six cousins by his dammy—Monica, Dolores, Pepón, Jessie, Suzette, and Pharaoh, jam-packed in a one-bedroom crib. Next to them, Cynda Alfaro and her moms, who works at the hospital—she's real cool, always puts my triage form on top. Two doors from the Alfaros on the right, them crackhead brothers Erwin, Erving, and Ernest. Plus, those fucking dykes Jocelyn and Lourdes on the left-hand side, with, for some unknown fucking reason, a rainbow flag on their door and in every damn window. Down from the lesbos, Genise Norris and her twin sons, Unique and Unique. Don't let me have to tell you who's on the second, third, fourth, fifth, and sixth floors because we'll be here all day. Shit, much drug running, breaking and entering, hiding out as I've done? I been on every block, in every apartment, Wilson Houses, Taft Projects, Jefferson Houses, George Washington. Wilson, Taft, Jefferson, Washington—ain't that a bitch? I never realized all the projects were named after presidents—what kind of twisted message is that? Anyway, I see these little flyers various candidates got up now. Wilfredo Cienfuegos, that motherfucker be selling illegal cellular phones in the back of Estrella's Restaurant. Any of y'all know that fool?"

"Naw."

"Course not. I know him because I know everybody."

Jordy opened Winston's thighs and clawed his way through the mass of flesh and muscle to his father's crotch. He lifted Tuffy's sagging stomach and was about to land a punch to the bulge before him when Winston punched him in the chest, knocking him to the seat of his diapers. Jordy just giggled and charged in again.

"Who else running?" Fariq asked, his interest piqued.

"Margo Tellos. She live over on one-eighteen. Got a big, fat, juicy ass and a little boy who goes to private school on the West Side." Winston held up Collette Cox's campaign flyer. "I know Ms. Nomura knows her. This one used to teach here at the school. I remember one day she was subbing for Ms. Dunleavy, we fucking around not doing the assignment, throwing shit out the windows, woman could've died and no one would've noticed or cared. Out of nowhere she starts crying, mascara all down by her chin, talking about, 'When I look at you people, I see failures. Wasted talent. The ghosts of students who could've become lawyers, doctors. It's like you people are zombies.' "

Winston looked cockeyed at Yolanda and Fariq to see if they'd shared his umbrage. Smush asked Inez for another cigarette and Yolanda just sat there, studying Tuffy for signs of bipolar disorder. "You two might not give a fuck, but I ain't no zombie. Damn if you see me walking in a straight line, arms stretched all out in front of me, hands choking the shit out of the air, going 'uuurrggghhhh, uuurraaaagggghh,' waiting for some teen hero to bash my head in and put me out of my misery. Fuck that. I'm sick of being . . ."

"Disenfranchised," volunteered Spencer.

"I was going to say 'left out.' But your word sound better."

"You flipping," said Smush.

"You're still my campaign manager."

"And Landa, you don't got no choice, because our thing is till death do us part."

"Don't tempt me."

"Ms. Nomura, Daddy, I know you with me, since you two are so supportive of everything I do."

"I raised a fool."

"Nigger, you didn't raise nobody." Angrily Winston pushed the tin of food scraps away from him. His chin dipped into his chest. His eyes closed. He squeezed them tighter, then covered his face with his hands.

"You all right, son?" Fariq asked.

Winston didn't move. Yolanda couldn't tell if he was about to cry or snap the neck of the person closest to him, which unfortunately was her.

TUFF

Just contemplating the absurdity of a nigger like him running for political office was making Winston's head hurt. He knew there was no point in talking about his future. He shut his eyes and patted the gun in his pocket. *Fuck am I doing?* he thought. *If it'd been winter and the flyer said, "Macy's—Extra Christmas Help Needed," I'd have said, "That's it— I want to be a department-store Santa!"* He slowly ripped Collette Cox's campaign flyer into four squares. Almost instinctively he whispered a verse from an old rap song:

> *. . . Bullet with my name on it*
> *Knife with my bloodstain on it*
> *Coffee table with my brain on it*
>
> *Pallbearer grab a coffin latch*
> *Another nigger snatched*
> *In the ghetto it's Catch-*
> *22 slug to the mug . . .*

Inez winced. It wasn't hard to envision a bullet-riddled Winston sprawled underneath the White Park monkey bars, gargling his blood, his head lolling in her lap, while his friends tried to coax his soul back into his body. She was determined not to be too late to save Tuffy, like she was too late to save Malcolm.

Winston slowly lifted his head and opened his eyes. "I ain't serious with this election bullshit. I'm not running for a damn thing. Fuck it."

Inez raised an index finger in the air like a committeeperson making a point of order. "Fifteen thousand dollars, Winston," she said. "I'll pay you fifteen thousand dollars if you run. Maybe a little more after I look into how much it costs for posters and things. It doesn't matter if you win or lose. It'll be like a summer job." Winston immediately flashed to the restitution check hanging on Inez's bedroom wall. "Come on, Ms. Nomura, don't joke."

"Inez, don't encourage the boy," pleaded Clifford. "He's going to think you mean it."

"The election is a little over three months away. Let's see—that's five thousand dollars a month."

Inez's eyes locked with his. She was serious. "It might be fun." Winston stole a glance at Yolanda. She looked skeptical. *She don't like*

Ms. Nomura nohow. He shifted his gaze to Fariq. Smush would eventually come up with some nefarious plan to make money this summer. It depended upon the riskiness of the venture, but at best Winston's end would be between four and five thousand a month. *Ain't that a bitch, crime and politics pay about the same.* "Ms. Nomura, I want all the money up front."

"Done."

Inez sighed. No one else said anything as they waited for her to come to her senses and renege on the offer. The phone rang. Winston pressed the Speaker button and snapped, "Who this?"

"Winston, is that how you answer the phone?"

"No ma'am."

"Okay, then. What did you decide to do?"

"I'm running for Congress."

"City Council," hissed Yolanda.

"That's nice, son, you have my blessing. Take care."

"Thanks, Mama, you always there for a nigger. I mean, you wasn't really there for me, but yeah, thanks. I'll call you soon. Bye. Love you." Winston picked Jordy up off the floor and dangled him over the phone with one hand and tickled his stomach with the other. "Say goodbye to Grams, Jordy." Jordy purred a slobbering gurgle into the phone.

Clifford backed away from the table. "Inez, is the auditorium ready?"

"Ms. Dunleavy is taking care of everything, but we should get going. I'll be there in a minute." While Clifford gathered his books and strode into the hall, Inez walked up to Winston and gave him a long hug. "You know what we haven't done lately?"

"Naw."

"Gone to the top of the Empire State Building. Let's meet next Sunday. Spencer, you come too."

"Sure."

"Winston, you mind?"

"Naw."

"Coming to listen to your father read?"

"Maybe."

Winston rose from the table, began cleaning up his mess. He crumpled Collette Cox's campaign flyer and tossed it with the food scraps into a wastebasket. "Ms. Nomura?"

TUFF

"What?"

"You think my pops would've come to this meeting if he didn't have this reading scheduled for today?"

"I don't know."

"You better vote for me."

"You have to earn votes, Winston. You can't strong-arm folks into voting for you," Inez said, scooting out into the corridor.

As he buckled Jordy into his stroller, Yolanda eased up to him and rolled his T-shirt over his beach-ball paunch. "You look hot, baby. You bring an extra shirt?"

"I forgot."

Yolanda hiked the shirt to Winston's underarms, exposing his chest. "I don't like how Ms. Nomura looks at you."

"Now who paranoid? You notice my father didn't even say goodbye?"

"I noticed."

With two fingers Yolanda skied a path down Tuffy's breastbone, jumping moguls of fat, slaloming in and out of his carbuncles and assorted battle scars, leaving wavy tracks on his sweaty skin. Winston's stomach quivered as her fingers schussed around the rim of his navel. "What did you mean when you said I don't have a choice—that I have to support you if you run for office?"

"You my girl—if I do something, you follow. And vicey-versey."

"It's much easier following a nigger who got fifteen grand, I know that much."

"Ain't that a bitch. But *no te preocupes*, I'm just going to take the money and run."

"Thought you said you wasn't going to run?"

"You know what I mean. Ms. Nomura wanna play social worker, I don't care."

Fariq grabbed Spencer by the elbow and guided him out of the room. "We be right out here, all right?"

"All right," answered Winston.

Yolanda cleared the layer of perspiration off Tuffy's chest with her hands, then blow-dried each nipple, watching his skin fill with goose bumps. "Yolanda, what are you doing?"

"You ever think we married too young?" she asked, driving an index finger into the abyss that was his navel. Her finger two knuckles deep into his belly button, she probed for the pressure points in her husband's soul.

She wanted to arouse the real nigger within, hear him scream, and beg her, and only her, for mercy. Winston clenched his abdominal muscles, causing the walls of his belly button to clamp down on her finger like a set of fleshy Chinese handcuffs. "Landa, you not going nowhere, so stop fronting." Yolanda tugged violently, trying to extract her finger from Winston's suction hold. "Tuffy, stop playing!" Winston exhaled and released her finger. It was moist. She smelled it before wiping it dry on Winston's pants. Yolanda lifted her shirt and they hugged, their sweaty bellies stuck together like wet tissue paper.

Outside, Spencer turned to Fariq. "Are Winston and Inez serious?"

"Jewboy, I don't know about Ms. Nomura, and I doubt Tuff will be out there campaigning and shit, but I know when he was talking about who he know in the neighborhood and all, he was coming from the heart. He only has two emotions: serious and serious as fuck, straight up. Only time I ever heard the nigger tell a joke was when we was working in Brooklyn, that shit was just a freak thing. Even when Tuffy jokin', he bein' dead real. He a sensitive nigger. You know how niggers be snappin' on each other, 'You so ugly,' 'so black,' 'so stupid'? Don't no one get into it with Tuffy. Not since him and Carter got into it. One day we was comin' from the beach and Carter was all over Tuffy, 'Nigger, you so fat, you jumped into the sky and got stuck. Motherfucker, you so big, you wear pillow cases for socks. You so big, you shit cannonballs. You so fat the only things on earth the astronauts can see from space is the Great Wall of China and the crack of yo' ass.' This wasn't no when-you-sit-around-the-house, you-sit-around-the-house, seafood-diet bullshit; this session was heated. Carter was rockin' that nigger, and all Tuffy could do was take the blows. But Tuffy can't play the dozens, 'cause he can't lie. If he ever say to a nigger, 'I'm going to kill you,' that boy will have fewer friends than Israel. So Carter breaking on Tuffy so hard he has to stop and catch his breath. Tuffy, tired of Carter fucking him up, right out of the blue says, 'Yeah, nigger, like I fucked yo' mama.' Now normally when a nigger go into the 'I fucked your mother' bag, the other niggers start groaning, saying, 'That shit's a dud.' But in this case they start laughin', fallin' off the stairs, runnin' into traffic, giving each other pounds—niggers is straight dyin'."

"Why?"

"Because they knew that if Tuffy had said it, then he'd really fucked Carter's mother."

"Oh, shit."

TUFF

" 'Oh, shit' is right. A nigger who honest as Tuffy just said he fucked your mother in front of your boys? You gots to fight. Tuffy should've just let Carter hit him, he don't weigh but a hundred twenty pounds. But Tuff play for keeps. Nigger hit Carter so hard—you ever see a matador stab a bull? Bull staggers for a quick second like, 'Goddamn, this punk mother- fucker stabbed me,' then just fall to his knees. That's how hard Tuffy hit Carter. Nigger dropped to his knees *olé* like a motherfucker. His nasal passages is all permanently crushed. The poor guy got to keep his mouth open to breathe. You give that nigger a lollipop and he'll die."

Fariq's gaze shifted and Spencer looked over his shoulder to see Winston and Yolanda standing arm in arm behind him. Spencer now understood why little boys ran to Tuff in the streets, tugging on his shirt, begging to be "put down" on some invisible ghetto roster of the termi- nally bad. He knew why his hubcaps were still on his car after that initial visit to Winston's apartment. Winston Foshay—a living African-American folk hero whose mythos lay somewhere between that of the angelic John Henry and the criminally insane Stagger Lee. Spencer had his newspaper story.

9 · THE READING

Winston paused at the auditorium's entrance. The stragglers hurried by, and he saw very few neighborhood faces. Whatever their ethnicity, these were people who only came uptown for the meager portions of soul food at Sylvia's Restaurant, or to hear a career Negro such as his father pontificate on the challenges faced by black Americans and those enlightened few genuinely sympathetic to the cause. Each loyalist mention of his father's name from a patron's lips was preceded by a slew of adjectives that convinced Winston that if he ever wanted to get to know his father, he'd have to read his books, because the dynamic, insightful, devoted Clifford Foshay was a man he didn't know.

"Tuff, you coming, yo?" asked Fariq. "Popduke be dropping bombs."

"No, y'all go ahead."

Yolanda and Fariq eagerly sought out seats in the small but crowded auditorium. Spotting Spencer about to settle into a front-row seat, Fariq called out, "Hey, Jewboy! Wait the fuck up! Save me a seat, can't you see I'm crippled?" Yolanda shoved Fariq ahead of her. "Do you have to say 'Jewboy'?"

"You sensitive to the word 'Jewboy'?"

"No, I'm just tired of hearing you say it."

"What else is there?"

TUFF

"I thought you were a follower of the Nation? What about 'Hebe,' 'kike,' 'hymie,' 'Yid.' Anything but 'Jewboy' all the damn time!"

" 'Yid,' " Fariq said thoughtfully, smacking his tongue as if he were tasting a fine wine. "I like that one."

Winston stood just inside the exit. On stage, Clifford's band was in the middle of their preperformance primping. Sugarshack tuned his saxophone with puffs of sound, peering down the bell and then shaking the horn every few notes, hoping to dislodge some invisible clog. Gusto sat behind a small drum kit practicing his licks and his distorted drum-solo faces. Duke adjusted and readjusted the congas propped between his legs. Winston recalled how he used to drive Duke crazy by asking him to explain the difference between congas and bongos. Dawoud rummaged through his duffel bag of percussion instruments, his choices for the evening's entertainment seemingly based on nonmusical attributes such as blatant Africanness and the dexterity required to play them.

Pointing Jordy's finger for him, Winston followed the nervous pacing of his father. "That's your grandfather, Jordy. He's an asshole." Clifford Foshay had changed into his poetry garb. The black fakir was resplendent in a Bengal tiger–patterned djellaba, topped off with an intricately woven macramé kufi, accessorized with wooden beads and yellowed lion's teeth. Unintroduced, Clifford strode across the rostrum, carefully set his watch on the lectern and produced a shotgun, which he fired into the air, silencing the crowd. "That's for Huey." *Blam!* "That's for Fred Hampton." He opened the barrel and inserted two more cartridges into the breech. *Blam!* "That's for raping my great-grandma." *Blam!* "And that's one to grow on." A sleet of particleboard and ceiling plaster began to fall. The audience leaned forward in their seats.

When Winston was younger and forced to attend his father's readings, Clifford's ostentatious militancy embarrassed him. He would return home obsessed with one question: what would happen if his dad turned white overnight? One day his father was a panelist on a Sunday-afternoon television news forum. The guests, no matter their political bent, argued, threatened, and insulted one another. Winston realized that every guest reminded him of his father and that if his dad had been born white he would be the same person, bellicose and belligerent, spewing his rhetoric from overstuffed recliners and television-studio swivel chairs instead of prison cots and bar stools. When his father called him later that day asking if he'd seen him on television, Winston said yes, then asked his father why, if he talked so much about the glories of Africa and the repressions of America, he didn't drop his slave name for an African one. Clifford replied, "Because then you can't cash the checks."

After invoking the requisite Yoruba spirits, Clifford was finally ready to read. There was a cannonade of shotgun fire, and Winston turned to leave. There was no purpose in his staying; he knew the program by heart. Poems about Clifford's expatriation to Cuba: repetitive paeans layered with images of mangos, rusty automobiles, sugarcane, and raven-haired beauties who like to fuck until the roosters crow. To break the revolutionary reveille there would be some poems about basketball, drums, and of course John Coltrane. The freedom suite would be followed by intermittent tales of how Clifford, drunk on Cuban rum and missing his mama's cooking, made a pontoon out of coconuts and fishnet, waded into the waters of Matanzas Bay, and extradited himself to Florida. For an encore Clifford would read an ode dedicated to Winston and his dead sister, Brenda. The poem would rumble incessantly onward, like the *Iliad* read aloud by a summer-school teacher on a gorgeous August afternoon. The first canto was the story of Clifford sending cross-country for Winston and Brenda when Huey P. Newton died tragically in the streets of Oakland, California. It would be read with dramatic caesuras inserted, not between musical phrases, but between poignant images, for maximum pathos. After a three-day bus ride, Winston and his sister arrived the day of the funeral. Winston, lacking a pair of clean underwear, was forced to attend the burial wearing a pair of his sister's panties. How he cried—not because the snake head of black-American rebellion had been severed from its body, but because his undergarment was thin, pink, and had "Tuesday" handwritten just under the waistband.

Canto 2 retold in quatrains how Clifford discovered his daughter was dead when the amount of the court-ordered alimony payments that followed him through four address changes had been halved. The third canto was a recounting of young Winston's African-American-warrior training. His thirteenth birthday present the very same twelve-gauge shotgun balanced on Clifford's right hip. The hunting trips took place in the swampy reeds of Wards Island, where shotgun fire scattered homeless men like park pigeons. Winston was made to fetch the kill, mostly buckshot-shredded possums and cats.

Tears of regret would pour down Clifford's face, and he would remove his reading glasses, take a sip of water, and read the poem's envoi, hammering home the point of how in fighting the war humane he'd sacrificed his humanity. Then Winston's father would bow his head; the audience, unsure if the poem was over, would remain silent. After the whispered "Thank you" into the microphone, everyone would stand and applaud this lyrical airing of dirty laundry. Clifford would scan the crowd looking for his bereaved son. Finding him, he'd ask Winston to stand. And the crowd would then turn toward Winston and smile, their clapping growing even more intense in recognition of the revolutionary's son who wore pink panties to Huey P. Newton's funeral. Finally, when his father had finished signing all the books, exchanging phone numbers with all the agents and groupies, the redeemed freedom fighter would make his way to his son and heartily embrace him, fooling Winston into thinking they might head into the night together, Ajax and Telamon after the siege of Troy. *I love you. No, you can't come with us, we're going to get some drinks. Call you tomorrow. Love you.*

Winston lay Jordy in his stroller and backed quietly out of the room, leaving Clifford on a Dadaist roll, turning wordplay riffs on Fidel Castro:

Fidel's fidelity
Hi-fidelity
Sieg heil fidelity

Two tablespoons of Castro Oil
Castro-castrate the bull market

Winston decided he would celebrate his candidacy at the movies. He bought a pint of gin and a bottle of lemonade, then flagged a livery cab.

The burgundy Buick Electra sailed down Second Avenue like an obsolete dreadnought full steam ahead on its way to the dry dock. Father and son poked their heads though the sunroof. Shirtsleeves flapping in the downtown traffic sirocco, they ahoyed everything from the prostitutes to leashed Pomeranians. "Vote Winston Foshay—City Councilman!" Winston shouted, his arm stretched into the dusk in imitation of Debs's pleading pose. "Vote Winston Foshay—City Councilman!" He didn't have anything else to say. He didn't have a political platform—no programs for reform, no admonitions for society. "Vote Winston Foshay—City Councilman!" As people turned to see who this crazy man yelling from an old

Buick was, he could almost see his words drifting away in the slipstream of the muggy city air, like skywriting. "I'm mad as hell, and I'm not going to take it anymore!" He laughed, took a sip of his drink, then screamed, "All for a spoonful of borscht!"

"Here?" asked the driver, cruising the car past the multiplex. The marquee displayed six films, none of which Winston had any interest in. It was the usual dreck: a low-budget music video passing itself off as an African-American feature film; the summer blockbuster chock-full of special effects; three white independent "mosaics" of risqué subject matter, flat asses, dime-novel plot twists, and lots and lots of driving; and one big-budget masturbatory vehicle written, directed, and produced by an aging white Academy superstar playing a vile, bitter, successful old curmudgeon who finds humility and understanding for his fellow man in the arms of a young nubile. *Fuck this garbage.* He said aloud, "Take me to Chinatown."

There is nothing darker than a Chinatown movie theater, and for a moment the gloom fooled Winston into thinking he was dead. After checking to make sure his heart was still beating, he groped his way down the aisle, his hand going from seat back to seat back, occasionally touching the sweaty neck of a sleeping old man. He found found two empty seats and rubbed the worn velvet cushions, checking for freshly chewed gum. Out of blankets and two small stuffed animals he made a pallet for Jordy, who quickly fell asleep, a parakeet in a covered cage.

Winston slouched in his seat and peered through the swirling cigarette smoke at the giant screen. Two Hong Kong brothers, obviously on different sides of the law, were arguing over who'd make the penultimate sacrifice. *I'll kill for you. No, I'll die for you.* Winston left the theater wondering if he would've thrown himself in front of the bullets that claimed his sister, dying in her arms with a noble look on his face. He headed north on Bowery singing the theme song to the second feature, *Once Upon a Time in China,* a picture he'd seen at least a dozen times. He was still singing when he walked into a pet store two blocks up from the theater. *"Ao qi mian dui wan chong la-a-ang. Re xie xiang na hong ri gua-a-ang!"* The proprietor greeted him with a smile and finished the chorus, *"Dan si tie da-a-a.* That's a great movie."

"The best."

TUFF

Winston asked to see the baby turtles, and the storekeeper placed a fishbowl full of dark-green inch-long turtles on the counter. Winston picked out a turtle and placed it in Jordy's palm. "What do the words in that song mean?"

" 'Stand proud when you face wars. Hot-blooded like the red sun. Courage like iron.' "

"That's good advice. How much them turtles?"

"One for a dollar, ten for eight."

Hunching over the counter, Winston whispered into the owner's ear, "You got them piranhas?"

The man looked around suspiciously, called for his attendant to watch the cash register, then headed to a back room, returning with a menacing-looking fish in a sandwich bag.

"That's what I'm talking about! Let me get some of those little rocks, too—blue ones."

When Winston got home, he placed the rocks into a corner of the casserole bowl that held his goldfish, sticking a plastic palm tree in the cobalt-blue mound, forming a makeshift tropical isle. He pried open Jordy's hand and resuscitated the dried-out turtle with a globule of saliva, then dropped it into the water with the goldfish and a dead fly that was floating on the surface. Waving the sandwich bag over the casserole dish, Winston teased his pet, "Fishy, come out to play! Dustin, I want you to meet Sir Laurence Olivier." The piranha swam out of the Baggie and into its new environs. "Is it safe? Hell naw, it isn't safe." The turtle scrambled for the rocks. The goldfish backed into the corner, cautiously eyeing his new neighbor. The piranha ate the dead fly. Winston took Jordy to bed, chuckling in his Ming the Merciless laugh.

10· PARADISE EX NIHILO

On a low-visibility day, from the observation deck of the Empire State Building, the Manhattan skyline looked like a giant histogram, the lofty edifices stretching upward along the X axis of greed. Beyond the midtown skyscrapers lay the meaningless statistical outliers, the barren flatlands of East Harlem. Tuffy looked back at Inez and Spencer, who were busily noshing on a plate of hot Empire State nachos, letting Winston have his moment.

The view always evoked mixed emotions in Winston. This high off the ground at the base of the clouds, he experienced the dissonant symptoms of social vertigo. He didn't know whether he was flying or falling. Today, the view was more apropos of Tuffy's life than ever before. Since declaring his halfhearted candidacy for public office, he'd begun to look at his neighborhood from the outside in. When he visited friends, the overwhelming stench of buckets that served as toilets for the people who lived on the top-floor landings no longer caused him to gag and laugh in ridicule, but to daub his stinging eyes in shame. At night from his bedroom window, he counted the buildings on his block, stupefied that abandoned dwellings outnumbered occupied ones by two to one. He fell asleep watching the nocturnal drug addicts flit out of the concrete caves like bats, and the diurnal homeless return to burrow into the dilapidated warren.

TUFF

. . .

The foreign tongues, drawls, and dialects of the tourists buzzed in Winston's ears like forest mosquitoes. Their gaiety almost fooled him into believing that he too was a foreigner to the urban chaos down below. A gale of hot wind rustled the city map he was holding. Winston struggled to hold it at a readable angle. A German tour guide and his group surrounded him. *"Im Norden liegt Harlem,"* the tour guide said, his hand raised for attention, *". . . die Heimat des schwarzen Amerikas."* The German language made his epiglottis itch, but Winston distinctly heard "Harlem" and wondered what the tour guide was saying. He knew the man wasn't saying anything about his Harlem, *Ost* Harlem.

There was little East Harlem folklore. There had been no Spanish Harlem Renaissance, only Ben E. King's catamitic reference to a rose in his soul song "Spanish Harlem," three poets of some renown (Willie Perdomo, Piri Thomas, and Doug E. Fresh), and a playground basketball legend (Joe Hammond). It would be impossible for any tour guide to convey the absurdity of daily life in the neighborhood. How could one even translate Winston's chaotic morning?

The East Harlem dawn bathed his casserole-dish aquarium in reddish-gold light. *Beautiful,* thought Winston. *Shoot, my set up lookin' kinda tropical.* But when he checked up on his beloved piranha, he found the metaphor of his election campaign floating on its side, dead; the goldfish and turtle frolicking around its corpse.

East Harlem was where the real excitement was, but black Harlem seemed to have better marketing. Tour guides with a textbook knowledge of Harlem weren't the only ones to profit by its mystique. Before the sanitized tour companies invaded Harlem with their double-decker buses and walking tours, Winston and Fariq provided services to European tourists. They plied their trade outside the Port Authority Bus Terminal. Near the cab stand they'd wait for a couple of tall, pale youths who displayed that distinctive European mien of being descendants of the great civilizations, along with cowlicks, black jeans, and a backpack, to stagger wearily out of the station. At the crinkle of a map unfolding, Fariq would break out his shortwave-radio-soccer German. *"Achtung,* motherfuckers!" he'd say, wobbling over to the youths, gold teeth glinting in his "Welcome to New York" smile. *"Nicht scheißen! Nicht scheißen!* Just kidding."

"Sprechen Sie Deutsch?" the tourist would ask skeptically. "A little,"

Fariq would reply. "Check me out: *Bayern München gegen Kaiserslautern; zwei zu eins. Borussia Dortmund gegen Herta BSC; eins zu null.*" The tourists would back away, unsure of how to respond to the irony of a crippled American boy who loved *Fussball*. If there was a piece of trash about, with a swing of his crutch Fariq would "kick" it between two rubbish bins, then exclaim, "*Klinsmann mit links—Tor!*"—a pinprick in the travelers' Social Democratic sensibilities. "Do you need any directions?" Fariq would volunteer. "Where you going? What are you planning to see? Have you thought about Alphabet City, or the Botanical Gardens?" "Botanical Gardens" was Winston's cue. "Harlem. What about Harlem?" he would say robotically, his voice barely audible over the Ninth Avenue traffic. It was his only line. Whenever he complained to Fariq demanding a bigger role in the con game, Fariq would explain to him that he had to say the line. "You big, black, and ugly. You everything they've ever imagined Harlem to be." "Yeah, great idea, Tuff. What about Harlem? Have you guys thought about Harlem?" At the mention of the magic word the European wayfarers would fidget like naughty children about to accept a dare. Soon the tourists would be purchasing fake tickets to a nonexistent Motown revue at the Apollo. If they were especially gullible, Fariq would bid Winston load their luggage into the cab, while he asked where they were staying, then relayed the information to the cabdriver. "Let's see, the Upper West Side will be twenty-five dollars. You give us the money and the driver will take you where you want to go." After a while the con stopped working. The new Eurotravelers were a wiser breed. They'd look at the counterfeit tickets and say, "James Brown never recorded for Motown."

The German tour guide was pounding and kicking the telescope. He cuffed the telescope with the heel of his hand one last time. "*Eine scheiß Optik.*"

Tuffy's gaze shifted back and forth from the distant rooftops of his neighborhood to the section of map Inez had marked off in red marker as his electoral district. While the German sightseers gawked at the lights of Times Square, his eyes traced the jagged borders of the unremarkable Eighth District. His mind filling in details invisible from eighty-six stories up and three miles away. According to Inez he needed nine hundred people to sign a petition that would place his name on the ballot. No one knew the district and its constituency like he did. The eastern boundary bisected the East River from 96th to 129th Streets, and Winston knew that somewhere along the concrete banks of the river, maybe by the 103rd Street overpass, crazy old Siddhartha Jenkins was minding rod and reel.

Today, like every day, Siddhartha was fishing for fluke, porgy, and the occasional albacore, wildly wrestling with his pole as if he'd hooked Hemingway's giant marlin. "I wish the boy were here with me. Blessed Mary, pray for the death of this fish, wonderful though he is. I wish the boy were here." If Siddhartha would sign the petition, Winston would be the boy.

The northernmost outpost of the ward was the intersection of Lexington Avenue and 129th Street. Winston envisioned constituent Jaimito Linares standing in front of Manny's Superette, sipping on fifty-cent cans of malt liquor, hissing at any female who strayed too close to his lair. *Psst, Mamí, com'ere. No, I really like you, you make me want to settle down.* Next to him, in the shade of an orange beach umbrella, Wilma "La Albina" Mendez. Legs cocked open like a bronco-busting cowboy on break, Wilma would be running her pink-margarita eyes over Jaimito's spillover. Her quasar-white skin set off with sparkling twenty-four-karat gold necklaces and dental caps, she would be searching for lesbian tendencies in the faces, walks, and haircuts of those who rebuffed Jaimito's advances or talked to him but couldn't keep their eyes off her. Wedding rings be damned. *It's fucking hot, right? You want some cold wine cooler. Come on, don't be that way, tómelo. Come sit in the shade.* Jaimito and Wilma would sign just to impress the ladies with their political savvy.

Down Lexington to 110th Street the streets would be lined with locals seeking relief from the heat. Some would have washrags dipped in ice water pressed to their foreheads, moving and speaking only when absolutely necessary. Others would be sitting on the porch listening to the block's interlocutor provide the latest "*Oye*, you heard about" gossip, basking in the air-conditioning of someone's problems. Up and down Lexington, youngsters would keep from stalling in the heat by lubricating their idling engines with various coolants, both legal and illegal. On 121st Street, next to the record shop, Carl Fonseca would be tending his quarter-acre vegetable garden, bragging that the only thing that matched the size of his tomatoes was the size of his balls. Between 114th and 115th Streets a pair of towheaded Mormon boys would be knocking on doors, clicking open attaché cases like movie hitmen, threatening the local heathens with their pamphlet weaponry. Maybe, Winston thought, he could use the Mormon evangelism to his advantage. He'd let the Mormons open the doors, get the doomed descendants of Cain talking, then he'd swoop in and, catching the hosts in be-polite-in-front-of-the-white-man mode, have them sign his petition.

Winston's eyes traveled west on 110th past the park, past the church of St. John the Divine, and down Broadway to what he approximated to be 96th Street. He struggled for an image of the area. *That's not my people. I don't know shit about the West Side. Don't white people live over there? Fuck.* The Eighth District included Central Park, the lines of demarcation excluding the residential sides of its eastern and western borders. Though Central Park wasn't a key voting bloc, the green was his jurisdiction. Right now Armello was playing baseball on diamond 10, nonchalantly scooping up hard-hit ground balls in the field and, after two feeble at-bats, being pinch-hit for in the fifth inning. *If I win the election I can pass a law saying Armello gets four strikes.*

"Ms. Nomura, it's so big."

"What is?"

"The district. I'm mean, I got the park, the West Side, everything but the fancy buildings on Central Park West and Fifth Avenue."

"Well, East Harlem's interests and their interests are different."

"Don't everybody pretty much want the same things—jobs, good schools, and shit?"

"Yeah, but they don't want you in their neighborhood, much less having any say-so over their lives."

Winston plucked a gooey tortilla chip from Inez's plate, making sure to hook a slice of jalapeño. "Man, for a second there I was excited about this shit. But from here you see how many people live in the neighborhood. I mean, look at all the windows. In every one there's a life being lived."

Spencer smiled. "Winston, you don't know it, but you'd be a really good city councilman."

"Man, I don't know shit about politics. No, wait, hold up, I do know something." Winston swallowed his food and began singing in a shower-perfected baritone that rarely graced the world excepting in drunken soft lullabies to his son.

I'm just a bill. Yes, I'm only a bill
And I'm sitting here on Capitol Hill.
It's a long, long journey

TUFF

to the capital city
It's a long, long wait
While I'm sitting in committee
But I know that I'll be a law someday. . . .

There wasn't an American born after 1960 who hadn't heard "School-house Rock." Not surprisingly, Spencer joined Winston in singing the last lines of the chorus.

At least I hope and pray that I will
But today I am still just a bill.

Winston grumbled. "I know that song. That's it, thank God. If I really knew something, my stubborn ass might get some ideas and actually try and make a change."

"But if you *could* make a change, what would you do?" Spencer asked, taking out his notebook. Tuffy glanced at his distant neighborhood, its dirt-brown facades barely visible, camouflaged in the smoggy haze. "First thing I would do is paint a yellow line on the ground that exactly matched the boundaries of the district. That way we'd know that the neighborhood is ours. 'This is our shit, step lively'—you know what I'm saying?"

Winston went on to create a paradise ex nihilo, an idyllic shtetl of midnight swimming holes and hassle-free zones where denizens would be free to "drug, fuck, suck, and thug" to their heart's delight. Where personal stereos wouldn't shatter into plastic shards when you dropped them, but bounce back into your hands undamaged, like rubber balls. Where children would never have to know what it is to eat sugar sandwiches for breakfast, frozen broccoli for lunch, and sit down to dinners of Spam, canned corn, and moldy pieces of bread, listening to Mother say, "Don't worry about the green stuff, that's where penicillin comes from, it's good for you." East Harlem would be a Shangri-la of moist weed, cold beer, and zesty sofrito.

"Then I would put up a huge sign that read 'Spanish Harlem' in bright red neon lights that flashed one letter at a time and then all at once. Some shit that make this GE, Citibank, big-business bullshit look small. Something that would make these foreigners say, "Over there is the Brooklyn Bridge, and over there, there is Spanish Harlem!" Winston shook his head. "I'm tripping, right?"

"Winston, those are things people need to hear," Inez said.

"Even that madness about fuckin', suckin', druggin', and thuggin'?"

"Well, maybe not the thuggin'."

Inez handed Winston a petition. "Here, this is the petition I have to turn in to the Board of Elections in three weeks."

Winston looked it over. "Nine hundred names? That won't be so hard."

"But they have to be registered voters and it has be done in three weeks."

"All we have to do is get a bunch of the registration forms and register motherfuckers as they signing the petition. Many times as I been caught up in the system, I know how it works, they'll never know."

"That's a good idea," Spencer said, wrapping his arm around Winston's shoulders, "You're feeling it today, huh?"

Winston shrugged off Spencer's hand. "You know, ever since I decided to run I'm thinking different. I can feel my brain working. Y'all remember those cards with the dots on them? You'd hold them up about six inches from your nose and stare at it, then real slowly a 3-D image appears. That's what's happening to me. My mind is slowly seeing the pattern. I hope it's not a fad like them cards were. What were those things called?"

"Magic Eye, I think."

"Then I got the Magic Eye. Woooo!"

Winston read the petition aloud. "We, the undersigned, do hereby state that as duly enrolled voters of the Eighth Council District and entitled to vote in the next blah, blah, blah to be held on blah, blah, blah, appoint Winston L. Foshay for City Council Eighth District. In witness whereof, we have hereto set our hands. Signed, Inez Nomura, Fariq Cole, and Yolanda Delpino-Foshay." Winston thrust the piece of paper back into Inez's hands. "Yolanda using her maiden name now? What the fuck is up with that? And my father—what, he don't want to sign?"

"He said, 'Why waste good ink on a lost cause?' "

"He's probably right."

Inez grabbed Winston by the wrist, saying, "Come with me," and dragged him to the southeast corner of the observation deck. Spencer followed at a distance. Tourists excitedly taking photographs of the Statue of Liberty filled the corner, jostling for vantage points. Elbowing and cursing her and Winston's way to the precipice, Inez was worried. There was an uneasiness in Winston she had never seen before. Why had she pushed him? Had she overreacted because he'd finally hinted he wanted to channel his natural leadership in a positive direction? Maybe she should have suggested he coach a Little League team instead. *"Here's fifteen thousand, run for City Council." What was I thinking?*

Inez watched the ferries shuttle people to and from Liberty Island, remembering the days when she knew exactly what was right and what was wrong. In 1977 it was right for her and the Puerto Rican National Activists to seize Lady Liberty in the name of *libertad* and political prisoner Andrés Cordero. Shoving Japanese tourists and schoolchildren aside, they slammed the door in the statue's sandal and draped a Puerto Rican flag from the crown. Press releases fell to the ground like confetti. It was wrong of the men in the group to feel up the latticework under Lady Liberty's dress and harass the women by asking one another, "Have you ever been inside of a woman? No, I mean *really* inside of a woman." It was right for Nolan Lacosta to climb the stairway near Liberty's vulva and insert his penis into a rusted-out orifice and say, "Hey, look, you guys, I'm fucking America!" It was wrong for her husband, embarrassed by the publicity, to leave her the next day to raise the children in Philadelphia, satisfying their filial curiosity by telling them their mother died in an explosion while making a pipe bomb.

Inez elbowed Winston in the ribs, then pointed out over the river. "I know I told you about the time we arrested the Statue of Liberty for false advertising."

"You showed me the photos."

"Winston, there was a time when I could make a call and evacuate any building in the city."

"Mmm."

Winston dug his hands deep into his pockets and leaned against the ledge next to Inez, his back to Lady Liberty. He studied her out of the corner of his eye. Inez looked tired but hopeful. She was developing bags not only under her eyes but over them. If nothing else, the Revolution was exhausting. She looked like an ex–prohibition-era pug: punch-drunk, permanently welted, stumbling from gin mill to gin mill rambling on about a promised shot at the title, a victory for the common laborer. All around, faces stared into the horizon. *Fuck everybody look so optimistic about? That's why she brought me up here. Catch some of that on-top-of-the-world fever.*

Calling out to Inez and Spencer, Winston nodded toward the line waiting for the elevator. "Let's go. I've got to meet Smush and them in Brooklyn."

After a long wait the trio squeezed into the elevator. Winston tossed a piece of bubble gum into his mouth so his ears wouldn't pop on the way down. The fortune read: "You are a responsible person. When something goes wrong, people always think you're responsible." With a loud pop he sucked a pink bubble back into his mouth.

"Ms. Nomura, you really going to give me fifteen K?"

"I'm cashing the check Monday morning."

"Damn, a nigger goin' to be liquid. I ain't got to do nothing, right?"

"All I ask is that you make two appearances: the sumo exhibition in the park, and the debate a week before the election."

"So should I be a Democrat or Republican?"

"You have a preference?"

"They all the same to me. I really don't want to be neither."

"Then don't. But if you run as an independent, your party needs a name."

"What, start my own party?"

"Why not? All you need is a name."

"How about 'The Party'?"

"Where did you get that?"

"I remember all them freaky-looking people rollin' up in your crib talking about 'The Party says to do this, and The Party says we should do that.'"

"Winston, 'The Party' has connotations that have nothing to do with you. Besides, it's someone else's thing. You need your own thing."

"What about 'A Party'? That shit sound kind of good. 'A Party.' Sounds like we having fun. Niggers will like that."

A Party. Inez mulled the phrase over. A Party. She liked the way the name shifted between egalitarianism and hierarchy: A Party, one political party out of many; A Party, as opposed to B Party and C Party. "Niggers will feel that," Winston insisted, "believe me." Inez believed.

"Winston?"

"Yeah?"

"You know, your father was a beautiful man."

"If you say so."

"If you'd known him during the movement. Most men look stupid in a beret, but Clifford pulled it off. He used to stuff his natural into a black felt tam, tilt it so that one edge hung just above his earlobe. If you were to ask him what he did for a living, he could have said anything— revolutionary, concert pianist, poet, painter, professional Frenchman, dancer—and you would have believed him, and thought he was the best at whatever he said he did, even if you'd never seen him do it."

"Ms. Nomura, you and my father have something going on back in the day?"

"You know, I think deep down Clifford is very proud of you, Winston."

"You not answering my question."

"On the grounds it may incriminate me." The elevator doors opened. "Aren't you supposed to go to Brooklyn?" Inez said, and then, feeling like Sisyphus, pushed Winston into the stream of tourists flowing toward the revolving doors. Inez waved and under her breath said, "*Gambate,* Winston."

Winston refused Spencer's offer of a ride to Brooklyn but walked him to his car. On the way Spencer asked if he had something to fall back on in case Inez failed to come up with the money. Winston had it covered. "That's why I'm going to Brooklyn. I ain't too sure Ms. Nomura going to be able to cash that check, that shit older than baseball. So I'm about to learn some card tricks."

"You're going to be a magician?"

"Something like that."

11· WHERE BROOKLYN AT? WHERE BROOKLYN AT?

Brooklyn was in the throes of a muggy yet festive Saturday night. The borough, at least the area surrounding the Fort Greene projects, was one big outdoor juke joint, and the party was in full swing. There's a weekend adage Brooklynites utter on nights such as this: "It's not where you're from, it's where you're at." But Winston, feeling the effects of his Brooklynphobia, had no idea where he was at. He was nauseous and disoriented. Somewhere, a few blocks back, the east end of Myrtle Avenue had flipped up and attached itself to the west end, encircling Winston in a concrete band. The street began to spin. Dance-hall music boomed out of slow-moving sedans, and triplets of red and green dice bounded off brick walls. The ghosts of Demetrius, Chilly Most, and Zoltan circled overhead, spooking him into dropping his bottle of malt liquor. Winston was back in Coney Island's Hellhole.

He took corrective measures. He truncated his gait and slowed his pace to a chain-gang plod. The appropriate amount of bounce was applied to his diddy-bop, just enough spring in his step to rock his torso and head in an autistic half-beat. His shoulders rolled so that his arms paddled stiffly through the humid air like oars to a cruising Phoenician warship. His face arranged itself into a Noh scowl: eyebrows cinched tight like zipper teeth, eyes squinted, jaw jutted to a position not seen on a hominid since *Homo erectus.* No oncomers held his stare longer than it look to think, *Who that ugly motherfucker? Nigger look crazy.* The street stopped spinning. His demons fled.

If he couldn't help looking like an outsider, it was best to look like a dangerous one. Stopping at each intersection, Tuffy suspiciously looked both ways, as if he were on the lookout for the police when in reality he was searching for a landmark that would jog his memory of where his cousin Antoine lived. *Where that nigger rest at? There was a post office, a laundermat kitty-corner from that, and a basketball court down the block. Cool, there go the laundermat.* Relieved, he turned left and walked to the middle of the brownstone-lined block, stopping under an oriel window with a debauched red glow. Three preteen girls sat on the hood of a car parked out front, dreaming aloud, daring the world to listen. But the only person paying attention was a delighted little girl, elbows on the fender, chin in hands, a small tinker bell attached to a red nylon choker wrapped tight around her neck.

"When we sign our record contract, we going to be so big. Oh my God! I'm a buy a car, set Moms out. Damn, I can't fuckin' wait!"

"You iggin', girl, we need to write some songs first."

"We don't need no songs. We don't even need know how to sing. All we need is an image, some dance steps, and a good name for the group. The music comes last, yo."

"So what's our group called?"

"I was thinking of B-R-A-T-S."

"What's that stand for?"

"Being Real And True Sisters."

"Hell naw, that's too soft. We gots to come hard, know what I'm saying? How about S-H-I-T—Some Hos In Trouble?"

"We can't be a cuss word. How we going to get any radio play. 'Here's the latest single by SHIT.' I ain't never going to get a pearl-gray Jaguar like this."

"What about C-R-A-P, Coming Real At People?"

"That's wack, we should be called A-S-S. We get on *Soul Train,* and the host'll say, 'All the way from Brooklyn, put your hands together for ASSSSS!' " The girl leaped off the car, danced a quick heel-toe-jig butt-shaking routine, then, clutching a microphone as real as her singing abilities, conducted the postperformance interview. " 'What's your name?' 'Felicia.' 'Felicia, I hear you're the choreographer for the group, is that true?' 'I put together a little something something. Get the people excited.' 'And where do you hail from?' 'Brooklyn. Hey, Brooklyn in the house, y'all.' 'ASS has the number-one single on the charts, but every-where I go people ask me what does ASS stand for, what should I tell them?' 'Tell them it stands for Always Singing Sisters.' "

One girl lifted her chin in Winston's direction, alerting her friends to the presence of an older boy. As the would-be divas eyed him, Winston's posture straightened and his face softened. Stopping within speaking range of the young ladies, he patted his stomach and ran his tongue over his teeth. The choreographer, at thirteen years old the doyenne of the group, closed the gap with two bold, hands-on-hip steps toward him, her egg-sized breasts violating his personal space. Tilting her head at the obtuse angle one uses to make sense of an abstract museum piece, she said, "Mmm, you fine." The backup harpies slid off the car fender with all the seductiveness bony twelve-year-olds can muster.

"Where Antoine at?" Winston asked, looking skyward to keep from flirting, the tag line to male adolescence ringing in his head: "Old enough to pee, old enough . . ."

"He upstairs," the choreographer answered, brushing her bangs from her forehead, then pointing toward the red window. "You going to get your dick sucked? You don't look like no fag."

"That's my cousin."

"Your name Tuffy?"

"Uh-huh. How you know?"

"He said you was coming by tonight. Antoine be talking about you. Told me you was his bodyguard. He said you be running up on niggers, for real."

"Naw, it ain't like that."

Felicia was referring to the nights when Tuffy used to escort Antoine to the cab stand after long nights of working the peep show and fuck booths. Winston would tromp up the lighted spiraling stairs of the XXX Sex Palace to find his cousin on the second floor sitting on a bar stool, wearing high heels, a tight miniskirt, and a lavender bustier, striking pinup poses. After a 360-degree spin on the stool, Antoine emerged looking ready to be posted up over a homesick GI's bunk.

"Who's this?" he'd ask his coworkers, nose pointed to the heavens, back arched, hairless legs crossed with one hand resting limply over one knee. He'd flick one bra strap seductively off his shoulder, part his thin red lips ever so slightly, and flutter his eyelids. "I said, who's this?"

"Betty Grable!"

TUFF

"Jane Russell!"

"Susan Hayward!"

"No. No. No. How stupid can you be—I'm Ida Lupino!"

"Who the fuck is that?"

"You bitches better learn your history."

"Let's go, Antoine!" Winston would snarl, snatching his cousin's rabbit-fur coat off the wall hook and, with a matador snap of the jacket, coax him off the stool and into the night. "*Vámanos*, goddammit."

"Winston, don't call me Antoine. Here my name is Mons Venus, you know that."

For thirty dollars in sticky one-dollar bills or fifty dollars in peep-show tokens, Winston's job was to march Antoine past a sign reading

GIRLS!
GIRLS!
GIRLS!

(with penises) All sex acts non-refundable.

then guide him through a gauntlet of sexually frustrated and bewildered men. Men who after fifteen minutes of awkward light petting through a small window in a Plexiglas partition reached for the phone to negotiate the price of a vaginal display. Antoine would stall for time, prudishly suggesting that it was his time of month. Nervous, he'd scratch the razor stubble on his cheeks, his reluctance to "show some pussy" and the amplified rustle of his five o'clock shadow arousing the customer's suspicion. The client would begin to panic. Eyes jumping from titties to Adam's apple, back to titties, over to the hands and feet, and back to the titties. The man would jabber in clipped sentences, his anger and shock fusing the declarative, exclamatory, and interrogative into complete thoughts that accommodated any form of sentence punctuation. *This bitch got a beard? This bitch got a beard! This bitch got a beard.* "I demand to see the manager!"

After being shown the sign and laughed off the premises, the traumatized men lined Eighth Avenue, questioning their sexual orientation. With Winston as his escort, Antoine paraded past them like a debutante as they demanded recompense, threatened vengeance, and sometimes proposed marriage.

Felicia snapped open her lipstick case, then buried her face in the passenger's-side mirror of a nearby car. She slowly applied the frosted-white wax with the expertise of a thirty-year-old. "Exactly like Antoine," Winston commented. "Little girl, you need a new role model."

He was about to enter Antoine's building when he heard the tinny ringing of a bell. He turned just in time to see the smallest girl slither between two parked cars, yell a war cry, then charge toward him. Lurching forward, Winston stamped a hiking-boot-shod foot into the ground. The loud thud stopped the emaciated bell cow in her tracks, and she teetered like a nodding dope fiend trying to keep her balance. He recognized her immediately: it was the moppet who lived down the hall from the Brooklyn drug spot. "What are you doing here, you little thief?" The child averted her gaze and pointed at the red light in the window. "If you want to go upstairs and start pickpocketing faggots and transvestites, you in trouble, because they either wearing dresses or tight pants."

The girl folded her prehensile arms tightly across her chest. The doleful expression on her face made the gesture seem more a self-hug than the intended show of disdain. "Fuck you, you fat motherfucker." Winston had already picked out a spot on her leg to kick when the girl began crying, the sobs convulsing her skinny frame and causing the tiny bell to jingle eurhythmically. Winston cursed and spat at the ground, "Damn." He looked at the child hard. She was even dirtier and thinner than he remembered. "Y'all know her?" he asked the older girls, wondering what about him set off such a violent reaction in the youngster. Winston tucked in his shirt. "Naw, some lady dropped her off out here and then went inside."

The symptoms of poverty are timeless, and Winston knew exactly who the weepy kid looked like: an extra from John Ford's *Grapes of Wrath*. A Brooklyn Joad, sullied from head to toe with the grime of parental and societal neglect. She wore a pair of tattered running shoes, the frayed laces tied through every other eyelet. Bands of dirt ringed her droopy white socks. A pair of knobby knees extended from the legs of her denim cutoffs. The grease-stained pink T-shirt was too small, and her bare midriff was bracketed by the bony ribcage of a lion cub starving in an African drought. Tufts of unkept sun-reddened hair flamed atop her head like a brushfire. The little girl pounded a small fist on her thigh and bit down hard on her bottom lip to control her crying. Samaritan that he was, Winston fished in his pocket for a piece of bubble gum. The confection disappeared from his hand before it was even offered. She chewed quickly, as if she were afraid Winston might reach into her mouth and take his gum back. "What the fortune say?" he asked, and she held the wrapper out for him to read. *"Whoever said 'Words cannot hurt me' never got hit in the head with a dictionary."* That ain't no fortune, Winston thought, turning his back on the girl and lumbering up the stairs. *That's a saying or a phrase or some shit.*

The older girls resumed dreaming of success, imagining journalists writing rave reviews of their debut single and conducting fawning magazine interviews. "Yeah, I'm going be up in the magazine cruising through the neighborhood in my Range Rover. Waving and saying whud'dup to people on the street. Talking about, "These are the niggers I *used* to know.""

"I got a name! I got a name! We could be B-U-B-B-A—Blown Up Big By Afternoon."

"How about N-I-P-P-L-E—Naked In Public Places Like Escalators?"

The quiet little girl tried to blow a bubble that would turn her world a chalkish pink. A bubble so big that when it popped, it would startle the gods and stick to her ears. As soon as the gum was moist enough for bubble blowing, she flattened the wad against the roof of her mouth with her tongue. Then with a loud, wet tongue cluck she broke the suction and shifted the disk so its outer edges lined the insides of her incisors and the meat of the gum covered her inner lips. Slowly the girl parted her teeth and lips with the tip of her tongue, while taking a deep world-record-bubble-gum-blowing breath. Her breath control was excellent. The meditation-smooth exhale produced a nice clean softball-sized but rapidly thinning bubble. The girl panicked. She didn't have enough gum. Her breath came in stops and starts. Just one more puff of air . . . but her next blow was too strong and the entire wad flew out of her mouth and landed in the street, a pink waste of still-juicy, sweet, and sticky bubble gum.

Winston entered the foyer and touched knuckles with the doorman, who parted a burgundy curtain and bade him enter. Dancing couples packed the front room. Hands thrust out in front of them and eyes closed, they wafted in the crashing breakers of bass-heavy funk rolling over them. Submerged in the music, the dancers swam in syncopation like a school of fish, suddenly twisting, changing direction at some hidden signal in the vibrations.

Normally in such a setting Winston would scan the dance floor watching the rumps shake, timing the pelvic thrust of a shapely rear end so he could slide behind a cutie-pie, align his zipper with the groove in her behind, and ride her ass until he needed a beer. But there would be no dancing tonight, because to Winston's thinking, *It's crazy faggots up in this here motherfucker.* Winston checked his hands for signs of contagion. The red light turned his brown skin a mossy green. The pungent tobacco smoke, incense, and the saccharine stench of women's perfume on sweaty men combined to form a swamp gas that immediately saturated his clothes. Winston wanted a beer, but the wanton looks of the men embracing in the dark corners, the come-hither stares of the unattached wallflowers leadened his limbs. Aghast at the homosexual brazenness, Winston was hard pressed to move.

He asked around for Antoine, and a partygoer directed him to the VIP lounge in the basement. When he reached the foot of the stairs, the crew was waiting for him: Fariq, Charley O', Nadine, Armello, and Moneybags, the niggers he still knew. They occupied the far corner of the bar, sipping cans of Budweiser and silently watching a video on the overhead television. At the near corner six women stirred their drinks with the repose of regulars.

Trying his best to look like an overworked hostess, Cousin Antoine tended bar. Bar rag tucked into his waist, he scurried from the blender to the beer cooler, flipping his long ponytail, blowing the bangs off his forehead, and sneaking peaks at the TV screen. Behind Antoine, amongst the neon and mirrored advertisements for import beers the bar didn't stock, was a neon sign: the FTD logo—Mercury, ankles winged in mid-arabesque, delivering a bouquet. Antoine looked up from a Brandy Alexander. "Tuffy!" he yelled, scampering from behind the bar in a straight-legged wind-up-doll trot, his house slippers sloshing through the sawdust on the floor. "Damn, it's good to see you! I thought by this time you'd be upstate doing twenty-five-to-life. You ain't killed nobody yet?"

Winston pointed to the pair of hip-hugging dungarees that crushed his cousin's genitals into near-oblivion, and delivered his retort. "You ain't got a vagina yet?" The regulars at the bar laughed, and Winston noticed that two of the six women laughed like pirates, with guttural "hardy-har-har"s that belied their svelte bodies: the one in the turquoise blouse and Ms. Thing with the beehive hairdo and red halter top. He reminded himself no matter how drunk he got, to stay away from those two—they probably owned penises bigger than his.

TUFF

The cold snapping spritz of a newly opened Budweiser called Winston to the end of the bar. There the television loomed over his head at an angle that reminded him of being in a jailhouse day room. A beer can on a collision course with his own slid toward him. Fariq hobbled over and intercepted it, crutches swinging from his arms like pendulums. "Much faggots up in this piece, yo. I was surprised you suggested this spot, this being Brooklyn and all. Faggots and all. You right, though—ain't nobody going to look for us here." Fariq blew a kiss to Nadine, then raised his voice. "It was kind of tight coming through the disco, though. I remember back in the day when a motherfucker you didn't know looked you in the eye, you'd be like 'Hey my man, Fifty Grand, what's happening? Stay safe.' Now a motherfucker look you in the eye it mean he want to shoot you or stick his dick in your ass. Times is changed." The rest of the gang thumped their Budweiser cans on the bar to show their approval of Fariq's commentary. From the far end of the bar in a testy voice Antoine said, "How come boys always think that anal sex is the worst thing that could possibly happen to them?"

"I can think of something worse than being booty-busted."

"What, Fariq?"

"Having a dick in your ass *and* one in your mouth!"

Though he found Fariq's quip funny, Winston didn't laugh as hard as he normally would. The feeling of being an outsider again crept up on him. He was within an arm's length of his best friends, and yet he felt as if he were back atop the Empire State Building looking down on them through the reverse end of the telescope. They were in focus but very far away.

His discomfort had only a little to do with his antipathy for Brooklyn and being surrounded by men in search of ovaries arguing about whether or not they were homosexuals. It stemmed more from the fact that by bringing Spencer into his life and accepting Inez's money he'd made a half-ass commitment to his life. He knew his friends saw him as turning his back on them, but that wasn't the case. In the war zone that was his neighborhood Winston wanted to be a neutral nigger. He wanted to call time out, steal a Popsicle from the corner store, and rejoin the game when he felt like it. But for Tuffy there was no middle ground. He was either real or fake. Down or invisible.

He'd felt this way before, during a Rikers shakedown that didn't involve him. During a cell-block search someone had handed him some contraband. He didn't know what to do with it: swallow it, tuck it under a roll of fat, or give it back? He ended up with two months added to his sentence.

Watching his friends guzzle beer and chat, Winston wasn't sure what to do with himself. He had a notion to call Spencer and seek some Big-Brotherly guidance. But the phone was near the transsexuals, one of whom was flitting his tongue like a disturbed snake. Winston let out a cry of frustration. "What's wrong with you, son?" asked Armello.

"You niggers seem different."

"Fuck, you talkin' 'bout?"

"I don't know, Whitey, it's like tonight I don't know y'all."

Fariq moved from behind Nadine. He was a little drunk, and held his beer unsteadily, his middle finger off the can and pointing at Winston. "Nigger, *you* the one changed. Got a Jew and Ms. Inez running your fucking life. Man, I wouldn't run for no white man's City Council for no amount of money. Not fifteen thousand or fifteen million thousand."

"Easy for you to say, you got money in the bank. You got ideas."

Standing abreast at the bar, Fariq, Charley O', and Armello looked to Winston like the Three Stooges in an army episode, lined up for inspection. He knew what happened next: the major would ask for a volunteer for a dangerous mission and they'd take one step backward. He'd be left standing alone having "volunteered" for who knows what. The Fourth Stooge assed out like a motherfucker.

"And don't be handing us that"—Fariq was signaling for another beer and talking to Winston at the same time—" 'You niggers seem different' bullshit. That sound like whitey talking."

"What? I didn't say nothing."

"Not you, Charles. I mean real white people. You know how they always want to make like there's friction between niggers. Niggers can't coexist unless they on one fucking wavelength. Divide and conquer. These niggers are different from these niggers. Fuck that. Winston, you want to act a fool and hang out with a black fucking rabbi and playact like you running for City Council, that's your fucking business. You always have been, always will be my and our nigger. So don't come to me with that 'Y'all seem different' sad-song bullshit."

Winston's face flushed. "That's on me, son. You talking good shit. Respect, nukka."

"Tuffy, long as you don't come between me and my money green, we will always be boys."

Winston didn't think the gap had been quite closed shut. But he knew that this sense of otherness wasn't something to dwell on. He lifted his beer can off the bar. The condensation from the can left a wet ring on the wood. He thought of Musashi's oneness with the universe, and knew no matter how different he felt, or was treated, he would never be different or removed. Not from these niggers at least.

Charles slung an arm around Winston and pressed a cold can of beer into his hand. "I'm saying, son, you runnin' for office, that shit inspirin', B. You thinkin' big. You ain't goin' to win, but that don't make no nevermind. Because we all thinkin' big now." Winston soon found himself drowning in an affirmative tidal wave of "uh-huh"s "word"s, and "true, true"s. From the earnestness in their voices, the greed in their grins, the way Moneybags had his back turned away from the group and was peering into the pour spout of his Budweiser, Winston could sense that some grand scheme was afoot. Something bigger than the three-card-monte con they'd all come to Brooklyn to learn, some score that couldn't be discussed in public. He played coy, and looked up at the television screen. "You niggers ain't shit. I need some new cellies. Antoine!" The loud hail for someone outside the clan signaled to the rest of the bar that the meeting of the East Harlem Thieves' Guild was adjourned. Moneybags lifted his head. Forthwith all conversation was public domain, and the regulars turned the volume of their causerie up a notch. Tuffy continued to bellow. "Antoine! Why you showing this movie?"

The movie in question was *Lord of the Flies*. The troop of stranded boys was balkanizing into the savage and the civilized, and the bespectacled fat kid was vainly trying to maintain a semblance of prep-school decorum. "I have the conch. It's my turn to speak." Tugging on Tuffy's shirtsleeve, Armello mocked the fat kid's plea. " 'I have the conch'? Of course nobody is listening to his roly-poly ass—he's carrying around an abalone shell like he crazy. Who'd want to hear what this fool has to say? 'I have the conch.' Please!" On the screen, the leader of the rebels eyed a nearby boulder. "I love this movie," said Antoine.

"You would, you sicko. All excited over little white boys running around the jungle half-naked, ain't you?" snorted Fariq, slipping his arm around Nadine's waist.

"The leader—what's his name, Ralph?—he got some muscles on him for a twelve-year-old. Look at those abs."

"Change the channel," Winston pleaded. "This one is exactly like the original."

"I'm sure it isn't exactly like the original."

"You right, the original was in black-and-white and they wasn't wearing designer drawers, that's the only difference."

"Look at the peter muscle on the redheaded boy with the spear."

"Oooh!" the entire bar gasped. Jack, leader of the primitives, caved in the chubby boy's head with a boulder, ending his filibuster and his life. "I have the rock!" Armello shouted gleefully. "Now *that's* how you get people to listen!"

Winston pounded the bar top. "Man, I'm tired of the fat kid always getting fucked up. Why the fat guy always gots to be the star's best friend? If you the star's best friend, fat, and getting laughed at, you going to get fucked up. Plain and simple."

"At least there's fat people in the movies," Fariq said. "If by some miracle a handicap person is even in a flick, he's in a wheelchair plotting to take over the world, snickering like a fucking maniac. And I ain't never seen a movie with *two* handicapped motherfuckers in it. You might see two obese motherfuckers, twins or some shit."

Winston laughed, "Because you can't have two crippled motherfuckers in the same room. Don't think when the handicap van pulls up in front of the center I don't see you trying to stare down the deaf and retarded waterhead niggers."

"Very funny, son. But I'm sayin', if it's a handicap in the movies, he's a bank-robbing mastermind."

Nadine shushed Fariq. "Be quiet, Smush, you trippin'?"

"My shit," Fariq apologized, quickly setting about covering his slip by harassing Antoine. "Hey, Antoine, would you consider yourself to be an expert on fagness?"

Winston rolled his beer across his forehead, trying to mollify his frustration with the can's coolness. Charles's we-got-to-think-big-now remark and Nadine's admonishing Fariq for his "bank-robbing mastermind" comment made it obvious to him that one of the many golden nest eggs laid on the stoop was beginning to hatch. *These stupid niggers fixin' to rob a bank. This beer ain't cuttin' it.* Leaning over the bar, Winston nimbly fingered a bottle of Idaho vodka off the shelf. Fariq and Antoine continued to flirt with one another.

"Yeah, I know a thing or two about fagness. Fagocity. Fagology. Fagistics. You want me to give you a lesson?"

Nadine placed her hands on her hips and looked Antoine up and down. "I don't think so, not with my man, you fucking *maricón.*"

TUFF

Antoine rolled his eyes. "Shoot, I'll show you something too, young lady."

Winston unscrewed the cap and sneakily filled his voluminous cheeks with vodka. The swallow produced a concussive sound in his head that clogged his ear canals, cleared his sinuses, and stiffened his fingers. While he was on top of the Empire State Building talking campaign strategy, his boys had planned something without him. After sixteen years of being consulted on everything from the rules for an afternoon game of kick-the-can to the proper attire for an evening of teen skulduggery, his friends had planned a robbery without him—a bank robbery, no less. It hurt that he wasn't part of the heist's planning, but he was also glad he hadn't been. *One less thing to worry about.* The second swallow momentarily ceased all of Winston's brain activity, dousing his synaptic impulse for bitterness and fusing his short-term and long-term memories into a lump of neurons concerned only with the here-and-now and the never-was. *Good luck to you motherfuckers.*

"I was down in the Village the other day, all these lesbos was holding hands."

"You never see none uptown holding hands."

"That's because they'd get lit up. And Whitey, don't interrupt me."

"Winston, do you and your friends go around bashing gay people?" asked Antoine.

"Man, what you saying? If I recall correctly, when I was little *you* and *your* little crew of faggots used to tease me and then beat *me* up. I was one who was bashed. You always hear of violence against fags, but you don't never hear of fag violence against straight motherfuckers."

"Fuck you, Tuffy."

"Then don't start. I ain't about to take your side just because we cousins."

Fariq began screaming, "Will you all, please, stop interrupting me and let me finish my story?"

The others quieted down. "Go 'head, nigger, damn."

"Right. What the fuck was I talking about?"

"Lesbians."

"Right. To each they own, know what I'm saying? But what I want to know is why lesbians dress so fuckin' bad? I mean, they dress like they going to a cookout to roast frankfurters and eat discount potato chips. What they carry in their purses? Paper plates and plastic forks? Tan

shorts, hiking boots, purple socks, and a fucked-up haircut. Look like they
ready to pitch a tent and have a potato-sack race at a moment's notice.
How come these bitches ain't got no style? I mean, I know all these
bitches ain't working construction?"

Antoine sucked his teeth. "Smush, you need to be more sensitive to
the homosexual community. Especially since you, you know, is crippled
and all."

"Now what, I got to suck dick to be politically correct?"

"Ask Tuffy, he a politician," suggested Nadine.

"Am I?" Winston asked, forcing another burning swallow down his
gullet, and not so subtly sliding the vodka back on the shelf. By the gnarl
in his voice it was evident to Fariq and the others that this drunk was
going to be an introspective one for Winston. They almost preferred his
mean psychosexual binges, when he would rampage through a club robbing men pressed up against the urinals, stand in the middle of the dance
floor conducting the DJ by waving his penis like a flaccid baton. "Y'all better get off the politician thing. I ain't never said I was a politician—even if
I *did* say I was, it wouldn't make me one. Whatever you seen me doing,
that's what I am."

Armello raised his can in Winston's direction. "So right now you a
drunk motherfucker?"

"Yup, and ain't ashamed of it neither. I ain't like them cabdrivers.
You get in the cab the driver try to start up a conversation, not because he
a friendly guy, but to see if he fucked up and let the wrong nigger in his
cab. 'Hello, my friend. Back in my country, I am scientist. I am doctor.'
Motherfucker, shut the fuck up, you cabdriver!"

"But I bet if you was back there bleeding to death, you'd be hoping
he'd be saying 'I am doctor,' Fariq said, waylaying Winston's Sophoclean
complaint. "Come on, y'all, let's do what we came to do before Tuffy end
up doing something stupid."

Everyone agreed, reaching for their beer cans to take to the back
room, mulling over which of the identical cans belonged to whom, their
hands circling over the cluster of containers, wary of picking up someone
else's backwash. His lips pursed and making childlike airplane noises,
Winston's thick, flattened hand buzzed over the other hands; then, to the
screeching whistle of a dive bomber making a pass, pitched and yawed its
way through the other hands, swooping up a can from the middle of the
pack. Satisfied, he scooted toward the back room, happily chugging his

beer. "Nigger, how in fuck you know that's your brew?" Armello shouted at Winston's back. Winston flipped the now empty container over his shoulder. "Man, I twist the thingamajig on the lid." Nadine reached out to catch the can. The pull tab was cleverly twisted to three o'clock. "Oh snap, that's pretty smart."

"I thought you motherfuckers was supposed to be ghetto," Winston said, disappearing into the darkness of the back room.

Moneybags blocked his actors around the card table, which was nothing more than a cardboard box propped up on a milk crate. Though he was speaking in a barely comprehensible drunken brogue, Moneybags was more lucid than Winston had ever seen him. With the efficiency of a Broadway taskmaster, he rehearsed everyone for their roles in a three-card-monte production set to open in one week's time. Armello, the leading man, stood behind the box, his magician-quick hands making the cards flip and leapfrog at will. Nadine was to play the ingenue. It would be her job to lure the marks to the game with a subtle squeeze of her breast, a slow lick of her upper lip, a foolhardy hundred-dollar bet. "Nadine, you have to sell that line: 'Fuck, I'm losing my daughter's birthday money.' Make a man want to come and stand next to you. A whale with deep pockets, who thinks he can show the lady how it's done—win some money and take you home." Charles and Smush would be the supporting players, shills whose duties were to purposely obscure the mark's view of the table, arousing his curiosity. Having enticed the mark into the game, the duo would advise him on its finer points, explaining that if they united in their efforts, they could turn the odds against the dealer. Charles was especially good at this. Winston remembered the time they'd stolen boxes of perfume from a broken-down van on FDR Drive, unloading it for five dollars a bottle in midtown, Whitey pitching the shag in an impeccable British accent: "Straight from France and Italy, the finest scents for your mum, your luv, and for you git wanker puftahs, your mates. Sixty dollars at Saks Fifth Avenue, five dollars at just Fifth Avenue." Upon hearing the princely argot of the United Kingdom, West Indians on their lunch breaks fought each other to purchase bottles of perfume from the benevolent Brit.

Typecast as the heavy, Winston played the same part in the sham as always: he was to be the stick man—a bit player who stayed away from the action, vigilant for the police and the suckered, who having lost face in front of their girlfriends invariably returned demanding a refund. After he lobbied for a speaking role, Moneybags gave Tuffy a tryout as the lead shill, directly across from Armello. But Winston was in Armello's light, and as Moneybags said while shunting him once more to the side: "Tuffy, you too big. Can't nobody see the cards!" Winston kicked the milk crates, scattering the cards to the floor. Only Fariq deigned to speak up. "Look, Tuff, every nigger got to do what he do best, and motherfucker, can't nobody regulate like you!"

Winston brusquely stepped past Fariq toward Whitey. Reaching into Charley O's trouser pocket, he pulled out a sack of weed and dangled it in front of his nose. The curl in the corner of Whitey's mouth gave Winston tacit "But don't smoke it all" approval, and he sauntered out of the room.

"What's wrong with you?" Antoine asked.

"Nothing," Winston replied, gazing up at the television set. Antoine laughed through his nose. Though he hadn't seen his cousin in nearly two years, he hadn't changed very much. "Tuff?"

"What?"

"Why don't you sit?"

Winston backed onto a bar stool. When he was younger, he thought the television screen was a mirror: a telepathic reflecting glass that sucked the thoughts from his mind, then played them back, so that he would know what he was thinking.

"Antoine?"

"What?"

"Movie is this?"

"You don't know? Get out, I thought you'd seen everything ever made! It's one of Carl's movies, *The Green Berets*. John Wayne joint with this big-eared motherfucker as a nosy reporter. Sulu from *Star Trek* plays an Uncle Tom Vietnamese."

"I hate war movies. Especially ones with a reporter or a writer in it, always too good to shoot at the enemy until the very end, then they pick up a gun. Like if a *writer* has to kill, then war must *really* be horrible. And they never get killed. The writer never dies."

"Nigger, you must hate your father. Fuck was Uncle Clifford doing to you, man?"

Both men watched the war reporter, David Janssen, smash a

TUFF

machine gun against the trunk of a tree. Winston giggled. "White people so fucking obvious." He eased the bottle of vodka off the shelf and held it next to his leg. "Antoine, is there somewhere I can be alone in this place? I ain't trying to hear John Wayne right now. I just want to smoke my get-high and chill, know what I'm saying? Carl still got them crazy videos?" Antoine handed Winston the key to his brother's room upstairs. When Winston pinched the key's blade, Antoine held tight onto the bow. Little Tuffy was growing up; he was just about at the age when cousins go from being trusted playmates to near-strangers seen only at funerals and on errands to the post office. Antoine let go of the key. "Thanks, cuz." Tuffy headed for the stairs, keeping the bottle of vodka out of Antoine's sight. "How Aunt Ruthie, by the way?"

12· THE LITTLE BELL

arl's room, the cupola of the brownstone, was cramped with war memorabilia. Winston bypassed the swords, Nazi flags, Croix de Guerre and went straight to the army footlocker stuffed with videos. He rummaged through the pile, reading the labels, then tossing them aside: *AC/DC Live at Budokan; Faces of Death; Lynyrd Skynyrd; The Maginot Line; GG Allin; All-Time Greatest Hockey Fights—The Probert Years; Fuckman #144.* "This one looks good," Winston said, inserting a tape labeled *Any Niggers Who Ain't Paranoid Is Crazy—The History of Conspiracy* into the VCR.

The video opened with a washed-out fourth-generation dub of the Minister of the Nation of Islam standing behind a podium, dabbing his glistening brow with a meticulously folded handkerchief and addressing an auditorium filled with true believers.

The history they teach us is incomplete! If you believe them, the black man wasn't invented until the first day of slavery. The red man didn't show up on the planet until Thanksgiving, the brown man until the Alamo, and the first time they set eyes on the yellow man he was dropping bombs on Pearl Harbor. You want to get somewhere in this world? Then you have to learn about them, the white man. I don't know why black children do so badly in school, their version of history isn't very difficult. Lesson One: The white man was the first to do this and that. Lesson Two: The white man is the best at such and such. If you're lucky they tell you, then quiz you on the white man and the black man. And all you need to know is the white man did X, Y, and Z to and for the black man on such and such a date. But they'll never teach what the black man has done independent of the white man. No multiple choice, true-or-false questions on the history of the black man that have nothing to do the white man, his wars, his foibles, his laws. And they definitely don't . . . *won't* teach you about the relationship between the white man, the black man and the sharks in the Pacific Ocean. What they don't . . . what they *won't* tell you is that sharks are in the Pacific Ocean because they followed the slave ships from Africa, eating the Africans as they were thrown overboard.

Settling back in a desk chair, Tuffy made a makeshift marijuana pipe by puncturing the base of a stray beer can with a bloodstained bayonet. He pushed the Minister's slave-trade lesson from his mind. *Fuck this nigger talkin' 'bout?* Critical thinker that Winston was, it wasn't the historical implausibility of slave ships sailing the Pacific, when the middle passage was a transatlantic voyage, that caused him to dismiss the Minister's claims. His ghetto cynicism was bathyal. A deep nigger-you-ain't-said-shit doubt that looked below the ocean's rolling surface. *Come on now, sharks in the Pacific 'cause they was following slaves, that's bullshit. Why the sharks still there then? What, they swimming in circles talking about "Gee, Harold, ain't been no niggers around in a while—hell, they was good eating"?*

Needing an ashtray, Winston turned a Nazi SS helmet on its crown. "I'm good to go now." He covered the mouth of the can with his, lit the mound of weed in the dented chamber, and took a long pull. Through the exhaled smoke he watched the Minister's left arm reach past the border of the screen and reel in a heavyset, middle-aged black woman. The tight embrace wedged the woman's left side into the Minister's underarm, creating the impression that the two were Siamese twins. The Minister introduced the woman as an embattled victim of the Philadelphia justice system, and the crowd received her with an empathetic warmth. His voice boomed throughout the hall. "Now you all know that this kind, beautiful black woman"—the handkerchief made another cameo—"a teacher of beautiful black children"—the woman nodded her head in agreement, thankful that someone cared enough to defend her honor—"a highly trained educator, did not hit that white woman like they say she did. How dare they accuse her of beating that devilish woman to a pulp?" The woman looked down and demurely covered her mouth with her hand, but she was unable to prevent a grifter's grin from breaking out across her face. Instantly, everyone in the auditorium knew she had hit the anonymous white woman. Titters of laughter reached the podium. The smile on the Minister's face broadened, and he hugged the woman even tighter. "And even if she did . . ."

Winston's own cannabis-coarsened laughter drowned out the guffaws somersaulting out of the television speakers. *Maybe I can learn something from this clown,* he thought, *"My niggers, right or wrong."*

The marijuana was potent, an *indica* strain. Winston blew smoke rings and watched them expand. There was a twinge in his neck; then suddenly he lost his sense of touch. The state of insensation lasted only for a few seconds, but he enjoyed the feeling of being unable to differentiate his body from the rest of his surroundings. *Yo, I feel like I'm the air. No, no, the air is me. Niggers are breathing me. Hold up, I'm breathing myself. Take a deep breath, yo, you buggin' the fuck out.*

Winston karate-chopped the last few smoke rings still wafting in front of him and returned his concentration to the television. The Minister vanished under a blizzard of television static, and a well-dressed white man announced the existence of a secret society called the Illuminati. According to the nasal-voiced host, the Illuminati, all graduates of an institution known as the Invisible College, had surreptitiously ruddered the course of world history since 1500 B.C. The University of Sumeria–Ur Campus was the alma mater of its founders; current members received their training in a basement lecture hall at Yale. Pythagoras, Mohammed, Martin Luther, Isaac Newton, Voltaire, the Logical Positivists of Vienna, Umberto Eco, and every American president excepting Taft, Carter, and Reagan (pawns) were alumni of the Invisible College. The crucifixion was a fraternity stunt that received an unanticipated amount of publicity, resulting in the forced spiriting of Jesus to France and the publication of his Master's thesis in creative writing, *Sermon on the Mount,* the text now known as the Bible. World War I was a practicum for honors students Mao Zedong, Lawrence of Arabia, and the mustard-gas manufacturers. Using the Nazis as patsies, World War II was nothing more than an elaborate ruse to set up a showdown between communism and capitalism. The Illuminati's machinations were responsible for every late-twentieth-century conundrum, including the energy crisis of the 1970s, the chain letter, and Buster Douglas's improbable knockout victory over Mike Tyson.

At the mention of Buster Douglas, the paranoia adjunctive to good marijuana kicked in and kicked in hard. Winston could hear the footsteps and muffled voices of the Illuminati's henchmen speaking in cipher behind him. The true world-beaters were coming to get him and he would remain conscious throughout the plotting, the interrogation, and the torture.

"Tuffy, that boy."

"What you watching?"

"That weed fucked your shit up, didn't it?"

Winston said nothing, cotton mouth having starched his tongue to the roof of his mouth. Fariq, Nadine, and Armello sat on the bed. Charles seated himself on the footlocker. "Smush, tell him about the bank job, kid."

"Tuff, you know the new bank on Sixth and Second, around the corner from Kentucky Fried?" Winston nodded. He was interested in the heist, but his focus was on the television. A new white man entered the screen stage-right. The host stood in front of a paneled wall and pulled down a retractable movie screen, tugging at the bottom a few times to make sure it locked in place. "Since November twenty-two, nineteen sixty-three, the United States government has defrauded the American people concerning the truth about the Kennedy assassination. I know the truth. And soon you will know the truth. . . ." Winston leaned forward in his chair, trying to find the threshold in his immediate airspace where Fariq's and the conspiracy theorist's voices ceased to overlap. The best he could do was to turn sideways, the television broadcasting to his left ear, Smush to his right, their voices fading in and out like two distant shortwave radio stations on the same frequency. "I went in there with Charley O's moms. Wednesday she hit the number at the travel agency, playing two thirty-seven—some Met's batting average, Marvelous Marv Throneberry, or some motherfucker I ain't never heard of. Anyway, me, her, and Whitey chilling on the roof smoking reefer. You, I don't know

where you was. Charley's moms listening to sports talk radio, trying to figure out what she going to do with six thousand tax-free dollars, when a
commercial come on. Man talking real fast: 'Experts predict that unrest in
the Middle East, combined with the increasing use of farm equipment in
the corn belt now that the drought has ended, will result in a rise in the
price of oil. If the price of oil goes up as little as ten cents a barrel, an initial investment of five thousand dollars can expect a return dividend of
twenty thousand dollars in the next six months.' I seen her eyes get big
and I marched her right down to the bank, explaining the difference
between fixed-rate and variable checking."

"The grassy knoll—bullshit. The book depository—hogwash. Oswald,
Ruby, Oliver Stone—CIA subterfuge . . ."

"But peep this—Whitey's mother walk in, 'I want to open a high-
yield savings account,' and the new-account bitch like, *Oh shit, a white
lady,* 'Let me get my supervisor.' The supervisor like, *A white bitch in
the bank,* 'Let me get the branch manager.' In two minutes everybody
in the bank falling over themselves trying to take care of Mrs. O'Koren.
The branch manager is opening up the account and the security guard is
pulling out a chair so she can sit down. You hear me? The branch manager opening up a savings account is like the president washing dishes in
the White House. All that because Charley O's mama is white. I'm like,
'Somebody need to take these motherfuckers off. They sleeping. White
bitch come in the place and they lose they minds.' "

"Who you calling a bitch?"

"I'm sorry, Charley, no offense. So what we going to do is go back to
the bank, send in Whitey's moms, and while they acting like she Princess
Diana come back from the dead, rob the fucking place blind. But that's
more than you need to know, now that you running for City Council like a
little bitch."

"I'm going to run the Zapruder film. I'm sure you've seen it before,
but you've never seen this, the new print blown up to thirty-five milli-
meter. What you're about to see is more than you need to know, but everything you've wanted to know. . . ." The grille of Kennedy's limousine
emerged from the shadow of a Dallas overpass. Winston was so high the
image looked three-dimensional. He felt as if he could reach out, lift
Jackie's skirt, and take a peek at her panties.

Winston turned around to look in the faces of his friends, gauging
their resoluteness. To his surprise they looked half-serious. If he were to

say, "You niggers is full of shit," they'd probably rob the bank tomorrow just to prove him wrong. "You niggers full of shit," he said. His friends looked as if they'd been slapped in the face. Fariq poked Winston in the shin with his crutch. "For real, son. On TV I seen a documentary on these fucked-up Japanese war criminals. They was using the drug knowledge they got from experimenting on the prisoners of war to rob banks and shit. They put on lab coats and ran up in the place telling the employees they'd been exposed to some poisonous gas and had to take an antidote. The antidote of course knocked them out, and *boom,* it was on. A white lab coat and white skin will get you in anywhere."

Winston spoke very slowly in the lilting voice of the deeply intoxicated. "You going to poison the whole fucking place?"

"No, we just going to knock them out," Nadine said. "Ain't you listening?"

Armello clapped his hands, "I still got these date-rape pills from my baseball days. Roofies. Been saving them for something important."

"That ain't nothing new. It's basically the chloroform dog-snatching bit. You on some coward shit, as usual."

"It's not cowardly, it's slick. There is a difference. Want-to-be-brave, flex-they-muscles–type motherfuckers get shot. Like your boy Kennedy fittin' to get."

Turning back toward the television, Winston brushed the dust from the screen with his hand. The electrostatic crackle underneath his palm stood the hair on his arms on end. Kennedy's limo was rounding the corner. Jackie's left hand was atop her pillbox hat, keeping it from blowing away in the wind. The president was smiling like her right was buried in his groin. "All y'all, shut the fuck up."

The dowdy white man halted the film and tapped the movie screen with a wooden war-room pointer. "Keep your eye on the limo driver. From this point on I'll advance the film in slow motion, the chauffeur will turn around slightly, extend his right arm behind his head and over his left shoulder, you'll see the gun, hear the shot, see a puff of smoke, and Kennedy's head will snap back grotesquely. It wasn't Oswald, the Cubans, the mob, it was the limo driver." The film advanced frame by grainy frame. The driver turned his head. The driver's arm reached back as if he were scratching the back of his neck. "Oh shit." The report of a gun, the smoke, the snap of head, all the events unfolded exactly the way the man said they would. "Oh shit." Amazed, Winston leaned in closer to the television, examining the fuzzy black blip the white man said was the gun. *Is that a gun? That ain't no gun. Fuck, I'm too high to see the gun.*

Charles walked in front of the television. "That's what's going to happen to you if you run, Tuffy." He held up the *Fuckman #144* videocassette. "You mind?"

Winston shrugged, replaying the image of Kennedy slumped in the backseat of the limousine in his head. The echo of the shots reverberated, recalling his brush with death the last time he was in Brooklyn. *Man, this politicking dangerous. If I won I'd be dropping so much truth, niggers would have to shoot me.*

Charles backed away from the TV set, revealing a ponytailed middle-aged white man fingering a brunette who looked as if she'd been eighteen years old for all of ten minutes. Properly moistened with saliva and pillow talk, the young woman readied to receive the gray-bearded man, legs spread, eyes open. The lech, a saggy-skinned convulsion of grunts and grimaces, mounted the woman.

"You know he rolling, old man fucking with his socks on."

"And his glasses."

"But he ain't doing no damage to the pussy."

"Come on, bitch, get your feet into the fuck. Dig your heels in, girl."

For the next few minutes the group watched the video in rapt silence, each caught up in a private pornographic peccadillo, Winston's being that he loved watching a woman's breasts bounce during sex. Armello, wringing his hands and bursting with the need to share, blurted out, "Ah shit, now she licking the asshole! Ever have your asshole eaten?" he asked, looking around, not really expecting an answer. "I did. I was in Memphis in a Budgetel. Mamí had *me* in the buck. I was the bitch, my knees all in my ears, her tongue showing a nigger's anus much love. I completely forgot I struck out four times in that night's game, twice with the bases loaded."

Pointing emphatically at the TV, Fariq called everyone's attention back to the video. "Now Fuckman working the pussy, that's how you do!"

Whitey slapped Fariq in the back of the head. "Smush, what your scoliosis-crippled ass know about working pussy? You probably can't even control your thrusts, flopping on the cock like a fish out of water. Bet you catch an epileptic fit on the pussy, talking about 'Honey, did you spasm?' "

"Nadine, what you laughing at? When we get home, watch."

"Look at this white girl, yo, she fucking like a wet blanket."

TUFF

"Any of you niggers ever tag a white bitch?"

Winston, beginning to sober up, spun around in his chair, raising his hand like a schoolboy. "I did."

"Nigger, what? You ain't never said shit."

"You know me, before Yolanda I was sticking dick in all four inputs."

The males nodded in agreement, though none of them, as they ran down the list of bodily orifices, could figure out exactly what the fourth input was.

"All right."

"Word life, kid."

"My boy."

A quizzical look on his face, Armello stopped in mid-hurrah and began counting on his fingers. "Anal, oral, vaginal. Hey, yo, what's number four?"

Winston laughed haughtily and said, "I be mind-fucking hos, stupid."

"Where you meet this girl?"

"Remember in junior year we used to go to that underground spot in the meat district near the piers?"

"Uh-huh."

"White bitch and black bitch about ten years older than us sipping Scotch near the speaker?"

"The redheaded freak?"

"You know when you see a white girl and black girl together at the club, the white one looking for some black dick, and black one wants to hook up with a white boy, ain't no two ways about it. So I hit Red off with the digits on the sly. Trick called back and the next day I was up in her crib sucking titties and didn't spend nary a dime on drink, dinner, or daffodils. What was her name? Holly, Markie, some shit. I think it was Holly."

Nadine's faced puckered. "Eeww. What's a white girl like?"

"It was weird, man. She was so comfy all the damn time. She was a computer consultant. Had an office in the crib. I ain't never been in no black person's house with an office. I ain't even heard a nigger say 'I'm going to the office.' I just let her carry on. Suck my dick right, you can talk about gigabytes and zip drives all you want. Then one day we chillin', then out of the blue she start talking this 'You know, when I was growing up I had a black nanny. I loved her like she was family. She loved me too. At her funeral her children told me so.' "

"She went there on you, kid?"

"She went straight plantation *Gone with the Wind* on a brother. My father used to tell me that every fool he knew who ever been with a white girl who was from even a little bit a money has heard that shit. Shoot, I was trying to be 'peace and love, we're all human beings' with the bitch. I thought that madness my father was talking was old-fashioned. I'm like, 'She white? Big deal, it's the twenty-first century. People are people. So what if she brush her teeth with fennel-flavored all-natural toothpaste from Maine? So what?' "

"Wait a minute," Armello interrupted. "What's fennel?"

"Some nasty-tasting flavor." Winston sighed, then continued, " 'Black nanny.' Pissed me the fuck off. I'm like, 'Why this bitch feel the need to tell me this? "Black nanny?" What, she think I want to know that shit?' "

"Why you think, God?" Fariq said, all too eager to answer Winston's question. "What she was really saying was, your mother ain't shit, and that you ain't shit, because she's the white princess who everybody loves and worships. She think she special because she was raised by a black woman."

"Shoot, a black woman raised me too, but that don't make me special. But I was in the cut behind that comment. Stuck in the back of my mind. We be having a good time, then I look at her and think, *This stupid bitch, said that stupid shit.*"

"You should've said, 'Fuck her. Later for that bitch.' "

"If I could've would've should've, but you know how a white girl do. Ol' girl was kicking out gear, jewelry, sucking balls. Set a nigger out with a pass to the entire New York Film Festival. One time that crazy ho grabbed my arm, cut me with some scissors, and started sucking my blood."

"Come on."

"I'm serious. Wiped her mouth, talking about 'Now we are both Negroes.' I was like, 'Negro? You ain't Negro, bitch, you delusional.' "

"That's what you get for messing with a white girl," Charles said, nodding his head knowingly. "I'm telling you, white women is evil. Why any motherfucker would fuck with a white girl is beyond me."

"Charley, how can you say that? Your mother and your sister is white."

"Then don't you think I should know what I'm talking about?"

Fariq slapped palms with Charles. "Charley O' right. Any nigger who marry a white girl is marrying her because she white and no other reason. Unless a nigger meets a white bitch because they the sole survivors of an airplane crash and stranded on a desert island, he marrying her because she white. I don't give a fuck what he say about true love, pretty eyes, and a nice disposition."

"Who said anything about marriage? Me and a white babe, picture that. Smush, what you looking like that for?"

"I'm picturing."

"Don't even feel it. None of y'all would even know what to do with a dark-skinned babe. Yolanda is . . . man, please."

"You and Landa still fucking?" Fariq asked, somehow phrasing the question in an innocuous manner.

"Of course."

"You know what I mean when I say 'still fucking'? Is she invisible yet? I'm not talking about when you be fucking and thinking, 'Why am I fucking this bitch?' but when you be fucking and thinking, 'Why am I fucking?' That's when your woman becomes invisible."

"Come on now, we been going out for two years, married for one. The attraction piece there, but hey, it ain't easy. Before we get down to business I be sitting on the edge of the bed sipping a brew or smoking some cheeb, sometimes both. Gettin' primed, know what I'm sayin'? Yolanda looking at me all sad, holding her breasts like food, like she'd give them to me if she could, if it would make me happy. She say, 'Why you have to drink and smoke that shit before we make love? Shouldn't I be enough?' and I'm hitting the joint for all I'm worth, talking about, 'Yeah, bitch, you should.' " To show his precoital exasperation, Winston took two hard pulls on the imaginary marijuana cigarette in his hand, then said, "I be like, 'Man, this shit ain't hitting right.' "

When the laughter died down, Nadine tried to bring the conversation back to the lovemaking distinctions between the Caucasian and the Negro. "You never said, was there a difference in how a white girl fucks and how we do it?"

"It ain't like I been with a whole bunch of white girls. All I know is Latin babes like to pull on your ears, but I'd say, no difference in the coochie—pussy's pussy."

"I fucked a woman who didn't have a pussy," volunteered Armello, reluctantly tearing his eyes away from the sex video. "*Una vieja*—bitch was about fifty. Met her in Zebulon, North Carolina. She didn't have a pussy, had a hysterectomy when I got with her. Stuck my entire hand up in there," Armello slowly opened and closed his fist. "So much room in that mug, I could feel the wind blowing. *Coño,* if I'd've had a flashlight, I could have made shadow puppets on the insides of her stomach."

Using the light from the television, Armello illustrated his sexual escapade by producing shape-shifting silhouettes, substituting the bedroom wall for some aging southern belle's cervix. Barking canines metamorphosed into jellyfish. Pachyderms transformed into craning swans. Finding Armello's story a repulsive anaphrodisiac, Winston excused himself from the room. *"Me voy. Smush, dame chavo."*

"How much?"

"A pound."

Winston took the five-dollar bill from Fariq, and said his goodbyes. "Tell Antoine I'm gone."

Making his way downstairs, Winston could see the party was winding down. The living room smelled of musty men and spilled beer; plastic cups were strewn across the sticky floor. The bay windows, fogged from the night's activities, were beginning to clear. The few remaining couples held hands and made out in the corners of the living room. A tall man slow-danced by himself, spinning, dipping, and softly crooning lyrics to a saccharine love ballad.

Once out the door Winston saw the little Joad girl sitting alone on a car bumper, fingering her bell, the preteen divas having gone home for the night. "Your moms still ain't come out?" Winston asked.

The girl shook her head no and asked, "Did you see her in there?"

"What she look like?"

"Like me, but a little older."

Suddenly, Winston was in a hurry to get home. He held the door open and waved the girl inside. Crossing the threshold, the girl stopped and punched him in the stomach. Before she could scamper inside, Winston lifted her by the collar, ripping the bell from her neck before setting her down. "You don't need to let her know you coming, you just let her know you there."

On his way to the subway he hoped that Yolanda would still be awake when he got home. He pictured her wearing a sheer silk teddy, two sticks of Black Love incense burning, a bottle of baby oil resting on the nightstand.

TUFF

To avoid the stifling heat of the subway station, he waited at the top of the stairs, ears cocked for the roar of the next Manhattan-bound train, eyes on a group of cornrowed turnstile jumpers hurrying past him into the bowels of the transit system. He thought about what Fariq had said earlier: how women become invisible. Sex becomes routine. A salvo of gunfire rang out on the street above him. Winston was looking forward to the routine.

Girl, you my shorty, my wisdom, my Earth.

13· TIPPECANOE, TYLER, AND TUFFY TOO

ook at Ben Franklin. Tuffy, holding a starched one-hundred-dollar bill up to his face, was scrutinizing the old statesman's portrait. *Nigger look upset. Like somebody just told him, "You discovered electricity? So what, the radio ain't been invented yet."* Crisp notes of the same denomination as the one in his hands swelled his pockets. So much so, he barely had room enough for his keys and bubble gum, much less his pistol, which he now toted in his sock. *And Ben look like he about to say, "Motherfucker, if I was twenty years younger I put my pilgrim shoes so far in your ass . . ."* Winston smelled the bill, aahed, then stuffed it back into his pocket.

On every corner of the intersection of Lexington and 106th Street his newly hired support staff, consisting of Inez, Fariq, Charley, and Yolanda and Jordy, canvassed the Monday-morning commuters. Fariq handed a woman a flyer, then shoved a clipboard in the drowsy worker's face. "That's him, right there," he said, pointing across Lexington Avenue in Winston's direction. "Hell yeah, he's a good man—the best." Fariq called out to his candidate, "Tuffy! Come over here, yo!" Winston kept his head down, his eyes fixed on his new shoes, looking for scuff marks on the burnished leather. "Get over here, son, and shake this lady's hand. She wants to meet you!" Pretending he couldn't hear Fariq's request over the traffic noise, Winston cupped his ear, mouthed "Thank you" and greeted the woman with a grand-marshal parade wave. The woman waved back and signed the petition. Shouting over the woman's head, Fariq cursed his friend's lethargy. "Tuffy, you want these people to vote for you, you supposed to come running. You they servant. You doing for them. Don't let that little chump change in your pocket fill your head, nigger!" Winston juggled his testicles and shouted, "Suck my dick, motherfucker!" The potential voter slunk into the subway, looking at the composed figure on the flyer, then crazily at the real candidate holding his crotch and yelling obscenities.

Winston thrust his hands into his pockets and squeezed the knot of bills. A jolt surged through his body. It was as if the bills were electrified. His joints jumped. His skin tingled with privilege—proving Ben Franklin's research on conductivity is still incomplete.

A slim-hipped woman in a receptionist-tight black skirt walked past Winston and did a double-take. "That you on that poster?" she asked. He peered over his shoulder at the campaign poster in the restaurant window behind him. He and Inez had designed it two nights ago over gin and lemonade. It read:

THE REVOLUTION MAY BE DEAD,
BUT THERE IS A GHOST IN THE MACHINE

EAST HARLEM—VOTE FOR WINSTON FOSHAY
CITY COUNCIL 8TH DISTRICT

A SCARY MOTHERFUCKER

✓ AMBIVALENT ON DRUGS, GUNS, AND ALCOHOL IN THE COMMUNITY
✓ AGAINST CATS IN THE SUPERMERCADOS
✓ ANTI-COP
✓ ANTI-COP
✓ ANTI-COP
TOPPLE THE SYSTEM: VOTE SEPTEMBER 9TH—A PARTY

Underneath "A Scary Motherfucker" was an eighteen-by-twenty-four-inch photo of a sullen-faced sixteen-year-old Winston staring directly into the camera. His features were ashen. His eyelids drooped to an angle two degrees from slumber. An unlit cigarette hung in the corner of his mouth. Inez had taken the snapshot moments after a judge cleared him on drug-trafficking charges because the arresting officer was two hours late to the proceedings. She had implored him to smile. "You're free," she said. Winston looked relieved, not free. He made the obligatory vow to go straight, but never smiled. Soon after taking the suit and bow tie back to the Nation of Islam member Fariq had borrowed it from, he returned to his old ways.

"Yeah, that's me," he said to the woman.

"I thought so." The hesitancy disappeared from her voice; her posture slumped with a friendly casualness. Her hand dropped away from the flap of her purse. "Why you look so mean in that picture? You a rapper or something?"

Winston frowned. The woman's misconception was a common one. There was a slew of overweight rap artists, and rarely a week passed in which someone didn't mistake him for Chub Boogie, Fat Max, or Tonnage, and request that Winston "kick a verse" or "bust a rhyme." "Why a fat nigger always got to be a faggot-ass rapper?"

"I'm sorry. I just thought since you out here handing out flyers and got a poster up, you was promoting your album. You never see a poster of a nigger your age on the wall unless he selling records."

"True, but I'm running for City Council."

"Oh snap, you really running? I thought City Council was the name of your posse or something. You serious?"

"I guess so."

Winston gave her a flyer and showed her his clipboard.

"You registered?" he asked. The woman shook her head.

"Well, fill out this card, sign right here, and you can vote for me come September."

As she scribbled in the pertinent information, Winston looked over her shoulder. "Mmm, you smell good. Let me ask you something—what's that you wearing?"

"Let me ask you something—how you funding your campaign?" Snapping to attention, Winston stalled for time. He wasn't about to admit that this morning Inez gave him fifteen thousand dollars, two thousand flyers, the campaign's single poster, and a pep talk. With tears in her eyes, she explained half in Japanese and half in English, how at seven-fifteen this morning, she stormed into the local congressman's office, an ex-socialist ally turned capitalist pawn, and threatening his lone staffer that she knew her reparation check was old, but if the United States government didn't cash it immediately, she'd rally every concentration camp survivor, bus them down to Washington, D.C., bind their wrists with barbed wire, and sit them down on the steps of the Capitol building until they bled to death trickle by trickle or her check was cashed. Then she handed the staffer a photo of the congressman as a young radical intern proudly showing off his birthday gifts, a framed photo of Stalin, a plastic Sputnik model, a signed copy of *Das Kapital*, and a lid of grass—Maui Wowee to be specific. A call was made to D.C., and an hour ago Inez gravely pushed fifteen thousand dollars across her coffee table.

Winston had seen ten times that amount in various neighborhood drug spots, but he knew how much suffering the money represented, and like the millionaire Hollywood megastar who acts flabbergasted at having found one hundred thousand dollars in a duffel bag, he perfunctorily bulged his eyes and dropped his jaw. As he jammed the money into his pockets, his mood changed. He began to feel a sense of indebtedness to Inez. "Ms. Nomura, I'll help collect the nine hundred signatures, but I ain't doing shit else but the sumo thing and the debate. No shaking hands and kissing babies."

"I know," she had said, and handed him an extra five hundred dollars.

"I got a little scratch saved up," Winston told the woman. "You know, gots to be prudent with your funds."

The woman brushed aside a loose braid and tucked it behind her ear.

"Where I know you from?" he asked her.

"Didn't you run with Eric and Tango over on Mount Pleasant?"

"Yeah, how you know?"

"I'm Isabel's sister."

"You shitting me. So you must've been there when Alex and Kayson got into their little thing."

"Who you think mopped up the blood? I knew I knew you. Now I know how you got your money—that place was a goldmine. You the only one I know who held on to any of it. You must've broke out before Lester got popped."

"Right after. Fifty came in and blew up the spot, next day my shit was ghost."

"You know T.J. got a thirty-year bid behind that."

"I heard."

"Well, anyway, I got to go to work," the woman said, handing back the clipboard. "I'm going to vote for you—I like a man who supports the community. You better not get in office and start fucking up."

"What could I possibly do to make things worse?"

When the morning rush hour ended, Fariq and Charley surrendered to the tedium. Turning their clipboards in to Inez, they abandoned the struggle, going home to catch up on the sleep they'd lost the night before. Winston spent the rest of the day fending off the advances of aggressive women who were just glad to see a young nigger doing something positive, listening to people's problems, and shrugging his shoulders when they asked what would he do for them if elected. "At least you honest," they'd say, signing the petition while prattling on about an inept mayor, a do-nothing school board, disrespectful kids.

It was now late afternoon. The old-timers were out in force, trolling the streets for opportunity; yet their protégés, those wild-eyed, disrespectful kids, were missing in action. Now that Winston had noticed it, their absence was off-putting, and he was angry with himself for not being aware of it earlier.

Winston counted the number of signatures on his petition. *Eighty-six. That ain't so bad. With what everybody else got I'm probably damn near halfway there.*

A voice came to Winston from above. "You got my vote, you fat motherfucker! Anything to keep your crazy ass off the streets, *moreno*." Tuffy looked skyward, not bothering to shield his eyes from the sun. "Amante, what up, bro? Where the party at?" Perched on a rooftop, Edgar Amante, the local party promoter, was running wires from a small transformer into a washtub-sized satellite dish, working his day job. "*Qué te pasa, papi?* I heard you was running for City Council, I ain't believe the shit till I seen the poster."

"But I'm saying, where the set at tonight? I need to get loose."

"No party tonight. Everybody's gone to the Rock or to the Tombs."

"What?"

"Word up, son. You ain't know? The task force was rolling deep last night. UCs was popping niggers left and fucking right, bro. The news said it was something like nine hundred niggers arrested. Matter fact, what you doing out here?"

TUFF

"I was in Brooklyn last night."

"You lucky, B."

"Thanks, yo. I'm out."

"How's the descrambler I hooked you up with working out?"

"Straight."

Winston ran across the street toward Inez, Yolanda, and Jordy. "Honey, I'm going down to the precinct. I know where I can get some signatures."

Winston kissed Jordy, then reversed course and tromped up the hill to 102nd Street. He was headed for the police station with a dumbfounded Yolanda and Inez in tow. Halfway down the block he spotted a police cruiser backing out of its parking space and blasting hip-hop music through the PA system. Winston threw himself into the backseat, slamming the door behind him. Both officers stopped bobbing their heads and wheeled about, guns drawn, yelling commands over the music: "Hands, motherfucker!"

Slowly, Winston peeked around the barrels of the guns pointed in his face. "Bendito, that you?" he asked the driver.

"Tuffy? *Puñeta,* I almost blew you away."

"Bendito!" Tuffy lowered his hands, "You're a real cop now? Gun, badge, and everything? Shit, man, congratulations." Bendito's partner went ballistic. Leaning over the seat, he jabbed the gun into Winston's cheek. "I said hands, you son-of-a-bitch!"

Winston glowered at the officer and dropped his hands into his lap. "Son, you best to get that gun out my face before I take it from you and beat you to death with the butt end. Bendito, you better tell your boy something." Bendito lowered the music and his partner's gun. "It's okay, I know this one." The officer holstered his weapon, "You don't know how close you were to getting lit up."

"You don't know how close you were to a bagpipe funeral and a plaque on the wall: 'In memory of Officer—' "—Winston tugged on the officer's nametag—" 'Officer Bitch-Ass.' " Insulted, the officer raised a fist, but Winston slapped him before he could deliver the punch. And until Bendito separated them, the two flailed at each other like children fighting over dinner scraps. "Tuffy, get out of the car, now!"

"Naw, Bendito, man, you've got to arrest me."

"It's our first day, I can't arrest you. And it's not Bendito anymore, it's Ben."

"I need to go to jail and I don't feel like taking the bus, *Ben.*"

Bendito turned the music off. "Listen, if I arrest you on day one, fifteen minutes into my tour, we'll look like gung-ho supercops out to impress the brass and none of the other guys will trust us."

"Officer Negro here a new jack?"

"Dave's been on a year. Why do you want to get arrested anyway? Because you rappin' now, you want some bad publicity for your album or something?"

"I'm not rappin'," Winston protested.

"I had breakfast at Delia's, I seen the poster."

"I'm running for City Council."

"You're what?"

"I not really running, I'm . . ." Winston looked hopelessly out the window. He could see Inez and Yolanda, carrying Jordy like a bag of groceries, huffing their way toward the car. "Look, do me this solid. Just take me in."

"And charge you with what?"

With the heel of his hand, Winston cuffed Dave in the temple just hard enough to knock the officer's hat askew. "Slapping Officer Negro upside the head."

"First arrest, assault on an officer? I don't think so. I'd be the laughingstock of the precinct."

"Bendito, why you acting like I shot your dog? Just give me a break."

Fueled by memories of his beloved Der Kommissar lying dead in the gutter, Bendito gunned the car into reverse, just as Inez, Yolanda, and Jordy reached the passenger-side door. "Winston, where in the hell you going?" Yolanda asked, holding on to the door handle and jogging alongside the car.

"Jail."

"Motherfucker, if you leave me to go to jail, don't bother comin' back. You hear?"

"Calm down, damn. It ain't serious. I'll be out tomorrow—Wednesday at the latest."

Winston knew that if he had any outstanding warrants Tuesday or Wednesday could easily be February, and as a precaution, he peeled off two one-hundred-dollar bills from his bankroll, then, knowing Bendito wouldn't say anything, brazenly reached into his sock for his gun. "Hold this for me," he said, tossing the pistol and the rest of the money out the window. They continued to back down the street, while Inez and Yolanda stared at the money and the automatic. Yolanda picked up the gun. "Somebody get my money from out the goddamn street!" Winston ordered, his head sticking out the window. Inez and Yolanda both reached for the money. Inez yielded, and Yolanda slipped the cash into her purse.

As Bendito backed the cruiser into the precinct parking lot, Winston, hoping to speed up the time it took to process him, removed his belt and shoelaces. Hands cuffed behind him, struggling to keep his baggy britches from falling to his knees, he entered the station looking like a maladroit circus clown. His size-fourteen boots flapped against the linoleum floor like shower slippers. Bendito shoved him into an empty cell and Winston began the interminable wait. Thinking the worst, he resigned himself to being Rikers Island–bound. Three dull months in a hangar-sized white fiberglass tent, trying his damnedest to stay out of trouble. *Yolanda, right. I need to stop being so "impetuous." Fuck am I doing? It's easier to get jail time in jail than it is on the outside. I'll be in Rikers forever. Fucking with them niggers and catching charges just for defending myself.* In the cramped dampness of the holding tank, head against the bars, Tuffy heard his name. Someone reported to the process officer that the check came up clean, he didn't have any outstanding warrants. The desk sergeant asked Bendito what charges he was filing. Bendito cited cruelty to animals and illegal possession of a firearm. Then the sergeant began adding what he termed "obligatory counts": loitering, endangerment of public safety, criminal negligence, resisting arrest.

"Well, no, Sarge, he didn't exactly resist arrest."

The Tombs were overcrowded because of the previous night's sweep, and Winston was hustled to a storage space that had been converted into a temporary billet. Designed to hold forty men, it currently held fifty, not including the seven corrections officers. Winston walked directly to an empty cot, shook the pillow, lifted the foam rubber mattress, then ran his hand underneath the bed frame. Turning to face the rest of the inhabitants of temporary holding pen D-6, he said, "Any motherfuckers got some shit hid up in, near, around, over, or under my area, come get it now. I'm not trying to catch no kind of charges on this bid, but I will get in your ass if I have to." Winston immediately recognized at least two-thirds of the inhabitants, and his caveat, though earnest, was inflected with a bit of whimsy. No one spoke, though judging by the grins on their battered faces, most of his bunkmates were happy to see him.

"Stop woofing, yo! This is a Blood thing, son." A slim boy of about seventeen with a red bandanna tied around his neck stepped out of a pack of twelve rumpled, red-clad black men languishing about the center of the room. "We'll hide anything we want, where we want." Winston glanced at the nearest corrections officer, who was reading the paper and not paying much attention to the conversation. "I know you will," he said, opening his hands and taking an easy stride toward the goateed young man. "But I'm just letting you know, you *don't* want to hide jackshit my way."

Winston knew who he was talking to: Yancey "Whip Whop" Harris, member of the upper echelon of the Spanish Harlem Bloods, and once a gifted comedian. When he was younger Yancey was as far from the thug life as a boy could be. An honor student, he was the neighborhood funny man, whose antics and impressions made two hours' worth of grade-school detention fly by. Whip Whop was the type of guy people fought to sit next to on the subway. When a merchant killed his two brothers during an armed robbery three years ago, Yancey stopped telling jokes, stepped off the stage, and joined the shock troops.

Winston and Yancey both knew that in a fair fight Winston would beat Yancey like a slave, but none of the soldiers standing behind Yancey were fair. They also knew that after a night of police brutality from arrest to arraignment, Yancey wasn't spoiling for a fight, just asserting his leadership. "Zero-zero-one," Yancey said to his aide-de-camp, relaying some command in their coded binary language. The acolyte muttered back, "One-Zero-One-One-Zero," then asked a guard to turn up the volume on the boom box, an implicit okay that it was now safe for Winston to turn his back.

There was some temptation for Tuffy to throw his lot in with the Bloods—sit at their table, playfully pinch their wounds, thump their bruises, and stare down the Puerto Ricans. Though he remained alone, he found himself staring at the Puerto Ricans anyway. Not long ago they ran the city's jails. Powered by overwhelming numbers and a loose coalition, the Latin Kings and La Ñeta regulated every aspect of a prisoner's life, from what hand he ate his meals with to when he could defecate. The two groups feuded and the Bloods stepped in to fill the breach. Now reduced to being the French Résistance of the New York State prison system, the

Latinos sat on their beds, observing the occupying forces. Scattered about the makeshift holding pen were the independents, most of their anuses puckered tight with fear. Three Asian boys huddled in a corner doing cigarette tricks. Two stray white boys, arrested on the wrong weekend for minor violations, changed positions every few minutes, trying to stay within the guards' sight lines. The unaffiliated colored kids congregated in the corners. Those who had their sneakers stolen wore orange foam-rubber slippers that made a sickening crinkly noise when they walked. The mentally ill were the only ones who mingled.

Tuffy, the collective eyes of the Bloods hawking him, approached a stocky Latin King, Brody Onteveras, known as King Bro. "You got case quarters for a dollar?"

"Here." King Bro slapped three quarters in his palm.

Winston straightened. "Give me my fucking quarter, motherfucker. How you going to show, charging me a quarter for a dollar change?"

"You lucky I don't charge you four dollars a quarter."

"You better stop playing. Did I charge you when you needed a place to stay after Marisol . . . ? Motherfucker, don't let me put your shit in the street." Blushing, King Bro handed Winston the fourth quarter.

Winston cut the line of inmates waiting for the phone and placed a call home. No answer.

"What's this I hear about you running for City Council?" King Bro asked, his question quickly followed by a chorus of "For reals?" from every corner of the room.

"For reals. I'm running."

"Why you doing something foolish like that?" asked Whip Whop, rising from his seat and almost treading into the Latin King side of the bunker.

Winston grabbed a chair, spun it backward, and sat in it so that his chin rested on the top of the seat back. He positioned himself between the Latin and the black camps. "Because I was talking out the back of my neck and said some shit without really thinking. Then someone put some money in my pocket." The prisoners gathered around Winston as close as warring factions could gather around anything. "Man, can you imagine if a nigger like you won?"

"No, I can't."

"That be some out shit, though."

"But if I did win, you know what I'd do?"

"What?"

"I'd sit in the meetings, take my shoes off, and put my funky feet on the table, and say, 'I don't know what you stupid motherfuckers is making laws about, but don't forget the poor smelly motherfuckers like me.' At the very least I'll tell y'all niggers when the next roundup is."

"On the real, though," Whip Whop and King Bro said simultaneously. With a nod Whip Whop yielded the floor. "We need a voice. One of us speaking, instead of some television nigger speaking for us. Tuffy, if you ran I'd vote for you just on some ol' humbug-I-don't-give-a-fuck-type-shit."

Winston took out a couple of empty petition pages and some voter registration cards, items neither the police nor the guards who frisked him deemed dangerous weapons. "CO," he called out, "pen, please. I'm writing a letter to my lawyer." The guard tossed him a felt-tipped pen. "All y'all sign here then, put me on the ballot. You nonfelony motherfuckers, fill these out. I'm going to send you misdemeanor bench warrant niggers absentee ballots."

While the men passed around the petition, Winston spoke until lights out, not politicking a bloc of potential voters, but just simply getting some thoughts off his chest. "Look at us—in jail, treated like animals. Take a last look at the white boys, because they fixing to get desk appearance tickets. Judge going to wave his finger in their faces, 'Don't do it again.' For us it don't matter if we do it once or two million times, we headed for Rikers to spend sleepless nights listening to jet airplanes take off and land, and niggers getting tossed. Look at y'all niggers, niggers I've known since back in the day when we was shorter than shorties. I played in the johnny-pump with Ramón, Peehole, Felipe, Point Blank, Carlos, Tony Bump-off, Yancey. Stolen petty shit with Foster, Pan-Pan, Hard Top, and Hennessey. Lent money, borrowed money from damn near everybody in this piece. But I realized soon as I walked in here, seen so many niggers I know to be down decent motherfuckers, I was like, 'Damn, there's some good niggers in jail.' Most of us in here because we was in the wrong place at the wrong time. Been that way since our births, if you think about it." As he spoke, the circle tightened around him, cinching like a drawstring to a felt bag of valuables. With Winston as the midpoint of the circle, the friction between the gangs eased. The arc of each gang circumscribed a disjointed circle around him. Winston imagined the ghost of Musashi Miyamoto, stick in hand, filling in its gaps. The young gangsters listened, sucking on razor blades lodged alongside their callused gums, rubbing the crescent-shaped scars on their faces with their fingertips.

Ten minutes before his arraignment hearing, Winston was in a small holding cell behind the upstairs courtroom. Across from him sat his legal aid lawyer, Ms. Rachel Fisher. Rachel had the sniffles. As she leafed through the stack of Winston's files, hawking and wiping her runny nose with the back of her hand, errant droplets of snot fell on his docket. "Mr. Foshay?" Winston grunted, offended and pleased she didn't offer to shake his hand. "You got some record here. Because of your propensity to skip bail and miss court appearances the Criminal Justice Agency has decided your bail should be set at three thousand dollars. Since there's no way you can afford that amount, I'll try to get it reduced."

"I can afford it."

Rachel looked up with a snort. "You can? We'll make a plea, then they'll send you home," she said with a lawyerly finality.

"Yeah, but I ain't paying it. I need that money for other things."

"Well, then no matter how you plead, there's a chance you'll be remanded to Rikers if you don't post bail. I think if we plead guilty now to the cruelty charge the district attorney will drop the other counts without much of a fight. Possession of firearm—there's no evidence of a firearm. The rest of these are bullshit. I think you'll get four months max, maybe a fine. Maybe nothing."

"I ain't pleading guilty to shit. I ain't done shit but get arrested."

"But Mr. Foshay, you're charged with a weapons violation and cruelty to an animal. Specifically the shooting of a pit bull"—the lawyer lifted a sheet of paper—"named Der Kommissar in the head, so they arrested you for something."

"Nobody arrested me. I made a citizen's arrest on myself because I needed to go to jail to take care of some business, but I ain't done nothing."

"You were arrested, but no crime was committed, per se?"

"No, I didn't commit no crime, per se."

"Per se." Winston allowed the phrase to dangle on the tip of his tongue, enjoying its foreign tang. " 'Per se'? What language is that?"

"It's Latin."

Fighting to breathe through her clogged sinuses, Rachel tilted her head back. For the next five minutes she counseled Winston on the efficacy of making a guilty plea with her nose pointed to the ceiling. "Any questions, Mr. Foshay?"

"What's the judge's name?"

"Judge Weinstein."

"He Jewish?"

"Yes, I believe he is."

"Then I might got a chance. Maybe I'll represent myself."

"You want to make a fool out of yourself, too cheap to hire a lawyer or post bail, you go *pro se*, be my guest."

"I don't know about no *pro se*, but I arrested myself, and I'm going to represent myself. Shouldn't be a problem. If I start losing I'll just go Al Pacino in *And Justice for All* on them. Start screaming, 'No, *you're* out of order. In fact the whole system is out of order!' " The lawyer cleared her nasal passages with a loud sniffle, pinched her red-rimmed nostrils closed, and gathered her papers. "Fine, whatever," she said. "Have you ever seen *To Kill a Mockingbird*?"

"Of course."

"Then I suggest you do a Gregory Peck and charm the judge."

Before she stood to leave, Winston grabbed her wrist. "Can you do like Gregory Peck and get an innocent nigger like me out the door?"

Rachel affected a southern drawl and asked Winston, "You ain't raped any white women, have you, boy?"

Winston played along. "No, ma'am. Least not nones that's lived to tell the tale."

"Winston, did you shoot the dog?"

"Yes, but he tried to bite my son."

"I'll talk to the DA."

As they entered the chambers Winston had a small panic attack when he remembered that in *To Kill a Mockingbird*, Gregory Peck lost the case.

Judge Weinstein was presiding, barricaded against the hordes of miscreants seated in front of him by a nameplate and a tall mahogany bench. The cases heard before Winston's moved like clockwork. Lasting no longer than forty-five seconds, each arraignment moved efficiently down the assembly line. The conveyor belt of justice moved its manufactured goods, the defendants, from their courtroom seats to the front of the judge's bench. The assistant district attorney looked at a sheet of paper, recited the charges, and recommended that bail be set at x amount. The defense lawyer cited a mitigating circumstance, such as the defendant's being the sole provider for a destitute family, and requested the bail be reduced by a third. The prosecution would say the substantial bond was more than fair, since the defendant was a previous offender, a danger not only to law-abiding citizens of the community but to his own physical well-being. The judge would agree; the defendant would be stamped "Made in the USA" and shipped out on a bus to Rikers Island. During the paper shuffling between hearings, Judge Weinstein stuffed a transistor-radio earplug into one fleshy ear. He was listening to the Mets' game.

The bailiff called Winston's docket number and motioned for Winston to approach the bench. As he walked through the swinging gate, the balding magistrate pulled the earplug from his ear and said, "The Mets are up five to three in the bottom of the seventh. Jenkins just hit a two-run homer." There was scattered applause from the pews. Winston could see Weinstein was pleased with the progress of the baseball game and took it as a good sign. The bailiff called Winston's name. He and Rachel approached the bench. The district attorney read the long list of charges. Judge Weinstein paused and put the earplug in his ear for about ten seconds. "Two strikes to Henderson. Mr. Foshay, do you understand these charges against you."

"Yes."

"Then how do you plead?"

Winston looked at Rachel. Rachel looked at her watch.

"Guilty."

"My client means guilty to the animal cruelty charge, Your Honor."

The DA announced that the people of New York would drop the remaining charges. Before he could be sentenced Winston blurted out, "The dog was attacking my son, Your Honor, he's a baby."

Weinstein lifted his glasses to get a better look at Winston. Somewhere in Queens a Met hit a line drive that caromed off the shortstop's mitt and into center field. *This one looks like Mookie Wilson,* the judge thought. *God, I loved Mookie.*

"Mr. Foshay, what breed was the dog you shot?"

"That would be a dog of the pit bull variety, Your Honor."

Judge Weinstein nodded his head. "Good, I hate those dogs. But Mr. Foshay, I'm concerned about the possession of an unregistered firearm."

"That charge has been dropped, Your Honor," Rachel said, forcing a phony smile.

"I know that, Counsel. But I'm more concerned with the gun than the dead dog."

"No smoking gun, Your Honor," Winston said.

"And if there *had* been a smoking gun?"

"I took the gun from a little girl so she wouldn't hurt herself or nobody else with it."

"Did *you* hurt anybody else with it?"

"No, Your Honor. Just the dog. I ain't never used a gun to do nothing."

Judge Weinstein asked the bailiff to bring up Winston's criminal record. He looked down the list for gun violations.

"Where's the gun now?" the judge asked.

"In the East River, Your Honor," Winston lied.

"Mr. Foshay, anyone ever tell you you look like Mookie Wilson?"

"No, Your Honor."

"The people of the state of New York hereby sentence you to ninety hours' community service."

To the consternation of the drug-sweep detainees and the prosecutors, Winston pounded his breastbone. He thanked Rachel, then strode out of the courtroom, not quite a free man, but more an indentured servant. Close enough. As he exited, a court officer, his hands clasped in front of him, whispered, "You know who Mookie Wilson is?"

"No fucking idea."

Winston shadowboxed his way out of the courthouse. Haymakers landed on the chins of Judge Weinstein, Rachel Fisher, and the assistant district attorney. With each punch he grunted and spat out a phrase of legalese. *"Pro se"*—jab. "Defendant"—jab, jab, right hook. "Penal code"—body blow. "The state sentences you to—" Winston fired an uppercut at the state, wondering exactly what the state looked like.

When he got back home he found the lock on his front door had been changed. After a few desperate knocks, he walked down the block, stopped outside Fariq's building, and whistled the shrill bar that for over ten summers had called his best friend to the window. He whistled again. One more time.

Armello's lockless front door opened with a haunted-house creak. The apartment was empty. He took a half-eaten Jamaican beef patty from the Salcedos' refrigerator and washed it down with two gulps of ginger ale. Then it was on to Whitey's. *"Hey, Ms. O'Koren, is Whitey home? . . . Where he at? . . . Come on, they ain't going rob no bank. Plus, they need a white lady to go in with them. . . . Well, as long as you only thinking about it. . . . Do mind if I use the phone?"*

Winston couldn't remember the last time he'd had one of these lonesome summer weekdays. He felt betrayed. How dare his friends live the portions of their lives that didn't include him? On days like this, he used to shovel breakfast cereal into his mouth, then bolt outside to play, only to discover nine-tenths of his world missing. Downcast, he'd return home and skim his sole Hardy Boys mystery, *The Missing Chums*, blind to the title's irony. After a few boring pages, he'd behead a few of his sister's dolls, then fight her off with the knife. Then they'd share a cantaloupe half, arguing about whether it tasted better with or without salt.

Thinking of Brenda, Winston rubbed the two one-hundred-dollar bills in his pocket, went back to Armello's apartment, and made a phone call.

14- MUSKRAT LOVE

Top down, the faded pink Mustang convertible chugged up 106th Street, serenading the block with a selection from *America's Greatest Hits*. Before Spencer could bring the car to a stop, Winston leapt into the passenger seat secret-agent style. He slunk low into the tattered leather. "Man, this ride is a piece of shit."

"Big and Little Brother out for an afternoon jaunt. How quaint."

"Don't push it. But thanks for coming, yo." Winston paused, his attention on the airy-voiced singer. " 'Muskrat Suzy, Muskrat Sam do the jitterbug out in Muskrat Land'? What the fuck you listening to, yo? A song about animals fuckin'?"

Spencer turned up the volume even louder and asked where to.

"The Ville," Winston said. "The Ville."

Some niggers like hanging out in the East Village, finding its effete bohemian sensibilities, if not exciting, at least freakish. Tuffy wasn't one of them. He hated the place. It used to be a good spot to pass off bags of oregano as weed, and glassines of toasted bread crumbs as crack, on stupid white kids from the hinterlands, but that was about it. To him the neighborhood, with its hodgepodge architecture and populace, looked like the bottom of somebody's shoe.

He and Spencer strode across St. Mark's Place until Winston found what he was looking for, a sidewalk vendor selling glossy eight-by-ten black-and-white head shots of entertainers and sports figures.

"How much this one?" Winston asked, holding up a photo of Michael Jackson.

"Seven dollar."

"You got any of him when he was dark-skinned and had a nose and 'fro?"

"Yes, only four dollar."

"Prince?"

"Five dollar."

"Todd Bridges?"

"Fifty cent. I give you Gary Coleman also. Free, no charge. You want MC Hammer? Arsenio Hall?"

He purchased twenty dollars' worth of photos, mostly of has-been television actors and rhythm-and-blues one-hit wonders from the eighties and nineties. However, he did spend three dollars on a Denzel Washington. He also bought a roll of tape at a magazine stand, then asked Spencer to drive him to New Jersey.

"What's in Jersey?"

"My sister."

"I didn't know you had a sister."

"I do and I don't."

They drove to the Evergreen Cemetery listening to *America's Greatest Hits,* Winston unconsciously bobbing his head and tapping his fingers to the chorus of "Horse with No Name."

A wrought-iron fence separated the cemetery from the Weequihac Golf Course. Brenda was buried in the northwest corner of the grounds. Errant approach shots had nicked the tombstone. Tuffy knelt beside the grave, scraping the bird droppings from the headstone with a piece of bark. Taking out the stack of photographs and his marker, he began scribbling inscriptions and forging signatures on the faces of the washed-up heroes of his sister's youth. Sometimes, to heighten the effect, he signed with his left hand.

To Brenda,

R.A.W.

Kool Moe Dee

Brenda,

Paz Mamacita!
Feliz Navidad!

Los chicos de Menudo

To Brenda,

My biggest fan,
thanks.

Much love,
Denzel Washington

After taping the signed publicity photos to the headstone, Tuffy bored a small cavity in the burial mound with his index finger. He rolled a hundred-dollar bill into a tube, placed the money in the hole, then covered it with mulch. "One for me and one for you," he said, kissing the marker. As he stood to leave, a black foursome of golfers ambled up to the tee box on the other side of the wrought-iron gate, chattering loudly as they smacked their balls onto the fairway. *Who are these niggers?* Winston thought, as another foursome of black men tromped up the hill searching for golf balls in the rough. As he read the inscription on the headstone, he had a sobering thought. He wanted Jordy to grow up to be like the golfers: successful, carefree, suburban, independent—the kind of nigger he couldn't stand. Carefully, as if he were peeling away a Band-Aid covering a tender blister, Winston removed the snapshot of Denzel Washington from Brenda's marker, then tore the photo to pieces.

Two hours later Winston found Yolanda in a corner arcade playing a video machine. Spencer drove off and for five minutes Tuffy leaned against a post and watched her do battle with a computer villain, raining a torrent of thundering kicks and punches on her hapless opposition. Yolanda's fighter grabbed the opponent by the nose and pulled the skin off its body with the ease of a magician snatching a satin sheet off a caged assistant. The gargoyle collapsed in a heap of muscle tissue and bone.

Looking at her surreptitiously from the rear gave him a perverted chill of satisfaction, a feeling similar to a breeder's pride in watching his prized mare fly around the racetrack. When Yolanda first moved into his apartment, Winston, full of common-law jealousy, would follow her around the neighborhood, spying on her from behind double-parked cars, eavesdropping on her conversations to the best of his lip-reading ability. Once he saw Player Ham, the neighborhood ladies' man, run out of Danny's Cuts, still cloaked in the barber's towel, smelling of coconut oil and hair sheen. "Damn, girl, you fine." Cracking his knuckles, Winston hid behind a van, ready to pounce at the first peck on the neck or affectionate squeeze of the hand. "Thank you," said Yolanda, going on about her business. "I just had to tell you, because you a looker." Then softly to himself he said, "Boy, I'd tear that shit up."

Winston emerged from behind the van, glowering at Player Ham. He waited a couple of beats and, when Yolanda was out of earshot, whispered, "Nigger, if I ever . . ." Shaking, Player Ham dug into his pocket, saying "Tuffy, come on now, I didn't know," and slapped forty dollars into Winston's hand, paying back a debt he never owed. "We straight, right?" Jogging to catch Yolanda, Winston realized how lonely she was in the neighborhood without him. Her family and friends in Queens had written her off for moving in with an obese unemployed habitual offender, and the local women her age were just too fast for her. With Player Ham's money he treated her to a bouquet of bird-of-paradise flowers and a dinner of bacalao and white rice.

Belted into his stroller, Jordy tried to alert his mother to his father's presence, but she was too engrossed in the game to pay any attention. Tuffy nudged Yolanda aside and dropped fifty cents into the machine's slot, interrupting her duel with a turbaned, scimitar-wielding Sikh caricature. As the coins plunked into the change box, the machine's screen flashed A CHALLENGER COMES in bold red letters. Each player was presented with a cast of fighters from which to choose. Yolanda stuck with her warrior, Kashmira, a ponytailed ninja assassin. Winston selected a scaly green behemoth. He pressed a button and the video game roared "Rotundo" in a deep electronic voice. "That's right, Rotundo in the house.

Ro-fuckin'-tun-do about to get busy." Yolanda said nothing, mentally rehearsing the intricate joystick-button combinations that would unleash a flurry of secret moves upon Winston's fighter. Yolanda toggled her joystick with her left hand, the fingers of her right hand darting over the red, white, and blue set of buttons. Her dexterity resulted in a samurai sword assault that dropped Rotundo's arms to the ground like pruned tree branches. Unfazed, Rotundo parried by raising his stumps and squirting a stream of his blue acidic blood in Kashmira's face. Temporarily blinded, Kashmira endured a barrage of flying kicks that sapped her strength, turning her energy bar from green to yellow to red.

"Girl, you about to get laid the fuck out."

Yolanda didn't panic. Holding down the red button, she calmly jiggled the joystick left, right, up, then tapped the white button twice. Kashmira let out a threatening "Kiai!," unsheathed two swords, and, raising her arms to the side, began to spin. The swords, twirling like helicopter rotors, lifted her up and sent her flailing toward Rotundo. Winston tapped his joystick twice to the right, causing Rotundo to back off, but before he could assume a defensive crouch Kashmira decapitated him, slicing the character's balloon-sized head in half before it hit the ground. "Kashmira wins," the machine announced.

"No fucking shit."

Yolanda walked away from the game and pushed Jordy's stroller outside. "Where you going? It's still two more rounds left. Landa, you better get back here and finish." Winston had Rotundo throw a couple of punches at the defenseless Kashmira, then gave up and followed Yolanda outside.

"How in the hell you come at me with 'You better finish'? Winston, you leave me like that again and I'm done."

"I know, Boo. I'm sorry. I got caught up. It won't happen again, I promise."

"You know how Jordy get when one of us isn't around. You know he had an attack."

"He did? When?"

"Last night. The asthma hit him and he stopped breathing. If I wasn't up doing homework, I wouldn't have noticed. He was fucking turning blue. Like an idiot I called your name three times before I remembered your ass was in jail. I had to walk to Metropolitan. Three hours until the doctor saw him."

"They put the oxygen mask on him?"

TUFF

"I mean it, never again. Next time a locked door ain't all you going to come home to."

Winston gingerly took the stroller from Yolanda. In doing so commandeering his son and his status as head of the household. Yolanda hooked a finger around his belt loop and the trio slowly hiked back to the house. Winston played father at the steering wheel, his avuncular blather shortening the trip back home. "Long as you don't lock up the coochie, Boo, you can lock anything up you damn well please. Because you know, sooner or later I'm going to fuck up. It's in a nigger's nature. All I ask is you two accept my apologies. I ain't saying forgive and forget, but remember I'm just a young nigger trying to break the cycle."

"Winston, unless you start acting right, I'm going to break your cycle."

15· YORI-KIRI

lthough his stalwart expression didn't show it, Oyakata Hitomi Kinboshi was enraged. Sumo wrestling, his cherished livelihood, was dying an ignoble death in Spanish Harlem's White Park. Here in a small local playground, the fifteen-hundred-year-old traditions of his sport were being violated like fourteen-year-olds at sleepaway camp. Instead of the *yobidashi* sitting cross-legged high up in a tower and announcing the start of the tournament with the customary playing of the sumo drums, a spindly-limbed herald sat atop a basketball hoop beating on a white plastic janitor's bucket. In fifteen centuries a woman had never set foot on the *dohyo,* but a Japanese-American woman stood in the center of the hastily constructed ring, yelling inanities into the microphone like a Communist screech owl. The Oyakata's English wasn't very good, but he understood something to the effect of "No justice, no peace."

Sumo wrestling, once the sport of the gods, was now a Japanese minstrel show, the wrestlers no longer warriors, but entertainers. They were Japan's goodwill ambassadors, sent out by the government to make amends for each administration's invariable breach of ethnic etiquette. Last year it was Vancouver to make amends for the foreign minister's calling Canadians "junior Americans." This time the justice minister blamed the country's growing crime rate on Japanese youths' desire to emulate

TUFF

American culture, specifically the wastrel and violent attitudes of blacks and Hispanics, characteristics inherent in most nonwhite races, but not the Japanese. Three months later, in an attempt to appease the unquieted ghetto masses, the Sumo Kyokai sent the Oyakata and the wrestlers to East Harlem.

The strange Japanese-American woman gestured to the crowd and a large black man rose to polite applause. The Oyakata smiled. It was the same sullen-faced young man he'd seen in the poster on the bus ride from the hotel—the one he thought looked like the Delta bluesman Robert Johnson. Standing up in the crowd, a child on his shoulders, a stuffed tiger on the child's shoulders, the black man looked like the bottom of a totem pole. "What did the Japanese girl say?" Kinboshi asked his translator. The interpreter bowed. "She introduced the young man as Winston Foshay, a politician who is running for public office. There's a petition circulating through the crowd. He needs fifty more signatures and he'll be on the ballot." Kinboshi shook his head in disgust. The translator must have made a mistake. That boy a politician? Never. Any fool could plainly see the impudence festering underneath a warrior's I-don't-give-a-damn expression. This Winston Foshay never had a civic thought in his life. With the body and face of a bullfrog, he was born to be either a sumo wrestler or blues singer. "Did she say something about Chairman Mao?" The interpreter answered yes, fumbling for a way to translate "Mao more than ever" into Japanese.

One of the *sumotori,* a Yokozuna named Takanohana, was in the ring performing the traditional *dohyo-iri.* Rising from his squat, he clapped his hands; then, with a hand behind his knee, hoisted a massive leg high above his head. His foot stamped down on the clay surface with a resounding thump. Instead of responding to the demonstration of the Yokozuna's uncanny balance with the customary shout of *"Yoisho!"* the audience answered each heavy stomp with a boisterous "Aiiight!" Under the searing New York City sun Oyakata Kinboshi reddened.

Ms. Nomura, how come they raising their arm to the side like that?"

"To show that they aren't carrying any weapons."

"Fair fight—I likes that."

The ancient sport immediately appealed to Winston. Never had he been in the presence of so many men his size. And in the world of sumo, he was on the small end of the scale, as most of the *rikishi* outweighed him by fifty to eighty pounds.

"Look at them two motherfuckers, they huge!"

"That's Akebono and Musashimaru," Inez said, referring to the two largest *rikishi,* each of whom stood well over six feet tall and weighed over four hundred and fifty pounds.

"They black?" asked Winston, puzzled by the wrestlers' swarthy skins and wavy hair tied into oily topknots.

"No, I think they're both from Hawaii."

"Hawaiians always looked kind of black to me. Big noses, grass skirts, and shit. They seem real African but more laid back."

Two lower-ranked *rikishi* prepared to enter the ring. Each man stoically tossed a purifying fleck of salt onto the *dohyo,* before determinedly stepping into the circle of inlaid straw and assuming their starting positions. Crouched down in football-like four-point stance, the half-naked titans, without any visible signal from the formally dressed referee, fired into one another. The sound of a slab of meat landing on a butcher's cutting board echoed throughout the park. The crowd, momentarily stunned by the ferocity, suddenly burst out in cheers, wildly applauding when one wrestler dumped the other unceremoniously out of the ring with a deftly executed leg trip. *"Takanishiki, sotogake no kachi!"* said the ring announcer.

Tuffy sat back in his seat, deeply impressed by what he'd just witnessed. "Man, I likes this. May the best and biggest motherfucker win. These niggers ain't just fat. Look at the leg muscles. The goddamn pecs. These boys is yoked. It ain't a whole lot blubber just jiggling around like I thought it'd be. Ms. Nomura, why you never told me you like this stuff?"

"It's embarrassing. So old-fashioned. So feudal. You know how you get crazy whenever somebody mentions slavery? 'Why you have to bring that up? That was in the past.' Sumo makes me feel that way. Makes my insides itchy, but sometimes when nobody's around I scratch the itch and watch it on NHK."

Normally, Winston didn't have much use for sports or the mob mentality of the sports fan. He found the events repetitive, pointless, and armchair analysis of the contests even more so. It didn't take long for the residents of his block to learn not to approach him after one of his frequent street fights saying, "Tuffy, you kicked that fool's ass, but when you had him in that headlock what you should've did was . . . ," because the speaker would find himself on the ground, holding a dislocated jaw in place, in too much pain to beg for mercy. Winston triumphantly straddled over his victim, taunting him like Diomedes sans spear and armor. "What *you* should've done is kept your fuckin' mouth shut." But sumo wrestling tugged at his corpulent pride. He soon found himself choosing a wrestler at the introduction for some indiscriminate reason—unusual sideburns, a gangster smirk, an especially serene countenance—then unabashedly urging him on until the bout's all-too-quick conclusion. Sometimes his allegiances changed mid-bout, touched by a smaller man's cunning and quickness overcoming the stronger, larger man's plodding orthodoxy. By bringing his street-fighter mentality to the matches, it was simple for him to figure out the rules. First man out of the ring or to touch the ground with something other than the soles of his feet loses. If Winston saw an opening in a wrestler's defense that wasn't exploited using the vicious tactic he'd employ under similar circumstances, then he knew his way was illegal. "Man, all the shit I'd do is outlawed. Because if that motherfucker grabbed me like that I'd kick him in the nuts, punch him in the face, yank on his ponytail, choke him with one hand, and gouge out his eyeballs with the other."

As the *yobidashi* introduced the fighters before each match, Winston strained to make out what sounded like a proper name among the slurring Japanese. "Takanohana? That's that nigger's name, Ms. Nomura?"

"It means Noble Flower."

"Wakanohana?"

"Flower of Youth."

"Musoyama?"

"Two Battling Mountains."

"Akebono?"

"Rising Dawn."

"Takatoriki?"

"Noble Fighting Sword."

"Mainoumi?"

"Dancing Sea."

"Kitakachidoki?"

"Northern Victory War Cry."

Just as Inez translated Kitakachidoki's name, the pint-sized Mainoumi picked him up and slammed him down onto the mat. Kitakachidoki hobbled out of the ring in pain, the fall having wrenched his knee.

Fariq, gesturing to the limping fighter, suggested, "That man need to change his name to East Harlem I Just Got My Ass Kicked and Blew Out My Knee and I Can't Stop Crying."

Oyakata Kinboshi watched his son-in-law Kotozuma amble onto the *dohyo*. Currently ranked at Maegashira 6, the former Seiwake was in free fall, tumbling down the ranks since his arranged marriage to Kinboshi's daughter. His weak *taichi-ai* and lack of fighting spirit were becoming an embarrassment to the entire Satogatake stable. Kinboshi thought he needed a kick in the ass. Arms folded tightly across his chest, he stared at Kotozuma's opponent, Tochinaru, who, seated cross-legged on the east side of the ring, was slow to get up. When Tochinaru caught his eye, Kinboshi made a slashing motion past his throat with his finger, the signal for a wrestler to throw a bout. Confused, Tochi furrowed his brow, since these were exhibition matches and nothing was at stake other than pride. The Oyakata shook his wrist and Tochi's face cleared with comprehension. Slowly rising from his seat, he bowed to the referee, reporting that he would be unable to fight due to injury. He bowed again and walked back to the mobile dressing rooms, shaking his wrist. The referee scurried toward Kinboshi, nodding his head as the Oyakata whispered in his ear, then dashed over to the ring announcer. The ring announcer, very plainly dressed in a black coat and gray Japanese knickers, walked to the center of the *dohyo* and raised his hand for quiet. "As a show of goodwill between America and Japan and Spanish Harlem, Kotozuma is willing to fight a challenger from the audience. Are there any takers?" Fuming, Kotozuma kicked up a cloud of clay dust. He wanted to leave, but knowing the fine would be at least a hundred thousand yen, he held his ground and spit on the *dohyo*. He'd pay the thirty-thousand-yen expectorate penalty.

So mad was Kotozuma that he didn't hear the raucousness in the stands as a few hundred of Winston's neighbors yelled his name and fifteen friends and family members pushed and pulled him out of the bleachers. "Ladies and gentlemen, we have a challenger." As some attendants escorted Winston to the dressing room, Inez stood up and shouted, *"Gambate!"* Without looking back, Winston punched the air with a fist.

TUFF

" *'Gambate,'* you always sayin' that. What's it mean, Ms. Nomura?" asked Armello.

"It means 'hang in that shit.' "

After a few minutes, Winston emerged from the dressing room. A sparkling white *mawashi* snaked around his body like a disheartened boa constrictor unsure of how to handle a victim whose girth was akin to that of a Parthenon column. The thick satin belt wound snugly around Winston's waist, hoisting his paunch almost to his nipples, cleaving his buttocks, and firmly knotting itself behind his back. Winston strode toward the *dohyo,* his broad back and massive haunches lotioned to a shiny obsidian black. To his surprise no one in the crowd mocked him with diaper jokes or commented on how his thighs rubbed together. His boys trailed him like wizened corner men, clapping his back and massaging his shoulders as he climbed up the straw-bale steps dug into the side of the ring. Charles, looking across at the imposing Kotozuma, grabbed the nape of his friend's neck and said, "Be careful, Tuff, this one look like he know karate."

"But he don't know me."

Before Winston stepped into the circle, the translator approached him with a deep bow. He told Winston he must perform the ritual movements and to simply copy whatever Kotozuma did. He also assured him that he would be perfectly safe from harm; since this was a demonstration bout, the professional *rikishi* would take it easy on him.

The clay surface of the *dohyo* was warm and dry. On reflex Winston, with his big toe, scratched "Tuffy 109" into the light brown powder just outside the rim of the circle. The announcer's voice boomed from the PA speakers, "Ko-o-o-to-o-zu-maaa!" Upon hearing his name, Kotozuma stalked into the ring, sprinkling a dash of salt on the *dohyo* and beating on the side of his *mawashi* with the heels of his hands. After a beat, a slightly garbled but deafening "Kuuu-rooo-ya-maaaa!" echoed throughout the park. The noble-sounding temporary *shikona* and the crowd's cheers caused Winston's left eyelid to twitch with nervousness. One long stride, a pinch of salt, and he was inside the ring of straw. The ring, about twenty feet in diameter, looked bigger than it did from the bleachers. Winston's thoughts flashed to Musashi and the monk, but it was hardly time to contemplate oneness with the universe. Judging by Kotozuma's glower, someone had forgotten to tell him that this was an exhibition bout. Facing each other, the two men squatted, clapped their hands, then swung their outstretched arms to their sides, turning their palms to the sky. The wrestlers stood up, and the limber Kotozuma slowly raised one foot above his shoulder, then the other. Trying to balance on one foot was somewhat more difficult for Winston, but he gamely locked his knees and raised his legs till his thighs burned, doing his best to keep his planted foot from twisting and his body from wobbling. Kinboshi stared at Winston's broad feet. "Like snowshoes," he said aloud to no one in particular. "He'll be all right."

Smirking, Kotozuma exited the ring and reentered flinging one last offering of salt. Kotozuma's cockiness relaxed Winston. *Ain't nothing but a fight. A little Friday-night scrap between men. Except that it's Saturday afternoon and I'm butt-ass naked.* He gazed into the stands; Yolanda was holding Jordy high overhead, Inez was staring at Kinboshi, and Spencer was furiously taking notes. At the foot of the ring Fariq, Whitey, and Armello were giving him a thumbs-up. Winston scooped up a handful of salt and tossed it high into the air. It fell to earth like a fountain of dying firework embers. He stormed into the ring ready to do battle. The crowd stood and roared its approval. "Wax that ass, Tuff!"

"Don't start none, won't be none!"

"Uptown!"

Winston and Kotozuma settled into the hunkered starting position, one hand on the ground, butt cheeks touching the backs of their calves. Kotozuma's puffy face was less than two feet away. *Goddamn, this motherfucker big,* Winston thought. *He so fat I can barely see his eyes. Eyebrows touching his cheeks and shit. Eyes look like apostrophes. I know this nigger don't wear contacts.* As they slowly raised their haunches, Winston blew Kotozuma a kiss and watched his opponent's ears turn red. At a silent signal privy only to the two wrestlers, their left hands dropped to the ground and they launched into each other with a crushing impact force that might have been Enrico Fermi's inspiration for nuclear fission. Winston's lungs emptied like two fireplace bellows, and a shoving Kotozuma slid him toward the edge of the ring. Winston marveled at the hardness of his opponent's stomach; it was as if a layer of rubbery skin had been stitched over a giant tortoise shell. Strangely, Kotozuma's warm, clammy skin had a familiar feel to it; where had he felt it before? Splaying his toes and digging his heels into the ground, Tuffy stopped his backward progress. *The beluga whale at the Brooklyn aquarium—this nigger feels just like that dirty white whale!* Deciding to take the offensive, he locked in

Kotozuma's extended arms at the elbows, which forced him to straighten and negated his leverage. Winston marched him back to the center of the circle. Using his right hand he grabbed Kotozuma's belt with an underhanded grip. With his left he vainly reached out for a grappling point as Kotozuma swiveled his hips, keeping that side of the *mawashi* just out of reach. With a sudden burst of speed and strength, Kotozuma freed himself and slapped Winston across his jowls so hard his vision doubled. If Kotozuma had done anything else—twisted Winston's arm behind his neck and thrown him to the ground with a perfectly executed *kubi-nage,* or grabbed his wrist and kicked his inner ankle—Winston would have succumbed. But in the streets to be slapped in front of anyone who even remotely knows you is the ultimate insult. Mothers slap children, wives slap husbands, pimps slap hos, but nobody slaps Winston, and before Kotozuma could release a follow-up smack, Winston blasted him with a "What, motherfucker?" two-handed push to the chest that sent the *rikishi* reeling backward. Just as Kotozuma was about to regain his balance, Winston blasted him out of the ring with a well-placed shoulder tackle and belly bump. Kotozuma landed in a clump at his Oyakata's feet. Unassisted, his jostled topknot resting over one eye, Kotozuma clambered back into the ring and squatted down. Winston did the same, returning Kotozuma's slight bow. *"Kuu-roo-ya-maa no kaa-a-chiii!"*

After the day's festivities were over and Winston had changed back into his street clothes, Kinboshi and a few of the wrestlers went over to congratulate him. The wrestlers greeted him with firm soul shakes, the two Hawaiians accompanying their grips with American street slang. "Yo, my man, you rocked Homeboy."

"Thanks, yo."

When the backslapping was over, the Oyakata began speaking and everyone stopped talking. Without prompting, the interpreter translated. "They tell me your name is Winston Foshay. I'm Oyakata Kinboshi, I trained the fighter you beat. They announced you won by *yori-kiri,* frontal force-out, but it was really *yori-taoshi,* frontal crush-out, a more powerful technique. Your style is unorthodox but effective."

Unable to hold the Oyakata's stare without smiling, Winston looked down at the ground feeling like the unassuming hero in a martial-arts movie: trained by wind, trees, and the monkeys, the country bumpkin makes a name for himself.

"Is it true you are running for political office?"

Winston nodded, wishing it weren't.

"Then not only do you win the match, but you probably won a lot of votes today."

"There is a loosely enforced ban on foreign wrestlers entering Japanese sumo right now. The Sumo Kyokai is afraid of big black men dominating the sport. I don't know why they are afraid. Whenever Japan gets a chance to prove its superiority complex, we cringe in fear. If you were Mongolian, or even an Argentinian Jew, I could get you in."

The translator whispered something in the Oyakata's ear, and the coach's eyes widened. "That's right, I forgot Sentoryu," remembering the mediocre Juryo *rikishi*, a half-Japanese, half-black wrestler from St. Louis. "You aren't part Japanese, or that loud woman who introduced you wouldn't want to sign an affidavit swearing she was your mother, would she?

"I'm sorry, I go too far. You are a politician. Obviously, your first thoughts are for your people and community, and a proud man like yourself wouldn't abandon his mission for selfish reasons."

Winston studied the expensive Rolex and Movado watches banded around the thick wrists of the Oyakata and the other *sumotori*, their fine silk robes, and the retinue of attendants shading their heads with parasols. Clearly there was big money to be made in sumo wrestling. Tuffy wanted to say, "I could give a fuck about an election. Man, put me and mines on a plane and let's do this. When do I get a couple of slaves?" But he recalled a television documentary he'd seen on the rigors of the Japanese school system. He pictured a college-age Jordy, a mathematics whiz but unable to think for himself. To survive on the streets of Harlem knowing how to factor polynomials wasn't going to help much.

Kinboshi took Winston's silence for a refusal of his offer and handed him a small book, *The Science of Sumo: The Seventy Techniques Diagrammed and Explained in Great Detail.* Winston thanked him and asked if the other wrestlers were ghetto kids like himself. The Oyakata smiled and said most of the *rikishi* were the sons of farmers and steelworkers, a few were Japanese-born Koreans trying to pass as "traditional" Japanese, and there was a sprinkling of college boys who would do anything to avoid the business world. There was a long, awkward silence as the two men pondered alternative destinies: Winston, a chubby Japanese boy pushed into sumo by overbearing parents. The Oyakata, a running buddy of Tampa Red, hitchhiking from town to town swigging whiskey from cough-syrup bottles and playing a mean blues harmonica. He couldn't get over how much Winston looked like Robert Johnson. Tuffy began to say something and Kinboshi expected the words to "Ramblin' on My Mind" to tumble out of his mouth, complete with vinyl scratches and pops.

"Say, yo, what was the name they introduced me as?"

"Kuroyama."

"What that mean?"

"Black Mountain."

As city workers disassembled the ring and the bleachers, Winston was back on the stoop, listening to his friends rehash his bout with Kotozuma. "Tuffy said, 'Blaw! I don't play that, you Jap motherfucker. Remember Pearl Harbor. Bip!' Even the police was clapping for you, son."

"I ain't seen Tuff that mad in a while. Nigger had on that berserko face. Tuff like to kill that nigger."

Winston's generic soda tasted funny and wouldn't go down his throat. He spat the contents of his mouth onto the sidewalk and listened to the carbonation sizzle on the sidewalk. "Don't call me Tuffy no more. I want y'all to call me Kuroyama."

Fariq drew back. "What, son? 'Kuroyama'? What the fuck that mean, 'Fat Bastard' in Japanese?"

The gang broke out in an avalanche of laughter that sent them rolling down the steps and into the street like brown boulders. Even Winston giggled, the paunch underneath his green shirt quivering like dessert gelatin. "Y'all not right," he said, flinging his soda can out into the street. "Won't even let a nigger dream. I could be in Japan tomorrow clocking mad loot."

"You are dreaming."

"Armello, like y'all ain't dreaming with this bank robbery shit." Winston's voice took on a pouty tone. "We going to give tellers the potion, wave the magic wand, and we'll be toodle-oo with the cash."

Armello spread his arms to the side. "Tuff, I seen the documentary, it's going to work."

"Man, even if it don't work, I think the shit will be fun," Charley O' said. "How many fools can say, 'I robbed a bank with my moms'? That right there will be worth it."

Fariq stood up on his crutches. "And even if it is a dumb idea, you supposed to be down for whatever. Until Brooklyn none of us ain't never vetoed an idea by saying it was stupid. If you think about it, whatever we do is always stupid. So stupid or not, you supposed to be there."

Winston opened his book of sumo techniques, saying, "Man, I'm on some other shit now." On page one was a sketch of two entangled Buddha-esque wrestlers. *Just as basketball is not only a matter of being tall, sumo is not simply about being fat and strong. The sumo novice often overlooks the mental aspects of the sport; a well-thought-out strategy and a level head will win more bouts than sheer brute force.*

16· FREE PARKING

pencer hadn't seen much of his supposed disciple in the two weeks since his profile of Winston appeared in the paper. When he handed him a copy of the Sunday edition over a game of Monopoly, Winston glanced at the unflattering photo of him swathed in a sumo belt, read the headline, THE HIP-HOP POPULIST, and handed it back.

"Don't you want it?"

"Why I want a paper I never read?"

"Put it in your scrapbook and show it to Jordy when he gets older. Besides, you should read the paper."

"I read it once."

"I don't mean the tabloids, I mean the *paper.*"

"I know what you mean. One day I was on the train and somebody left it in the seat next to me. I picked it up looking for the comics and came across an article on Stanley Kubrick. Loved that nigger, good article too. I folded the paper like the Wall Street motherfuckers do on they way to work. I swear to you, white people was looking me at different. Smiling and shit. Like they wanted to come up to me and ask, "What a nigger like *you* doing reading a paper like *that*?""

"If you want to know what's happening in the world you have to read the paper."

"I don't want to know. And Smush and them don't want to know neither, so don't go showing them that picture, okay? Got enough problems with them clowns as it is now."

Winston rolled, moved his game piece, the iron, to Kentucky Avenue. "Shit, I never land on Free Parking."

"Let's see, with three houses that's seven hundred bucks."

Winston paid the rent in small bills just to be annoying. "Rabbi, now that you've written the article you going to stop comin' over?"

Spencer, counting his earnings answered, "No, it's a three-part feature, so I'm in it for the long haul." The money counted, he lifted his head and smiled. "You're short twenty dollars."

Tuffy flung two blue Monopoly-money tens at him. "Here, goddammit! I'm tired of this slow-death bullshit. What kind of asshole only puts three houses on a property? You got more money than the bank. Just put a hotel on these shits and get the game over with."

"Quit."

"No, you coming around on my streets. You in the ghetto now, yo. Light blues and purples like a motherfucker."

Spencer rolled double fours and, to Winston's delight, tap-danced his shoe to Oriental Avenue. "Oriental Avenue. Let's see, two tenements . . ."

17 · THE HUSTLE

The opening article had generated some interest in inner-city politics. Part two would detail Winston's whistle-stops on the campaign trail and part three the election's aftermath. The problem was, Winston's campaign activities ceased, so Spencer decided some behind-the-scenes orchestration was needed. "It's for the good of the politically disenfranchised," he told himself. "I'm not going to be one of those journalists who write about starving children, then don't give them any food."

Whenever an interested political organization called asking how they could contact Winston, instead of protecting his source, Spencer volunteered to arrange a meeting, insisting he go along as an "independent observer." Usually the meetings took place in a Times Square restaurant after Winston stopped working the three-card-monte games.

Winston peeked out from behind the Broadway ticket booth and waved Spencer over. "*Ven acá.*"

"Hey, Winston."

"We still going drinking tonight?" Tuffy asked, looking past Spencer at the pedestrian traffic.

"Yeah, yeah, I promised to expose you to some real beer. Wean you off that malt liquor you drink."

"Who is it tonight?"

"Bruce Walsh from the New Progressive Party."

"Whatever. Give me about forty-five minutes, Armello hot as a motherfucker."

Armello was standing behind a large upended cardboard box with a page from the newspaper's financial section draped over it. Spencer sauntered over. Armello's hands maneuvered three cards across the day's stock quotes. His siren madrigals lured the Argonauts of the world to their financial ruin.

Round, round it goes,
Black like crow,
Red like a rooster.

Pick the chicken
And I'll watch you grow,
'Cause that means you beat me
Like my mama used to.

A Swedish sailor stormed away from the table two hundred dollars lighter, his shipmates laughing and pounding his back. In turn each of Armello's confederates acknowledged Spencer's presence with a subtle signal. Charles, dressed like a banker, straightened his suit jacket and twisted a cuff link. He placed a wad of "winnings" in a Gucci wallet, then nudged Spencer. "Easy money to be made here, chap. I don't need the money, of course, I do it for the blasted thrill. For Christ sakes, lad, get in on the action." Finished with his shuffle, Armello moved his hands away from the table. Three red-backed cards from a well-worn Bicycle deck lay on the table. Winking at Spencer, Nadine slid two fifty-dollar bills onto the table. "Don't nobody jump in. This one's mine. I got this money, yo." A man sporting a Stalin mustache stepped into the spot where the Swedish sailor had stood earlier. Nadine turned over the king of hearts. "All right!" Armello paid her without complaint and began to reshuffle the cards. As the cards leapfrogged over one another he "accidentally" flipped the king of hearts, the money card, face up on the table. In picking it up, he bent its upper left corner. The crimp was clearly visible as he slowed the shuffle to a halt. "Point to it, girl," he said to Nadine. "Point to it so I can win my money back." Nadine turned over an unmarked card, unleashing a stream of curses. "That was 'posed to be the fucking card."

TUFF

Ike, Mike, Spike
It's the king you like.

Fariq, bedecked in a flowing white linen robe and a white knit kufi, yelled, "My money!" and threw down eighty dollars and turned over the three of clubs. Armello plucked the dollars from his hand, then flipped over the king to show the crowd the losers had lost their money fair and square. "That's okay. I'll get the next one. I'm thinking Jew-like now," Fariq said, looking out the corner of his eye at Spencer. "By observing the Jew, I've learned how to magnetize my mind to money. Point my spirit in the direction of the tender legal." He faked a sneeze on Spencer's shoulder. "Ah-Jew! Sorry about that, sir. Anyone have a tissue?"

Armello's hands were moving faster now, his movements a blur; the cards seemed to hop about under their own power, the hands just passing over them. Every few passes Armello held up the king to show the gathered crowd the golden fleece. Through all the shuffling Spencer tried to keep his eyes glued to the king.

> *Red king, black deuce and trey,*
> *Choose the two you lose,*
> *Trey you pay.*
> *Bring the king*
> *Make your mama sing.*
> *Use my money to buy some chicken wings.*

"Who seen it?" Armello shouted, the crested cards facedown on the table looking like tract-house roofs viewed from the sky. "You seen it?" he asked Spencer, poking a finger solidly in his chest. Spencer shook his head no and backed a pace and a half away from the table. Dog-eared like a cropped Doberman pinscher, the middle card lay on the table screaming to be picked. "Who seen it? You? You? You? Point to it for free." No one stepped up. Armello was about to redeal when Stalin's hand shot across the table toward the bent card. Armello beat him to the card, but just barely. Holding the card down, he pressed the man to show him some money. Stalin took out a twenty. "I don't play for twenty," Armello said. "Show me a hundred, I'll give you two hundred." The man hesitated. Charles opened up his wallet and removed a stack of twenties. "I'll take this chap's bet."

Stalin dug into his pocket, pulled out three crumpled hundred-dollar bills. "Oh shit," the knot of onlookers gasped. Hands shaking, Fariq placed a small rock on the card, then quickly went through his pockets and soon fanned out six hundred dollars in bills of various denominations. Nadine unfolded Stalin's money, slowly scooting it closer to Fariq's edge of the table. Hands no longer shaking, Fariq slowly raised the rock off the card. Stalin turned it over: two of spades. He started screaming that he'd been cheated, that the cards had been somehow switched. "I demand a refund!"

"Refund?"

Nadine cooled the mark out, then turned to Fariq. "Give him a free shot. Slow it down. Let my man go for free."

Fariq refused, stuffing the wrinkled bills into a money clip already filled with cash. "Hell naw, if he would've won would he have given me *my* money back?" he said, knowing that even if by some improbability the man had chosen the king, the only way he'd have received his winnings was at gunpoint, and the only way he'd spend them would be to shoot Winston. Nadine ran a finger down Fariq's cheek. "Come on, baby." Smush reshuffled the cards, held the king to the man's nose, flicked his wrists and dropped the cards on the table, the bent king no longer available. "Pick, motherfucker!" Stalin's hand paused over every card, finally settling for the one on the far right: three of clubs. "Now get the fuck out of here! I hate a sore motherfucking loser." Nadine quickly lost a hundred dollars and the crowd, growing suspicious, thinned.

> La-di-da-di, I got enough money to pay everybody.
> Ding, ding, ding, I pay like a slot machine,
> Show me the red, I'll show you green.
> I bluff you, I beat you
> But I would never cheat you.

Spotting two beat cops coming up the boulevard, Winston cupped one hand over his mouth and in a muffled voice that went unheard except by those who were meant to hear it, said, "Ease up." The game and its players disappeared from the street as if they'd fallen through a trapdoor.

18· THIRD PARTY OVER HERE

Winston, Spencer, and Bruce, the New Progressive Party's representative, settled into a Theater District steakhouse. Winston pulled his nose out of a goblet of Belgian beer. The aroma was pleasant. Spencer suggested apricot with a hint of caramel. Winston disagreed, "Shit smell like alcohol to me. Maybe a little like Halloween candy." Holding his glass up high, Bruce proposed a toast. "To Winston, forwarding the progress of American third-party politics like no one since Zachary Taylor." Spencer seconded the toast with a hearty "Hear! Hear!" though he knew Bruce's claim of Taylor's being a third-party candidate was specious, Old Rough and Ready's being a Whig at a time in American history when the Whigs and the Democrats were the two major parties in a two-party system. Tuffy raised his glass a centimeter off the table, grunted, and made a silent toast. *To the three weeks until election day going by with the serious quickness.*

During the past two weeks nearly every American third party had tried to wine and dine Winston over to their side. The gratuitous liberalism had added ten pounds to his frame. Sushi and alligator teriyaki compliments of the Green Party. Coq au vin, pâté fraîche, and lemon mousse with toasted coconut and blueberries courtesy of the Working Family Party. The Welfare Recipient Faction treated him and his "advisory staff" to grilled Bay of Fundy salmon with Israeli couscous. The New Party spared no expense and insisted that Winston order a second helping of yellowfin tuna au poivre with Szechuan peppercorns. The New Alliance Party sat him down to a heaping portion of shrimp and okra étouffé.

The feasts followed more or less the same agenda. His hosts, often a white charter member and two or three colored officers, opened up with a statement that Party X was a multiracial organization. But if during the ensuing conversation Winston mentioned race, the dithyrambic chorus was quick to tell him that race was a dead-end issue. That if history has taught us anything, it's that using ethnic oppression as the basis for social and political upheaval is doomed to fail. No matter what you do, racism will be still be, if not prevalent, at least present. Social and economic class must be the rallying points of the future struggle for democratic dignity. The next line would be "More Calvados, Winston?" and he would silently sip his ten-dollar aperitif as daintily as possible, intuition telling him that if racism was an immutable oppression, so was poverty.

Bruce was well past the color, gender, class, sexual-orientation trivialities. When the waitress placed the appetizers on the table, Bruce, who matched Winston in portliness, was already on his second dinner salad and waist-deep into the tautology of third-party politics.

So much as he understood the language of political rhetoric, Winston agreed with the litany of New Progressive principles. If the New Progressive Party's platform was idealistic, it was an idealism worth advocating: a constitutional amendment that guaranteed every American equal rights to shelter, health care, and education; community control over both public and private institutions, permitting cross-party endorsement in all elections; a minimum living wage. The cold facts had been presented, and from being a fly on the wall at countless of Inez's cell meetings, Winston was well versed in leftist liturgy. He knew that after the wish list came the emotional plea. Bruce addressed him in a voice so sincere it lifted his head from his plate of apricot-basted quail. "Winston, the New Progressive Party believes in you. And from all that I've read about you, heard about you, and witnessed this evening, the New Progressive Party is ready to have you as its next candidate for whatever city office you wish to pursue in the next election, because the New Progressive Party believes that ordinary people have the ability to govern themselves." While on the surface Bruce's avowal was a show of support, it was dripping with a political rectitude Winston found condescending; but in the spirit of coalition politics, he kept his thoughts to himself. Why upset the man who's buying bottles of the best beer he'd ever tasted at eight dollars a pop? *"Ordinary"?* thought Winston. *Who you calling ordinary? "Ability to govern themselves"? What you really saying is that people like me can't run people like you.*

"Do you have any questions, Winston?" Bruce asked.

Winston sipped his beer. "Yeah, how do you pronounce this beer again?"

"Chimay," said Spencer, cutting Bruce off.

"And you say this shit is brewed by priests?"

"Trappist monks, to be exact."

"Monks don't have sex, do they, Rabbi?"

"I suppose they don't."

"That's why this beer is so damn good. They have to devote their energy to something that will take their minds off fucking. And this stuff is damn close to doing that. Prayer alone ain't going to keep your hands off your dick, your mind off the pussy." Winston lifted the bottle and read the label, " 'Chimay Grand Reserve.' It even sounds like the shit. Strong too. But you can't just drink it down. You have to bitch-sip it. Savor it. Smoke a cigar and talk politics like we been doing. Say shit like 'per se' and 'deprivatization of the banking industry.' "

"I agree, Winston, it's an excellent beer, but do you have any questions about the New Progressive Party?"

Winston signaled the waitress for another round before asking his question:

"Um, how many white people in the party?"

"I'd guesstimate that at this stage the NPP is eighty to eighty-five percent white."

"Damn."

"I know the numbers sound disproportionate, but remember the United States is almost seventy-five percent white and the NPP is working diligently toward meeting our goal of a forty-percent-white membership."

"That would still be forty percent too many whities for my taste. Most times when a white boy just say a simple 'Hello,' I feel like I'm being talked down to."

"I understand your reluctance. But give us a chance, Winston. I think you'd find the progressive white a bit more amenable to your political aspirations." The waitress set down three more bottles of beer, and

Bruce filled Winston's glass, topping with just the right amount of a frothy head. "Winston, have you never worked with white people you felt you could trust?"

"There's a white nigger live down the block from me, Charley O', but I've known him and his people my entire life. If he'd have moved on the block when he was, say, nine years old, he'd still be on my *cuidado* list, like every other person I haven't known since I was five."

"So you have an almost inherent distrust of whites you haven't known since you were born?"

Winston thought a moment, swirling the maple-colored beer in his glass. "Firemen. I trust firemen. I never seen or heard of a fireman not doing they job. You trapped in a burning building, them motherfuckers come and get you. Don't matter how old, ugly, black, retarded, they turn on the hoses and do they thing. Long as they wearing them big rubber boots and those heavy-duty yellow jackets, I trust 'em."

Winston went on a philosophical tangent in which he pondered why the Chimay had to be served in a goblet. For practical purposes the recruitment of Winston into the New Progressive Party was over. "I'm sayin', would the beer taste any different from a paper cup?" The NPP would have to scour the grass roots and find another ordinary citizen to pin its hopes for dismantling the corporate oligarchy on. "Why can't I drink it straight from the bottle?" This one was too drunk.

19- FEELIN' GROOVY

Winston writhed in the passenger seat of Spencer's Mustang. The whiny harmonies of Simon and Garfunkel were torturous. He rolled down the window, gasping for air and the inveterate New York City funk. "Come on, Rabbi, you gots to change this, I'm dying here."

"Listen to the melody, Winston. Forget Paul Simon. Listen to Garfunkel, man. Garfunkel! Doesn't it make you feel wonderful?"

"No, it makes me feel like I should be skipping barefoot in a meadow. Holding hands with a hippie white girl wearing a see-through dress and daisy in her hair. Please, yo, turn this off, G."

Spencer turned the volume down a bit. Winston shifted in his seat. Arm propped in the window, he took in the passing streetscape. Traffic was heavy. The car nudged forward in stops and starts. There was no conversation from Forty-ninth Street to Sixty-third. Winston had suffered through "The Sounds of Silence," "I Am a Rock," "Mrs. Robinson," and "Cecilia." During "The 59th Street Bridge Song (Feelin' Groovy)" he almost bolted from the car to seek respite in a turkey-and-cheese deli sandwich.

"What these people want from me?"

"What?"

"Bruce and the rest of those weirdos."

"They saw the article and wanted to meet you. I suppose it makes them feel like they have ties to poor people. They call me up, 'Loved your article. The hip-hop community is exactly who we need to communicate our message to. It's so exciting to see an authentic inner-city representative,' blah, blah, blah."

" 'Hip-hop community'? What the fuck is that?"

"Young urban African-Americans—preferably bald-headed."

" 'Hip-hop community.' Where the hell is the opera community? The heavy-metal community? How the hell you define people by the kind of music they listen to? And man, to be honest with you, I don't even like rap music too tough. Inner city. Don't get me started."

"Too late for that." Spencer sighed.

"And how come you never hear about the outer city? Tell me if I'm wrong, but shouldn't there only be one inner city per city? In New York City there's umpteen thousand 'inner-cities,' none of them nowhere near each other. Where the fuck is the outer city? Anywhere niggers like me ain't? 'Inner city.' 'Hip-hop community.' Give me a fucking break!" Winston mimicked Bruce's midwestern twang: " 'We're in the struggle together.' Then how come whenever I'm strugglin' I never see motherfuckers like Bruce around? Don't get me started."

"That's the second time you said that. Admit it to yourself, you've started. Now let's see if you can work on finishing."

"I know, but I'm sayin', though, I have had it."

"Winston, I think the real question you have to ask yourself is, why do you come to the meetings?"

"I'm not going to any more dinners."

"But you could've said that after the second or third one. Why didn't you?"

"I don't know. The food. All Smush and them is talking is this stupid bank—" Winston caught himself. "Yolanda on my case about how much of the fifteen thou I got left, Ms. Nomura in another world, acting like I'm really going to win."

Winston dug his hand into his belt line and pulled out his automatic. "Sometimes it's just easier being with you and those stupid people. Y'all don't know me. I don't care about y'all. So nothing that anyone says or does can really upset me, you know? I just have to listen and pretend."

Spencer was hurt. Did Winston really not care about him? He didn't dare pose the obverse question: did he really care about Winston? "I learned something, though. Belgian beer. Some alternative political shit. And you know what's a trip? In some ways these third-party motherfuckers are the only people that take me seriously."

Winston opened the glove compartment, placed the gun inside, and closed the door. After two choruses of fidgeting through "El Condor Pasa (If I Could)," he opened the compartment and stuffed the gun back into his pants. He looked at Spencer's doleful expression and waited for him to say something. Spencer eased the car into a right-hand turn onto Seventy-second Street and drove east through Central Park, softly singing along to "The Only Living Boy in New York."

"Rabbi, you not going to say anything about my gun?"

"If I say get rid of it, are you going to?"

"Probably not. But you could show some concern."

"Winston, do you ever take any of my advice?"

"I finally rented *Schindler's List*."

"That's a start. And?"

"The shit was terrible."

"Yeah, the Holocaust was," Spencer said, turning left on Madison Avenue.

Tuffy continued his review. "I mean, the movie was terrible. I couldn't get past that there were no Jews as tall as Schindler. In all of Germany the tallest Jew went up to Schindler's belly button? Come on, man, too fucking easy. The flick's unbelievable right there. Manipulative Hollywood bullshit."

"Poland," Spencer said, his voice unable to hide the testiness he was feeling.

"Poland? The movie ain't Polish."

"The people portrayed in the film were Polish Jews."

"Fine, Poland, whatever."

Spencer looked for a street sign. Eighty-first Street—twenty-three more blocks and this black-hearted monster would be out of his car.

Winston continued with his film review. "And the scene where the Nazi on the balcony just shootin' at people? Don't get mad, Rabbi, I know I was supposed to be like, 'Ooooh, this is an evil motherfucker,' but I didn't understand it."

A taxicab nosed its way into Spencer's lane and he slammed the brakes, narrowly avoiding a collision. "You stupid fuck!" he yelled out the window, leaning on the horn for good measure. The outburst relaxed him and he loosened his grip on the steering wheel. "When one dog barks, he easily finds others to bark with it," he said in dreamy, far-off voice that scared Winston a little bit.

"What's that supposed to mean?"

"It's a quote from the Midrash. It popped into my mind . . . just seemed like the right thing to say."

"You think I'm prejudiced." Winston placed his chin on his forearm and spoke to his reflection in the side-view mirror. "Because I didn't like *Schindler's List* that mean I don't like Jews, or some shit, huh?" Winston rubbed the butt end of his pistol and mumbled, "I don't know, maybe it does."

"You upset with me, Winston?"

"I'm upset with people trying to tell me how to think."

"Why?"

"Because now I'm thinking."

"And?"

"And nothing. That's the fucking problem. And nothing."

"I think the scene on the balcony was meant to convey the Jews' powerlessness. How unreal the Holocaust must have been. André Breton once said something to the effect that the epitome of surrealism was shooting into a crowd."

"No, that's backward. The most surreal thing is being in a crowd getting shot *at*. Now *that shit* is bizarre." Winston ducked back inside the car and leaned against the headrest. "I guess I seen too much fucked-up shit in my life. You say the movie supposed to show how unbelievable those camps was, but man, I already believe it. I seen niggers set motherfuckers on fire. I seen niggers hold a gun to a mother's head and piss on her babies because her man didn't pay on time for some consignment rock. People are fucked up? Man, tell me something I don't know."

The last weepy notes of "Parsley, Sage, Rosemary and Thyme" were losing out to the uptown din. "Make a right here," ordered Winston. Spencer wheeled the car onto East 102nd Street. To his surprise the block was quiet. Rows of renovated brownstones and thin churches lined both sides of the street. The end of the block was dark, sealed off by the trestle for the Metro North train, which once past Ninety-sixth Street runs aboveground along Park Avenue. Branches of an overgrown oak diffused the streetlight, breaking it up into rays of imitation moonbeams. At the corner, on the right-hand side, barely visible through the oak in its front yard, was a decaying silt-brown building that loomed over the rest of the block like a haunted house. "Stop at the corner." Winston got out of the car and vanished around the corner, entering the building through a side entrance.

Spencer couldn't decide what tape to play next; it was between Bread's greatest hits and Harry Chapin's. A commuter train rumbled slowly past, the slogging clack of the cars almost lending an aura of rusticity to the setting. Harry Chapin's gritty warble clattered out into the darkness, buckled itself to the tracks, and took out after the departed Metro North train like a noisy caboose.

When Winston finally emerged from the building, his eyes were bloodshot and an indelible smile creased his face. In his hands was a shoebox full of marijuana and explosives. "Sorry about that, Money, but you know how it is when you doing business." Winston held up what appeared to be a small stick of dynamite and examined it in the amber streetlight. "Besides, I ain't been in that spot since I was twelve years old. Much memories up in there, boy."

"What is all that?"

"Weed, nigger."

"I mean the other stuff."

"Ain't nothing. Some M-80's and cherry bombs, two half-sticks, but mostly smoke bombs."

"Smoke bombs?"

"Yeah, I know some niggers who thinking about deprivatizing a bank, and supposedly the smoke bombs will fog up the surveillance camera."

"Winston, I'm going to have to insist that you never get in my car again with the intention of doing something illegal. If I find out that I'm taking you to or picking you up from some dope deal or something, then the Big Brother thing is over."

"Chill out. Don't get all self-righteous on me, when you just pick me up from playing three-card monte to meet with Bruce of the New Procession Party—but that served your purpose, so it was all right, I guess?"

"Progressive Party."

"Whatever. Man, I would never put you in no situation. Nigger, you'd be in my way."

Spencer started the ignition and asked his passenger to shut the door. Winston didn't budge. "Just pull out, getaway-style," he said. Gunning the engine, Spencer hit the gas and threw the car into gear, the momentum slamming the door shut just as the car rounded the corner onto Park Avenue.

The Mustang idled in front of Winston's building, neither man moving until Harry Chapin's son had grown up just like him. "You still want me to come over tomorrow and help you prepare for the debate?"

"Yeah, do that. But Yolanda got finals, so we have to do it outside."

"We'll walk around the neighborhood or something."

"Cool. One thing though, Rabbi—don't wear those shoes you got on."

"These? The clogs?"

"Yeah, nigger, the clogs. Don't wear them. If you think I'm going to be clippity-clopping merrily up the ave with your ass, you crazy. How much them things hit you for anyway?"

"One hundred and forty dollars."

"What? And they sweat us for buying sneakers that cost that much! It's the spending habits of you bougie niggers they need to address. A bill and a half for some wooden blocks! Shit, I'll cut up a two-by-four in two pieces, glue on some socks, and sell them to you for fifty bucks, yo." The belly rolls of laughter eventually rocked Tuffy out of the car. He stuck his head back in and offered his hand. Spencer hesitated, not sure if Tuffy was proffering the traditional or the soul shake. They shook quick and firm like dignitaries departing for their respective helicopters. "That's the diff between a nigger like me and a nigger like you," said Winston, backing out of the window. "One forty for some clogs or some tennies."

"White people can't tell the difference, though."

"True indeed."

"But it really hurts when other black folk can't tell the difference. I expect the white people to clutch their purses, and cross the street."

"Yeah, back in the day if I saw you coming, Rabbi, I'd cross the street too, but I'd be coming over to your side to take your money."

"Thanks a lot."

"Well, Rabbi, at least you sound white. You got that going for you. You spend the rest of your life on the phone, your shit be straight hunky-

TUFF

dory. But I got one for you, though. What's the difference between white people and black folks?"

"Is that a riddle?"

"No, I'm serious."

"White people eat ice cream year-round, even in the winter. And when they give you a ride home, they drop you off, then drive away as soon as you get out of the car. Black folks wait until you're safely inside."

"Thanks for the lift, Rabbi."

"Easy, Winston."

"All right then."

The boys standing in the vestibule parted like canal locks; Winston floated through, and they closed ranks behind him. Spencer waited a minute or two, then drove off with a tire squeal, closing the passenger door getaway-style.

20 · INFIERNO — DEBAJO DE NUEVA ADMINISTRACIÓN

The butt end of a flauta de pollo disappeared down Winston's gullet. His napkin already saturated with grease stains, he licked his fingertips and wiped his mouth with the corner of the linen tablecloth. "I don't know where all these Mexicans came from, but I'm glad they decided to move here. Fucking food is good." Spencer paid the bill and they left Puebla Mexico, Winston savoring the last of his cold horchata.

Headed north, they walked in silence, digesting the meal and their surroundings. Like the moors of the English countryside or the bogs of the Louisiana bayou in a late-night creature feature, at night the streets of East Harlem undergo a metamorphosis. Only fools and monsters trod in the darkness. Spencer splashed up Lexington Avenue, jumping at every hoot-owl screech. Winston slipped upstream, an urban alligator skimming the swamp's surface, eyes peeled for prey.

At 110th Street locals jammed the intersection. Oblivious to the automobile traffic, they dashed between cars, yelling and furiously signaling to one another like traders on the New York Stock Exchange floor, closing bell be damned. "It's hot out here tonight!" Winston remarked with a relish that made it obvious he was referring more to the street frenzy than to the muggy evening. Spencer read the lettering above the gated windows of the post office on the far side of 110th Street, 'HELL S

TUFF

GATE STA ION.' At their feet were a couple sitting on milk crates and dressed in T-shirts, cut-off denims, and foam-rubber thongs, watching a black-and-white television powered by an extension cord alligator-clipped to the innards of a lamppost. The Yankee game was in extra innings, and the play-by-play in melodramatic Spanish. The woman, her newly hot-combed hair dipping like an aileron behind her head, looked away from a pop-up and greeted Winston with a broad smile. "Hey, Tuffy Tuff."

"What up, girl? How you feel?"

When her man saw Winston, he grabbed and held his dog, a stocky black-and-brown rottweiler named Murder, by the collar. "*¿Qué te pasa, bro?*"

"*Suave.*"

Turning the bill of his baseball cap to an even quirkier angle, Winston stooped to pet Murder. When the dog went to lick his hand, he quickly put its head in an armlock. "What up, nigger?" he said to the animal, who answered him only with pleading brown eyes and a try to yank himself out of the grip. Winston tightened his hold until the dog whimpered. Satisfied, he released Murder and he and Spencer crossed the street.

"Now are you ready to study?" Spencer asked, handing Winston a sheet of paper. "I made up a list of questions I think might be asked at the debate." Winston took the paper and, without looking at it, rolled it into a tube. "Let's walk uptown," he said. "It'll be quieter."

Ahead of them a row of red traffic lights receded far into the distance. Spencer felt as if he were about to descend into the concrete depths of perdition, Dante to Winston's Virgil.

It had been a while since Spencer had walked the streets of East Harlem at night. The last time was when he and Rabbi Zimmerman sat shiva on 117th Street with Bea Wolfe, her husband laid out on the kitchen table, dead of lung cancer. For seven days he shuttled between the apartment and the market, sprinting through the chaotic streets for cat food and candles, reciting the kaddish to himself.

He glanced about, looking for Mr. Wolfe's ghost or another remnant of a Jewish presence. A vagabond wearing a weather-beaten sweater and grimy polyester pants sat cross-legged in front of a *panadería*. The smell of fresh-baked bread mixed with the stench of dried urine. There was an eerie lacquered sheen to the man, as if he'd been bronzed by gritty air and polished by the warm night winds. Catching Spencer's gaze, the vagrant put his thumb and forefinger to his lips. "You got a square?" Not knowing exactly what a square was, Spencer shook his head, sidestepping away from the man with a patronizing smile he hoped would placate them both. Winston handed the man a cigarette.

"Do you know if any Jews still live in the neighborhood?" Spencer asked. Tuffy shrugged, saying he occasionally saw old white people taking baby steps to and from the market, or store owners collecting the day's receipts and hopping into their Cadillacs. Maybe they were Jewish, he didn't know. A war whoop rolled down the street. Ahead of them a brood of rough-looking young men blocked the sidewalk. The boys jumped up and down like freshly oiled pistons, feverish with the boundless energy that comes from being on a New York street corner after eleven p.m. En masse the group moved toward Spencer and Winston. Spencer braced for an act of violence. He was thankful Fariq wasn't with them. Fariq would sense his fear, hear his insides knotting like a ship's lanyard, notice his eyes avoiding the boys as if they were lepers and he a gentleman too polite to stare.

Tuffy pointed to a second-floor bay window. Tucked in the corner of the window was a small sign, RAYMOND TENNENBAUM—ABOGADO Y SEGUROS.

"You asked if there are any Jewish people in the neighborhood—Tennenbaum sound Jewish, don't it?"

Spencer agreed, his head sinking toward the ground. The boys were within mugging distance. He could almost hear Fariq saying something about the irony of Tennenbaum making money off both ends: insuring the public against the crimes of colored boys like these, then defending the same kids after they'd committed the crimes.

"Rabbi, take your hands out your pockets," Tuffy whispered. "And lift your fucking head up."

Spencer did as he was told. The boisterous youths were only two steps away from him—so close he could feel the chill emanating off their ice-cold scowls. Winston walked toward the group, reached out, and, without breaking stride, shook the hand of the lead gargoyle.

It was the same with nearly every band of young people they met: a firm yet quick slide-'n'-glide handshake exchange that, like comets hurtling around the sun, seemingly propelled each party up the sidewalk to the next rallying point. "What up, kid?"

"Coolin'."

TUFF

"Tranquilo."

"Stay up, son."

Some handshakes ended with a finger snap, others with a light touching of knuckled-up fists. "Peace, God." One man, whom Winston apparently hadn't seen in a while, received a handshake that collapsed into a strong, spinning bear hug that chicken-winged their elbows out to the side. "Nigger."

"My man. Fuck's happenin'?"

Spencer asked why he warranted an embrace from Winston rather than the standard soul shake. "Rabbi, that nigger got stories to tell, but the fucked-up thing is, he so deep in the life, he can't tell them."

Not having spent much time with Winston on his home turf made it difficult for Spencer to determine if he was campaigning or just taking his leisurely nighttime stroll up the avenue. He knew so many people. And those who were too busy to hail him watched him knowingly.

"Winston, it's too late now but you should've taken the election seriously—you probably could've won." Tuffy looked at Spencer like he was crazy. He spat and put the rolled-up debate questions to his mouth. Through the paper megaphone he yelled to two sisters sitting on a fire escape three stories above them. "Where your brother at?"

"Wagner!" one shouted back.

Tuffy shook hands and exchanged pleasantries with many locals, but few received the bear hug. As with prime numbers, the farther uptown they zigzagged, the greater the distance between the persons who got the grip and the loving embrace. Between 109th and 112th Streets, Winston squeezed homeboys and homegirls 2, 3, 7, 11, and 13 like lost children found in the amusement park; 23, 29, and 37, all standing in line to get into the La Bamba dance hall on 115th Street, were crushed like sympathetic friends at a funeral. In the lobby of the Chicken Shack on 117th, Winston, 41, and his sister, 43, were hugged like football players in the end zone celebrating a Super Bowl touchdown. Now, at 119th and Second Avenue, Winston was tapping 73 on the shoulder.

Raychelle Dinkins was his first love. His first kiss. His first slow dance. His second fuck. His first regular drug customer. Back in junior high when Winston and Raychelle were an item, she was a thick-framed teen who had what Winston liked to call "a luscious, dark black, hard-ass gospel body." A heroin addiction had eaten away her muscle like jungle rot. Turned her into a wisp of a woman so thin her pregnant belly seemed to account for half her body weight. "Winston!" Raychelle shouted, raising her bony arms to hug him. Winston tucked her head into his chest, resting his chin on her flaky scalp. The familiar scent of the perfume she'd been wearing since seventh grade flared his nostrils and caused an involuntary growl to rumble from his throat, the sweet smell taking him back to ditch parties at Kevin Colón's house, where he spent school days sipping wine coolers and listening to Hector Lavoe sing love ballads he couldn't understand. "You speak Spanish, what he sayin', Raychelle?" Taking a break from notching a hickey on his neck, she would cock an ear toward the stereo. After a few bars she'd stick her tongue and her translation in Winston's ear. "He saying, 'Fuck math, fuck English, fuck me right now.' "

"Raychelle!" her boyfriend, an integer, a regular nigger, called from across the street. He was clapping his hands, a drill-sergeant coach urging his recruit through the obstacle course. "Let's go!" As she turned to leave, Winston hooked an arm around her waist, swept a lock of stringy hair from her ulcerated face, and planted an affectionate kiss on her cheek. "How many months?"

"Seven and a half."

The boyfriend, seeing the kiss, took three strides into the street. "Bitch, come on!"

"Hold up, motherfucker!" Raychelle licked her thumb and brushed it across Winston's eyebrows. "You know what I'm a name it, right?"

"Lonnie if it's boy. Candice if it's girl."

"You remember."

"Come on now, this Tuff."

"How's Jordy?"

"He all right. He don't never talk, but he cool."

"Raychelle, them niggers ain't going to be at the spot forever, and unless you got some works, you best to come on!"

Raychelle bussed Winston on the eyelids, then, stomach-first, waddled into the street, tumbling after her already-departed boyfriend, who seemed to pull her along as if she were a mangled kite he was trying to get airborne. The couple moved briskly past a brick wall plastered with graffiti and campaign posters. Winston spat. The street lamp hanging overhead began to flicker. The strobelike flashes illuminated Winston and Spencer as if they were caught in a silent-movie lightning storm. "Damn, she used to be fine."

"I bet she was. You can still see it. She still got some booty left."

"Check you out, Rab, showing a little zest," Winston said, still gazing up at the light. He handed Spencer his questions back, then clapped his hands. The beam steadied. "What they going to ask me at the debate, Rabbi? They going to ask about Raychelle?"

"They will. They'll hand out index cards and ask the audience to write down their questions and pass them to the front." Spencer unrolled the paper like a medieval herald. " 'Mr. Foshay, what do you plan to do about drugs in the community?' "

"You not hearing me, Rabbi. Are they going ask me about Raychelle? Are they going to say, 'Tuffy, you know all the troublemakers, if you get elected what you going to do about Raychelle, or Petey Peligroso?' "

"Winston, the idea of a debate is to address the issues on a broader scope. I doubt they'll mention anyone by name."

"That's because they know better. Because then I'd say, 'What you going to do about your son, your niece, your nephew, yourself?' I'd throw it back in they face, word."

They continued north on Second Avenue, Spencer tossing out prospective debate questions in the affected stuffy yammer of a television moderator. "Children having children. A problem. A moral disgrace. How do we prevent it? Mr. Foshay?" Although he was listening, Winston looked straight ahead, keeping his answers to himself, vainly trying to remember which one of the upcoming bodegas carried the Captain Nemo chocolate cakes he was craving. *You ain't never going to stop kids from having sex. Those that want to fuck going to fuck. What you need to do is be real with them. Hip them to the Astroglide. Squeeze it out the tube, slap it on the rubber, and the pussy feel normal.*

"Rap music . . . violent television programming . . . films that glorify crime. Are they influencing our youth and pushing them in the wrong direction? Isn't the answer censorship, and not warning labels and ratings?" *Has anyone ever thought that this type of entertainment is . . . what's that word Yolanda be using after we have one of our angry fucks? Cathartic. Maybe if niggers wasn't listening to rap music, and watching these bullshit films, they'd be even more violent. And for that matter, if the white man wasn't making these movies, he'd be more violent too.*

Soon they found themselves treading down a narrow footpath that cut through the innards of the massive Wagner projects. As they stood in the urban gorge there was a roar in the air. The sound of laughter and argument echoed off the sides of the tall brick buildings. Bands of residents could be seen navigating the housing development's cataracts, wittingly rushing headlong to the unseen cascades like daredevils in a barrel. *One way to keep people off the streets would be to provide them with air-conditioning,* Spencer thought. "Do you want more questions, Winston?"

"Naw, I'm just going to have to look stupid. But that's all right, I'm used to it."

A herd of grade-schoolers detoured around Winston and stampeded past Spencer, almost knocking him down in the process. He looked at his watch. "It's one-thirty in the morning—do you know where your parents are?"

An eleven-year-old boy, his hair already shorn in a gangster tonsure, moped up to Winston and clasped his hand with a vigorous shake. "When you going to put me down, big man?"

"You know I ain't out there like that right now, Shorty," Winston said, palming the boy's head in his hands.

"I know, I seen the posters. These bummy-ass niggers and some Chinese lady be putting them up all the time."

"She Japanese."

"Right, right, whatever. Niggers say you laying in the cut. Niggers say if you walkin' out of courtrooms free as a beetle, then the mafia backing you. Niggers say that you finally packin' a toolie. That if you win, bodies going to drop."

"I ain't going to win."

"You packin' heat, though?"

"That ain't none of your business."

"Niggers say you on some syndicate-type shit."

"Fuck out of here."

"Niggers say you holding twenty, thirty G's on the daily. I know you not pushin' no product, so how you get that kind of scratch? I know, you can't tell me—just when the time come, hook a young nigger up. I'd like a piece of that mafia lifestyle. Live that 'wack a nigger here, clip a nigger there' day to day."

Winston cut the youngster off with a ten-dollar bill. "You know where to get a Captain Nemo's chocolate cake around here?" The boy nodded, his hands posed to take the money. "Get me three loosies, a chocolate cake, Captain Nemo's now, not none of them no-name ghetto snacks, and a tall can of Budweiser." The boy snatched the money, but Winston held on tight to his end. He tossed his head toward a circle of teenagers standing under a lone elm tree. "I'll be over there with Bucknaked and them, okay?" Winston released his grip on the money, sending the boy flying through the projects like a pellet from a slingshot. Winston looked at Spencer, then, cupping his hands over his mouth, shouted down his runner. "Change that Budweiser to two foreign beers! Heineken or some shit!" The boy acknowledged the change in orders with a raise of his hand.

Sitting on top of a pipe rail bordering the walkway, they sipped their canned lagers, Tuffy somehow also managing to smoke a cigarette and lick chocolate frosting off the Nemo's wrapper. "Shit good, ain't it, Rabbi?" asked Winston, holding up his green can like an actor in a television commercial. Spencer grinned. Though the first taste of the mundane Dutch import had made him gag, and long for a foamy glass of a Flemish wit bier with a slice of lemon, he had to concur that nothing went better with a humid New York City night than beer—even this vacuum-packed aluminum swill. Beneath the branches of the elm tree, about five yards from Winston and Spencer, the cluster of young men had tightened. A Spanish kid, the color of wet sand, was blowing into his hand as if it were a trumpet's embouchure. His efforts produced a mélange of beats that varied between the sounds of flatulence, the pings of a drummer's high hat, and the burps of a jalopy chugging uphill. As his other hand alternately slapped his chest and muted his "horn," the percussives gained momentum. The other members of the clique, feet planted firmly against the cement like the roots of the nearby tree, began to dip at the knees. A few slowly bobbed and weaved their torsos like boxers practicing dodging punches in the mirror. The rest lifted their hands skyward and bounced in place like Sunday rollers in the first pew catching the Holy Ghost. Even the branches of the elm tree seemed to sway to the beat. And like the singing trees in *The Wizard of Oz,* the teens began spouting frenzied rhymes, trying to solve all the world's problems in one breath. Spencer wondered if among these young men was the anonymous neologist who invented the ever-mutable New York slang.

Experts in urban eschatology, the rappers' monodies and laments wove a dense skein of verse from the spindles of despair and cautious optimism that unraveled from the looms in their hearts and minds. Spencer could only make out the guttural call-and-response what-whats, uh-huhs, okays, mm-hmms, and yes-yes-y'alls. Even Winston, though somewhat better versed in ghetto colloquialism, understood only about three-quarters of the machine-gun poetics.

A shirtless young man wearing a Jackie Coogan cap and a pair of Tom Sawyer denim overalls peeled away from the group. He weaved toward Winston waving a paper-bagged pint of liquor like a metronome, spewing his freestyle like a drunken Nubian skald.

> *. . . this here is Bucknaked*
> *life expectancy of a fly,*
> *ready to die*
> *so no time for faking it.*
>
> *Bucknaked in your sphere —*
> *ass out, talking loud,*
> *farting rain clouds.*
> *Penis flapping,*
> *nuts hanging,*
> *lube the pubes*
> *'cause bitches I'm banging.*
>
> *Like my nigger Tuff*
> *call your bluff.*
> *My whole race got a poker face,*
> *treys over queens,*
> *and like they say I'm keeping it real.*
> *Don't what that means,*
> *but I know how it feels . . .*

After Bucknaked dropped his last "lyrical bomb," the session ended, the rappers' scorched-earth policy having temporarily defoliated the briar patch that was once the quadrangle of the Wagner projects and left the night as brittle as rice paper. Exhausted and speaking in wheezes, the boys gathered around Winston to catch their breath with small talk.

"With them posters up, nigger, everybody think you rapping."

"I know."

"When's the election?"

"Next Tuesday. Y'all niggers going to vote for me?"

A slender snaggle-toothed boy waved his hand in front of his face.

"Get real, dog. I'm from the projects, dog. That vote shit ain't for niggers like me."

Tuffy raised a hand, feigning a backhanded slap in the pessimist's direction. "Who you think you talking to, a nigger from Mars? What your birth certificate say—'Place of Birth: Projects'? You better save that 'I'm from the projects' bullshit for a somebody that give a fuck."

The boy shuffled his feet and with sanguine eyes looked up at Winston.

"I ain't saying waste your vote on me, because I ain't the somebody that give a fuck, but you need to vote for somebody."

"Check, Tuff out, son!" one of the group exclaimed. "You been around Smush and Five Percenter shit too long, because you talking in circles now."

Bucknaked was staring intently at Winston, rubbing his chin. "On the real, yo, I would vote, but that shit just puts me in the system, B. Give them motherfuckers one more address to bust up. Feel me?"

"Man, the worst that can happen is they call you to jury duty."

"You been called?"

"Had to serve last November. Paid me twenty-five dollars a day or some shit."

"Federal?"

"I wish. Some joker was suing the electric company."

"I'm sayin'," said Bucknaked, feeling his apathy vindicated by Winston's jury experience, "that right there is why I ain't registered. What if I get on some boring-ass long-drawn-out case where you have to live in a Roach Motel for six month? I got no time for the city, not for no measly twenty-five a day. I could steal that out my mama's purse."

"You would, nigger," commented the project baby.

"Damn straight. And I have, too," snorted Bucknaked.

"It ain't all that. If you don't like the case it's ways to get out of it."

"Like how, nigger?"

"Motherfuckers tried to put me on that electric-company-blew-up-my-house madness. I wasn't having it—Joe Whiteman vs. Amalgamated So-and-So, who give a fuck? So we broke for lunch, I came back eating a bean pie and holding a copy of *The Final Call*. Headline in big-ass letters: MINISTER CITES SCIENTIFIC EVIDENCE—WHITE MAN IS THE DEVIL. They wasn't going to pick me for shit after that. But I got to thinking, as much as I been in court, I ain't never seen a nigger like me in the jury box."

Bucknaked reconsidered his stance and in a fit of giddiness started jumping up and down like he'd won some local raffle. "Word life, son. If I was on the jury I be like, 'Let my people go! Videotape, smideotape! DNA, NBA! The nigger didn't do it!' "

Spencer unzipped his rucksack. The group was startled by the sound like a herd of bucks catching a whiff of the hunter. Their relief was palpable when his hand produced nothing more than a notebook and a pen. For a second Spencer thought he saw a gun in the hands of the buck-toothed kid. Now his hands were empty and Spencer couldn't guess where he'd stashed his weapon. "Who this nigger, man?"

The pen and paper had increased the discomfort in regard to his presence, and the rappers backed away from him. Spencer waited for Winston to introduce him to his friends to ease the tension. He wondered what would be the term of endearment: Big Brother, Rabbi Spence, Ace? *He's a Jew, but he's all right.*

Winston snatched the pad out of Spencer's hand. "Fuck you doing?"

"I'm just jotting down some thoughts for the next installment. I don't want to forget anything." Winston tossed the book back to Spencer and said, "Big Brother, Little Brother over. Rabbi, you need to be out. This ain't no zoo."

"Who is this nigger, G?"

"Nobody. Motherfucker just writing some article about me for the paper. Some King-of-the-Jungle-type shit. But the safari over now."

Spencer wanted to defend his actions but knew that anything he'd say would sound hollow. Goose bumps rose on his skin. He felt as if he were shrinking before Winston, soluble in his own bullshit, his body bubbling and floating toward the sky in tiny pieces like an antacid tablet dissolving into the night. Before disappearing completely, he turned to leave. "See you tomorrow afternoon at the debate, okay? Two-thirty?"

Winston wrested the paper bag from Bucknaked, took a long pull from the bottle, then slung an arm around his friend's shoulders. Together they and rest of the boys bopped down a labyrinthian walkway and into the depths of the Wagner Projects. This level of hell was off limits to Spencer, and he began the trek back to his car, feeling slighted he hadn't been introduced, and guilty for taking out his notebook. He knew that he'd never have the access to Winston the others had, and it suddenly dawned on him why: he was more afraid *of* Winston than *for* him. Afraid of his reputation. Afraid of his latent intellect. Afraid of being judged— and being judged fairly.

TUFF

As Spencer walked to the edge of the apartment complex, the boy who'd fetched Winston the beer and cake jumped in front of him. "Hey yo," the imp said, stepping directly in his path. "My man say you gave him a Frisbee." Spencer followed the boy's outstretched arm across a small patch of grass and recognized the child he'd given the Frisbee to after his first visit to Winston's. "Yes, I did."

"Do you have any more, mister?"

It was an innocent request, and for the first time the kid's tone of voice matched his age. Regretfully, Spencer shook his head and lightly reached out to touch the youngster's forehead. He'd just started to mumble a benediction when the boy slapped his hand away and yelled, "Well, fuck you then!"

21· "VOTE WINSTON FOSHAY—KING!"

n the stage of the community center's auditorium, Winston, dressed in pleated slacks and shirt and tie, was fidgeting in his seat, fighting the tedium of democracy. He'd finished his pitcher of water before the associate director of the New York chapter of the NAACP had finished welcoming the sparse audience to the debate. Now the moderator, the managing editor of *El Diario* newspaper, was reviewing the ground rules. Each candidate would have three minutes for opening remarks, after which the moderator would read questions submitted by the audience on index cards.

"I'm qualified to represent District 8 because I am a mother. . . ." Margo Tellos was at the microphone, giving her opening remarks. Tuffy studied the other candidates seated on either side of him. Two seats to his left, Wilfredo Cienfuegos, dressed like he was going ballroom dancing, was softly rehearsing his speech. "*Buenas noches* to the barrio. *Mi barrio, su barrio, nuestro barrio* . . ." Next to Cienfuegos sat Collette Cox. She had her head in her lap, faking a meditative pose, but was clandestinely scratching an instant-win lottery ticket, praying for a third dollar sign. Coming up empty, she ripped the ticket in half and adjusted her campaign button. On Winston's immediate right was Tellos's empty seat. Beyond it, a sharp, conservatively dressed middle-aged man he'd never seen before, taking notes on a yellow legal pad. *Who this nigger?* Leaning forward, he tried to read the man's paper nameplate. Just then Margo Tellos took her seat to polite applause, forcing Winston to sit back in his chair and join in. She scooted her chair under the table, condescendingly smiling at him as if she were Kennedy looking down his nose at Nixon in 1960.

"And now our most accomplished candidate . . ." The unknown man stood up. "German Jordan is a noted philosophical, political, and critical thinker. He's written a number of scholarly works, his most recent being *Setting My Sights Low: Why I Chose to Be a City Councilman Instead of President.* Ladies and gentlemen, just back from a space-shuttle mission to resume his campaign, I give you professor, theologian, astronaut, renaissance man, and the Eighth District's incumbent councilman, German Jordan."

"Astronaut?" Winston said, embarrassingly covering his mouth when he realized his bafflement was audible. Winston looked up at the ceiling. It was still riddled with shotgun holes from his father's poetry reading. *What the fuck am I doing up here?*

Jordan addressed the audience in the bold, clear voice of an old-fashioned orator, his Hitlerian stare and backwater Baptist inflections holding them spellbound. "What we as a community need to do is start imagining ourselves beyond race. . . ."

Winston gazed into the crowd. Inez sat in the front row, her angry face trembling with hatred, reddening with Jordan's every word. She knew that despite his representing the district, Jordan's only real connections to his constituency were a couple of second cousins he saw once a year at the family reunion and a post-office box he didn't have the key to. Two rows behind her, Spencer sat on his hands. He'd seen German Jordan speak before, and once counted himself a devout Jordanite. Two years ago they even shared the podium at a conference on identity held in Minneapolis. Jointly chairing a workshop on multifarious identity, they succeeded in affirming the oxymoronic confab of black Jews, hermaphrodites, white niggers, and the walking dead. It was at the conference he first became disenchanted with Jordan. It wasn't the rampant rumors of a white mistress salted away in a New England log cabin or the cocaine habit that led to his disillusionment; it was the realization that no matter the topic, if there was an African-American subtext (and isn't there always?), Jordan gave the same speech. Every aspect of black culture from art to athletics had its roots in the church. Louis Armstrong was the trope for all things black. The ills faced by America's impoverished could be righted by embracing radical Christianity and never wearing anything less dressy than a cardigan sweater. To Spencer's way of thinking, Jordan's regimented cures for colored America amounted to tweed-jacketed fascism. *I know Stephen Jay Gould,* Spencer thought, *and you're no Stephen Jay Gould.* Most of the audience vigorously applauded Jordan's every point, and occasionally, shouts of "Amen!" rang throughout the hall.

Where's my peoples at? Winston asked himself, scanning the rear of the auditorium, where his friends and family were seated. They weren't listening to German Jordan; they were fixated on Winston, their pride evident even through their efforts to make him laugh with hand signals and distorted faces. Winston shyly waved at them, like a child playing an elf in the school Christmas play.

"Though for the past four years I've represented the concerns of this district to the fullest extent of my abilities, I am ashamed to say that to this day I am afraid to park my Mercedes-Benz in this neighborhood. We must do something about . . ." Inez caught Winston's eye and made the yap-yap-yap sign with her hands. Winston rolled his eyes in agreement. When they centered, he saw his father, arms folded, standing underneath the Emergency Exit sign. His left eyelid twitched as he recalled the times his father had embarrassed him from this very same stage.

"I have traveled in space, seen the stars, and know that they are within our grasp if only we . . ."

How this fool get to space? Why him? How does he get to do the one thing I really want to do? What a nigger got to do to get to the stars? Unable to hold off the jealousy, Winston covered his ears with his hands. German Jordan's mouth was moving, but no words were coming out. His silent podium pounding and stiff oratorical gestures were reminiscent of a nineteenth-century wooden whirligig toy come to life. Tuffy's eyes closed. He hummed an impromptu tune to himself, pretending the pastel flashes dancing on the insides of his eyelids were novas and nebulas beckoning him onto the dance floor like house-party trip lights.

Margo Tellos tapped Winston's shoulder. Awakened from his disco daze, he moved his hands away from his ears and the audience's laughter replaced his daydream. The moderator beckoned him to the microphone. "Next up is one of our young charges, who's following in the activist footsteps of his father, ex-Panther Clifford Foshay, who's standing over there in the back of the room. Please welcome Winston Foshay." Tuffy sheepishly approached the mike, unsure what portion of the applause was for him and what belonged to his father. From the back of the auditorium Clifford slapped palms with his boys, then pumped a black-power salute in his son's direction. Winston answered the encouragement with a subtle middle-finger scratch of his temple. *Nigger, I'm fixing to embarrass you, so that you ashamed to be my father like I'm ashamed to be your son.*

"Like Ms. Tellos over there, I too am a mother . . . a motherfucker."

The foul language thrust the audience back into their seats as if they were fighter pilots pulling g's in a steep climb.

"I don't know why you looking so shocked. Most of y'all know me and know it's true. I know you motherfuckers too. I see you goin' to church Sunday morning, walking your kids home from school. Y'all the normal nine-to-five people. Don't think I don't be hearing what you say at your block association meetings. Ms. Nomura tells me what y'all be whining about. Nothin' different from what everybody has said so far. 'We have to support our youth. We have to find ways of reaching these kids.' Well, here standing in front of you is a nigger who been reached. And the question is, now that you have a brother like me by the scruff of the neck, what you going to do with him? If you think me standing up here in slacks and a tie means that me and other thug niggers like me is going to settle for the drab life y'all niggers livin', well, you got another think coming. 'Support the youth. Support our youth.' That's all I ever hear, and here before you is a youth asking for your support—y'all goin' to give it to me? I doubt it. Most of you already set on votin' for that slick nigger over there, German Jordan, the renaissance man, whatever the fuck that is. A motherfucker you can tell wasn't even born and raised in the neighborhood. Because if he was, he'd be a lazy bitch-ass pimp nigger runnin' prostitutes on Mount Pleasant Avenue."

Winston walked over to the table and poured himself a glass of water from Cienfuegos's pitcher.

"I wasn't listening too hard, but I heard him say something about we need to imagine ourselves beyond race. Look at me," Winston said, raising his arms to crucifixion height. "What you see is what you get, a big black motherfucker from a low-budget environment. If I'd been to outer space, written books, had dollars, drove a Mercedes-Benz, I'd imagine myself beyond race too. I'd imagine myself *way* beyond race. I'd imagine myself right out of this fucked-up neighborhood. Leave y'all motherfuckers behind to fend for yourselves. This nigger up here talkin' about he afraid to park his Benz on the block. Wants to make the block a place safe enough to park his car. Like he the only nigger in the world got a fancy car. Much uptown niggers got Mercedes-Benzes. Tommy Touch got a brand-new fuckin' Mercedes that does everything but tuck you in bed at night, and that nigger park his damn car anywhere he pleases. Why? Because unlike German Jordan, niggers know who Tommy Touch is. Tommy known on the block and in the community. Whether you know Tommy personally or just know of him, you know not to fuck with his car. 'Imagine yourself beyond race.' Shit, imagine owning a brand-new Mercedes-Benz. If you goin' to fantasize, go all the way.

"Imagine Jordan, Ms. Tellos, Mr. Cienfuegos, or Ms. Cox goin' to the hospital with you to watch your uncle die of AIDS, posting your bail, writing you letters while you upstate, sending commissary money, defending you on the street. Shit I've done for and with many of the sons, daughters, and grandchildren of many folks that's up in here tonight. I don't need to mention no names. You don't think it's true? Ask the person next to you. If you about supporting the youth, vote for me this Tuesday. Remember—'mi barrio, su barrio, nuestro barrio.' "

The speech drained Winston. Too dazed to hear anything other than Fariq, Armello, and Charley stomping their feet and yelling "Damn!" he slumped back to his seat, his face beaded with sweat. He looked up to see if his father had a smile or tears on his face. He'd never know, because Clifford was gone, replaced by a newspaper photographer.

Tuffy struggled to occupy himself during the remaining speeches. He rolled and unrolled his tie. Doodled on his notepad. Interrupted Wilfredo Cienfuegos to ask for more water. Inverted the nameplate, scribbled 'Tuffy 109' on the blank side, and placed it back in front of him. Apologized when the snickers discombobulated Collette Cox during her speech. Winston welcomed the moderator's first question. *Forty-five more minutes and I can go.*

"The first question is from Juanita Navarro of East 111th Street. What strategies do the candidates have for reducing juvenile crime?" Each of Winston's fellow aspirants answered the query with the requisite campaign forthrightness, their responses identical save for German Jordan's couched verbiage: "It is imperative we provide our children not only with the physical infrastructure for advancement, but also a bold social and mental infrastructure. Just as the streets need sewers, the children need community centers, midnight basketball, tutorial services. . . ."

TUFF

Winston's answer set the jocular tone that would be his for the remainder of the debate. "What would I do about juvenile crime? I'd lower the age when niggers are no longer minors to five years old. Juvenile crime would be eliminated just like that," he said, snapping his fingers for emphasis.

Slamming his hand on the table, German Jordan stood up and demanded Winston respond to the question with the sincerity it deserved.

Tuffy snorted. "That's how they lowered welfare. Kicked me and everybody else off and said, 'We lowered the number of niggers on welfare.' When they did that I bet you didn't jump in the mayor's face talkin' 'bout 'Would you be serious?' So sit your punk ass down, you little astronaut bitch!"

When the debate ended, it was apparent from the number of strangers wishing him good luck come Tuesday, that Winston had won over a few of the electorate's more cynical voters. His friends invited him to a celebratory dinner, but he begged off, saying he needed to be alone for a while. He kissed Yolanda goodbye and told her he'd be home in about an hour. On his way out, he stopped to hug Inez, who was in German Jordan's face, lambasting him about his duplicitous policies. Stopping in mid-tirade, she squeezed Winston. "You did good. That speech alone was worth fifteen thousand dollars. Thanks." She held at him arm's length. Winston had survived another summer. "What, Ms. Nomura, what?"

"Nothing, just looking."

"Ms. Nomura, I ain't changed."

"Yes you have."

"How?"

"I don't know."

"Same as I ever was," Winston said, returning her hug.

Spencer came over, looking contrite. "Winston, I want to say—"

Tuffy raised his hand. "Look, man, I have an idea. I'll call you about it in a week or two."

"About the articles . . ."

"Look, write whatever you want, I really don't care."

As he walked outside, his muttering loitered behind him like the putting of a small outboard engine: "No shame in my game."

He passed Spencer's car, knelt down, and retrieved his gun from the hollow of the rear bumper. Suspecting a police presence, he'd stashed the pistol before the debate when no one was looking. He slid the automatic, now as much of an accessory to Winston as his belt, into his pocket and walked west. He was going to lie down on the grass of Central Park's Great Lawn, soak in the last of the summer sun, and read his sumo book.

During the walk he didn't ruminate on the previous two hours like an ordinary politician would have. Though he felt good about his performance, he didn't care whether it appeased his supporters or moved the swing vote to his side. He had said what he had to say, nothing more. It simply felt good to be out of the auditorium, well away from the posturing civil servants and concerned public.

Winston's legs and spirits were light, and they quickly carried him to Eighty-sixth Street and Park Avenue, the southern hinterlands of the Eighth District. Long gentrified by the private university that owned most of the land in this section of the city, the vista was of wine and specialty shops, and luxury condominiums named after Native American tribes: the Iroquois, the Dakota, the Oneida, the Pequot. Like a child hesitant to jump into an unheated pool, Winston toed the curb, afraid to step into the street. *Fuck, I have to piss. I shouldn't have drank all that water.* He knew there was no sense in going to a nearby restaurant to use the bathroom. He'd only be rebuffed under the guise of not being a patron. Unable to hold his bladder any longer, he urinated on the walls of a dormitory, not even bothering to tuck into one of the facade's crannies. He took a deep breath, and after a few seconds he began sidestepping his way along the base of the building. As he moved right, dripping wet letters spelled out, "Vote Winston Foshay—King!"

Their skins burned pimiento red, white people soaking up more than their share of the sun filled the Great Lawn from the far softball fields to the turtle pond. The air smelled of Brie, grapes, and Australian white wines. Normally, Winston would've avoided a mob of white folks as if it were, well, a mob of white folks. But this time, the iron lance of King Wladyslaw II's statue prodding him in the back, he plunged into the throng, settling between the tartan blankets of two Upper East Side preppy families. After checking their immediate surroundings, ensuring that nothing valuable was within Winston's reach, the blond family smiled and politely offered him a plate of wafers and Roquefort and a clear plastic cup of wine. Winston's refusal was his churlish "Hey, yo!" to the scruffy merchant selling cans of beer out of a Styrofoam cooler he carted along in a red toy wagon.

Lying there on his back, beer can in hand, Tuffy swore he could feel the earth moving, its rotation gluing him to this patch of grass. He opened his sumo book to a page at random and shaded his face with it.

Two unheralded yet important components of a wrestler's training are his diet and sleeping habits. The post-practice meal is rice and hearty helpings of chanko-nabe, a tasty miso-based stew of meat, fish, vegetables and noodles. After lunch it's straight to the futon for a metabolism-slowing afternoon nap.

Winston, his metabolism slowed to a crawl, dreamed of rough-and-tumble sumo matches fought inside the rings of Saturn.

22- IF ELECTED I WILL NOT SERVE

On election day, Tuffy was in the kitchen roasting a hot dog over the stove's gas burner. Using a fork as a spit, he rotated his lunch, flaming, sizzling droplets of grease falling onto the stove top. "Come on, Winston. Let's go vote, I have to get to the computer center before it closes. I ain't got time to be waiting on you. Plus you talking about going to the movies."

"The polls are open till nine. If you want, go on to school and vote when you get back. I'll watch Jordy. I ain't doing nothing."

"Just hurry the fuck on up. Every fucking time."

When the meat was bubbled and burnt to perfection, Winston wrapped the frankfurter in a doughy slice of wheat bread, covered it with loops of ketchup and mustard, then stuffed half of it into his mouth. On his way out the door he stopped in front of the casserole dish. Plucking his pets out of the water, he gave each a loving kiss on the lips, then dropped them back into the ersatz aquarium.

Three abreast and hand in hand, the Foshays looked like a trio of paper-cutout dolls on their way to join the rest of the foldout accordion. But any similarity to the mythical happy-go-lucky American family on their way to exercise their inalienable rights was purely superficial.

"I need something to drink."

TUFF

"Winston, you promised, no alcohol before eight o'clock at night."

"I don't want no beer. I'm going to get me a malta," Winston said, referring to the small bottles of carbonated molasses.

Yolanda protested. "No, baby, that has alcohol in it."

"Less than point five percent," Winston countered. "I probably drank more alcohol than that this morning when I was eating your stank-stank."

"Winston!"

"For real, that strong-ass douche you be using probably ten times the proof of a malta."

"God, you're nasty."

"You wasn't saying that this morning."

"No malta."

Resigned to a soda pop, Winston entered a bodega just as two young children carrying book bags and ripping open bags of goodies with their teeth exited. "What time is it?" he asked Yolanda.

"These kids just getting out of school, so I guess it's about three o' clock."

Pulling on Yolanda's hand, Winston steered her and Jordy toward 108th Street. "Come on, we late." The dress rehearsal of the bank robbery was scheduled for three. When they arrived at the corner of 108th and Second Avenue, the bank's security guard was holding the door as the day's last customers filed out. He saw Armello calmly waiting in an idling Dodge Winston didn't recognize, but he thought the baby seat in the back was a nice attention-deflecting touch. Armello gestured toward the side of the bank, where Fariq, holding a box, was leaning against a brick wall. Next to him was an extension ladder, Ms. O'Koren, Charley O', and a dreadlocked male whom Charles was busy manhanding.

"What's up, nigger?" Charles asked. "Yolanda."

Winston noticed Charles was wearing only one shoe; his other foot was bare and soiled. Whitey twisted his hostage's right arm so severely his knuckles touched his forearm. The dread lifted his head and yelped. The tube sock stuffed in his mouth muffled his cry. It was La Mega, the boy Winston had beat senseless a few months ago. Winston slipped a hand under his shirt and rubbed the keloid scar La Mega's box cutter had raised. La Mega saw Winston and cowered into a fetal position. Winston's eyes followed the rungs of the ladder. Nadine was on the roof, her hands filled with smoke bombs. She waved hello.

Fariq lifted a white lab coat from the box. "Got an extra lab coat for you. It's not too late."

Winston knew the basics of the plan. When the next-to-last customer left the bank, on Armello's signal Ms. O'Koren was to approach the guard, claiming that she had some urgent business and needed to see the manager. After the guard let her in, she'd wait a few moments, giving Nadine time to light the smoke bombs and drop them into air ducts. When the bank filled with smoke, Ms. O'Koren would spill a vial of ammonia, say "What's that smell?" and pretend to pass out. Fariq and Whitey would enter the bank holding handkerchiefs over their mouths and flashing phony tags that identified them as city terrorism experts. In his best British accent, Charles would quickly explain there'd been a sarin gas leak and if the employees wanted to live they'd have forty-five seconds to drink the antidote—the antidote being a concoction of blueberry-flavored Thirstbusters, Armello's Rohypnol, and some knock-out drug Fariq had gotten from who knows where. Plan B? There was no Plan B. "Why La Mega here?"

"Man, we forgot to test the antidote," Fariq explained. "We about to go home, and this unlucky motherfucker walked by."

Winston knew the plan would never work but was curious whether the antidote would. He grabbed La Mega from Charles, lifted his dreads off his face, and pressed his finger into the soft spot behind his earlobe. La Mega dropped to his knees. Fariq tossed Whitey a spiked Thirstbuster. "Charley, tilt his head back and pinch his nose," Winston ordered. "When he start gagging, Ms. O'Koren, you pull the sock out his mouth." Charles squeezed La Mega's nostrils shut. "Yolanda, take Jordy around the corner." Yolanda stayed put. With two hands Ms. O'Koren gingerly pulled on the knee-high sock like a magician's assistant removing a rope of knot scarves from his mouth. The toe of the sock caught on one of La Mega's incisors. Ms. O'Koren yanked. La Mega gasped for air. Another yank. The sock was still tangled. La Mega was blabbering in radio Spanish, *"Foxes Nightclub de Jersey City—Damas cinco dolares y caballeros diez . . . Western Union es confianza . . . llame al dos uno dos seis, cuarenta cinco . . . ,"* when Tuffy dislodged the sock with a boot heel to the jaw. Still holding La Mega's nose, Whitey poured the liquid into his mouth, careful not to get any blood on his clothes. Fariq set his watch. La Mega went limp and fell to the ground as Winston released his hair.

TUFF

"Six seconds!" Fariq said, looking up from his watch. "That shit works quick."

With his shod foot, Charles nudged La Mega's head. "That nigger's out, but I don't know, I think Tuffy's kick did it."

Armello honked his horn, the signal that there was only one customer left in the bank. Nadine climbed down the ladder. "We can't go through with it now. We don't even know if the stuff works or not." Looking at Yolanda, she jabbed her thumb in Winston's direction. "Your man fuckin' shit up as usual." Not knowing what was causing the delay, Armello, trying to be inconspicuous, lightly beeped the car horn. Charles knelt down beside La Mega and thumbed open one of his eyelids. "Damn, Tuff, you forever knockin' motherfuckers out."

Fariq shook his head. "I ain't too sure it was Tuff who did it. That nigger's eyes was rolling back in his head before Tuffy put the boot to him."

"I don't know, Winston kicked him pretty hard."

Everyone stared at La Mega. Armello gave a long blast of the car horn, and rolled down the window. "What the fuck?" Ms. O'Koren tugged at her dress, hiked her purse high on her shoulder and walked around the corner and into the bank. Winston wanted to tackle her, but did nothing but look quizzically at Charles. "Don't ask. That six thou she won didn't do nothing but wet her whistle."

"Y'all fuckin' insane," said Yolanda.

"Probably," Whitey replied, putting on his lab coat. "But if you think I'm about to let Moms go in alone, *you* insane. Rest of you motherfuckers come on if you want."

Fariq motioned for Nadine to scramble back up the ladder, then he hobbled over to Tuffy. He handed him his crutches. "Let me lean on you for a second." Slowly, Fariq put his arms through the sleeves. "You know we voted for your ass before we came down here, nigger. I didn't believe it but your name is on the ballot. I thought I'd walk in there and have to be all loud and shit: 'How do you vote for Winston Foshay in this bitch? But your name on the paper."

"I got three votes at least."

"Naw, just two, Nadine voted for German Jordan."

"No, Tuffy got three. My mother voted for him," Charley O' said, patting Winston on the back. "But I didn't expect to be so nervous. The curtain and shit. I didn't know if it was naked lady behind there or priest.

Voting is fuckin' weird, what they need to play some music in there to set the mood." Whitey ran a comb through his hair, placed a stethoscope around his neck, then put on a pair of thick black-framed Medicaid glasses. "How I look, yo?" he asked.

"Like a doctor, I guess," answered Winston.

Nadine stuck her head over the edge of the roof. "Okay, all the smoke bombs is lit."

Fariq grabbed his crutches. "Well, we be right back."

"Except we going be rich and shit," laughed Charles, picking up the Thirstbusters and easing in behind Fariq.

Winston watched them disappear. Yolanda pulled on his elbow. "Let's go." Eyes glued to the bank's entrance they walked past Armello and the Dodge. Winston stopped and backtracked to the getaway car while Nadine and Jordy kept walking to the intersection. "What are you doing?"

"I'll be right there."

He leaned against the car's rear door. "Let me get some of them potato chips." Together they waited for the smoked glass doors to open. At any moment Tuffy half-expected Smush, Whitey, and Ms. O'Koren to come stumbling out of the bank drenched in blood, one hand clutching a bag of money, the other a bullet wound to the stomach. "What you still doin' here?" It was Nadine, down from the roof and clapping the dust from her clothes.

"Waiting."

Without asking she dug her hand into the bag of chips and pulled out more than her share. Aroused from his slumber, La Mega slithered past them, cautiously staying outside of arm's reach, but still blathering. *"La nueva Mega! La emisora oficial para salsa y merengue. La nueva Mega con mas música contigua cada hora! La nueva M-e-e-g-a-a!"*

"Jesus, that fool's crazy," Nadine commented, spitting overcooked bits of chips onto the sidewalk.

"Somethin' wrong."

"Ain't nothin' wrong, Tuffy. It ain't been but four or five minutes. Give them some time."

"I don't know, somethin' not right."

Armello drummed his fingers on the steering wheel. "You right, kid. La Mega wasn't out long enough. Even if the knock-out potion work, he wasn't out long enough for them to rob shit."

Winston sucked his teeth, raised up off the car. "Smush always got to be so elaborate all the damn time. Why didn't y'all use guns like some normal motherfuckers?"

"Niggers not try to catch no armed robbery charge, that's why."

As Winston walked toward the bank, Yolanda put Jordy on her hip and marched toward him, joining him at the entrance. Faces pressed against the glass and hands cupped over their eyes so they could see through the tinted window, they evaluated the situation.

"Blue smoke, Tuffy?"

"I guess."

"But why is it all in one corner?"

"I don't know."

"Look at Whitey's mother. She look like she really passed out. Everyone in the bank standing around her looking all concerned. And look at Whitey checking her pulse and listening to her heart like he's a doctor. But where are the Thirstbusters?"

"I have no idea."

"Well nobody's behind the counter. Smush should be robbing the place. . . . Where Smush at?"

"He over there in the smoke. See him? Near the safe." Though the dense cloud of blue smoke obscured him, the spindly figure had to be Fariq. And judging by the way he was squirming on the floor, downing pills and sucking on his inhaler, he seemed to be having a grand mal seizure of indeterminate origin. Panic-stricken, he unwrapped a hypodermic needle and jammed it into his thigh. The shaking stopped.

"He don't look good."

The smoke around Fariq began to thin. Worried about being seen by the security cameras, he stuck his inhaler in his mouth, discreetly removed a smoke bomb from a lab-coat pocket, lit the fuse, placed it on the floor next to him, and vanished in the billowy haze like a cheesy television genie. Winston noticed the security guard, though unconcerned about the O'Korens, seemed to be getting edgy about Fariq's being so close to the open safe.

"I don't like how that security guard lookin' at Smush."

"Why? You thinking about doing something?"

"I don't know."

"It doesn't look like anyone suspects them of trying to rob the bank, so they can end this fiasco anytime they want. All they have to do is get up and go. And you can do the same thing."

"Smush don't look like he got the strength to walk. And look at him, he can't take his eyes off the safe."

"So what are you going to do?"

Winston stuck a hand in his pocket and clicked off the safety of his gun, then he picked up a paper bag off the sidewalk, and poked two eye holes into it. "I'm going to go in there and stick my gun in somebody's face," he said. The comic struggle of him trying to slip the medium-sized sack over his large head almost negated his seriousness. Disgusted, Yolanda snatched the bag, which fit him like a brown chef's hat, off her husband's head. "Don't be stupid."

"What then?"

"Just go in there and get Smush."

Winston motioned for Nadine to get in the car, and for Armello to be ready to drive off. He took a deep breath and balled his fists so hard his knuckles cracked. "Don't go in there all Nigger Tuffy from Ninth Street," Yolanda cautioned, slipping her hand into his pocket and clicking on the pistol's safety. "Don't be all 'What? What?' You're liable to get everybody shot. Go in there and be *another* nigger. All right?"

Who? Winston wondered as he walked in the door, stepping over the threshold and into a puddle of spilled Thirstbusters. As soon as the door closed behind him, the security guard and a well-dressed man Tuffy took to be the bank manager rushed him. Winston's first thought was to emulate an action hero and slam their noggins together like orchestra cymbals. *Always wanted to do that. I wonder if it works like in the movies?* But as the men approached him, they walked past an easel that displayed one of his campaign flyers next to the interest rates for CDs and treasury bills. Winston now knew who the other nigger was.

"Sir, we're closed."

"That's okay, I'm Winston Foshay, that's my picture on the flyer."

Seeing that the burly local in front of them was indeed the politician on the flyer, the men calmed down appreciably. Winston shook each man's hand. "I came to . . . uh . . . check on my medical staff. . . . We're . . . uh . . . giving out free checkups around the corner, and they were supposed to get some money because we ran out of . . . uh . . . uh . . . those wooden things they stick in your mouth."

"Tongue depressors."

"Yeah, tongue depressors. What happened?"

"This woman," the bank manager said, pointing to Ms. O'Koren who was just starting to come around, "one of our most valued customers, came into the bank, when all of a sudden there was blue smoke coming from the vent and the smell of ammonia. She passed out. We called an ambulance, then, thank goodness, these two doctors came in a few seconds later, but the handicapped one had some sort of attack. He knocked the blue drinks out the other one's hands and staggered into the smoke, saying to stay away from him, he was a doctor, and he'd be okay."

Winston punched his palm in pretend disappointment. "Those drinks was for the kids."

Charles stood up and helped his mother to her feet. "Is this citizen okay, Dr. . . . Dr. Whitey, I mean Dr. White?" Winston asked Charles, biting the insides of his cheeks to keep from smiling. "I say, I believe she's starting to show some life. It was nothing more than a dizzy spell brought on by the smoke and fumes and all that rot. Some proper rest, a spot of tea, and she'll be fine," Charles answered, barely hiding his own grin and enunciating like an Oxford graduate. "Bit of a fright, though."

Winston jogged over to Fariq, who, groggy from the medication, was working his crutches like chopsticks, trying to pick up a loose bundle of hundred-dollar bills that was just out of reach. "Come on, kid, let's go," Winston whispered, as he lifted his limp friend by the knees and armpits.

"Yo, Tuffy, we came in ready to get this money, yo. Ms. O'Koren fakin' a seizure, and my ass get a real one." Fariq raised a crutch toward the vault. "Look at all that money, son. What you doin', nigger? Go back! Go back!"

"Chill, man. You 'posed to be a doctor."

Tuffy hustled Fariq past the bewildered employees. "Dr. Allah seems a bit woozy." Stopping at the doorway, he thanked everyone for their help and reminded them to vote for him. When they got to the car Winston placed the gelatin-jointed Fariq in the backseat, folding each loose limb into the cramped space like a puppeteer putting his favorite marionette back in the box. Everyone thanked him for his efforts, Charley O's gratitude laced with his usual aspersion. "Yeah boy, your shit was on time like German railroad, but you did come in kinda pussy. All 'Howdy, y'all. Glad to meet you,' and shit. You supposed to come to the rescue toolie out, blasting shots U.S. cavalry style." Armello put a fist to his lips and blew into his air bugle. "Dit doot dit doot ditooo. Charge!"

Charley O' nodded his head, "Yeah, Tuffy, if you not going to use the gun, give that shit to me."

Winston backed out of the window, his hands still gripping the car

door. He looked at his boys, Armello at the wheel, Fariq and Charley O'
smashed shoulder to shoulder in the backseat, crowded with a baby chair
and Ms. O'Koren. They reminded him of the doomed gun-boat crew in
Apocalypse Now headed upriver to Cambodia, the Bronx, to who knows
where. He could hear Robert Duvall yelling in his ear over the shelling:

> *"Do you want to surf soldier?"*
> *"Yes, sir!"*
> *"That's good, son, because you either surf or fight."*

Winston wanted to surf like never before. He pressed down the car
door's lock. "We out, y'all."
"You got your pager, nukka?" Fariq asked. Tuffy nodded. "Then I'll
beep you in an hour or so. We'll go to Old Timers'. Smoke some isms. Get
some drink."
"We probably goin' to be at the movies, so . . ."
Fariq tapped Armello on the shoulder and the car pulled away.
On the way to the elementary school Winston held Yolanda's hand so
tight they could feel one another's pulses.
"You kicked that guy on purpose, didn't you?"
"It wasn't no accident."
"You know what I mean. You meant to knock him out." Tuffy raised
a foot in the air. "Timberland makes a hell of a shoe. These shits is water-
proof. No-skid soles. Reinforced heels."
"Thanks, Boo."
"For what?"
"Nothing."
A block away the band of addicts and derelicts hired by Inez
stormed a municipal bus like Entebbe commandos. After handing out flyers to the passengers, they poured into Second Avenue, halting traffic,
slipping the handbills under the wipers of stopped cars, tossing them
through open windows. The chaos caused an onslaught of blaring car
horns. Winston squeezed Yolanda's hand even tighter. Her knuckles
cracked. She was the only thing in his life that was real. Even Jordy plodding in front of them, nose to the ground like an anteater scouting bug
lairs, seemed imaginary. *Little light-skin motherfucker don't even look like
me.* The pressure from Yolanda's return squeeze quieted his fears.
When they got to the school the flag over the entrance was flying at

half-mast because the pulleys had rusted shut. A cracked-out man stood outside the door exchanging goo-goo eyes with a preteen. "What you doing, Marvin? I thought Ms. Nomura hired you to hand out flyers today."

"I'm talking to my girl."

"My flyers better not be in the Dumpster, nigger." Winston spat. "You vote?"

Marvin shook his head and tried to gauge Winston's mood. Tuffy looked calm, but he took a step back just in case. "Didn't I register you at Papo's spot?"

"Uh-huh, you stepped on my jumbo too."

"That was an accident."

Marvin pursed his lips and shifted them from side to side.

"It was, nigger." Downcast about the memory of his lost crack rock and allowing Winston to punk him in front of his girlfriend, Marvin stared at the ground. "Listen, you go vote, I'll give you your twenty dollars back."

Marvin hurried through the entrance, the school's thick metal doors closing slowly behind him. Winston turned to the girl. "That nigger not for you, hear me?" The girl remained standoffish, her hands on a set of bony hips cocked at an angle.

"She waiting for her tip," Yolanda said.

"I should've never told Marvin I was giving him twenty dollars. I should've just threatened to beat his ass." Tuffy handed the girl twenty dollars. She walked away, switching her nonexistent behind like an anorexic flapper full of whiskey.

"They growing up fast."

"How much of that money you got left?"

"Enough for the movies."

Marvin poked his head out from between the doors. "Tuff?"

"What you doin' out here, man? You supposed to be voting!"

"I don't know your real name."

Winston chuckled. "This shit's insane." Climbing the stairs, he held the door open and said, "Foshay. Winston Foshay."

The voting booths were downstairs in the cafeteria. Bendito, on election day duty, leaned against a soda machine, looking bored. He spotted Winston first. "Truce."

"Truce."

Inez stood behind the volunteers, looking over their shoulders like an exam proctor. Yolanda checked in and headed to an empty booth, leaving Jordy with his father.

"Lighten up on them, Ms. Nomura, dag."

"Winston, you have no idea what the city will do to rig the election. I just came from the polls at P.S. 57 and they've got six cops standing out in front of the place. Now people in this neighborhood, especially the people who'd vote for you, wouldn't walk through six policemen to get free beer, much less vote."

"Come on, now, Ms. Nomura, it can't be that serious."

"Oh, it can't be that serious? Before that I was at Carver projects next door to the old folks' home. Do you know where the voting booths in Carver projects are located?"

"No."

"They're in the rec room on the eighth floor."

"But the elevator in Carver ain't never worked."

"Exactly. You think those old people who were so proud of you at the debate are going to walk up eight flights of stairs to vote?"

So the volunteers wouldn't hear, Winston mouthed, "How many votes I got?"

Inez flashed her fingers in sets of ten. It was either sixty-four or seventy-four, Winston having lost count.

With a sharp pinch Yolanda let him know the booth was ready. Winston, Jordy in his arms, entered the booth and closed the curtain behind him. He primed the ballot by moving the red lever to the right.

"Tuffy, that you?" It was Marvin whispering from the booth next to Winston's.

"What up?"

"How you spell your name?"

"W-I-N-S-T-O—nigger can't you read?" Exasperated, Winston began directing Marvin in a voice loud enough to lift the heads of the volunteers from their rosters. Following his own directions, he showed Marvin how to vote. "Put your finger on the top box in the first row of boxes."

"Okay."

"Go down to the third box."

"All right."

"See the little metal lever next to the box?"

"Yup."

"Pull it down."

"Done."

"It's a little black X in the box?"

"Uh-huh."

TUFF

"Pull the red handle to the left." Without pulling his lever, Winston listened for the loud kerchunk of Marvin casting his vote. "There you go, son. You just voted."

"That was easy. I should vote more often. When you running again?"

"Hopefully, never."

"Winston." Marvin's voice had returned to its original hush. "About that twenty?"

"I'll get you tomorrow. Come by the crib."

"Promise?"

"Yeah, nigger."

"Don't be like the rest of them politicians, making promises you can't keep."

Winston didn't worry about breaking any political promises. He figured there was no way for him to win.

Tuffy puzzled over the rest of the ballot. He examined the judgeships, then voted for the surnames he thought sounded Jewish. He let Jordy flip the rest of the poll's switches. In a local election with a pitifully low voter turnout, the baby's whims would go a long way in determining the outcome of the assorted city offices, propositions, and referendums, the particulars of which Winston understood as much as Jordy. When he stepped out of the booth Yolanda looked so proud that for a moment he thought he had a chance to win.

Man, if I won, I wouldn't even know where to show up for work.

23. THERE WAS A FATHER

The Foshays were sitting in the back row of a small art-house theater, sipping herbal teas and watching an Ozu film. The film, *There Was a Father,* was an early work and so absent of dialogue it might as well have been silent. From Yolanda's perspective the slow-moving tale with its static camera work might as well have been a still photograph. "Winston, this movie's awful. Ain't shit happened since the kid drowned in the lake, and that was just a glimpse of an overturned boat in two feet of water."

"Lots of things is happening. You just don't how to look for them."

"What, the old man getting even older? His son talking even less then he did when he was a boy? Long shots of stone statues? If nothing's happening, then there's nothing to miss."

A brave viewer shushed the couple. Winston ignored the reprimand and explained the movie's subtext to Yolanda. "You supposed to be a psychologist. Can't you see the father going through some heavy shit? Nigger in crisis. He's lonely. His wife been dead for who knows how long. His student died, he feels responsible, now he afraid to raise his son. The kid feels abandoned, but still got mad love for his pops. When you watch these shits it's not about what's happening, but what ain't happening." On-screen, the father and son were fishing in a shallow stream, casting their lines, their poles moving in perfect sync, like windshield wipers. Without turning to face the boy, the father said, "I'm sending you away to school." The boy stopped fishing while his father kept snapping his line into the water. "That's deep as fuck," Tuffy said in a loud voice. The audience launched a chorus of "Shhh"s and "Be quiet"s in his direction. But Winston was unshushable, and the chiding only encouraged him. "What you all crying about? None of y'all can't understand Japanese no way." His *benshi*-like exegesis continued unabated. "If you think about it, Landa, all I have to do is kill you and this movie be just like me and Jordy's life. Father and son against the world." Yolanda playfully slapped him across the jowls. A couple of patrons stormed out to alert the theater manager.

Winston looked at his beeper. Nothing from Fariq. He imagined Fariq and the others joyriding in the stolen Dodge, convinced the traffic helicopters flying overhead were the police radioing their whereabouts to the ground forces. They had rehearsed the plan of escape many times on the stoop: Drive by the airport, where the helicopters aren't allowed to violate the airspace. If they weren't near an airport, drive to the nearest college campus, park the car, and pile out. From five hundred feet up they'd look just like students.

Winston turned his attention to the film. The father was on his deathbed, the now full-grown son at his side, fighting back tears for a man he never really knew. As the father passed away quietly, the son left the room and began crying uncontrollably.

Winston's eyes were moistening when Yolanda whispered in his ear: "Smush and them all right?"

He shrugged.

"You crying?"

"Naw."

The son and his new bride were on a train to their new lives. The son suggested to his wife that she invite her father and her brother to move in with them. The woman sobbed into her hands at her man's kindhearted resoluteness. Yolanda shook her head in disgust. "This movie is a trip. Japanese people must cry at the drop of a hat. They could never live in the ghetto. They'd be a fucking wreck."

"Ms. Nomura live on the block, and she do all right."

"Well, when the next movie start, let's move up to the front a little bit?"

"We can't. I have to sit behind my seat."

"What do you mean, your seat?"

"I'll show you in a sec."

When the houselights slowly brightened, Winston tapped a small metal plate stapled to the seat back in front of him. Yolanda ran her hands over the silver-plated tag and sighed, "Unbelievable." Neatly engraved into the plaque was WINSTON FOSHAY—PATRON OF THE THEATER FOR CLASSIC CINEMA. "That's where all Ms. Nomura's money went? How much that cost?"

"Two thousand dollars."

"Winston, how much money is left?"

"About fifteen hundred."

"Where the rest go?"

"I don't know—beer, your tuition. And I gave Spencer five thousand." Yolanda stood up. "For what?"

"He's going to be my screenwriter."

Reentering the theater, the pack of disgruntled patrons pointed Winston and Yolanda out to the manager. Yolanda sat down in a huff, ready to take out her anger on the manager. "That's them. Those two right there." The manager slid into the seat next to the troublemakers. "How you doing, Mr. Foshay? Good to see you again." The men shook hands and Winston introduced Yolanda and Jordy. "How did you like the film?" the manager asked. "Have you seen the next one, *What Did the Lady Forget?* It's about a henpecked husband and how he regains the upper hand in his marriage."

Winston groaned, "Oh, man, I seen this one," then raised an eyebrow at Yolanda, who, fed up, had pulled out a psychology text, deciding she could study during the intermission. "He hits her and she straightens right up." Yolanda ignored him and highlighted a passage with her fluorescent orange marker.

Tuffy looked around suspiciously, making sure no one was eavesdropping, then tugged on the manager's shirtsleeve. "Look, forget about Ozu for a second," he whispered. "Listen to this idea . . . *Cap'n Crunch—the Movie.*" The manager bolted upright, covering his open mouth with his hand. "My God, that's brilliant!"

Now it was Winston's turn to shush for quiet. "Calm down, yo. I got a guy who writes for the paper working on the screenplay. If you want in, let me know."

When the manager had left, Yolanda spoke without looking up. "You pitching that idea to every white man you know. And one of them going to steal your idea."

"I know, but I don't care—I just want want to see it get made. Look up at the screen and say, 'Yo, there go my idea.' "

"Wouldn't it be better to look at the screen and say, 'There go my idea and I made crazy dollars off it'?"

"That's why you going to college. You the one who going to be making the money in this family."

"Shit."

Winston stuck his head in her lap. "What you studying anyway?"

Yolanda tapped a finger on a chapter heading that read, "Perception Psychology—Gestalt."

"What's that?" Winston asked.

"It like studying why the brain perceives things a certain way. Like how come certain colors make us feel a certain way."

With a sly expression Winston cupped her breast and said, "Like what is it about your fine ass that make me feel so good?"

"Something like that."

"And who is Guest-alt?"

"Ge-*stahlt*."

"Ge-*stahlt*."

"Gestalt is a theory of perception. When we see something that is divided up in parts, we tend to see the whole thing, not the individual units. Say you order a large pizza pie, you see a circle not six triangles."

"Eight."

"However many."

"Like when I look at those little bumps around your nipple I see a circle?"

"Exactly." Winston started to get grabby and Yolanda elbowed him off her. As the houselights dimmed, he leaned back in his seat and lit a cigarette. "You know if I went to college what I'd take up?"

"What?"

"Space."

Inez trudged up Second Avenue to Park East High School. It had been a long day. Streaks of sweat pasted her shirt to her spine and the small of her back. Her feet ached from hiking from poll to poll challenging voters and monitoring the clerks. She entered Room 202 in a dither. She brushed away the strands of hair stuck to her face and looked up at the clock—ten-thirty-five. *Shit, I'm late.* She'd sworn to herself there would be no ballot stuffing this election. That repeat of the great voter fraud of 1977 would not happen on her watch.

There were four other people in the room. At the teacher's desk, behind the small pile of remaining ballots, sat the district inspector and a clerk. Seated at a student's desk in the front row was one of German Jordan's lackeys. And in a back corner of the room, Bendito Bonilla, still in uniform, was absentmindedly spinning a globe.

The inspector, a dumpy woman about Inez's age, wore a lime-green pants suit and a string of black pearls. She picked up a ballot and said, "Collette Cox." The clerk, probably her husband, pressed his pencil hard on the tally sheet, dutifully tabulating the vote. "Collette Cox," he repeated, pulling on the crew neck of his T-shirt. *"Hace calor, coño."*

Inez took a seat next to Jordan's flunky.

"German Jordan."

"German Jordan."

The clerk's pencil broke. The snap echoed for a long moment. The clerk got up to sharpen his pencil, and Inez interrupted the proceedings. "May I ask your name?"

"Lourdes Molina."

"Ms. Molina, may I request an announcement of the results as they now currently stand?"

"You'll have to wait until all the votes are counted."

The hireling hunched over the piece of paper on his desk like an overachieving pupil unwilling to let anyone cheat off him. Inez whistled, looked at her fingernails, then snatched the sheet of paper. It was an official tally sheet missing only the bottom right-hand corner, which was still in the manservant's hand. Inez scanned the columns. The clerk returned to his seat and the count resumed.

"Winston Foshay."

"Winston Foshay."

It looked to be a two-person race. Quickly, she counted the votes. *Wait a minute.*

"Winston Foshay."

"Winston Foshay."

Holy shit.

"German Jordan."

"German Jordan."

Inez handed the sheet back to the minion, and took out a thick mimeographed copy of the *State of New York—Election Law; Rules and Regulations.*

"German Jordan."

"German Jordan."

"Winston Foshay."

"Winston Foshay."

Tuffy wasn't winning, but it was close. She looked up at the desk. The pile of votes was shrinking. There looked to be only five or six left, and a stack of about ten absentee votes still in unopened envelopes.

"Wilfredo Cienfuegos."

"Wilfredo Cienfuegos."

"Margo Tellos."

"Margo Tellos."

The absentee ballots reminded her of Winston's Rikers Island whistle-stop, a prison cot serving as a campaign stump.

"Winston Foshay."

"Winston Foshay."

But even if all of the remaining votes were for Winston, they wouldn't be enough for him to win. However, Inez didn't know if Jordan had enough votes for a plurality. She hurriedly flipped through the book, looking for the requirements for a run-off election. "German Jordan."

"German Jordan."

"German Jordan."

"German Jordan."

Fuck. There was no run-off for City Council seats. It was majority wins.

"Winston Foshay."

"Winston Foshay."

The inspector slapped the last ballot down on the desk. And with a sharp fingernail slit open the first absentee ballot.

"Winston Foshay."

"Winston Foshay."

The envelope fell to the floor, sliding under Inez's seat. There had to be a loophole somewhere, but there were almost four hundred pages of picayune New York State election law to pore over. She needed more time.

"Winston Foshay."

"Winston Foshay."

Inez was about to ask if the total number of votes counted matched the number of ballots cast but she didn't have the energy. She looked down at the envelope under her desk. The return address was for Rikers. She smiled, sat back in her chair and closed the book of election laws with a satisfying thud. Instinctively, she reached into her bag for her bottle of rum. She kissed the label, and took a long sip.

"Winston Foshay."

"Winston Foshay."

The rum went down easy. Inez lightly stamped her feet, enjoying the tingle in her toes. For a grassroots campaign in a community with no grass, Team Tuffy had done well. Now all that had to be done was to make sure Tuffy would live to see his twenty-third summer. *Just one more sip.* Inez raised the bottle to her lips, whispering a toast. *"Gambate,* Winston Foshay, *gambate."*

A NOTE ABOUT THE AUTHOR

Paul Beatty has published two volumes of poetry and has been profiled in magazines ranging from Newsweek *to* Vibe *to* Harper's Bazaar. *He lives in New York City.*

A NOTE ON THE TYPE

This book was set in Caledonia, a Linotype face designed by
W. A. Dwiggins (1880–1956). It belongs to the family of printing
types called "modern face" by printers—a term used to mark the change
in style of the type letters that occurred around 1800. Caledonia
borders on the general design of Scotch Roman but it is
more freely drawn than that letter.

Composed by Creative Graphics, Inc.,
Allentown, Pennsylvania

Printed and bound by The Haddon Craftsmen,
an R.R. Donnelley & Sons Company, Bloomsburg, Pennsylvania

Designed by Iris Weinstein